ANDY McDERMOTT

THE TOMB OF
HERCULES

Also by Andy McDermott and available from Headline

The Hunt For Atlantis

ANDY McDERMOTT

THE TOMB OF
HERCULES

headline

Copyright © 2008 Andy McDermott

The right of Andy McDermott to be identified as the Author of
the Work has been asserted by him in accordance with the
Copyright, Designs and Patents Act 1988.

First published in 2008
by HEADLINE PUBLISHING GROUP

1

Apart from any use permitted under UK copyright law, this publication
may only be reproduced, stored, or transmitted, in any form, or by any means,
with prior permission in writing of the publishers or, in the case of
reprographic production, in accordance with the terms of licences issued
by the Copyright Licensing Agency.

All characters in this publication are fictitious and any resemblance to real persons,
living or dead, is purely coincidental.

Cataloguing in Publication Data is available from the British Library

Hardback ISBN 978 0 7553 3913 6
Trade paperback ISBN 978 0 7553 3914 3

Typeset in Aldine 401BT by Avon DataSet Ltd,
Bidford-on-Avon, Warwickshire

Printed and bound in the UK by
CPI Mackays, Chatham ME5 8TD

Headline's policy is to use papers that are natural, renewable and recyclable
products and made from wood grown in sustainable forests. The logging
and manufacturing processes are expected to conform to the environmental
regulations of the country of origin.

HEADLINE PUBLISHING GROUP
An Hachette Livre UK Company
338 Euston Road
London NW1 3BH

www.headline.co.uk
www.hachettelivre.co.uk

For my family and friends

Prologue

The Gulf of Cadiz

One hundred miles off the southern coast of Portugal was hidden one of the greatest secrets in human history.

For now, it would remain hidden, guarded by another secret of much more recent origin.

Officially, the giant six-legged floating platform was listed as SBX-2, a sea-based X-band radar station. Nicknamed the Taj Mahal for the huge white radar dome dominating its upper deck, the high-tech US Navy behemoth swept the skies to the east for thousands of miles, its stated purpose to monitor North Africa and the Middle East for ballistic missile launches. In function and application, it was what it claimed to be.

But that was not the real reason for its presence. The truth lay eight hundred feet below.

Fifteen months earlier, the citadel at the heart of the lost civilisation of Atlantis – long believed to be nothing more than a legend – had been discovered directly beneath where the SBX was now anchored. Though the only visible structure, the huge Temple of Poseidon, had been destroyed, radar surveys had revealed many more buried beneath the silt covering the sea floor. Since the discovery of Atlantis had ultimately turned out to be part of a conspiracy to exterminate three-quarters of humanity with a biological weapon, the Western governments which stepped in after the plot was foiled decided that not only the circumstances of the ancient city's discovery, but also the mere fact of its existence, should remain a secret. At least, until a more benign story of its finding could be concocted – and any danger of a repeat of the genocidal plan eliminated.

So while the SBX stood vigil over the skies, beneath it scientists and archaeologists explored the site in secrecy under the auspices of the International Heritage Agency, a United Nations organisation established a year earlier with the remit of locating – and securing – ancient sites such as Atlantis. The central leg on the starboard side of the giant radar platform had been converted into a submersible pen, a section of the pontoon at its base now open to the sea. Shielded by concrete walls six feet thick, the IHA scientists were normally able to conduct their explorations with no interference from the outside world.

But not tonight.

'Jesus,' muttered Bill Raynes, the IHA's expedition director, clutching a handrail as the rig swayed again. The SBX was so massive and securely anchored that normally even an Atlantic storm did little more than gently rock it.

This was clearly a much bigger storm than usual.

One of the two bright yellow two-man submersibles swung on its chains as it was winched out of the water. Raynes watched it anxiously. Its twin was already secured over the dock, but if conditions got much worse there was a danger that the loose sub could become an uncontrollable pendulum and smash right into it.

'Get a line on the damn thing!' he ordered. Two of his men hurried to obey, staggering round the edge of the moonpool as the floor lurched beneath them. They waited for the sub to swing back towards them, then snagged one of the chains with a boathook, damping its motion. The dangerous swaying reduced, the winch operator raised the submersible fully into position above the dock, where more chains were quickly attached to secure it.

'Okay! Good work, guys,' Raynes called, letting out a relieved breath. Both subs were now safely in place, which meant the day's operations were concluded. On most evenings, that would have been the cue for him to go up to the main deck and enjoy a cigar.

Not tonight, though. He wasn't going to set one foot outdoors if he didn't have to. He felt a brief stab of pity for the Marines stationed aboard the platform, who had guard duty no matter what the conditions. Poor bastards.

The unexpected drama aside, it had been a good day. The high-resolution sonar mapping of the citadel was ahead of schedule, and the excavation of the first site had already produced results, an exciting haul of Atlantean artefacts valuable in both historical and monetary terms. He may not have *discovered* Atlantis, but Raynes had already decided that he was damn well going to be the person famous for *exploring* it.

The actual discoverer of Atlantis was Dr Nina Wilde, fifteen years Raynes's junior and – on paper at least – his IHA superior.

He wondered if the red-haired New Yorker had any idea that by accepting a senior post in the IHA she'd effectively ended her archaeological career before even turning thirty. Probably not, he decided. While she was certainly cute to look at, Nina also came across to Raynes as naive. It seemed to him that she'd been given the position of Director of Operations as a way to keep her – and her bodyguard-turned-boyfriend Eddie Chase, whom Raynes regarded as little more than a sarcastic English thug – quiet and out of trouble while more experienced hands got on with the *real* work.

He made his way to the elevator cage running up the inside of the support leg, glancing at the dark void overhead. The SBX's main deck, the size of two football fields, was twelve storeys above sea level. Carrying the case of artefacts, Raynes slammed the gate closed and pushed the button to ascend.

Water sprayed up into the dock below as waves slapped noisily against the sides of the pool. He had never seen conditions inside the sub pen so bad before. Normally, the ocean surface inside the moonpool did little more than ripple. If it were this bad inside, he didn't even want to think about what it would be like outside.

Spray blasted almost horizontally over the surface of the Atlantic, waves pounding explosively against the forward leg on the rig's port side. The metal staircase that rose from the submerged pontoon to a ladder stretching up the towering structure rattled and moaned under the onslaught. It was not a place where anyone in his right mind would choose to be.

But someone *was* there.

The man was a giant, six feet eight inches tall, with every hard-packed muscle in his athlete's body picked out by his skin-tight black wetsuit. He emerged from the water and made his way up the stairs, hands clamping round the railings with the force of a vice, even the thunderous impact of the waves barely throwing him off his stride.

Once clear of the churning ocean, he paused to remove the scuba regulator from his mouth, revealing perfect white teeth – one inset with a diamond – surrounded by ebony skin, then began his climb up the ladder. Considering the distance and the conditions, most men would have been lucky to make it in under five minutes, and exhausted by the time they reached the top.

The intruder made it in two, and was breathing no more heavily than if he'd climbed a single flight of stairs.

Just below the top of the ladder, he stopped and carefully raised his head above the edge of the deck. The blocky grey superstructure of the SBX was three floors high, catwalks running along each level at the platform's bow. Sickly yellow lights made a feeble attempt to illuminate them. Rain spattered on the man's diving mask, obscuring his view. He frowned and pulled it from his face, revealing calculating black eyes before he flipped down another pair of goggles from the top of his head.

The weak yellow lights disappeared, replaced by shimmering blobs of videogame-vivid red and orange. Almost everything else was either blue or black. Thermographic vision, the world represented by the heat it gave off. The metal walls of the rig, lashed by freezing rain, were visible only as shades of blue.

But there was something else that stood out against the electronic darkness, even in the storm. A glowing shape in green and yellow and white moved closer, gradually taking on human form through the false-colour fuzz.

One of the platform's US Marine guards, on patrol.

The intruder silently lowered himself so that he was poised just below the edge of the deck, barely moving even as the storm pummelled him.

The Marine came closer, boots clanking on the metal as he reached the end of the catwalk. One hand holding the railing, the other on his gun, he peered down the ladder—

Fast and fluid as a snake, the intruder's hand snapped up and seized the Marine by his gun arm. Before the startled man could react, the giant almost effortlessly yanked him over the edge of the platform and flung him to his death in the spume over a hundred feet below.

The killer flipped up his thermographic goggles and looked along the catwalk to see his next target only a few metres away. An electrical junction box, protruding from the metal wall. He hurried to it.

The rat's nest of wires and cables inside seemed impenetrably complicated, but the man already knew exactly where to find the main feed for the rig's security cameras. He tugged one particular skein of wires clear of the others, then sliced a combat knife straight through them. A few sparks popped, but the blade was insulated. He returned the knife to its sheath and reached down to click the key of the radio on his belt.

Go.

In the submersible dock, a man's head broke the surface of the sloshing water. Eyes glinting behind his mask, he turned in a full circle to survey the surroundings. Two of the rig's crew were on the dock, backs to the moonpool as they secured their equipment.

He sank back under the dark water and took a gun of unusual design from his belt. Then he resurfaced, raising the weapon out of the water. Trickles of seawater ran out of the drainage holes along its barrel as he took aim. Another man emerged next to him, doing the same.

Two flat thuds, so close together that they could almost have been the same sound, echoed around the concrete chamber. The guns were gas powered, compressed nitrogen blasting the darts they fired across the dock to slam into the backs of the two crewmen. They gasped in pain, hands clutching behind them . . . then collapsed to the floor, unable to move. The dart guns were designed to fire tranquillisers. But these were loaded with something else.

Something deadly.

The men in the water swam for a ladder leading out of the moonpool. Other divers appeared, following them on to the deck. Seven men in all. They quickly shed their scuba gear and crossed the dock to the elevator.

The two crewmen still lay nearby, frozen; helpless. Only their eyes, bulging in fear and pain, could move. The darts were poisoned, paralysis of the voluntary muscles occurring almost immediately.

Paralysis of the *involuntary* muscles, specifically the heart, would soon follow.

One of the intruders bent down to pull out the darts, which he tossed into the moonpool. They sank out of sight. After a moment of consideration, glancing at the cylinder clipped under the dart gun's barrel that contained an antidote to the toxin, he tipped his head towards the water. His companions dragged the paralysed crewmen to the rim of the pool and unceremoniously dumped them into the sea.

Not looking back at the drowning men, the team entered the elevator cage and closed it. A security camera looked on uselessly with its dead eye. With a rattle, the elevator started its ascent.

The black-clad giant cautiously raised his eyes just above the level of the rain-lashed top deck. The flat metal expanse was dominated by the giant radar dome. It was illuminated from within, a colossal lantern glowing through the wind-whipped deluge. Everything else on the deck was indistinct, lost in the storm.

He lowered his goggles again. The view sprang to gaudy life. At the stern, beyond the dome, was a swirling red haze – exhaust from the platform's power plant, and heat pumped out by the banks of container-sized air conditioning units cooling the electronics of the enormous radar array.

But other shapes stood out brightly. Two more Marines flared in his thermal sights as distant amorphous blobs, shambling through the cutting rain towards each other. They were following a set path, meeting up to confirm that all was well before turning back along their patrol routes.

They would never make it.

The intruder raised a weapon. Unlike the dart guns used by his team in the submersible dock, this was a rifle, a telescopic sight mounted above the grip.

Flipping the goggles back up, he brought the sight to his

right eye. Without the thermographic enhancement the Marines were little more than grey silhouettes, flapping rain capes outlined in yellow by a nearby light. He fixed the crosshairs on his target, the closer of the two men. Waited for them to meet, to stop—

The indistinct figure in the scope spasmed, then fell to the deck. The other man reacted in surprise, dropping to his knees to help him.

Saw the dart protruding from his back. Looked up—

The assassin had already reloaded. He barely needed the sights, the rifle almost an extension of his body as he fired again. He didn't need to see an impact to know that he had hit.

He ran to the second downed Marine, ignoring the man's desperate, twitching eyes as he checked where his shot had landed. The dart had caught the man square in the chest, an inch below his heart. The sniper made a noise of annoyance. He'd been aiming for the heart itself. Sloppy.

But only his pride was affected. The end result was what mattered here. He tugged the dart out of the man's flesh and threw it across the deck, then did the same for the first victim. The darts would be swept away into the sea, lost. And nobody would pay any attention to the tiny puncture wounds when there would be a far more obvious cause of death.

The radio on his belt clicked, twice. A signal. The second team was in position.

Right on time.

The deck was clear. He returned the signal, clicking the key three times.

Take the platform.

★

The seven men had already shot the pair of surprised Marines in the cabin at the top of the support leg, immobilising them with darts as soon as the elevator emerged. Then they waited for the signal from their leader. As soon as it came they split up into three groups – one of three men, two of two – and headed into the superstructure.

The group of three quickly made their way towards the platform's stern and the power plant section. While the SBX resembled a stationary oil rig, it was actually a vessel in its own right, able to move under its own power. It carried a crew of around forty, not counting the platoon of Marines and the IHA contingent. With the radar station itself being highly automated, most of the crew actually performed the same tasks as sailors on a warship: running and maintaining the vessel.

Which meant the majority of the crew were concentrated in one area.

Dart guns raised, the trio advanced through the grey corridors, one man checking at each junction before signalling the other two to move on. They went up a steep flight of stairs to B Deck, listening for any sounds of activity around them.

A door opened ahead. A bearded petty officer carrying a toolbox stepped out, froze in surprise as he saw the three men—

A dart stabbed into his throat, instantly delivering its toxic payload. The sailor let out a choking gasp, his killer already rushing forward to catch him and his toolbox before they crashed noisily on to the deck.

The other two men checked the label on the door – an engineering storeroom – and flung it open, guns up as they checked it was empty. It was.

It took only a few seconds for the paralysed sailor to be dumped inside the storeroom and the hatch closed again. The men moved on, ascending more stairs to arrive at their target.

A hatch was set into one of the bulkheads, the low thrum of machinery audible behind it. Warning signs told the intruders what they would find within.

The primary ventilation shaft for the aft section.

The SBX's superstructure was essentially a sealed metal box. There were only three windows on the entire vessel, in the bridge at the bow, and even those didn't open. The only way to get air inside the rig was to pump it through the vents beneath the giant intakes on the upper deck.

The assault team forced open the hatch, exposing an access panel into the shaft. A huge fan whirled behind it. The three men donned insectile respirator masks before taking a cylinder that one carried on his back and manhandling it through the access panel. A twist of a valve – and the cylinder began to pump cyanogen chloride gas into the vent. Colourless, odourless – and deadly within seconds.

They jogged back to the stairs and slid down the steep banisters to B Deck, heading forward. They ignored the strangled, agonised gasps from dying men and women in the rooms they passed.

One of the two-man teams stealthily made its way to the platform's accommodation section. The SBX's small crew worked on a two-shift system: twelve hours on, twelve hours off. Right now, those on the second shift would probably be asleep.

Including half of the Marines.

The long room serving as the Marines' barracks had two doors, one at each end. One of the men waited by the first door until his comrade reached the other entrance. Then he took a small cylinder of cyanogen chloride from his harness and opened the door.

Most of the twelve Marines inside were asleep, though one man looked up at him. A moment of hesitation, replaced by trained response as he saw the black breath mask—

'*Marines!*' he yelled, before a dart fired from the open door at the far end of the room thudded into his back. Other men jumped upright in their bunks, startled into life by the shout of alarm.

Then they slumped back down as the two gas cylinders rolled through the room, spewing invisible death.

The second team of two headed for the front of the rig and the command section on A Deck. This area was always guarded, four Marines stationed at the entrance.

Poison gas was not an option in this part of the rig; there was one man who needed to be kept alive at all costs, and gas was too indiscriminate and unpredictable a killer. The dart guns were also unusable, too slow to reload and carrying the risk that a dart might embed itself uselessly in a target's equipment. At this critical stage of the operation, instant kills had to be guaranteed.

So the two men simply walked round the corner to face the unsuspecting Marines and shot each of them in the head with silenced pistols before any of them had a chance to respond.

The corpses would have to be removed when the attackers left the rig – a body with a bullet wound would give everything away. But that had been planned for.

One of the men clicked his radio. *In position.*

★

A single click came from the huge man's radio. He nodded to himself in acknowledgement, then cautiously looked round the edge of the rain-streaked window.

There was only one person on watch in the bridge, a young female lieutenant. Since the SBX was stationary and the Command Information Center behind the bridge acted as the vessel's nerve centre, there was no need for anyone else. He could see more people through the glass doors to CIC, including the platform's commander.

It was time.

Lieutenant Phoebe Bremmerman looked up from her console at the bridge windows. There had been a noise, something other than rain pounding against the glass.

And there was something on the glass itself, a dark grey object the size of a large coin.

She stood, about to call out to her commander in CIC—

The window exploded.

Fragments of glass sprayed into the bridge, the muffled rumble of the storm outside instantly rising to a howl. The lieutenant screamed as a chunk of the broken window slashed her cheek.

A huge black man in a wetsuit leapt through the window, a pistol aimed at her. Simultaneously, more wetsuited men burst into CIC, weapons raised. One of the radar operators jumped up, only to fall back over his chair, a dart protruding from his neck.

The giant grabbed Bremmerman and dragged her into CIC, the noise of the storm dropping as the bridge door thumped shut.

'Commander Hamilton,' he said to the SBX's commander, shoving the woman to join the other occupants of the room in a group surrounded by four armed men. 'Sorry for the intrusion.' He smiled, the diamond glinting in his flawless teeth. His Nigerian accent was smooth and sonorous. 'My name is Joe Komosa, and I'm here for one thing only.' The smile reappeared, but with menace behind it. 'Where is Dr Bill Raynes?'

The remaining crew of the platform were taken to the large lab on B Deck assigned to the IHA team and forced to kneel in the centre of the room.

None of the Marines had survived the assault. The Navy crew had also suffered severe losses; aside from Hamilton himself, there were now only ten alive, including the five others from the CIC. Of the ten members of the IHA contingent, three were missing.

The attackers had been joined by another three men, who had brought in the other survivors at gunpoint. Whoever they were, Hamilton realised, they were utterly ruthless; another sailor had protested when he'd been shoved into the lab – not even fighting back, just shouting – and been shot in the chest at point-blank range, dying on the deck right before Hamilton's eyes.

And there had been nothing he could do.

Komosa pulled off the headpiece of his wetsuit, revealing a gleaming shaven head with a row of piercings, silver studs, running back from each temple. Then he pulled down the zip to expose his bare chest, which was marked by lines of more glittering piercings. Pausing for a moment to admire his reflection in a glass partition, he slowly strode back and forth before the prisoners without a word, arousing nervous glances, then rounded on Raynes with his dazzling smile.

'Dr Raynes,' he said, 'as I told Commander Hamilton, I

have come here for one thing only. Do you know what this is?' He held up a small white object he had taken from a waterproof pouch.

Raynes peered uncertainly at it as if being asked a trick question. 'It's . . . a USB flash drive?'

'It is indeed a flash drive.' Komosa went to one particular computer in the corner of the lab – Raynes's own workstation. 'And I would like you to fill it for me.'

Raynes swallowed, voice dry. 'With – with what?'

'With certain files held on the IHA's secure server in New York. Specifically, those concerning the lost works of Plato held in the archives of the Brotherhood of Selasphoros.'

For a moment, confusion almost overcame fear on Raynes's face. 'Wait, you did all this to *access our server*? Why?'

'That's my concern. Your only concern right now is to do what I tell you.'

'And if I refuse?'

Komosa's arm snapped up. Without taking his eyes off Raynes, he fired a dart into the heart of one of the other IHA scientists. The man clutched weakly at his chest before collapsing.

Raynes flinched, eyes wide with fear. 'Okay, the server, okay! I'll–I'll – whatever you want.'

'Thank you.' Komosa nodded, and one of his men led Raynes to the computer.

'Don't do it, Doctor,' Hamilton warned. 'You know we can't let anyone else reach Atlantis.'

'Atlantis!' said Komosa with a dismissive laugh. 'I don't care about Atlantis!'

'I don't believe you. Dr Raynes, under no circumstances

whatsoever are you to give this man access to that computer.'

Komosa sighed. 'You *will* give me access, Doctor.' He crossed to the prisoners, taking Bremmerman by the arm and pulling her to her feet. She gave Hamilton a fearful look, unsure what to do.

'Leave her alone,' Hamilton barked.

Komosa moved behind the lieutenant, towering over her as he slipped one thick arm round her waist and the hand of the other to her neck. 'Dr Raynes.' He turned away from Hamilton, moving Bremmerman round with him as he faced the scientist. 'I'm sure you've noticed this young lady around the rig before. She *is* very pretty.' He lowered his head, stroking her hair with one side of his chin. Despite her fear, she slammed an elbow into his stomach.

He barely flinched. The diamond smile widened. 'And very spirited.' His thumb moved slowly up her neck, stopping an inch below her chin—

And *pressed*.

Something inside her throat collapsed with a sickening wet crunch. The young woman's eyes bulged, her mouth opening in a desperate attempt to draw a breath that could never reach her lungs. Komosa released her. She reached up to her face, fingers twitching. A drop of blood ran from the corner of her mouth as she convulsed.

'And very dead,' said Komosa, voice like stone.

'You *bastard*!' roared Hamilton. He tried to charge at Komosa, but one of the other wetsuited men viciously clubbed him down with the butt of his gun. The commander dropped to the floor. Bremmerman fell too – but, unlike Hamilton, she didn't get back up.

Komosa turned back to Raynes. 'I will kill one of your shipmates every minute until you give me what I want. Their lives are entirely in your hands. Are your computer files really so valuable that you're willing to let your friends die to protect them?' He aimed his gun at the head of one of the IHA scientists. 'Fifty-eight seconds.'

Sweat beaded on Raynes's face. 'B-but even if I wanted to, there's no way I could now! The security system, it—'

'I know about the security system, Doctor. Forty-nine seconds.'

Frantic, Raynes sat down at the computer and began working, his hand so slick with frightened perspiration that it slipped off the mouse. A password box popped up. He typed a string of characters and stabbed at the return key. The box vanished, replaced by an alert: THUMBPRINT VALIDATION REQUIRED. With a worried glance back at Komosa, he pressed his thumb against a black square set into the top right corner of the keyboard. A red light pulsed. The alert disappeared, replaced by another.

VOICEPRINT VALIDATION REQUIRED.

'Seventeen seconds to spare,' said Komosa, lowering the gun. 'Well done.'

'I can't get you any further. I can't!' Raynes pleaded. 'The voiceprint ID, it's got a—'

'It has a stress analyser, I know.' The giant moved over to the desk, his free hand reaching for something on his belt. 'It denies access even to authorised users if they seem to be under duress. But don't worry – in a moment, you'll be perfectly relaxed.'

And with that, he jabbed a syringe into Raynes's arm and pushed the plunger.

Raynes stared at the syringe in horror, opening his mouth to cry out . . . before a tremor ran through his entire body. He sagged, bones turning to jelly. What had started as a cry emerged as a long, almost orgasmic sigh.

Komosa leaned closer. 'Now, Doctor, I know you can hear me, and I know you're still lucid. There were seventeen seconds left on the clock. That is how long you have to enter the final code before I shoot your friend. Do you understand?' Raynes nodded, the muscles in his face slack. 'Your time starts now.' Komosa aimed the gun back at the other scientist, taking Raynes by his shirt collar and lifting him closer to the computer.

Raynes cleared his throat, then spoke, voice low and dream-like. 'In this island of Atlantis there was a great and wonderful empire.' A small microphone icon flickered, acknowledging that the computer had heard.

Nothing happened. The man Komosa was aiming at whimpered. Then—

The screen lit up with a directory window. The satellite data link had been established. A few of the prisoners let out relieved sighs.

'Thank you, Doctor,' said Komosa, plugging the drive into a port on the computer. 'I'll take it from here.'

That was the signal.

The flat hissing thuds of dart guns filled the lab. Those people who weren't hit by the first volley started to shout – only to fall silent within seconds as the guns were reloaded and a second round fired. Outside the main group, Hamilton jumped up with a roar of fury.

Komosa fired. The dart slammed deep into Hamilton's right eye socket, unleashing a welter of blood. The commander instantly fell to the swaying deck, dead even before the toxins took effect.

Turning back to the computer as if nothing had happened,

Komosa copied files to the drive before accessing a different directory. Even through the influence of the powerful muscle relaxant, Raynes managed a look of surprise when he saw the directory name.

Komosa caught his expression. He grinned. 'Yes, IHA personnel records. Don't worry, we're not going to kill them.' The grin hardened as he selected two particular files and copied them to the drive. 'Yet.'

The files transferred, Komosa pulled the drive from the computer and returned it to its pouch. He straightened, turning to his men. 'Disperse the bodies throughout the command section – it needs to look as if they were on duty when the rig capsized. I'll go to the bridge and flood the starboard pontoon – once the pumps start, we'll have five minutes to get back to the sub.' They acknowledged and hurried out, dragging the paralysed navy personnel after them.

Komosa tugged the zip of his wetsuit back up to his neck and followed his men out of the lab, stepping over the slumped, helpless civilians. He didn't look back.

All Raynes could do was stare at the computer screen as he waited to die. The names of the last two files Komosa had copied were still highlighted. He knew both of them.

CHASE, EDWARD J.

WILDE, NINA P.

1

New York City: Three Months Later

The lights of Manhattan shone like constellations of precision-aligned stars against the night sky. Eddie Chase gazed out at the spectacular panorama and sighed. He would much rather have been somewhere, anywhere, on the island – a restaurant, a bar, even a launderette – than here.

Not that the venue itself was a problem. The *Ocean Emperor* was their host's pride and joy, a 350-foot motor cruiser on which absolutely no expense had been spared. Chase had been on luxury yachts before, but this one represented a whole new level of opulence. Had he just been with Nina and a group of close friends, he would have taken full advantage of the experience.

But apart from a handful of senior IHA staff, so far he didn't know any of the hundred-plus guests. And he didn't have anything in common with them either. Diplomats, politicians, titans of industry, all busy networking and deal-making with every handshake. Chase, on the other hand, was here merely as Nina's 'and guest'. This wasn't his world.

It wasn't Nina's either, but she was doing everything she could to pretend it was, he thought with a frown. He knocked back the remaining red wine in his glass and turned away from the vista to face the crowd. Nina was standing with former US Navy admiral turned historian Hector Amoros, the head of the IHA, and shaking hands with a tall, distinguished yet smug-looking man. *Politician*, Chase knew at a glance.

Nina glanced through the open doors in his direction. 'Eddie!' she called, waving one hand to summon him. The champagne glass that had been in her other from practically the moment she boarded the yacht had been refilled again, he noticed. 'Eddie, come here and meet the senator.'

'Yeah, coming,' he replied without enthusiasm, fingering his stiff and uncomfortable collar. A blast of noise and wind swept over the deck as he re-entered the ship, another helicopter coming in to drop off more ultra-VIP guests on the yacht's helipad. Chase and Nina had been brought to the *Ocean Emperor* by boat, as had most of the other guests. Even in the world of the super-rich, there was still a pecking order. He imagined the only way to top arriving by helicopter would be to land in a Harrier jump jet.

Nina looked amazing tonight, he had to admit. The sweeping scarlet off-the-shoulder dress was a world away from the ruggedly practical clothes she had worn when he first got to know her a year and a half before, or even the Italian suits she'd adopted more recently in her role as the IHA's Director of Operations. Her normally red hair had been dyed a richer, darker tone for the occasion, swept and styled to highlight her carefully made-up face.

Chase ground his teeth at the mere thought of her hair. He'd complained about it all day before Nina finally made him promise to shut up.

But still . . . *five hundred dollars* for a fucking *haircut*?

'Eddie,' said Nina, 'this is Senator Victor Dalton. Senator, this is Eddie Chase, who works for me at the IHA. And he also happens to be my boyfriend,' she added.

'Nice to meet you, Senator,' said Chase, shooting Nina a subtly annoyed look as he shook Dalton's hand. He recognised the name – Dalton was in the running to be the next President of the United States. That explained the two stone-faced men in dark suits watching him coldly from nearby: Secret Service agents.

'You too, Mr Chase,' Dalton answered. 'English, huh? Not a Londoner, if I'm right about the accent.'

'Too blood— I mean, yeah, that's right. I'm from Yorkshire.'

Dalton nodded. 'Yorkshire, right. Nice part of the world, I understand.'

'It's not bad.' Chase doubted the senator knew where Yorkshire was, or cared.

'Senator Dalton's on the IHA's funding committee,' Amoros told him.

Chase smirked. 'That right? Any chance of a pay rise?'

Nina's glossily lipsticked mouth shrank into a tight line, but Dalton laughed. 'I'll see what I can do.' He looked past Chase, his eyebrows flicking in recognition. 'Say, our host approaches! Monsieur Corvus, good to meet you again!'

Chase turned to see a sleekly groomed, black-haired man in a dinner jacket. He looked to be in his mid-fifties. 'Please,' he said to Dalton as he shook hands, 'René. This is a social event, yes? No need for tiresome formality!'

'Whatever you say . . . René!' Dalton chuckled.

'Thank you . . . Victor! And Nina,' Corvus continued as he turned to Nina, taking her hand, 'such a pleasure to meet you again.' He leaned forward and kissed her on both cheeks. Nina blushed. Chase glared at the Frenchman, quickly forcing a neutral expression when he turned to face him. 'And you, you must be . . .'

'Eddie Chase,' Chase announced brusquely, sticking out his hand. 'Nina's boyfriend.'

'But of course,' said Corvus, smiling as he shook his hand. 'René Corvus. Welcome aboard the *Ocean Emperor*.'

'Cheers.' Chase looked round at the oak-panelled room. 'It's a really nice boat you've got here. I suppose being a shipping magnet has its perks.'

Dalton suppressed an amused noise, while Nina let out a fluttering, slightly desperate laugh. 'René's not just a shipping *magnate*,' she said to Chase, emphasising the pronunciation of the word through clenched teeth, 'he's also one of the IHA's directors.'

'Non-executive, of course,' Corvus added modestly. 'It's only proper that the experts like Nina should make the decisions about protecting the world's archaeological wonders.'

'Yeah, well,' said Chase with a big fake smile, 'she really does like to be in control of everything, I can tell you.'

Nina took a gulp from her glass before treating Chase to an equally false grin. 'Honey, sweetie?' she said, tugging at his jacket sleeve. 'Can I speak to you? Over here?' She tipped her head towards the doors.

'Of course you can, *darling*,' he replied. He nodded to the other three men. 'Excuse us for a second.' The trio exchanged knowing looks as he and Nina backed away.

'What the *hell* are you doing?' Nina hissed as soon as they were what she mistakenly thought was out of earshot.

'What're you talking about?'

'You know damn well what I'm talking about! Making an ass of yourself and embarrassing me!'

'Oh, *I'm* embarrassing *you*?' snorted Chase. 'What about you and your "Here's Eddie, my dogsbody at the IHA – oh, and he's sort of my boyfriend as well"?'

'I *didn't* say that!'

'You might as well have! And *pardon bloody me* for getting a word wrong that no bugger uses in normal conversation. Not all of us could go to the University of Poncy Vocabulary. Or afford a five-hundred-dollar haircut,' he added before he could stop himself.

Nina's eyes narrowed into angry slits. 'You *promised* me you were going to stop going on about that! Jesus! The one time, the *one goddamn time* I need to look good to impress these people, and all I get is you complaining how much it cost!'

'It was *five hundred* fucking *dollars*!' Chase reminded her. 'I can get a haircut for ten bucks!'

'Yes! And it looks like it!' Nina snapped back, waving a hand at his close-cropped, receding hair. 'Besides, I've got a high-level job with the United Nations now, I'm earning a hell of a lot more than I was at the university – it's not like I can't afford it.'

'Yeah, there's a lot of things you can afford now, aren't there?'

'Meaning what?'

'If you can't . . .' Chase tailed off as he saw two people descending the stairs from the upper decks. New arrivals, brought to the *Ocean Emperor* by the helicopter. One was a Chinese man, like Chase in his mid-thirties, surveying the crowd of wealthy guests with an arrogant smile that suggested he considered himself to be far more important than any of them – or all of them. The other . . .

' 'Scuse me,' Chase said, his fight with Nina completely forgotten. He started for the doors. 'I need to get some air.'

Nina blocked his way, confused and still angry. 'What? No you don't! What did you mean, I can afford a lot of stuff?'

'Forget it. I . . .' He looked at the stairs again.

It was too late. She'd seen him.

The Chinese man swaggered through the crowd towards Corvus, people moving out of his path as if he were sweeping them aside with an invisible force field. Following a couple of paces behind was a younger woman. Unlike him, she was Caucasian. Brunette, stunningly beautiful, expensively attired . . . and wearing an expression of quiet sadness.

The only person she looked at as she crossed the room was Chase.

'Shit,' he said under his breath. There was no way he could simply disappear now.

'Yo, René!' said the man loudly, opening his arms wide as he came up to Corvus. His features may have been Chinese, but his accent was entirely American, upscale Californian. 'Nice boat! I've got one like it on order myself. Bigger, of course. Senator Dalton!' He grabbed Dalton's hand and pumped it exuberantly. 'Or I guess

I'm going to have to get used to calling you "Mr President" before long, huh?'

'Well, I still have to win the primaries yet . . .' said Dalton with a sly smile.

'Ah, you'll ace it. You know you've got my vote, Vic. And my funding. Unless the other guy can offer me a better deal!' He laughed, Dalton joining in with rather less sincerity. 'And Hector, hi! Good to see you again.'

Amoros looked at Nina and Chase. 'Nina! I'd like to introduce you to someone.'

Nina and Chase both hurriedly adopted masks of bland sociability as they walked over. 'Nina,' said Amoros, 'this is the newest non-executive director of the IHA, Richard Yuen Xuan.'

'Good to meet you, Mr Xuan,' Nina said, holding out her hand. Amoros's face froze, and Dalton held in another amused grunt.

'*Actually*,' said Chase, cutting in before Amoros could correct her, 'Chinese family names traditionally come *first*. Am I right, Mr Yuen?'

'You're right,' said Yuen. He smiled at the mortified Nina. 'Hey, don't worry about it! I'm not gonna get your name wrong, though. I already know it.'

Nina blinked. 'You do?'

'Dr Nina Wilde, Director of Operations for the IHA. Historian, archaeologist, explorer . . . and *discoverer*,' he said, with meaning. 'I've been reading all about you.' He shook her hand.

'Uh, thanks,' she managed to reply, completely thrown. 'So what do you do, Mr Yuen?'

Yuen smirked. 'Call me Rich. 'Cause I am!' He laughed loudly at his own joke. 'I was in telecoms – still am, got satellites, phone companies, the biggest ISP in China – but I've been diversifying recently. Hell, why not, I can afford it! Got a microchip plant in Switzerland, and I even bought a diamond mine in Botswana off René here. Shoulda kept it, René, production's gone through the roof! And here's why I took an interest in diamonds.' He turned to the woman waiting silently behind him and took her left hand, raising it to reveal a huge diamond ring. 'May I introduce my beautiful wife of the past six months? Sophia – Lady Blackwood.'

'Wife?' exclaimed Chase, almost a yelp. Nina looked at him disapprovingly.

'Delighted to meet you all,' said Sophia, a distinct flatness to her cut-glass English accent.

Yuen introduced the others to her, stopping when he came to Chase. 'I don't think we've met before, Mr . . .'

'Chase. Eddie Chase.'

'Okay . . . Eddie. And this is my—'

'We've met.'

This time, it was Nina's turn to let out a yelp. 'What?'

For the first time, Sophia's expression changed, a hesitant smile blooming as she lifted her right hand. 'Hello, Eddie. It's . . . been a while.'

'Yes.' Chase didn't return the smile, nor did he acknowledge her raised hand. After a moment she lowered it again, the smile withering to hurt disappointment. 'Well, I see you've done all right for yourself.' He turned to Yuen. 'Good luck with your marriage, *Dick*. Excuse me.' He turned for the door.

Sophia stepped forward, reaching out to touch the side of his jacket. He stopped, but didn't look round. 'Eddie, I . . .'

Chase remained still for a long moment, then strode away.

'Eddie!' said Nina, not sure what had just happened. Something about Chase had changed – his voice, even his stance – but she couldn't pin down exactly what. 'Where are you going?'

'For a *piss*,' he barked over his shoulder as he walked out.

Nina stared after him, cheeks flushing pink with humiliation. 'I – I'm very, *very* sorry about that,' she stammered, taking a mouthful of champagne to calm herself.

Yuen shrugged. 'Don't worry about it, no harm done.' He turned to Sophia. Nina expected him to ask how she knew Chase, but instead he just said, 'You okay?' She nodded. 'Good. Anyway, Dr Wilde – Nina?' Nina nodded. 'I'm really glad to meet you. I've been fascinated by your work. I know there are some things you've found that the IHA wants to keep under wraps for now, but I'd love to know what ancient wonders you're going to hunt for next!'

Nina hesitated before answering. As one of the numerous non-executive directors the IHA had taken on around the world, primarily to facilitate connections and grease the political wheels in places where a UN-backed archaeological survey might otherwise be regarded with suspicion, Yuen ought not to have been told exactly why the IHA had been established; his knowledge should have been lacking in certain specifics. The full details of the discovery of Atlantis were restricted to a relatively small number of people. On the other hand, he had certainly hinted that he knew about it . . .

She decided to play it safe and avoid any mention of Atlantis. Much as she wanted to unveil her discovery to the world, she knew she couldn't until the IHA and the governments behind it were in agreement that the time was right. Revealing just how

29

close over five billion people had come to being exterminated by a genetically engineered plague had the potential to cause a lot of problems.

However, her current project was almost infinitely less controversial. And in this case, when she *did* discover the truth of the supposed myth, she would be able to take full credit for it right away . . .

'Well, actually,' she began, 'I'm looking for the Tomb of Hercules.'

Dalton raised an eyebrow. 'As in the Greek mythological hero?'

'The same.'

'Pardon me for stating the obvious,' Dalton said, a slight tinge of sarcasm to his voice, 'but if he's mythological, how can he have a tomb?'

'As a matter of fact,' said Sophia, causing all the men to look round at her almost as if surprised that she had a contribution to make, 'many figures from Greek mythology have tombs. Whether there was ever anyone buried in them was immaterial to the Greeks – they were more like temples, places where they could pay tribute.'

'That's right,' Nina said, feeling slightly upstaged. 'You're very well informed, Lady . . . do I call you Lady Blackwood, or . . . ?'

'Just Sophia, please.'

' "Lady" is what we call her when we want to impress the rubes,' Yuen added smarmily. 'You'd be amazed how much value that old Brit aristocracy thing can add to a deal. Main reason I married her!' He laughed again, in a way that suggested to Nina that he wasn't entirely joking.

'Benefits of a classical education,' Sophia explained to Nina.

Either she was untroubled by her husband's boorishness, or she was well practised at hiding her feelings. 'But to be honest, my speciality is more in Latin than Greek. Please, you were saying about the Tomb of Hercules?'

'Right, okay.' Nina polished off her champagne, then waved her glass at a nearby waiter. He smoothly swept in and refilled it. 'As Sophia said, many Greek mythological figures have tombs dedicated to them. Hercules – or Heracles, the original Greek form of the name – is actually quite unusual in that he *doesn't* have a tomb. At least,' she added theatrically, 'not one that's been discovered.'

'And you think you've found it?' asked Yuen. The arrogant jokiness was suddenly gone, the question posed with intensity.

'Well . . . much as I'd *like* to say yes, I'm afraid I haven't. Not yet. I've been piecing together clues for several months, but so far haven't managed to pin down a location. Hopefully that's going to change soon, though!'

'And where did you find these clues?'

Even through the champagne, Nina reminded herself to be discreet. 'There were references in some ancient Greek parchments in the archives of . . . a private collector.' That the parchments contained *Hermocrates*, the lost work concerning Atlantis by the Greek philosopher Plato, and the 'private collector' was actually a secret society willing to kill to prevent anyone from rediscovering the ancient civilisation, were facts to keep to herself. 'The IHA made a deal to examine the collection last year. Well, photos of them, anyway. Although I'm actually meeting a guy tomorrow to arrange a viewing of the *original* parchments.'

Yuen looked intrigued. 'You think the originals will tell you something you can't get from photos?'

Nina took another drink before replying. 'Yes, definitely! That's what archaeology's all about – actually seeing things for real, not just looking at pictures. Going to a real site or having a physical object to work with, something you can hold in your hands, makes all the difference. You get to see things in a whole new light.'

Yuen nodded thoughtfully, and Corvus said, 'But surely in your role as Director of Operations, you can't have many opportunities for field work?'

'No, afraid not,' said Nina, shaking her head. 'I spend most of my time at a desk or in meetings at the moment.' More so than ever following the loss in a storm of the rig exploring Atlantis; most of the IHA's field projects were on hold pending the results of the ongoing investigation. 'But on the other hand, there are compensations. Like this!' She indicated the opulence of the ship around them. 'Thank you for hosting us.'

'I thought it was time the IHA's profile was raised,' Corvus said, smiling.

Yuen gave her a smile as well, though his was rather more slippery. 'Well, good luck with your tomb raiding!' He looked over one shoulder at another group of people nearby. 'But anyway, gotta go circulate. René, thanks for the invite, and Vic, remember to invite me to the White House! Come on, Soph.'

'Nice to meet you,' Sophia said to Nina, before Yuen took her hand and drew her away.

'Little punk,' muttered Dalton after they had gone. 'I don't care how many billions he has, he's still a jackass. Still, damn! He knows how to pick a wife.'

'He's a very fortunate man to have found somebody so perfect,' agreed Corvus. He turned to Nina. 'And you, Nina. Are you and Eddie planning to marry?'

Nina was caught off guard by the question, hurriedly gulping down another mouthful of champagne before answering. 'Uh, well, I don't know.' Although after Chase's little display tonight, it certainly wasn't on her immediate agenda.

She glanced round, wondering whether, now that Sophia had gone, he was on his way back. There was no sign of him. She decided to find him and express her annoyance at his behaviour.

After she finished her drink.

Chase wandered aimlessly through the *Ocean Emperor*. Coming to the function had definitely been a bad move, what with Nina's new high-and-mighty attitude – and then meeting *Sophia*, of all people . . .

He didn't even want to think about her. She was a part of his past that he thought he'd successfully forgotten. Apparently not.

He emerged on to the aft deck, noting with relief that there were fewer guests here. The cold wind was an encouragement to stay inside the ship. Heading to the railing by the ship's retracted swimming platform to look out over Manhattan again, he was surprised when somebody called his name. He looked round. 'Matt?'

'Hey, Eddie!' Matt Trulli padded over to him, the tubby, spike-haired Australian looking decidedly out of place amongst the other guests in his scruffy knee-length shorts and garish shirt. He pumped Chase's hand with genuine enthusiasm. 'Haven't seen you for ages! How you doing, mate?'

'Fine, thanks. What're you doing here?'

Trulli gestured up at the *Ocean Emperor*'s bridge. 'I work for the boss now!'

'Corvus?'

Trulli nodded. 'Normally work in the Bahamas, but I was in the States 'cause I'm going up to MIT tomorrow for a seminar. I was kind of surprised to get an invite, but thought what the hell, free booze!' He held up his glass.

Chase realised that he didn't have a drink of his own, and couldn't see any waiters nearby to give him a glass. Whatever; he didn't want any more. Unlike Nina . . . 'So, you still in the submarine business?'

'Yeah. After Frost's business went belly up I started working for René, designing underwater hotels.'

Chase gave him a sceptical look. 'Underwater *hotels*?'

'You laugh, mate, but they're going to be the next big thing!' Trulli assured him. 'They're already big in Dubai, and the design I came up with? Modular, so you can bolt one together wherever you like. Wake up in the morning, look out the window and bam! Fish, right there. René's actually been living in the prototype in the Bahamas. Pretty cool. Wouldn't mind one myself, but it's a bit more than I can afford for an apartment!'

'I know what that's like,' said Chase ruefully, looking across at Manhattan.

'Anyway,' Trulli continued, 'now I've got the hotel stuff all done and dusted, I'm working on something way cooler.' His face changed to a definite 'oops' expression. 'Only, well, I can't really talk about it. Top secret, y'know?'

Chase gave him a half-smile. 'Your secret's safe with me.'

'Aw, cheers, mate. But I will say this much – it's bloody *awesome*!

You know how the subs I built for Frost were like bulldozers? This is more like a Ferrari. It's going to be fantastic! When I get the bugger working properly, anyway.' He took another drink, then leaned back on the stern railing. 'So, what about you, mate? How'd you swing an invite to this shindig?'

'I'm here with Nina. She got the invite, not me.'

Trulli reacted with curiosity at his cutting tone, but didn't comment on it. Instead, he said, 'So you and her are . . . ?' Chase nodded. 'Aw, great stuff!'

'Don't get too excited; we're not married or anything. Not sure exactly what we are at the moment, to be honest.'

'O-*kay* . . . So she works for the IHA, then?'

'Yeah. So do I.'

'Gotcha. What do you do?'

Chase puffed air from his cheeks before replying. 'Well, most of the time I sit on my arse at a desk and do absolutely fuck all. My official job title's "Assistant to the Director of Operations", my *actual* job's to look after Nina when she's out in the field, but since she hasn't been out in the field for over a year, there's not really a fuck of a lot to do all day.' The words came out with rather more frustration in them than he'd intended.

'So Nina's your boss, then? That must make things interesting.'

Chase shot him a dark, humourless smile. 'You have no idea.'

Trulli looked slightly awkward. 'Right . . . Is she around? Wouldn't mind saying hello.'

'Speak of the devil,' said Chase at the sound of high heels clicking rapidly towards him. He turned to see Nina approaching with an irate expression, her dress fluttering in the wind.

'I've been looking all over for you,' she snapped, before seeing

Trulli next to him. 'Matt! Oh my God, how are you? What are you doing here?'

'Just telling Eddie that I work for René Corvus,' said Trulli. 'Still building subs. I hear you're big at the IHA now. Congrats!'

'Thanks. Look, Matt, I'm sorry to interrupt but I need to talk to Eddie. In private.'

Trulli gave Chase a concerned glance, then drained his glass. 'Sure thing . . . I need to get a fill-up anyway. Maybe see you guys around later?'

'Maybe,' Chase said. Trulli clapped him on the arm, then kissed Nina on the cheek before heading inside.

Chase watched him go, then looked round to find Nina glaring at him. He indicated her glass. 'So, on red wine now? Is that your sixth or your seventh drink of the evening?'

'Don't try to change the subject.'

'You haven't *told* me the subject.'

'You know *exactly* what the subject is.' She stepped closer. 'I've never felt so humiliated in my life! I don't care what your problem was with Sophia, you could at least have *pretended* to be civil. There are *ten-year-olds* who act with more maturity! For God's sake, René and Sophia's husband are directors of the IHA!'

'Non-executive,' Chase noted sarcastically.

Nina's face tightened angrily. 'Do you have any idea how bad you made me look in front of all those people?'

'Oh, *now* we're getting down to it,' said Chase, leaning back against the railing. 'That's what *really* pissed you off, isn't it? You were there knocking back the champagne with the billionaires and the wannabe presidents and her fucking ladyship, and then suddenly you remember – oh, shit! My boyfriend's just some thick ex-soldier, how embarrassing! Better put him in his place or my new friends might think I'm more like him than like them!'

'That – that's *not* what happened at all, and you know it!' said Nina, open-mouthed with outrage. 'And what *is* your problem with Sophia? Where do you know her from?'

'That's none of your business.'

'Oh, I think you've *made* it my business!'

Chase shoved himself upright, face just inches from Nina's. With the extra height of her heels, she was as tall as him. 'All right, you want to know what my problem with Sophia is? She thinks that just because she was born into the right family, everyone else is beneath her. But you know what?' His face pulled into a sneer. 'I didn't mind it so much from her, because that's how she's always been, and she doesn't know any better. But from *you*? You get a fancy job title and a bit more money and start schmoozing with politicians and all these rich dickheads, and suddenly you think you're better than me and you can treat me like shit?'

Nina flushed with fury, lips drawn tight and quivering. Then—
Splash!

'Fuck you, Eddie,' she spat, turning on her heel and stalking away, leaving Chase with red wine dribbling down his face on to his shirt and jacket. He took a deep breath, then wiped his eyes. The handful of other people on the deck quickly looked away.

'What?' he said, offering them a broad grin that exposed the gap between his front teeth. 'It's not a proper party until someone gets a drink thrown in their face.'

This particular party being on a yacht out in New York Harbour, simply getting a taxi back to their apartment wasn't an option for either Nina or Chase. Instead, they had to wait for one of the boats to return, then sit through the unhurried journey to shore, before finally taking a cab all the way uptown to the Upper East Side. The whole trip took close to forty-five minutes.

Neither said a word to the other the whole time.

2

'Ow.'

Nina squirmed painfully across her pillow, desperately searching for a cooler patch that might ease her headache. She didn't find one.

The music thumping from the next room, seventies and eighties rock, wasn't helping matters. Nor was the 'singing' that accompanied it.

She reluctantly shuffled across the bed, the long T-shirt she was wearing creased and sweaty. One glance in the mirror as she rolled out from under the covers told her that her hair would require some serious restorative work before her meeting.

The meeting . . .

Suddenly filled with panic, she rushed into the apartment's living room, squinting at the bright morning light through the balcony windows. 'What time is it?' she demanded.

Chase, in shorts and a grey T-shirt, was lifting weights. He broke off from his tuneless rendition of 'Free Bird' to say, 'Morning, sunshine,' in a decidedly sarcastic tone.

'No, Eddie, really, what time is it? I need to get ready, I'm meeting—'

'It's only seven o'clock, relax. Even you don't take that long to sort yourself out.' He resumed his bicep curls.

'Seven o'clock? Wait, you got me up that early – can you turn that down?' She jabbed a finger at the stereo, into which Chase had plugged his iPod.

He grudgingly stopped lifting long enough to lower the volume by a tiny amount, then picked up the weights again. 'It's Wednesday morning. Training day.'

Nina winced. 'Oh, God, do we have to? I really don't feel up to it today.'

'It was your idea in the first place,' Chase snorted. He put on a nasal and shrill impersonation of her accent. *'Eddie, can you keep me fit? Eddie, can you teach me self-defence?* You were the one who nagged me into doing it.'

'I *didn't* nag,' Nina complained. 'Look, can't we just skip it this week?'

'You should be doing it at least *twice* a week if you want it to be any use.' He changed stance. 'I'm going to work out anyway. I might be stuck at a desk all day, but at least *I'm* not going to turn into some blob.'

Nina didn't like his emphasis, but wasn't sure whether he'd meant it deliberately or not. She decided to let it pass. This time. 'Okay, okay. But keep it short, twenty minutes. I really need to get ready for this meeting. And let me freshen up first.'

When Nina emerged from the bathroom five minutes later, Chase had shoved the glass coffee table and black leather Le Corbusier couch aside to make room for a blue padded mat in the centre of the room. She had donned a pair of sweatpants, padding barefoot across the floor. 'Damn, I'm cold.'

'That's bare wood floors for you,' Chase said dismissively. 'Your old place was much nicer. You know, cosy and warm, carpets . . . None of this poncy stuff.' He made a sour face at the elongated carved statue of an African warrior that was the room's showpiece.

'You live here too,' Nina reminded him, with an equally disapproving look at the Cuban pottery cigar-box holder in the shape of a beaming Fidel Castro, now used to keep loose change, that Chase had insisted on displaying on the kitchen counter. Exactly what Chase had been doing in Cuba during his time in the Special Air Service was yet another thing about his past she'd never been able to prise out of him. She understood the figurine's sentimental value – it had been a joking gift from his friend Hugo Castille, who had died on the Atlantis expedition – but God, it was ugly!

'You wouldn't think so,' he muttered, taking a martial stance. 'All right! Let's get started.'

The training session began with a warm-up, then moved on to judo, each of them in turn trying to throw the other. It didn't take long for Nina to realise that Chase was offering considerably more resistance than usual when she tried to throw him. And as for his treatment of her . . .

She let out an angry gasp as she was smacked down – hard – on to the mat for the third time, Chase's knee digging into her chest as he pinned her. 'Eddie, that *hurt*!'

'That's why it's called *fighting*. Otherwise it'd be called fannying about.' He held her down for a moment longer, then stood. 'Okay, let's try something else.'

Nina waited for him to help her up. When he didn't extend a hand, she glared at him and got to her feet. 'What's your problem?'

'*I* don't have any problems.'

'Yeah, you do. You've got a bug up your ass about something. You have for a while, actually. And I don't just mean last night.'

He gave her a smile devoid of any humour. 'Wow, I'm impressed. You mean you can actually *remember* anything about last night?'

'With the way you behaved, I'd rather forget it.' She knew he was about to make some scathing comment, and cut him off before he had the chance. 'Come on, then. We were going to do something else.'

Chase grunted, then reached into his sports bag and took out a gun – not a real one, but a garish orange plastic toy. 'Fair enough. You want me to be the bad guy, I'm the bad guy. Let's see if you actually remember anything I've taught you.' He took a step back, then raised the gun and aimed it at Nina. 'Disarm me.'

Nina shook her head. 'For God's sake.'

'What? You wanted self-defence training. This is self-defence training.'

'Yeah, but that was when I still thought there was a chance we might run into trouble, like if someone wanted revenge for Atlantis. Now? To be honest, all I want is a bit of a cardiovascular workout.'

'And you'll *get* a cardiovascular workout if someone sticks a gun in your face. Come on.' He thrust the gun at her. 'Give me your purse.'

'What? Eddie, come on—'

He pulled the trigger. The toy gun clicked. 'Bang! You're dead. Try again. You killed my boss. Now I'm going to kill you.'

'Eddie—'

'Bang! Dead again. Useless.' Nina frowned at him, growing annoyed. 'Try again! I'm Giovanni Qobras's brother, and you're the bitch who got him killed—'

Nina lunged, twisting her body away from the gun and grabbing Chase's forearm with one hand as the other tried to prise the weapon from his grip—

Whump!

The room spun around her, and she found herself flat on her back, the breath whooshing from her lungs. The muzzle of the gun hung over her.

It clicked. 'Bang,' said Chase, smirking.

Nina stared up at him angrily. Then she shoved herself upright and stormed into the bedroom, slamming the door behind her.

Forty minutes later, Nina was ready to leave. She would have preferred to spend longer on her hair, which was proving more resistant to styling than she'd hoped, but she just wanted to get out of the apartment. Despite coffee and some painkillers, her headache still hadn't gone away.

But that wasn't the main reason she was in a rush to get out into the open air.

'So this bloke you're meeting today, what's it all about?' Chase asked. He was still in his T-shirt and shorts, slouched on the couch with his feet up on the glass coffee table and showing no sign that he intended to go with her.

'Put your feet down,' Nina told him. He ignored her. 'It's classified, IHA business.' It wasn't, but she had neither the time nor the inclination to go into details with him.

Chase rolled his eyes. 'Oh, is that right?'

'And what're you doing? You're not even ready.'

He waved a casual hand at the window. 'Thought I'd take the morning off.'

'You did, huh? And did you bother checking if that was all right?'

'Well, since it's pretty obvious you don't need me for anything, I thought, why the fuck not?'

Nina took a long, slow breath in a fruitless attempt to suppress her frustration. 'The IHA's a professional organisation, *Eddie*. You're supposed to get permission.'

Chase put both hands behind his head and stretched out even further. 'Okay then, *boss*, can I have your permission to take the morning off? Seeing as I need to go to the dry-cleaner because *somebody* got red wine all over my jacket.'

'God!' Nina snapped, finally losing her patience. 'Whatever! Take the morning off, take the *week* off! I don't care.' She grabbed her bag and walked out, closing the door with a bang.

Chase thumped a fist on the sofa cushion and got to his feet, his own frustration coiled up inside him. 'Buggeration and fuckery!' he snarled, glaring at the African statue. 'And you can fuck off, an' all.' It stared back in wooden silence.

Still fuming, he went into the bedroom and retrieved his jacket. Even on the dark material, the stains stood out clearly. 'Well, bollocks,' he told it. 'Suppose I really will have to get you cleaned.' He went through its pockets, emptying the contents—

His fingers touched something unexpected. A sheet of paper, tightly folded into a small square. Anger giving way to curiosity, he opened it out.

He recognised the handwriting even before looking at the

signature. *Sophia*. She must have slipped it into his pocket when she tugged on his jacket at the party.

He read the note. Then his eyes widened and he read it again, just to make sure it really said what he thought. It did.

'Fuck me . . .' he whispered. Forget the dry-cleaner – he needed to go to the IHA after all.

But not to see Nina. This was definitely over her head.

Nina's office had a small private bathroom, in which she tried to make herself appear as polished and professional as possible for her visitor. She looked at herself in the mirror and touched the pendant hanging from her neck. The curved piece of metal was actually a scrap of an Atlantean artefact she had discovered years earlier without knowing its true nature; she had instead always regarded it as her good-luck charm. She hoped its luck would help her get what she wanted today.

Satisfied that her hair finally looked worth five hundred dollars, she checked that her Armani jacket and skirt were straight and her black stilettos clean, then looked at her watch. Almost time for her meeting.

There was something she had to practise first, though.

Nina left the bathroom and sat at her desk, turning to face the view of Manhattan from the window of the United Nations building. 'Okay. I can do this, I can get this right.' She took a breath. 'Good morning, Mr Popadol— *dammit!* Popo, Popadolapis . . . shit!' She ground a palm against her forehead. 'I'm still drunk! Mr Nicholas Popadopoulos,' she finally managed to say, carefully enunciating each syllable. 'Pop-a-dop-ou-los. Popadopoulos. Finally!' She giggled involuntarily. 'Okay, I'm ready for you now,

Mr Nicholas Popadopoulos. And you *are* going to give me what I want.'

The man in question arrived a few minutes later. Nina had spoken to him by phone on several occasions, but this was the first time she had met him in person. For such an obstructive personality, he was not terribly impressive to look at. Popadopoulos was in his sixties, stooped, with thin black hair plastered greasily down in a vain attempt to hide his bald spot. He had a little pencil moustache, and beady spectacles through which he peered suspiciously at Nina as she welcomed him into her office.

'Good morning, Mr Popadopoulos,' she said, mentally congratulating herself even as she held back a smile. 'It's good to finally meet you.'

'Dr Wilde, yes,' he replied. His accent was Greek, not surprisingly, but with a hint of Italian – the Brotherhood of Selasphoros was based in Rome, and, from what Nina understood, Popadopoulos had been in charge of the secret society's archives there for over three decades. 'I really don't see why you had to force me to come to New York, no, no. There are these marvellous inventions now, telephone, fax, email. Perhaps you have heard of them?'

'Do take a seat,' Nina offered, already wanting to strangle him. Popadopoulos grunted, but sat down. She drew up another chair to sit facing him. 'The reason I *asked* you to come to New York is because I haven't been able to persuade you to help me by telephone, fax or email. And since my bosses at the IHA and your superiors in the Brotherhood are finally in agreement that my research into the Tomb of Hercules is valid, and since the Brotherhood has agreed to assist the IHA—'

'An agreement made essentially at gunpoint,' Popadopoulos cut in. 'It was not as if we had a choice!'

'However it was made, it *was* made. And I wanted to do you the courtesy of meeting face to face to explain why I need to see the texts of *Hermocrates* – the *originals*, not copies or photographs.'

'There is nothing in them you cannot already have seen!' protested Popadopoulos, waving his hands. 'They have been in our possession for over two thousand years, they have been studied by the Brotherhood's own historians! If there were any clues to the location of the Tomb of Hercules in there, do you not think we would have found them by now?'

'You had Plato's other lost works about Atlantis for all that time as well, but you didn't find it. *I* did,' Nina pointed out sharply. Popadopoulos looked stung. 'Critias says on several occasions in the text of *Hermocrates* that he will reveal to Socrates and the others the location and secrets of the Tomb, as given to him by Solon, but he never does.'

'That is because the text was never finished!'

'I disagree. In every other respect, *Hermocrates* is a complete dialogue. The only thing not neatly wrapped up by the end is the matter of the Tomb of Hercules – which would have been one hell of an oversight by Plato if he'd just happened to forget about it!' Nina softened her voice, remembering that she was trying to persuade Popadopoulos to co-operate. 'I'm *convinced* that there is something else to be found, some clue that isn't obvious from transcripts of the text or photos of the parchments. Mr Popadopoulos, we're *both* historians – preserving and documenting the past is what we do, it's our passion in life. It's what *drives* us. I honestly believe that if you allow me to see the original texts, I'll be able to find some clue that will reveal the location of the Tomb of Hercules. We both know why the discovery of Atlantis can't be revealed to the world, but this is something, a genuine ancient treasure, which *can*.'

Popadopoulos said nothing, but at least seemed to be considering her words. She pressed on. 'Every precaution will be taken to ensure the safety and preservation of the parchments. The only members of the IHA who will see them will be myself and whomever else you authorise, you will have full control over access to them, and the security arrangements will be entirely up to you. The only thing I ask is that I be allowed to view the text here in New York, so that I have access to all my research and the IHA's facilities. The Brotherhood's archives are an incredible source of knowledge – please, let me put them to good use. For the benefit of history.'

Nina sat back. She'd said her piece; everything was now in Popadopoulos's hands. He stayed silent for several seconds, Nina's anxiety increasing with each tick of the clock. If he said no, she was back to square one . . .

'I will . . . consider your proposal,' he finally said. Nina could tell from the resignation in his voice that he was going to let her see the text; knowing that the Brotherhood had already agreed in principle would make it very hard for him to refuse. His 'consideration' was just for show. 'And I will also need to speak to the Brotherhood in Rome.'

'Take all the time you need,' Nina told him. 'Please, use my phone to make your calls.' She gestured at her desk. 'I'll give you some privacy – when you need me, just dial zero to have somebody page me.'

'Thank you, Dr Wilde.' They both stood and shook hands, then Nina left the room. As soon as she closed the door, she punched the air and mouthed a silent *Yes!*

Feeling triumphant, she headed for the IHA's lounge. Coffee wasn't exactly a celebratory drink, but after the previous night champagne wasn't currently high on her list of options—

She froze. Farther down the corridor, a man emerged from an office, his back to her, and headed for the elevators at the far end. A man in jeans and a battered black leather jacket.

Eddie Chase.

Nina opened her mouth to call out to him, then clamped it shut again, not sure what she would say. And what was he doing here anyway, after all the fuss he'd made about taking the morning off?

Her confusion increased when she realised from which door he'd just come. It was the office of Hector Amoros. Not somebody with whom Chase dealt regularly . . . so why had he gone to see him now?

The elevator doors closed on Chase – if he'd seen her down the corridor as they shut, he gave no sign. A chill suddenly hit her.

Had he quit? Was that why he'd gone to the man in charge of the IHA, to hand in his resignation?

The chill intensified. If it were because of her, then the IHA might not be the only place he was leaving . . .

Nina was about to go to Amoros's office and ask him what had happened when she heard her name over the PA system. Evidently Popadopoulos had come to a quick decision.

She vacillated for a moment before turning and heading back to her office. One thing at a time. Get rid of Popadopoulos, and then find out what the hell Chase had just done. And hope it wasn't too late to stop him from doing anything stupid.

Not, she reflected ruefully, that she'd had much successs at *that* lately . . .

The hunched historian stood waiting for her as she entered. 'Dr Wilde,' he said, somewhat reluctantly, 'regarding the *Hermocrates* text . . . the Brotherhood has agreed to allow you to view it. Here in New York.'

'Thank you,' she said, though without the pleasure she'd expected.

'I have certain conditions that must be met regarding security and the handling of the pages, of course – I will email the details to you by this afternoon.' His eyes narrowed behind the gold-rimmed glasses. 'These conditions are not negotiable, no.'

'I'm sure they'll be fine,' said Nina, distracted, still concerned about Chase. Popadopoulos seemed surprised by her ready agreement, geared up for a confrontation and slightly disappointed not to get one.

'Very well,' he said. 'I will make the necessary arrangements to have the text flown over from Italy by tomorrow. I, of course, will be in attendance at all times while you – you alone, no one else will have access – examine the pages.'

'Yeah, that's great.' She blinked, snapping back to full awareness of the conversation. 'I mean, thank you, Mr Popadopoulos, thank you! I look forward to it. Thank you.' She shook his hand, then almost bustled the little man out of the office before sitting down, one hand over her mouth.

What had Chase done?

She was about to reach for the phone to call Amoros when it trilled. Startled, she picked it up. 'Hello?'

'Nina, hi.' It was Amoros himself. 'When you're free, can you come by my office?'

'Is it – is it about Eddie?'

'Actually, yes.' He sounded surprised. 'I didn't realise you knew. He said he hadn't told you about it.'

'About *what*?' she asked, feeling panicked.

There was a pause. 'Maybe you'd better come see me . . .'

'You're going *where*?' Nina demanded. As soon as her meeting with Amoros ended, she'd raced out of the building and jumped into a cab back to the apartment.

'Shanghai,' said Chase casually, as if flying to China on a moment's notice was no more remarkable an event than taking the subway, while he stuffed clothes into a bag.

'Why are you going to *Shanghai*?'

He gave her a condescending smirk. 'It's classified. IHA business.'

Nina bristled. 'The hell it's classified! Tell me what you're doing!'

'Sorry, love, it *is* classified. Amoros agrees with me – and so does the UN.'

She stepped up to him, hands on her hips. 'Is this about us?'

'It's got nothing to do with us,' he said. 'Something came up, I thought it was an IHA security issue, Amoros agreed, so I'm off to Shanghai to check it out.'

'Why you? Why not somebody else? Like somebody actually *in* Shanghai already?'

'I can't tell you.'

'Can't tell me, or *won't* tell me?'

Not looking at her, Chase shut the bag, then slipped his passport and other documents into the inside pocket of his leather jacket. 'I've got to go.'

'And how long are you going to be gone?'

Chase shrugged. 'Long as it takes.' He started towards the door, but Nina stood in his way.

'You seriously expect me to believe that you're flying halfway around the world at a moment's notice, and you won't tell me why, and it has *nothing* to do with what we're going through right now?'

'I don't really care *what* you believe. Now, if you'll excuse me, I'm going to work.' He pushed past her and left the room.

'Son of a *bitch*!' Nina growled, shooting a venomous look at the back of the apartment door as it closed behind him. Fists clenched, she went over to the Cuban souvenir as if about to sweep it from its perch and smash it into a million pieces, but then turned away and threw herself on to the couch, shaking with anger.

3

Shanghai

It was over two years since Chase's last visit to Shanghai, and he was impressed – though not surprised – by the scale of the change in the city's skyline. New skyscrapers had sprung up wherever he looked, and the spaces between them were filled with towering construction cranes, gangly silhouettes against the dusk sky.

The new structures weren't the boring boxes that dominated cities in the West. Flush with money and determined to show off the fact, the booming corporations of Shanghai were engaged in an architectural arms race, competing to have the tallest, the coolest, the most outrageously designed headquarters. Ancient Chinese temples stretched vertically to a hundred storeys or more, gleaming silver spires, domes, corkscrews and even some bizarre organic shapes that defied easy description, everything blazing with neon.

The building Chase took a particular interest in as the taxi drove along an overpass on the city's eastern side was not as tall as some, but it still made a statement with its size and design. The headquarters of Ycom – pronounced *yee-com* – were around thirty floors high, one side of the building a sheer cliff of black glass while the other dropped away in a smooth curve that reminded him of a skateboard ramp. The roof of the building was festooned with communications masts, all picked out in neon, with what looked like a helicopter pad at the centre.

Ycom, he knew, was one of Richard Yuen Xuan's corporations.

'So, Eddie, you still like Shanghai?' said the woman driving the cab. Her petite frame made to seem even smaller by her oversized, boyish clothes, Chao Mei appeared to be barely out of her teens. In fact, she was several years older than she looked, and her pretty, innocent face, partly hidden below the brim of a floppy turquoise beret, belied some of the less-than-legal activities Chase knew she'd been involved in through her family's connections to the Triads.

'Yeah, it looks pretty cool. All these towers, though – the whole place is like one giant dick-waving contest.'

Mei giggled. 'You still always joke about sex, Eddie. Maybe if not for this—' she patted her stomach. Not even her padded jacket could disguise the fact that she was several months pregnant – 'we could have finally done it for real, hmm?'

'Yeah, bloody Lo and his powerful sperm,' said Chase, knowing she was joking. 'But I'm probably going to need to get out of town fast when I'm done.' His voice dropped. 'Also, I'm sort of involved with someone.'

'You are?' She looked back at him, pleased but also a little surprised. 'Good for you! What's she like? Is she beautiful?'

'Eyes on the road, Mei,' Chase reminded her, trying not to wince as the taxi drifted out of its lane towards a bus. She jerked the cab back into line, then watched him in the mirror. 'And yeah, she is.'

'I knew it! When I told Lo you were coming, he got very jealous. Wanted to know how someone with your face always ended up with beautiful women.'

Chase snorted, rubbing his flat, oft-broken nose. 'None taken! Guess it's because I'm just such a great bloke.'

'That's what I told him! So, tell me about her. Are you in love?'

The skyline disappeared as the taxi descended into the tunnel under the river bisecting the city. 'I . . . I don't know. I dunno *what* we are right now, to be honest.'

In the mirror, Mei gave him a look of sympathy. 'How long you been seeing her? A year, two years?'

'Year and a half, about.'

'Ah!'

' "Ah!" what?'

'Tricky time,' Mei explained. 'Past first love, now you get to know each other properly. And maybe, you find there are things you don't like so much.'

'You could say that,' Chase muttered, not wanting to discuss it.

'Lo and I, we go through the same thing,' Mei went on chattily. 'He hated my hats, I can't stand his idiot friend Fong or him always playing computer games, yah yah yah.'

'But you sorted things out?'

She gave him a slightly sarcastic look as she patted her belly again. 'Guess.' Chase couldn't help but laugh. 'If you are really in love,' Mei went on, 'if you're meant for each other, you'll know it. If something's good, it's worth fighting for.'

'I'll keep that in mind,' said Chase, wanting to change the subject. He looked out at the skyscrapers again as the taxi emerged from the tunnel on the city's western side.

Shanghai's Grand Theatre was an ultra-modern structure of steel and glass on the western side of the People's Park. Mei pulled the taxi over by the plaza in front of the building. 'Okay, this is it. You got everything you need?'

'My ticket's right here,' said Chase, holding it up.

'Sorry I couldn't get you a better seat. Very short notice.'

'I didn't come here to see some fat bloke singing,' he reminded her with a grin.

'What about a signal when you want me to get you?'

'Just keep your eyes open. You'll know it when you see it.'

Mei frowned. 'Eddie, *please* don't blow up the Grand Theatre. I like it, I saw *Les Mis* there.'

'Sounds like a good reason to blow it up!' The frown deepened. 'Okay, *okay*, I promise I won't completely destroy the place.'

'Thank you.'

'Might be some breakage though.'

'Eddie!'

'Just kidding. Okay, time to go.'

'Hold on.' Mei reached back and adjusted his bow tie. 'There. Perfect.'

'Aren't I always?' He tugged the lapels of the tuxedo she had obtained for him.

'Take care of yourself,' she told him as he stepped out of the taxi. He winked in reply, then set off across the plaza.

Chase had deliberately arrived early, and hung around in the Grand Theatre's glass-walled foyer to observe the other audience members as they came in.

He was quickly able to distinguish the genuine opera fans from the corporate show-offs. The former were excited to be there, filled with anticipation for the performance. The latter were more interested in braying loudly, displaying a dismissive, seen-it-all-before attitude to prove this was just another in a long line of expensive perks. Fancy phones, expensive watches and showy jewellery were on open display. Yuppies were as obnoxious in China as anywhere else.

There was another division, as well. The auditorium in which *Don Giovanni* was being performed was on two levels, floor and balcony. According to the seating plan in Chase's programme, the balcony level was mostly private boxes. He had no doubt that his target would be found there.

Keeping watch on the main doors, he familiarised himself with the lobby's layout, then climbed the stairs to the balcony level. Theatre staff at the end of a velvet rope cordon examined tickets to make sure that only the wealthy gained access – and beyond them were a couple of heavy-set, thick-necked men in dinner jackets. Private security. Holstered guns bulged noticeably under their jackets, and Chase was sure that was deliberate. A show of force.

He looked back down at the main entrance – and saw the people he had been waiting for.

With four men surrounding him in a protective square, tuxedoed hulks who could have been stamped from the same mould as the guards along the corridor, Yuen swept into the lobby as if it were his own personal domain. A few of the yuppies made moves as if hoping to get a personal audience, but glares from the goons deterred them.

Sophia followed a couple of steps behind. She was wearing a long cheongsam dress in shimmering red silk, and even her hair had been pinned up in a traditional Chinese style. She was also carrying a little handbag and wearing shiny black spike-heeled shoes – the platform soles making the heels even more ridic-ulously high, at least five inches – secured to her feet with a web of thin straps. Chase frowned. That could make things awkward.

The group headed for the lifts at the back of the lobby. Chase made his way through the guests on the balcony level, also heading for the lifts.

The doors opened and the four bodyguards emerged to clear a space, followed by Yuen and then Sophia. Chase stepped forward. One of the goons moved to block him—

'Eddie!' Sophia cried.

Yuen froze, regarding him suspiciously. 'Mr . . . Chase, isn't it?' he said slowly. The bodyguard stepped back, allowing Chase to approach. 'This is kinda unexpected.'

'I'm a huge opera fan,' Chase said. 'Never miss a performance.'

Yuen's suspicion deepened. 'It's a long way to come from New York.'

'I get around. But it turned out well, because it means I can apologise to your wife.' He turned to Sophia. 'I was . . . rather rude to you the other night. I'm sorry about that.'

'Thank you,' she replied. 'I know we had some problems in the past, but I wouldn't want you to still be angry with me.'

'I'm not. So, where are you sitting?'

'Box number one,' Sophia told him. 'Best seats in the house.'

'I'm down in the cheap seats, I'm afraid. Oh well, maybe we can meet up later.'

'We'll be leaving as soon as the performance finishes,' Yuen said pointedly.

'That's a shame. Some other time, then?'

'It'd be a *really* big coincidence if we met again.' Yuen nodded slightly at one of his guards, who interposed himself between Chase and the group. 'Anyway, we have to take our seats. Enjoy the opera, Mr Chase.'

'Nothing I like more. Oh, by the way, Sophia . . . nice shoes.'

She stopped, tipping her right shoe on its toe to show it off to him. 'They are rather good, aren't they?'

'Very high heels. What are they, five inches?' Sophia nodded. 'They can't be good for your feet. You really should take them off once you're in your seat.'

'I didn't realise you were a podiatrist, Mr Chase,' said Yuen cuttingly. 'Or are you more of a shoe fetishist?'

'Hey, they're very handy when you need to get something off a high shelf.' Chase flashed him a grin. It wasn't returned. 'Anyway, nice to meet you again.'

'You too,' Sophia said quietly as she was led away.

From his seat on the auditorium's main floor, Chase used his programme to locate Yuen's box. By hanging around in the lobby until just before the performance began, he had spotted two of the bodyguards who arrived with Yuen heading downstairs, apparently not opera fans. With luck that meant there were only two men in the box with Yuen and Sophia.

There were still the two goons in the corridor, but he was sure he could handle them when the time came.

It came roughly twenty minutes into the performance. He left his seat, earning annoyed tuts from the other people on his row as he squeezed past them, then headed for the lobby and went up the stairs. As he'd hoped, the theatre staff manning the cordon had gone now that everybody was seated.

That just left the two armed guards.

Chase peered round the corner. They were stationed almost directly outside the entrance to Yuen's box. One leaned against the wall by a fire hose on a large reel, looking bored out of his mind, while the other fidgeted and ran a finger around his shirt collar. Chase knew the feeling.

He unfastened his dinner jacket, then stepped into view.

Or rather, he *staggered* into view. The two guards straightened, watching him cautiously. As he got closer, he saw that both men had radios, coiled wires running down their necks from small earpieces.

'Ay up, lads!' Chase said in a loud, slurred voice as he approached. 'Couldn't 'elp me out, could you? Think I've 'ad a bit too much to drink, an' I've got a bit lost. Lookin' for the bogs, but all the signs are in Chinese!' He was only ten feet from them, six . . . 'Can you point me int' right direction?'

One of the guards extended a fat finger at a sign on the wall. Directions were given in Mandarin and English, as well as the international symbols for male and female. Chase squinted at it.

'Oh, it *is* in English! Bloody 'ell, must be more pissed than I thought. Thanks, lads.' He gave the two men a bleary-eyed smile. They grinned back – and Chase drove his fist into the nearest man's face.

He fell backwards, out cold, a spray of blood radiating from his crushed nose. The other man gawped, then fumbled at his jacket. He barked a word in Chinese—

Chase leapt at him and body-slammed him against the wall. He clawed at the man's jacket, snagging the transmitter under his lapel and tearing it loose. A wire popped free as he threw it on to the polished floor, at the same time delivering a crunching kidney punch with his other fist. The guard's face contorted in pain.

But that didn't stop him from smashing his fist against the side of Chase's skull.

Chase staggered, this time for real. Filled with sudden fury, he threw himself shoulder-first against the guard's chest, ploughing him back against the wall with such force that it drove all the air from his lungs.

Before the man could even begin to catch his breath, Chase seized him in a headlock and hauled him back across the corridor. The guard's head hit the reel of the fire hose with a *bong!* that left a dent in the metal. He instantly collapsed, unconscious.

But he'd got off a warning, however brief. Yuen's other goons would burst out of the private box at any moment.

Chase grabbed the heavy brass nozzle of the fire hose and yanked it free of the reel, several feet of fabric-covered rubber playing out behind it. He swung it round his head, faster and faster, letting out more of the hose through his hand with each turn.

The door opened—

And the first of Yuen's goons to emerge took the full force of the nozzle across his jaw. It hit so hard that he flipped over backwards in an involuntary somersault, blood and teeth arcing across the corridor.

Shouts from the lobby. Chase glanced back towards it. He could hear footsteps clattering up the stairs: more of Yuen's bodyguards on the way.

And one more guy in the box.

Chase tilted his raised arm, still whirling the hose like a lasso but now bringing it down closer to floor level as the other guard vaulted his fallen comrade, pulling a gun from his jacket—

The hose whipped round his ankles.

The man stumbled, throwing his arms out to keep his balance. Before he had a chance to bring up the gun, Chase charged at him, bending to ram into him at waist height and scoop him off his feet. Without slowing, he ran into the darkened box, seeing the surprised faces of Yuen and Sophia as he shot past them and threw the guard over the edge of the balcony.

The hose snaked past him at frightening speed, the bodyguard letting out a high-pitched shriek of fear . . .

The shriek was cut off abruptly as the hose snapped taut, vibrating like a plucked guitar string. Chase looked over the balcony. The bodyguard's fall had been brought to a stop with his head inches above the auditorium's main aisle. The opera continued, the performers and musicians unable to see what had happened through the glare of the lights – though Chase did hear a chorus of '*Shhhh!*' over the singing.

62

He turned to the occupants of the box. Sophia stared at him in amazement, while Yuen's expression was one of disbelief and growing rage.

'Sophia, get up,' Chase ordered. She did. He hoisted her over his left shoulder in a fireman's lift, realising she still had her high heels on. Muttering a curse, he backed to the edge of the balcony. 'Hold on to me, and whatever you do, *don't let go.*'

She clung to him. 'What are you going to—'

He wrapped the hose round his right arm, lifted it clear of the balcony railing – then vaulted over the edge.

The hose hissed as he slid down it, feeling the sharp heat of friction through his sleeve. Sophia yelped in shock as they dropped towards the floor, the bodyguard still dangling below—

Chase tightened his legs round the hose, using the guard's upturned soles as a landing pad for his feet. He bent his knees to absorb the impact, then said, 'Brace yourself!' as he unravelled his arm and jumped the last few feet to the ground. He felt Sophia's stomach muscles tense against him just before the impact, body heat against his cheek. GALWAY COUNTY LIBRARIES

Old memories . . .

They hit the floor. Sophia gasped. Chase looked up the aisle towards the rear exit, seeing people in the audience gawking at him. Someone shouted from above. Yuen leaned over the balcony, pointing down at them. Chase gave him a cheeky salute, then ran up the aisle, Sophia still over his shoulder. Little coils of smoke wafted from his right sleeve. The black cloth had been scorched brown. He hoped Mei hadn't paid a deposit on the tuxedo, as she wasn't going to get it back.

'You okay?' he asked Sophia.

'I'm fine!' she replied, somewhat winded. 'That was . . . that kind of reminded me of how we first met!'

'Yeah, but I had a machine gun then, and there weren't any civvies around to worry about. Mind your head!' He turned sideways to slam open the double doors with his right shoulder, emerging in the brightly lit lobby. Sophia's legs waved in front of him, her spike heels glinting. 'I *told* you to take off your bloody shoes!'

'I didn't realise you were going to burst in like some crazed rhino halfway through the opera!' Sophia objected as he hurried for the exit. 'I was expecting something more subtle!'

'You really *didn't* know me at all, did you?' More shouts came from above. He looked up to see Yuen's two remaining bodyguards haring back down the stairs, guns in their hands. The handful of people in the lobby screamed when they saw the weapons and ran for the exits. 'Hellfire! Will these guys shoot at me if I've got you?'

'I certainly *hope* not!'

'Then make sure and tell them not to!' He looked back as Sophia shouted commands in Mandarin. He was only halfway across the lobby, and the two bodyguards were almost on him—

'Put down Lady Sophia!' one of the men yelled in heavily accented English. Whatever Sophia said had worked; neither guard had put away his gun, but nor were they aiming them at him. 'Put her down *now*!'

'Come and get her!' Chase called as he turned to face them, right arm outstretched to counterbalance Sophia's weight over his shoulder. They were moving to flank him, one on each side. 'You keep up with the fight training?' he asked her.

She was puzzled. 'Yes?'

'Good, because you just became my weapon! Get ready—'

One of the bodyguards rushed at them. Chase whirled round – and hit him square in the face with Sophia's feet as she kicked out, the heavy platform soles cracking into his jaw. The man's head snapped to one side and he dropped to the floor, dazed and bloodied.

'Nice one!' Chase told her, spinning to look for the second guard. He had been closing from the other side but had now stopped abruptly, realisation that Sophia was *helping* her kidnapper spreading across his face. He brought up his gun.

Chase turned faster, hoping Sophia still thought as quickly as she used to. She *did*, realising what he had in mind and lashing out with one expensively shod foot—

The gun flew out of the bodyguard's hand and clattered away across the lobby's marble floor. He stared in surprise at the tip of the spike heel protruding through his palm. Sophia pulled her leg back, a little spout of blood jetting from the hole in the man's hand as her heel withdrew. He howled – only for the cry of pain to stop abruptly as Chase punched him in the face and knocked him flat on his back.

'Aren't you glad I kept my shoes on now?' Sophia said.

'Okay, I'll give you that one,' Chase replied, jogging for the exit.

'It would have been much simpler if you'd just shot him, though.'

'I didn't bring a gun,' Chase admitted.

Sophia's voice filled with disbelief. '*What?* Why not?'

'I'm trying to cut down on shooting people. Too much paperwork.'

'Since when do *you* care about paperwork?'

'My life's changed!' He booted one of the glass doors open and hurried outside, looking back for signs of pursuit. Yuen was running down the stairs, and the bodyguard Sophia had kicked in the head was struggling to his feet.

A car horn hooted frantically. A taxi charged across the plaza towards the front of the Grand Theatre, pedestrians jumping out of its way. 'That's our ride!' he told Sophia, waving to Mei as she brought the taxi to a screeching stop in front of them. He pulled open the rear door, then quickly bowed to deposit Sophia on the pavement with a click of her heels. 'Get in, quick,' he ordered, now all business. Behind, Yuen was rallying his troops, the bodyguard now helping the second man up, and another coming down from the balcony level.

Chase shoved Sophia into the taxi, then leapt in after her. Mei stamped on the accelerator before he even had a chance to close the door, the taxi taking off with a shriek of rubber. He poked his head up to look through the rear window—

'Duck!' he shouted, shielding Sophia with his body. Yuen and one of the bodyguards were now outside the theatre, the guard raising his gun. Chase heard four shots, but none of them seemed to hit the speeding taxi.

'Good thing this isn't my cab!' Mei yelled, swerving the taxi on to a grass verge. It skidded over it in a shower of turf and careered across a pavement. People dived out of its path, yelling obscenities after them as Mei turned again, merging into a line of identical cabs as they sped along the street.

Chase looked back. Yuen was an angry silhouette against the illuminated glass foyer – then trees blocked him from sight. 'Okay, we're clear. Nice driving, Mei.'

'That was nothing. You should see me when I need to get home to pee!' She looked at Sophia in the mirror. 'So, you rescued your lady friend? Hi, I'm Mei.'

'Sophia Blackwood,' Sophia told her. 'I'm very happy to meet you!'

Mei's expression became confused. 'Sophia? But I thought . . .' She glanced back at Chase. 'Is she who you told me about before, the one you—'

'No,' said Chase emphatically. 'Let's get to the station. The sooner me and Sophia get out of here, the better.'

'We have to go to my husband's company headquarters first,' said Sophia. It was a command, not a request.

Chase raised an eyebrow. 'You what?'

'I can't leave the country otherwise – Richard keeps my passport in his office safe.' To Chase's disbelieving look, she went on, 'I said in my letter that he was controlling.'

'Wait, and you let him? *You?*'

'Can we not start, please?' Sophia sighed, exasperated. 'And there's more there than just my passport. I can access his private computer files – and give you the proof that he's connected to the sinking of the SBX rig.'

'And you couldn't have done this *before?*'

'Don't you think I *would* have done if I could?' she snapped. There was a brief, frosty silence. 'I'm sorry. Eddie, I'm so grateful that you would do this for me, you have no idea. But you don't know what Richard is like. He's very . . . suspicious. Paranoid, even. And now that I've found out what he's involved in, I know why.' She touched his hand. 'Once we're in his office, it'll only take me ten minutes, less, to get what I need.'

Chase looked down at her hand on his, thinking. Then he gave it the briefest of squeezes before leaning forward. 'Okay, Mei. Looks like we're making a detour. Take us to the Ycom building.'

4

New York City

Half a world away, Nina sat back and rubbed her eyes, frustrated but unwilling to admit defeat.

She had arrived at the anonymous Art Deco office building a few blocks from City Hall just after six in the morning, excitement blowing away any tiredness, eager to see the ancient parchments with her own eyes. Met in the lobby by an unsmiling – and almost certainly armed – man, she was taken to the fifth floor to meet Popadopoulos.

There was a second man with him, another well-dressed but grim-faced guy with the build and pug features of a boxer. He too was armed; Nina was now familiar enough with concealed weapons to spot the telltale bulge beneath his tailored Italian jacket. He carried a black leather case, which at first glance Nina took to be chained to a steel cuff round his wrist. On closer examination, she realised that the chain actually disappeared into the case, attached to something within.

'Good morning, Dr Wilde,' said Popadopoulos.

'Mr Popadopoulos.' Practice had made perfect. 'What is this place?'

'One of the Brotherhood's properties – a safe house, you could say. We have a number of them around the city.'

Nina regarded him coldly. 'Like the place Jason Starkman planned on killing me a year and a half ago?'

Popadopoulos shifted uncomfortably. 'I never met Mr Starkman. My role within the Brotherhood is concerned only with the archives. Now, come, come, you wanted to see something, no? Well, I have brought it. At considerable inconvenience, I might add.' The other man placed the case on the large old oak desk in the centre of the room and opened it. Popadopoulos carefully lifted out the object inside.

It was a book, in dimensions an inch or two larger than a sheet of typing paper, but as thick as a dictionary. The cover was bound in dark red leather and reinforced by a brass frame, held shut by a heavy clasp. The 'pages' were also framed in metal, each about half a centimetre thick. The whole thing seemed extremely heavy.

Popadopoulos spoke in Italian, and the other man took out a key and unlocked the cuff linking him to the book. To Nina's surprise, Popadopoulos then fastened it round his own bony wrist. 'What are you doing?' she asked.

'I told you that I will remain with the text at all times,' he said, sitting at the desk. The chain connecting him to the book was about eighteen inches long.

'What, you don't trust me?'

'People have stolen items from the Brotherhood before. I know you met Yuri Volgan, for one.'

'You think I'm going to *steal* it? Oh, come on!' She tipped her head towards the other man. 'You've got Rocky here and God knows how many other guys guarding the building, and we're five storeys up! I'm hardly going to jump out the window with it.'

'That is the arrangement you agreed to, Dr Wilde,' Popadopoulos said curtly. 'Accept it, or leave.'

Annoyed, she sat opposite the historian and brought out her laptop and notepad. The other man left the room, taking up a position outside the door.

Popadopoulos unfastened the clasp. 'So, Dr Wilde,' he said as he opened the book, 'here is the original text of *Hermocrates*.'

Despite having seen many photographs of the parchments, Nina couldn't help but be awed at the sight of the real thing. Each page of the ancient work was pressed between two sheets of glass. The parchments were discoloured and mottled, but they were still far more intact than any other documents from the same era that she had ever seen. The Brotherhood clearly took great care even of items it had stolen.

She looked more closely at the first page. The handwriting stood out clearly, the ink mostly a reddish brown but with darker impurities mixed in. There were even mistakes; ink blots, scratches, words crossed out. In a couple of places another hand had added annotations. Her heart beat faster. Plato had disapproved of written text, preferring the oral tradition of rote memorisation . . . but that didn't mean he never used it. Were these the notes of the great philosopher himself, passing comment on the students who transcribed his words?

Popadopoulos coughed slightly. Nina looked up at him,

belatedly becoming aware that she was grinning like a fool. 'You are impressed, Dr Wilde?'

'Oh, God, yes!' she replied, nodding. For a moment, Popadopoulos looked amused rather than irate. 'This is incredible! You've actually had these for over two thousand years?'

'In different locations, preserved in different ways, but yes. This book was bound in the nineteenth century. You are the first person from outside the Brotherhood ever to see it.'

'I'm honoured,' she said, meaning it. Popadopoulos nodded.

'But,' he said, 'I still do not believe you will find anything in person that you could not have got from photographs, no, no. There is nothing more to discover.'

Nina turned the page, finding with surprise that the back of the parchment was blank. 'I disagree – I've already discovered something I didn't know.' She tapped the glass. 'The photos never suggested that only one side of the page had been written on. Parchment was expensive – it's kind of unusual not to use both sides, don't you think?'

'Unusual, yes, but not unknown,' Popadopoulos said dismissively. 'I assure you, you will find nothing else.'

Nina gave him a crooked grin. 'I like a challenge. Okay – let's get started.'

But now, three hours later . . .

Reluctant as she was to admit it, Popadopoulos was right. Having already read the text from photographs and in translations many times over the past months, she was able to work through it quickly, turning each heavy page with the hope of discovering something new . . . and always being disappointed.

There were no hidden clues to the location of the Tomb of

Hercules, no additional paragraphs completing the tale. Plenty about Atlantis, yes, and about the wars between the Atlanteans and the ancient Greeks, a splendid treasure trove of knowledge for historians . . . but nothing new about her current obsession.

'Damn it,' she muttered, defeated.

Popadopoulos sounded almost sympathetic. 'As I told you, Dr Wilde, there is nothing. Either the text was never fully transcribed, or Plato had no more knowledge of the Tomb.'

'He wouldn't have brought it up in the first place if he didn't mean to discuss it,' Nina objected. 'Critias plainly says that he'll tell Hermocrates and the others where it is, how he was told its location by Solon, who got it from the records of the Egyptian priests. Just like Atlantis. There are phrases in the text that seem to be clues, like this one – "For even a man who cannot see may know the path when he turns his empty face to the warmth of the sun." It doesn't quite fit in with the rest of the dialogue around it.' She turned back through the pages, their frames clanking against each other. 'There *has* to be something more.'

Popadopoulos stood. 'It will have to wait. Now would be a good time to take a break, no?'

'I don't need a break,' said Nina impatiently.

'But *I* do! I am an old man, and I had a very large meal last night.' He clucked disapprovingly. 'American food, such huge portions. No wonder you are all so fat.'

'Wait, I know I agreed that I could only see it for a limited time,' protested Nina, ignoring the crack at her countrymen, 'but now you're going to take it away while you go to the *john*?' An idea came to her. 'Look, handcuff it to *me* if you're worried. I can hardly just stroll out with it without anyone noticing, especially with a guy right outside the door. It must weigh twenty pounds, at least! And I'm not going to damage it – I want to preserve it every bit as much as you do.'

Popadopoulos narrowed his eyes behind his glasses, considering it. 'I . . . suppose that could be done. But . . .' He unlocked the cuff, then looped the chain round one leg of the heavy table, making a steel knot.

'Are you *serious*?' Nina asked.

'I will not be gone long, perhaps twenty minutes.'

'Wow, I guess you really *did* have a big meal.'

He scowled. 'This is my condition, Dr Wilde. Either accept it, or I will take the text away with me.'

Nina relented. It was only for a short while, after all . . . 'Oh . . . okay.' Popadopoulos held up the cuff. 'But on my *left* hand. I want to be able to take notes.' She pulled her chair round the end of the table.

The handcuff closed round her wrist, the steel teeth clicking ominously. Nina felt a chill. The last time she'd been handcuffed, she'd been a prisoner, on her way to be executed. She raised her arm. With the chain would round the table's thick leg, it only had a few inches of play.

'I will return soon,' Popadopoulos assured her as he went to the door.

She jangled the chain. 'Well, I'm not going anywhere.'

The member of the Brotherhood keeping watch in the lobby looked up as a stranger entered. Instantly alert, he surreptitiously brought his hand closer to his concealed gun. 'Can I help you?'

The unexpected visitor appeared to be Chinese, a grey-haired, bull-shouldered man in his fifties with a long ponytail swinging behind him. He walked with a black cane, tapping the metal tip on the tiles. 'I hope so,' he said in a throaty voice as he stopped, both hands resting on the cane. 'My name is Fang. I'm looking for the offices of Curtis and Tom?'

The guard frowned. That was one of the Brotherhood's shell companies, ostensibly headquartered in the building, but as far as he knew the law firm never did any actual business. 'This is the right place,' he began, 'but—'

Fang's right hand flashed upwards with lightning speed, a thin line of silver trailing it. The guard shuddered, then collapsed to his knees, his clothes sliced cleanly open from crotch to neck – as were the skin and organs beneath. Blood and entrails gushed from the wound.

In a single smooth movement, Fang returned his blade to its sheath inside the cane, the sword making a metallic ringing sound as pure as a musical note. 'Thank you,' he said to the dying guard. He took a gun from inside his long black coat, a compact Heckler & Koch MP-7 machine pistol with a fat silencer attached to the barrel. Three more men entered, all Chinese, drawing identical weapons.

'Find her,' Fang ordered, heading for the stairs.

Nina was already regretting her decision. Every time she tried to turn a page of the ancient text, she instinctively reached out with her left hand – only to have it jerked to a stop by the chain. She wondered about lifting the desk to pull the chain out from under the leg, but after an experimental shove decided against it. The table was every bit as heavy as it looked.

Chase would have been able to lift it easily, she thought – and her anger at him, forgotten in her concentration upon the *Hermocrates* text, flooded back. She still couldn't believe what he'd done. Storming out was one thing, but storming out to *China* . . .

She hadn't believed a word of his story, but when she'd called Amoros to demand answers he'd told her the same thing – it was an IHA security issue. She didn't need to know.

Which, of course, had only made her more angry.

Fuming, she rapped her manicured fingernails on the desk, now unable to focus on the text – or anything except the idea of strangling Chase when he finally returned—

A bell suddenly rang, making her jump.

Was it a fire alarm? Worried, she made another attempt to lift the desk. She managed to slide it a little across the floor, but actually raising the unyielding leg high enough to pull the chain free proved more difficult. 'Hey! Rocky! I could use some help here!'

No reply. But she heard shouting elsewhere in the building. She pulled at the chain again. Maybe if she put the book on the floor to give herself more slack—

A noise, closer than the shout. She froze.

It sounded familiar. Frighteningly familiar. Like a bullet smashing into a wall.

But it couldn't be! There had been no gunshots . . .

Another shout from nearby. Only it wasn't a shout, it was a scream, cut off abruptly by more of the flat cracks of bullets against wood and stone.

Popadopoulos sat on the lavatory, waiting for nature to run its course as he read his newspaper. There was no point trying to rush things, he'd long since learned. Things would take as long as they would take . . .

He raised his head at an odd noise, like rapid hammering. As he listened, he became aware of another sound at the limits of his hearing, higher-pitched. A bell?

The noise suddenly became louder as someone opened the door of the men's room. It was definitely a bell . . .

His attention distracted, he lost his grip on a couple of pages and they slipped to the floor. Annoyed, Popadopoulos bent down to retrieve them—

The wooden door of the stall burst into splinters just above his head as a stream of bullets ripped through it, tiles on the back wall shattering and covering him with porcelain fragments.

Popadopoulos decided to keep his head down for a while longer. But at least now he didn't need to wait for nature.

'Shit! *Shit!*' Nina threw herself against the table, trying to move it to block the door.

Someone was outside. The door handle turned . . .

With a final desperate effort, Nina forced the desk against the door, slamming it shut. On instinct she ducked below the tabletop, pulling the book down with her—

The door erupted with ragged holes as whoever was on the other side blazed away at it with a silenced machine gun. Nina shrieked, throwing herself to one side. Bullets tore into the desk, blasting holes through the solid wood.

Armour-piercers!

The desk wouldn't provide her with any cover, and nor would anything else in the room – even if she could reach it.

The shooting stopped. The man outside shouted, calling others to him.

She wedged her shoulder under the edge of the table and pushed upwards, straining her muscles to their limits—

The leg lifted. Barely a centimetre – but it was enough.

Nina yanked the chain clear and grabbed the book, hunting for a way out or somewhere to hide. There was neither. She ran to the window and looked out. There was an alley behind the building, but five floors down and with no fire escape in sight.

A loud bang. Someone barged against the door. The desk jolted. More blows, and the door began to open, a little at a time.

If she tried to push the desk back, they could shoot her straight through the door.

The book was like a lead weight in her arms. She'd under-estimated how heavy it was; it felt more like thirty pounds than twenty, glass and brass and sheets of metal under the leather combining to turn the thing into her own personal anchor.

But on the other hand, it was solid . . .

Closing its clasp, Nina rammed one end of the book against the window, shattering the glass. She knocked out the largest shards and looked back. The door was open wide enough for her to see a man with Asian features on the other side peering through at her. His lips curled in expectant triumph as their eyes met and he read her trapped expression. He tried to squeeze a gun through the gap—

Nina scrambled through the window.

There was a very narrow ledge outside, a Deco demarcation of floor level, but it was barely wider than her foot. And apart from the window frame, there was nothing to hold on to. There was no way she could reach another window.

But there was a telephone line, a thick trunk cable serving the whole building, running down from her building across the alley . . .

More banging from behind her. The desk scraped across the floor as the door was forced open.

She was over forty feet up, and if she fell she would almost certainly die.

Not that she had a choice.

'Oh, *crap* . . .' Nina gasped as she hoisted the book over the phone line, then grabbed the chain as tightly as she could—

And stepped off the ledge.

She dropped almost two feet before the drooping cable snapped taut. Fire seared through her left wrist as the cuff ground against it.

Nina hung on as she slithered down the line. The alley whirled below. She was too scared to scream, watching helplessly as the wall of the building opposite rushed at her—

She pulled up her feet just before impact. The heel of her left shoe broke with a loud crack as it slammed into the brickwork, the jolt driving a hot spike of pain into her knee. The book was jarred from her grip and shot upwards, the chain rasping over the phone line. She fell with a shriek until the book slammed against the cable. The cuff bit into her wrist.

Dangling, Nina kicked off the ruined shoe and took in her surroundings. She was closer to the ground than before, but still two storeys up. Dumpsters lined the side of the alley below. Twisting round, she looked back up the phone line to see a face at the broken window – a ponytailed man. He seemed as surprised as she was that she'd made it.

But he still had a gun . . .

She swatted at the book, trying to flip it back over the top of the cable. It refused to budge. Her own weight was pinning it in place.

'Come on!' she hissed, bashing at the book. It went higher with each blow, but still not enough. *'Come on!'*

She looked round again. He was taking aim—

The phone line abruptly ripped free of the wall.

Nina screamed as she fell – to land with a wet thump inside an open dumpster, plastic sacks of trash exploding beneath her. Garbage sprayed everywhere. She sat up, blinking in confusion before shock passed and sensation returned.

Smell, in particular.

'Oh, *eurgh!*' she wailed, sheer revulsion overcoming all other feelings. But the weight of the book still chained to her wrist rapidly reminded her of her priorities. Struggling to find support on the squishy sacks, she peered nervously over the brim of the dumpster.

The phone line dangled slackly from beside the empty window. Her attacker had gone.

Her moment of relief was immediately stamped flat. *That meant he was coming after her!*

She forced herself upright, the contents of the dumpster squashing revoltingly under her bare foot, and climbed painfully over the side. Kicking off her other shoe, she worked out her location. If the main entrance to the Brotherhood's 'safe' house was to her left . . .

She went right, cradling the book in her arms. A lifelong

Manhattan resident, she only needed a moment to figure out where she was. Police Plaza – headquarters of the NYPD – was just a few blocks away. She would be safe there.

If she could reach it . . .

Nina emerged from the alley on to a street, and searched for help. Not a cop in sight, of course. But there was a guy strolling towards her, sharp suit and slick hair and Bluetooth headset as he chatted to someone on his phone.

He did a double take as she ran to him, weighing her dishevelled appearance against the Armani suit beneath the slime and rotting vegetables. 'Looks like you need help, babe,' he finally said.

'Oh, ya think?' Nina shrilled. 'Call the police, *now*!'

He gave her a smarmy grin and spoke into his headset. 'Have to call you back, bud, it's Good Samaritan time. Got a real life damsel in distress. Ciao.'

Nina glanced back up the alley as he ended the call. Four men charged round the far end, guns in their hands. 'Shit!'

'Hey, calm down,' said the guy, leisurely tapping the buttons on his phone. 'I'm here now, I'll look after you—'

A chunk of wall by his head was shattered by a bullet.

He let out a girlish shriek. 'Second thoughts, screw this!' he yelled as he ran away.

'Son of a *bitch*!' Nina shouted at his rapidly retreating back. She hared off in the opposite direction, heading for Police Plaza. Her pursuers had reached the alley much sooner than she'd expected – there was no way she could stay ahead of them for long, especially with the weight of the book slowing her down . . .

But maybe there was another way she could lose them.

A subway entrance at the end of the street led down to Brooklyn

Bridge station. She ran for it, already short of breath. Shouts of alarm rose behind her as other people on the street saw the armed men.

Nina hurried down into the station concourse. The directions to the nearest platform were marked with green – the 6 Train on the IRT line. She followed the signs, racing barefoot through the crowd.

There was no time to buy a ticket, but like any self-respecting New Yorker Nina knew how to jump the turnstiles, even hampered by her priceless cargo. A ticket inspector bellowed after her, but he stopped abruptly at sounds of panic from the concourse. The gunmen were making no attempt to conceal their weapons.

There was a train at the platform. If she could get aboard . . .

Its doors started to close.

She ran faster, feet slapping on the concrete as she sprinted for the narrowing gap.

The grubby stainless steel doors slammed shut. Nina reached the train just a moment later, banging on the windows, but she knew the driver wouldn't open the doors again. Brakes released with a clunk, and the train set off, motors whining.

The platform was empty, nobody to help her. Brooklyn Bridge was the terminus of the 6 Train, everyone having just boarded the departing northbound train.

More shouts and screams from the direction of the turnstiles. They were coming—

There was only one way she could go.

Nina ran along the platform towards the mouth of the tunnel at its southern end, then leapt, landing on the trackbed just inches from one of the rails. She flinched away from it. How many thousands of volts ran through it she had no idea, and had no intention of finding out first-hand.

The surface of the trackbed was treacherous, filthy and slick with oily grime. Sharp edges hurt her feet. But she forced herself to keeping running into the darkness.

The tunnel curved, the gleaming rails disappearing round a corner. Feeble, widely spaced bulbs on the walls were the only source of light ahead of her. She looked back.

Two of her pursuers emerged on the platform from the entrance she had used, looking round before spotting her. A moment later, the other two gunmen appeared from a more distant opening. They'd split up to surround her, not thinking that she would risk going into the tunnels.

They jumped down on to the track after her.

Nina kept running, the dull lights flicking past as she followed the curve of the track. Another look back. One of the two closer men was much faster than his companion, quickly catching up.

Too quickly. She knew where she was, what was down the tunnel, but he would reach her before she could get to it.

She could hear his rapid breathing, right behind her—

He snatched at the collar of her jacket. Nina wrenched herself free. But he was already trying again, this time getting a firmer grip on the material.

With a yell as much of anger as of fear, Nina spun round and smashed the sharp corner of the weighty book into the man's face.

Even in the low light, she saw that she had drawn blood, a large gash across his cheek and top lip. He reeled, the toe of his boot catching a bolt and pitching him over—

Across the tracks.

Nina jumped back as fat sparks briefly lit up the tunnel. The man convulsed, smoke sizzling from his body where it touched the rails and created a circuit. He was being fried alive, cooked as the full power of the subway's electric current ran through him.

She turned and kept running. The second man was gaining. She hoped he would be dumb enough to try to pull his friend clear, which would electrocute him as well—

He wasn't. There was a brief pause in his footsteps as he vaulted over the rapidly charring corpse, then they carried on as if nothing had happened. Catching up fast.

Nina became aware of two things at once. Both of them bad.

The sides of the tunnel were lined with red and white stripes. Signs for maintenance workers, warning that there was not enough room to stand between the tunnel wall and a passing train.

Which had suddenly become a life-threatening issue, as she felt wind against her face—

A train was coming!

The tunnel formed a loop, where trains arriving at Brooklyn Bridge could circle round to begin their journey back north. And one was doing exactly that right now.

The glow from the train's headlights rose as it approached. Metal screeched against metal, the rumble of its wheels becoming a roar.

Nina kept running, trapped between two dangers. She desperately scanned the walls for any kind of exit or alcove, but the warning stripes continued as far as she could see.

The noise was almost unbearable. Light flared ahead, the flat front of the train coming into view round the curve and still nowhere to hide—

Except *between* the tracks.

A trench, maintenance access for cables running under the track. No more than six inches deep, but it was all she had.

Nina dived into the filthy channel with the book held out in front of her, the driver reacting with shock as she flashed through his headlights. Sparks spat from the train's underside. The front coupler whooshed over her, catching her hair and tearing out a clump. She screamed, barely hearing herself over the noise of the train as its wheels pounded over joints in the line like colossal hammers.

Then she heard another scream, abruptly cut off by a crunch of breaking bones as her pursuer was hit by the train even as he tried to flatten himself against the tunnel wall.

The driver slammed on the emergency brakes. Nina screamed again, pressing her hands against her ears in a futile attempt to block out the noise. Carriage after carriage shrieked overhead, more sparks spraying out from the wheels, scorching her . . .

The train stopped. Silence suddenly descended. Nina wasn't sure whether it was because the train had shut off its motors or she had gone deaf. Cringing, she opened her eyes.

The last car hung over her like a black shroud. Lights inside the carriages illuminated the tunnel. Shaking, taking enormous care not to touch the rails, she lifted herself out from beneath the train. Looking back, she saw a huge splatter of blood along the wall, a ragged smear of red trailing away like a stroke of paint from a giant brush.

Hearing began to return, sounds fading in. The grumble of the train at idle, creaks and moans of metal still swaying from the emergency stop . . .

And voices.

The second pair of men, temporarily baulked by the stationary train blocking the narrow section of the tunnel, but it wouldn't take them long to bypass it.

Nina crawled along the side of the track, ducking under the train's overhanging tail end, then jumped to her feet and ran again. The tunnel opened out ahead, light bulbs and even a faint sheen of daylight gleaming on ornate patterns of tiles in cream and olive green and brick red . . .

City Hall subway station.

Nina had been here before, with her parents as a child. The family's interest in history wasn't limited to the ancient; New York itself had its own lost treasures. Built as a showpiece for the Interborough subway line, the station had suffered from low passenger traffic compared to its close neighbours, and its sharply curved platform made it impractical to extend when the length of trains was increased. As a result it was closed in 1945, forgotten and unseen by all except a handful of curious visitors on the rare occasions when it was opened to the public.

She had been one of those visitors. And she remembered the layout. Steps from the single platform led to a mezzanine, stairs from there emerging on each side of Murray Street just along from City Hall.

Where there would be cops.

Frosted glass skylights in the vaulted ceiling let in enough illumination for her to see the elaborately tiled walls, but Nina couldn't spare even a moment to appreciate the sight as she clambered up on to the platform and looked back. The rear lights of the train stared at her like demonic eyes. Somewhere beyond them she could hear her remaining pursuers coming after her, scrambling under the carriages.

She gripped the book to her chest and ran up the stairs into the mezzanine. The staircase to her right would emerge closest to City Hall—

Shit!

Nina stopped, cursing her own stupidity. The station was closed – *and so were its entrances.* There was no daylight visible at the top of either flight of stairs. They had been sealed off.

No way out.

Noises from the platform below. She couldn't go back into the tunnel—

A space in one wall, an alcove where there had once been a ticket booth.

And a hatch set into it . . .

Nina ran to it, having no other options. There was a handle – and a small lock.

She tugged the handle. It didn't move.

Running feet on the platform.

She slammed the end of the book hard against the panel, once, twice. Glass cracked, but she didn't care as she drove it against the closed hatch like a battering ram one last time—

The lock broke, pieces of metal popping free.

Nina threw the hatch open, not caring what was beyond as she climbed through and pulled it shut behind her. Low ceiling, a short passage leading to a vertical shaft.

Which only went down.

She looked over the edge. There was a very faint light below, a lone bulb at the bottom. The shaft went down deeper than the subway tunnel. She had no idea where it led.

Not that she had a choice. The running men drew closer.

Struggling to support the book in the crook of her elbow, Nina hurriedly descended the ladder.

5

Shanghai

The glass lift ascended the sheer face of the Ycom building, giving Chase and Sophia an ever more spectacular view out over Shanghai as it rose. Mei had parked her taxi in a lot beneath the building, and was waiting for them. There was a security station at the entrance to the lower ground lobby, but the two guards on duty had practically saluted at the sight of Sophia, quickly ushering her through.

They weren't alone in the lift. As an internet service provider, Ycom was a twenty-four-hour operation, and ascending with them was a nerdy young Chinese man in a *Buffy* T-shirt – like yuppies, geeks too were apparently the same anywhere in the world – who had just received a bag of delicious-smelling food from a delivery boy on a moped. He also seemed to recognise Sophia, smiling bashfully while never quite having the nerve to look directly at her.

He got off on the twentieth floor. 'Looks like you've got a fan club,' said Chase as the doors closed and the lift resumed its ascent to the top floor.

'Richard likes to show me off,' Sophia told him. 'I've been paraded round the building a few times.'

'Right. And I bet all the geeks like him couldn't wait to crack one off afterwards.'

'Eddie!' Sophia chided him. 'That's disgusting.'

He grinned. 'Well, you know me.'

'All too well, but you never used to be that vulgar.'

'Hey, I didn't have to come,' Chase said, raising a hand as if about to push a button to stop the lift. 'I can go home again if you want.'

'I'm sorry.' She looked away from him, out at the shimmering *Blade Runner* neon of the city. 'It's just that . . . I didn't know how I was going to feel when I saw you again. Especially after the way you reacted on Corvus's yacht. And in all truthfulness? I still don't know.' A sidelong glance. 'And I can tell that you've still got some issues. Eddie, I—'

'You asked for help, so I came to help,' said Chase firmly, not wanting to continue along the current line of discussion. 'Especially since it affects the IHA.' Something occurred to him. 'How did you know I worked for the IHA in the first place? You'd obviously written that note before the party; you knew I'd be there.'

'Richard has a file on you,' Sophia said. 'And one on your . . . your girlfriend. Dr Wilde.'

'Nina?' Chase exclaimed, filled with sudden alarm.

'Yes. I don't know why he has them, but they were with the other files I think he stole from the IHA.' She turned to face the door. 'We're here.'

Chase had more questions, but held them back as a soft bell chimed and the doors parted. Sophia stepped out into a reception area of black marble, her heels ticking on the polished stone. He followed.

Seated behind a large semicircular black desk was a single uniformed security guard. He reacted with pleased surprise on seeing Sophia, then wariness when he noticed Chase behind her. 'Good evening, Lady Sophia,' he said in a thick accent, standing and lowering his head in a slight bow.

'Good evening, Deng,' Sophia replied pleasantly. She rounded the desk, gesturing with one hand for Chase to stay where he was. 'How are you tonight?'

'Very good, Lady Sophia,' said Deng, breathing faster. Chase couldn't decide whether the man was nervous or excited. He got a fairly good idea a few moments later when Sophia stepped right up to Deng and whispered something in Mandarin. Deng's eyebrows rose with the distinct delight of somebody who couldn't believe their luck. He stuttered a reply. Sophia leaned even closer, whispering into his ear, then giving him a very soft kiss that left a little smudge of glossy red lipstick on his cheek. Chase narrowed his eyes.

Deng fiddled with his tie, then bowed again and hurriedly backed away through a side door into a washroom. 'What was *that*?' Chase demanded.

'Deng and I have an arrangement,' Sophia answered.

'Yeah, it bloody looks like it!'

There was a flash of irritation in her dark eyes. 'Not like *that*. Although that's what he thinks *now* – I just told him to, well, get ready for me in there. I've been nice to him, given him little gifts, and he's been useful in return. Like looking the other way when I need to get into my husband's office without anyone knowing.'

Chase glanced at the door. 'He's getting ready for you, eh?'

'Eddie, we don't have time for this. Come on.' She went to the double doors behind the desk.

'You go in,' he told her. 'Be with you in a sec.'

'Eddie!'

He ignored her, going to the bathroom door and quietly tapping on it. Deng's eager voice came from the other side. He slowly opened the door to be greeted by the sight of the security guard, back to him, pulling off his shirt. Deng said something else, full of enthusiastic anticipation, and turned round—

Chase punched him in the face. Deng wobbled backwards until he bumped against the wall, eyes crossed, then slowly slid down to the floor and passed out.

'In your fucking dreams, mate,' Chase told the inert figure with an angry jab of his forefinger. He emerged from the bathroom to find Sophia waiting, her arms crossed impatiently. 'What?' he asked, semi-innocently. 'You didn't seriously think I was going to let the dirty little sod get away with that?'

'Just come on,' she snapped, opening the door.

Beyond was a suite of interconnected rooms, softly lit and expensively decorated. Dominating the central hall were several large sheets of copper-coloured metal hanging down from the ceiling like stiff banners. 'What the hell are these?' Chase asked. The metal had a weathered, hand-beaten look to it, with long, coiling strips in other colours winding at random across its surface.

'Richard's latest installation. He changes them every month or two,' said Sophia, leading him past them to an office at the far end of the suite. 'They're by a German artist called Klaus Klem. Worth about eight million dollars altogether.'

'Eight *million*?' Chase cried. 'I wouldn't give eight *pence* for them!'

Sophia sighed. 'You never did have an eye for art, did you? Anyway, here we are.' She went to one wall and moved aside an abstract painting, which Chase imagined was probably worth another eight million dollars, to reveal the door of a small safe. Rather than a dial, it had an electronic keypad.

'You got the combination?' he asked.

Sophia gave him a sly smile. 'Some champagne and a big bed, and I can get whatever I want.'

'Yeah, that was never a problem for you, was it?' He turned away before she could reply, looking out of the huge floor-to-ceiling window behind Yuen's oversized desk. Below, the rear wall of the Ycom building dropped away in its long sweeping curve. At the base of the structure was an ornamental lake. Fountains swelled within it, lit from below the water by slowly pulsating coloured lights.

There was a bleep, and he looked round to see Sophia opening the safe. She held up a maroon British passport with a triumphant wave, then took out a couple of other items and went to the desk. A quick tap on the keyboard recessed into the desk's surface woke up a computer, a trio of large flatscreen monitors smoothly rising from slots in the black marble. Chase noticed that a list of folders in a window on the central monitor was sorted by names of politicians, including Victor Dalton, but then his gaze switched to the small white object Sophia held. 'What's that you've got?'

'Flash drive. I'm pretty sure this is how Richard obtained the files I saw, but I want to check.' She reached under the desk and plugged in the drive. 'The password I have to the copies on the server only has read privileges – I can't copy or email them.'

'Guess you couldn't get *everything* you wanted, then.'

As the computer accessed the drive, Sophia fixed Chase with a hard – but also somewhat pleading – look. 'Eddie, *please*, can you put your problems with me on hold for now? I know you can't resist making your sarcastic little comments at every opportunity, but *try*. This is too important.'

'Okay, I'll *try*,' said Chase, feeling uncomfortably chastened. On the screen, a new directory window appeared. 'Is that it?'

Sophia quickly scanned down the list of files. 'These are the files I saw, yes. And here's the one on you.' She pointed a glossy red nail at the title of one of the documents: CHASE, EDWARD J.

Chase was more concerned by the file below: WILDE, NINA P. But then his attention was seized by something else on one of the other monitors – a live feed from a security camera. It showed the marble lobby outside, and four uniformed men cautiously entering it from a side door. All were armed. 'Uh-oh.'

'What?'

'Company's coming. Time to go.' Sophia unplugged the drive and put it in her handbag along with her passport. On the screen, one of the men looked into the bathroom, then reacted with alarm as he saw the unconscious Deng. 'Well, I guess strolling out casually's not an option now. Are there any other exits?'

Sophia shook her head. 'Just the lift and the emergency stairs. We can go up to the helipad, take Richard's helicopter—'

'Can you fly a chopper?'

'No.'

'Nor can I.'

She looked dismayed. 'I thought you could!'

'Learning's on my to-do list,' Chase snarked. The guards moved out of frame on the monitor; he heard the doors at the far end of the suite open. 'You're still the boss's wife. They won't shoot you.'

'They might! What if they've been told what happened at the opera, that I helped you escape?'

'Trust me, when they see you looking like that it won't be their *guns* they'll be shooting. Just buy me a few seconds. Go!' He ducked and headed for an adjoining room.

'Lady Sophia!' came a shout from outside the office. 'We know you are in here. Please, come out – Mr Yuen has asked us to bring you to him.'

Sophia stepped into the hall, coming round one of the hanging metal art pieces to see the four men waiting for her. Their guns were in their hands, but not aimed at her. She advanced slowly, slinkily, one high-heeled foot in front of the other as she swayed her hips in the tight red silk dress. That caught the attention of three of the security guards, at least.

The fourth was more professional, however, looking cautiously into the nearby rooms. 'Where is the man?'

'What man?'

'You came here with a man. Where is he?'

'I don't know.' That was true; she had completely lost sight of Chase.

The guard sidestepped an installation piece and came towards her. The other men followed a few paces behind, on the other side of the hanging artwork. 'We do not want to hurt you, but Mr Yuen has told us to use force if you do not co-operate. Where is the—'

A noise to one side—

The guards looked round as Chase leapt from a side room almost at ceiling height, having jumped from a table. His outstretched arms grabbed the rail from which the artwork hung as he slammed his feet against the metal sheet.

It rang like a gong, swinging upwards with the force of Chase's weight behind it and sweeping two of the guards off the floor. One of them hit another installation piece, wrenching it from its hangings. It landed with an enormous bang, then toppled over and flattened him beneath it. The other man crashed against the wall so hard that he almost broke through it, embedded unmoving in the plasterboard beneath the expensive wallpaper.

Chase dropped to the ground, rolling to avoid the metal sheet as it swung back. Another startled guard was there – he scythed up with his legs at the man's knees. The guard was pitched on to his back with a yelp. Chase was already up, driving a sledgehammer blow from his fist into his face. The man instantly went limp.

The remaining guard aimed his gun at Chase—

Sophia swept aside the front of her dress and delivered a hard kick up between the guard's legs. The hefty platform toe of her shoe crunched into his crotch. He made a high-pitched keening noise, face contorted in agony, then dropped to the floor and curled up in a ball.

'I see you still know how to take care of yourself,' said Chase, kicking the other guards' guns away.

She picked up the fallen weapon of the sobbing man at her feet. 'Shanghai's a tough town.'

'Come on.' He took her hand and pulled her after him, heading for the lifts. She followed, still keeping perfect poise despite her heels.

They only got a few steps into the lobby before an alarm shrilled, red warning lights flashing. The display screen of the lift flashed up Mandarin characters. 'The lift's locked down!' Sophia gasped.

'They'll already be on their way up the stairs,' said Chase grimly. Cut off, and the only remaining escape route led to an aircraft they couldn't fly . . .

He turned and hurried back into the suite of offices. 'We can't get out down here!' Sophia protested.

'Then I'll have to do some DIY.' He stopped at the fallen art piece, one end of which had bent upwards when it hit the floor. Chase looked down the hall to Yuen's office at the end, the sloping windows . . .

'Give me a hand!' he ordered, grabbing one corner of the metal sheet and dragging it down the hall. Sophia obeyed, confused.

They passed the guard she'd kicked, who was showing signs of recovery. Sophia jabbed a spike heel between his legs. He curled up even tighter, tears streaming down his face.

'Stop enjoying yourself,' Chase told her. They pulled the metal sheet into the office. 'And take off those bloody shoes!'

'What are you *doing*?' she asked as she tugged at the straps and kicked off her stilettos. 'There isn't a way out in here!'

Chase took the gun from her and fired several shots at the window, the glass exploding. 'There is now!'

'What do you—' Realisation crossed her face, followed a moment later by genuine fear. 'Oh my God! Are you *insane*?'

'It's been suggested.' He dragged the metal sheet to the window, a cold wind blowing through the shattered hole. Sophia didn't move.

'We – we can go up to the helipad! You could pretend to take me hostage, demand a pilot—'

'They already know I came to *rescue* you, not kidnap you!' Chase leaned out of the window, looking down. The slope of the building's side was at least seventy degrees to the vertical on the floor below, but it became more shallow as it descended, almost horizontal at the bottom . . .

Sophia stared at him in horror. 'Eddie, we'll *die*!'

He dropped the installation piece so that its bent front end hung over the edge of the broken window, then held out his hand to her. 'Have I ever let you die before?'

'No, but—'

'I'm not going to start now.' He offered his hand again, more forcefully. 'Trust me.'

Sophia hesitated, then took it.

Chase pulled her to him. 'Okay, just hold on to me, and whatever happens, don't let go.' He kicked the metal piece further over the edge, its underside crunching on the broken glass.

Behind them, the doors to the lobby flew open. More guards.

Chase stepped on to the metal sheet and knelt down. Reluctantly, Sophia did the same, clinging to him. He grabbed the artwork's bent corners and jerked forward, inching it over the edge, then turned his head to Sophia. Their cheeks touched. 'Ready for a magic carpet ride?'

The guards burst into the room. 'Don't move!' someone shouted.

One last shove—

They tipped over the edge of the building and plunged downwards.

6

Sophia's scream was lost in the wind as they shot down the glass wall, the installation piece a makeshift sledge shrilling and rippling beneath them.

Chase held on to the raised metal corners with all his strength, feeling the edges cutting into his palms. He endured the pain – he had no choice, because if he let go then even the minuscule amount of control he had over the course of their descent would be lost.

Floors flashed past. Windows cracked and shattered in their wake as they skidded over them, a line of destruction gouged out of the face of the building. The wind blasted at Chase's face. He had no idea how fast they were travelling, only that it was *too* fast and his escape plan was looking like a very bad mistake—

The curve of the wall shallowed, forty-five degrees, less, as they hurtled past the halfway point.

But they weren't slowing.

The artificial lake at the bottom of the wall grew rapidly, a glowing swathe of surreal colours. Getting closer, *closer* . . .

They shot off the end of the last floor and hit the water, still moving fast. The window imploded behind them. A huge plume of spray burst from the front of the sledge as they aquaplaned across the surface.

Slowing rapidly, but the lakeshore was still rushing at them—

'*Jump!*' Chase roared, leaping off with Sophia still clinging to him. They landed on soft grass, rolling clear of their ride as one corner bit deeply into the turf and flipped the whole thing end over end in an eruption of soil.

'Bloody hell!' said Chase as he sat up, bruised but unbroken. 'That was better than Alton Towers!' He saw Sophia nearby and quickly went to her. 'You okay?'

'I've been better,' she said groggily. Chase lifted her to her feet. She grunted in discomfort but didn't cry out, which he took as a good sign.

He looked back at the Ycom building. The path they'd taken down the building was clearly visible, people gawping out through the broken glass on several floors. 'We've got to get back to Mei's taxi. Where's the nearest entrance to the car park?'

Sophia raised a shaking hand. 'That side—'

As if on cue, several men ran round the side of the building where she was pointing.

'Hellfire!' Chase grabbed her hand. 'Okay, Plan B.'

They hurried across an ornamental lawn. Busy roads ran along two of its edges. Chase made for the nearer one, looking first for unoccupied taxis and then, more pragmatically, for any vehicle they could commandeer.

The traffic was too dense, too slow-moving. They wouldn't be able to make much headway in a car. He needed a motorbike . . .

He saw one, parked at the side of the road as its owner talked into a mobile phone. It wasn't what he would have picked in an ideal world, but he didn't have enough options to be choosy . . .

'You must be *joking*!' Sophia said, looking aghast at the little red delivery moped. A large wooden box with a crude painting of a tiger on the side overhung the back wheel by almost two feet, the whole thing looking ridiculously unbalanced.

'It's all there is!' Chase ran past the rider, who stared in surprise for a moment before realising that he was being carjacked and shouting angrily. Chase briefly considered drawing the gun to enforce the issue, before instead reaching into a pocket, drawing out a wad of banknotes, and tossing them to him. 'I need to borrow your bike!'

The man caught the money, regarded it in bewilderment for a moment, then smiled ecstatically and gave Chase a thumbs-up. Chase mounted the bike and started the engine, Sophia climbing on behind him. He was about to set off when something occurred to him, and he took another roll of banknotes from his pocket. 'Shit!'

'What?' asked Sophia.

Chase looked round for the delivery boy, but he was already racing down the street as fast as his legs would take him. 'I meant to give him *Chinese* money!'

'What did you give him?'

'Five thousand dollars! It was emergency cash – that's going to be fun to account for on my expenses!'

Sophia almost laughed, but then saw the guards still running after them. 'It still *is* an emergency, Eddie!'

'Let's hope this thing's worth five grand, then!'

He revved the engine, which responded with an ear-splitting whine and a cloud of blue smoke from the exhaust, and released the brake. The rear wheel squealed against the pavement, then the moped shot off down the street.

Chase tried to get his bearings. They needed to head southeast . . . 'Hang on!' he shouted as he swerved the moped off the pavement and into the traffic. Horns blasted as he swept past the slow-moving cars, the box on the back of the bike almost scraping along them.

'Where are we going?' Sophia demanded.

'The maglev station! It's the fastest way to get to the airport!'

A car ahead was up on the kerb, blocking their path. Chase made a frantic turn, cutting in front of another car and moving further out into the road. They were now surrounded by traffic on both sides, and Shanghai lane discipline was far more ragged and disorderly than in England or America.

A car tried to force its way into the inside lane. 'Knees in!' was all Chase had time to yell as they shot past, his elbow missing the car's wing mirror by a fraction of an inch – only for the wooden box to shear it cleanly off the side of the vehicle.

'That's what happens when you don't indicate!' Chase yelled. The traffic ahead had stopped at lights. He needed to turn at the junction—

A cacophony of horns behind caught his attention. 'What was that?'

Sophia looked around. 'I think we have company!'

Chase risked a look back. A car – no, *two* cars had driven up on to the pavement and were racing past the stationary traffic, pedestrians leaping aside. Yuen's security forces had done some carjacking of their own.

'Well, that's bloody marvellous!' They reached the junction,

Chase putting out one leg to support the little bike as he leaned over and swept it into the turn.

Cars were coming the other way through the intersection, headlights blazing—

Chase turned harder, his heel scraping along the ground. The moped wobbled, threatening to flip over, before he regained control just in time to dart in front of a car. Its front wing clipped a corner of the wooden box, spraying splinters everywhere.

'Jesus!' Sophia gasped. Chase fought to keep the moped upright as he guided it between two more lanes of vehicles. He heard tyres screech behind, and more angry bleats of horns. A brief glance in the moped's round mirror told him that the two cars were still pursuing them, driving against the oncoming traffic.

And there was another white light amongst all the flaring red, the single headlight of a motorbike joining the pursuit. A *real* bike, not the crappy little 50cc toy he'd been landed with.

The traffic slowed again. He looked ahead. Red traffic lights, another junction. A crossroads, the road he was on meeting a wider street, buses and trucks zooming along it.

And an illuminated sign above the pavement. The entrance to a subway station.

'Hold on!' He pulled hard on the brake levers, the moped juddering as it sloughed off most of its speed. One end of the handlebars scraped against a car, prompting a howl of protest from its driver. Chase ignored him and guided the bike between the traffic until he reached the roadside, then bounced it up over the kerb. People stared in disbelief, only jumping out of his way when they realised that he really *was* going to ride along the pavement. The buzzing whine of the moped's little engine echoed back at him as they whipped past shopfronts, the street still busy even at night.

'They're catching up!' Sophia warned. With traffic on the other side of the road stopped by the lights, their pursuers now had a clear run.

The crossroads was just ahead, traffic speeding through it. The subway entrance yawned on the corner. 'This'll be bumpy!' warned Chase. He stood up on the moped's running boards. Sophia did the same, still clinging to his back.

Concrete steps pounded beneath the bike as they dropped into the underpass. Pedestrians tumbled after them.

The moped landed on the flat floor with a bang. Chase grimaced as he was slammed down on to the thinly padded seat, but he forced back the pain and twisted the throttle to weave through the throng. He found the button for the horn and pushed it. The sound was as weedy and annoying as the engine note, but it did the job, encouraging people to dive out of his path.

To his relief, directly ahead was a ramp up to the other side of the crossroads. He gunned the engine and sounded the horn in a frenzied staccato rhythm to clear his path. 'You all right back there?' he called out to Sophia.

'Oh, it's just like old times!' she replied sarcastically.

Chase grinned. 'You love it really!' he said as they reached street level again. He looked back for their pursuers.

The first car surged across the lanes of traffic on the main road, barely avoiding collisions with several cars as they locked their brakes. The second cleared the first lane—

The hulking flat nose of an articulated truck smashed into its side. The car flipped and crashed down on its roof, the passenger compartment pounded flat in an explosive halo of shattered glass.

'One down!' Chase crowed. In the mirror he saw the truck jack-knife and come to a stop, blocking the junction. At least nobody else would be able to follow . . .

Except the guy on the bike. The single headlight picked its way through the slew of stationary cars before accelerating after him.

With traffic behind stopped, Chase's side of the road was clear for the next few hundred yards. He swung off the pavement and speeded up.

But the first car and the bike now had a clear road too, and they could go much faster. Headlights filled his mirror.

He couldn't outrun them. Which meant he had to *outmanoeuvre* them.

A dark alley between two buildings, coming up fast—

Chase didn't need to tell Sophia to hold on – she'd already guessed what he was about to do and tightened her grip around him. He turned the bike as hard as he could, the handlebars shuddering in his grasp. The running board rasped against the road surface, the sudden drag almost pitching them both off.

Chase yanked at the handlebars. The moped lurched, centrifugal force pulling its riders upright again. He fought with the steering, trying to bring the bike back into a straight line before it rammed into the wall.

The protruding mirror hit the brickwork and snapped off, spinning past him. But the moped itself missed the wall by the barest fraction of an inch.

He straightened out. Older buildings rose on each side, a jumbled mish-mash of houses abutting commercial properties.

The alley itself was strewn with rubbish, empty boxes and pallets, even washing lines hanging across it.

Light shone down the alleyway from behind, shadows stretching away in his path. Chase looked back. The car had also made the turn and was coming after him. The bike shot past along the street, undoubtedly intending to turn at the next junction to intercept them.

He twisted the throttle, but with two passengers the moped couldn't match the car's acceleration. Its engine roared behind them—

Sophia shrieked as the car nudged the back of the moped, and even Chase let out an involuntary yelp. He regained control, but the car bumped them again, harder. The top of the wooden box popped open, flapping on its hinges.

'What's in the box?' Chase shouted.

'What?'

'In the box! Is there anything in it?'

Sophia twisted round. 'Food!'

'Throw it at them!'

He expected her to ask why, but instead she did as she was told and lobbed the contents of the box at the car like paper grenades. Bags of rice and noodles burst open on its windscreen, spraying stickily across the glass.

The car dropped back, the driver's vision impaired. Chase glanced at it. The wipers started up, smearing food across the windscreen, but it would only take a few seconds to clear.

He looked ahead again, saw a washing line spanning his path, the alleyway narrowing beyond it . . .

Sophia was out of ammo. 'Eddie!'

'Hang on!' He reached up with one hand as the moped shot beneath the line, plucking a hanging shirt from its pegs and tossing it back over Sophia's head. It landed on the car's windscreen, sticking to the glutinous mess and blocking the driver's view.

Chase swerved the moped over to the left to avoid a messy stack of barrels and broken planks. The car followed, the man in the passenger seat spotting the obstruction and yelling for the blinded driver to avoid it—

Only to smash into the corner of a building jutting out from the other side of the alley.

The car came to an abrupt and terminal halt. Both men were catapulted through the windscreen in a shower of glass and blood.

'Should've worn their seatbelts!' Chase said as he reached the end of the alley and made a sharp turn back into traffic, once again heading southeast. He raced between more slow-moving cars and buses, the stink of fumes stinging his nostrils. 'Not that far to go now—'

The motorbike suddenly swept out from an adjoining street and cut in front of them. The rider grabbed for Sophia.

'Shit!' Chase braked hard, swerving away from the bike and passing in front of a van. It didn't stop in time, hitting the wooden box and ripping it from its mounts to smash apart on the road. Out of control, the moped skidded and crashed into the side of another car. Chase's elbow slammed against it hard enough to crack the window.

'Eddie, keep going!' Sophia cried. The bike's rider, one of Yuen's uniformed security guards, waved a gun to make the traffic stop and let him through.

Grunting in pain, Chase shoved the battered moped off the car and looked for an escape route. There was nothing in sight. One side of the road was occupied by a shopping mall, all illuminated billboards and glaring neon.

The man on the bike was now in their lane and riding towards them, gun raised—

Chase revved the engine and turned the sputtering moped towards the mall, weaving between other vehicles. He heard the crunch of a collision behind him. The guy on the bike would be forced to go round the accident, but it would only take him a few seconds to catch up.

Glass doors ahead. He hoped they were automatic—

They parted just before the moped reached them, little more than an inch of clearance on each side of the handlebars as they zoomed through. Shoppers dived out of their path.

'He's still coming!' Sophia warned. Chase didn't need to look back to know that the motorbike rider had entered the mall as well, the sound of the bike's engine an echoing roar under the shrill stutter of his own ride.

There didn't seem to be anywhere to go, only a bank of escalators leading up to another level and the entrance to a department store—

Chase gritted his teeth and rode the moped through the doors. He felt the little bike slithering as the surface beneath its wheels changed from tiles to cheap purple carpet. Racks of clothes whipped past, women shrieking and jumping out of the way as he sounded the feeble horn.

He felt Sophia shift position behind him. 'What are you—'

She grabbed the clothes on a rack as they passed. The rack toppled and crashed to the floor behind them. Chase heard the motorbike's brakes lock, then a Chinese curse and the rasp of its engine as the rider turned to round the obstruction. 'Nice one!' he cried.

'I'm more than just a pretty face, remember?'

'Yeah, I remember.' They emerged from the other side of the store into a large atrium. Chase still couldn't see an exit. 'How do you get *out* of here?'

'That way,' Sophia told him, pointing at a large ramp spiralling up to the next level.

Chase drove for it, keeping his thumb on the horn button. The motorbike shot out of another exit from the department store, tyres screeching on the tiles as it turned to follow.

'Get out of the bloody way!' Chase roared at a line of dawdlers blocking the ramp, who seemed oblivious of the two rapidly approaching bikes. The handlebars clanged against the railings as he swung to the outer edge of the spiral to get around them. Shoppers tumbled like bowling pins in his wake. The motorcyclist swerved madly to avoid them, running over somebody's foot before thumping bodily against the railings. He paused for a moment to regain his breath before angrily gunning the engine and re-joining the pursuit, faster than ever.

Chase and Sophia reached the top of the ramp, finding themselves on a balcony overlooking the atrium. 'Which way?' he demanded.

'There!' Sophia pointed to one side, past a sporting goods shop. Chase turned towards it. The shop had displays set up outside its frontage, basketballs and brightly coloured golf umbrellas and dummies wearing football strips . . .

The guard was catching up fast.

Chase brought the moped closer to the displays and kicked out as he shot past. Basketballs flew in all directions, a bouncing orange roadblock. He looked over his shoulder. That ought to slow him down—

The smile froze on his face as he saw the guard weave past the first few basketballs before turning and riding *into* the sports store, avoiding the obstruction entirely. And as he looked ahead again, he realised he'd made a mistake – the shop was on a corner of the balcony, meaning his pursuer could take a shortcut through it and intercept them . . .

Unless he could get rid of him.

Chase yanked one of the big golf umbrellas from the last display as he passed, then braked hard to make the ninety-degree turn at the corner of the balcony. The guard sped through the store. The two bikes would meet in moments.

Chase accelerated again, turning the throttle with one hand as he wielded the umbrella like a sword in the other. As a weapon it was pathetic, and the guard clearly thought the same as he closed in, grinning mockingly. He emerged from the store alongside Chase and Sophia, raising his gun—

Chase swung the umbrella.

Not at the guard, but into the front wheel of his bike.

The umbrella whipped round to slam against the front forks. It crumpled – but didn't break. The wheel locked solid, instantly flipping the bike end over end and blasting its rider into the air as if fired from a cannon. He shot over the balcony railing and fell screaming into the atrium, plunging through a hanging display of lights which exploded in a shower of sparks, before obliterating a stall selling mobile phones on the lower floor.

'Eat your heart out, Jackie Chan,' said Chase, looking down at the destruction.

'You always were a master of improvisation, weren't you?' Sophia remarked.

'It's quicker than working out a plan. Okay, where's the way out?'

Sophia directed him through the mall, following the signs for the exit. The mall's security personnel were finally responding to the chaos, trying to close the doors and trap the moped's passengers inside. Chase took out the gun and fired a single shot up at the ceiling, which prompted the guards to reconsider their actions and flee for cover as he rode past and out on to a street.

He now had a fairly good idea where they were – Mei had driven him through this part of the city when she'd picked him up from the station. Not far to go. He re-joined the traffic and buzzed down the road. The buildings on either side were now mostly blocks of flats. He made another turn to get on to a wider highway—

A rush of noise from above, then suddenly they were pinned in a circle of glaring white light. The spotlight of a helicopter.

'Is that the police?' he asked, having to shout to be heard. The chopper was coming in low above the road, its rotors whipping up a fierce wind around them.

'Worse!' Sophia yelled back. *'My husband!'*

'Chase!' boomed Yuen, voice amplified and echoing through a loudspeaker. 'Stop the bike and let my wife go, *now!*'

'You up for that?' Chase asked. Sophia shook her head. 'Me neither.' He darted the moped between the milling cars, squeezing through every gap he could find. The spotlight followed like the pointing finger of God.

'Chase! Last warning! Stop right now!'

'Keep going!' Sophia ordered. 'We're almost there! And he's in a helicopter – what can he do?'

The answer came a moment later as the chopper dropped even lower and roared overhead, barely above the height of the street lamps and phone cables. The blinding spotlight was now pointing back at them.

Chase screwed up his eyes against the glare, narrowly avoiding the back end of a sharply braking car as its driver was dazzled. He realised what Yuen had in mind – the chopper was heading for the concourse outside the station, either to hover just above it and block their path, or even to land so that more of his men could come after them.

Vehicles screeched to a halt around them, their drivers blinded. The crunching bangs of collisions pierced the thunderous noise of the helicopter like gunshots. Traffic ground to a standstill, horns blasting.

Chase could see the station now off to the right, the metal and glass façade of the terminal building in front of the huge elevated steel tube housing the actual platforms. The helicopter drifted sideways away from the road, descending towards the concourse.

Last chance—

He revved the struggling engine and peeled away between the stalled vehicles, Sophia's arms tight round his waist. The helicopter kept the spotlight pointed at them as they reached the approach to the station. The main entrance was at the base of a convex glass wall halfway along the building – but the chopper was now hovering right in front of it, blocking their way.

'Whatever you do,' Chase shouted to Sophia, 'keep your head *down!*'

He changed direction, heading away from the entrance, straight for the wall of the terminal – and pulled out the gun to fire at the windows.

The glass burst into a billion fragments and cascaded downwards like jagged rain just before the moped hurtled through it.

Chase found himself in an office, most of the desks empty but some night-workers still screaming and flinging themselves clear as he raced past.

Another window at the far end—

He pulled the trigger again – and got only a dry *click*.

'Hold on to me!' he yelled as the moped rushed at the window. Sophia's grip tightened. *'Jump!'*

They dived off the bike, Chase taking the brunt of the impact as he hit the floor with Sophia on top of him. The riderless moped crashed through the window and skidded across the enclosed concourse beyond before finally toppling over and coming to a halt.

'You okay?' Chase asked.

'Yes, I think so,' said Sophia, standing and brushing off a few stray splinters of glass.

Wincing in pain, Chase staggered upright. He glanced down at Sophia's bare feet, then before she could protest hoisted her over his shoulder once more and lumbered through the broken window.

They emerged on the far side of the passenger turnstiles, station staff looking on in astonishment at the wrecked moped and shattered glass. Chase reached into his jacket with his free hand. 'Got my tickets here, no need to check them!' he shouted, waving them in the air. He hurried up the nearest escalator to the platform before anyone thought to try to stop them.

A train was waiting, a long gleaming metal caterpillar. There were no wheels, the whole thing floating just above the track, levitated by a magnetic field. The Shanghai maglev was currently the longest railway of its kind in the world – and it was also the fastest passenger service of *any* kind in the world. The nineteen-mile journey between the Shanghai terminal and Pudong airport southeast of the city took just seven minutes, at its fastest the monorail hitting 430 kilometres per hour.

Faster, Chase knew, than any helicopter.

He hurried to the nearest door, just behind the blunt curve of the train's rear cab, and put Sophia back down on her feet before ushering her inside. The doors closed behind them. They attracted more than a few curious looks from other passengers as they moved up the carriage to find seats. Looking down at himself, he realised that his tuxedo was smeared with mud, its sleeves ripped and glinting with fragments of glass.

'So much for my James Bond look,' he said sadly as the train began to move.

Sophia held his hand. 'You're far better than James Bond,' she assured him with a smile. He smiled back, then looked out of the window. Even though it had only been in motion for a matter of seconds, the train was already emerging from the steel cocoon of the station, accelerating with an almost unsettling smoothness, literally gliding along the track.

And rising up alongside the elevated track was Yuen's helicopter, the spotlight sweeping along the length of the train. Hunting for them.

Finding them. Locking on . . .

For just a moment. Then the train began to draw away, outpacing the chopper despite the pilot's best efforts to keep up.

Chase used one hand to block out the spotlight, making out Yuen in the co-pilot's seat. He gave him a cheerful wave. Even as the helicopter fell back, Yuen's expression of fury was clear.

But there was nothing he could do to stop them now, short of opening fire on the maglev. And however big Yuen's business, however many friends he had in the Chinese government, riddling the country's most prestigious technological wonder with bullets was not something he could easily brush off.

The train kept accelerating, glowing green LED displays in the ceiling of the carriage giving its speed. Already past 150 kilometres per hour, 200, and still rising fast.

The glare of the spotlight disappeared; Yuen's helicopter had been left eating dust.

Chase turned back to Sophia. She had come through the experience in better condition than him, grass stains on her dress and a few small cuts on her bare arms the only damage. 'Are you all right?' he asked anyway.

'I'm fine.' She squeezed his hand, then leaned over and kissed his cheek. 'Thank you, Eddie. Thanks for helping me. I knew you'd come.'

'I couldn't really say no, could I? But try not to make a habit of it.'

Sophia smiled. 'I'll try.' She sat back, looking out of the window as the outskirts of Shanghai whipped past in the darkness. 'So now what?'

'Now? We get to the airport, I pick up the rest of my stuff from a locker, then we get on a plane and go back to the States.'

'Just like that?'

'Just like that. Working for the UN can be pretty boring . . . but there are some perks. Once we're in the air I'll call my boss at the IHA. Then we can find out just how deep in the shit your husband's got himself.'

He thought about the flash drive in Sophia's handbag. What did Yuen want with the IHA's files, and what was his connection to the sinking of the SBX platform over Atlantis?

More to the point, what was Yuen's interest in himself – and Nina? He felt a brief flash of guilt for not having thought about her, wondering if she was all right.

She was probably fine, he decided. Whatever she was doing, it could hardly compare to what he'd just been through . . .

7

New York City

Nina picked her way as fast as she dared along the dark tunnel, cold water splashing up her legs. From the smell, she assumed that a sewer was leaking into the passage. Every so often she heard flurries of movement – rats scuttling away from her.

She wasn't sure how long she'd been running or how far she'd travelled from City Hall station – only that it wasn't far enough. While the narrow tunnel twisted, it only went in one direction. Barred gates blocked every side passage, leaving nowhere she could hide from her pursuers.

And they were getting closer. By closing the hatch in the abandoned station she had given herself a little extra time as they checked the stairs . . . but on realising there was no way out, they hadn't taken long to guess where she'd gone.

Her arms ached as much as her legs. The book was getting heavier, sharp edges digging into her flesh. But she couldn't get rid of it even if she wanted to, couldn't simply drop it so her hunters could take what they were after. It was still locked to her wrist.

Another turn. Nina rounded it, hoping to see an exit, or at least other passages to confuse the men behind her. But there was nothing except more feeble lights on the arched brick ceiling pointing her way further into the darkness.

And more water. The tunnel dipped before levelling out again, the stagnant pool at her feet becoming deeper. Somewhere ahead she could hear a low hiss of flowing water.

Running became harder, a layer of sticky ooze beneath the filthy surface engulfing her feet at each step. It felt like a childhood nightmare come to life, the sensation of trying to run through quicksand.

Her fear rose. The more slowly she moved, the closer the two men got – and they didn't need to catch her. Just shoot her. All they needed was a clear shot . . .

Gasping for breath, she ran faster, forcing her knees higher as her feet pounded through the sludge. The noise of running water ahead grew louder – as did the splashes from behind.

She didn't dare look back. Another bend in the tunnel, a faint glow of daylight on the walls as well as the greasy yellow of the bulbs—

One of the sets of chasing footsteps suddenly stopped.

Clear shot—

The flat thumps of the silenced shots were amplified by the confined space, but they were nothing compared to the splintering *crack* of bullets hitting the walls as Nina threw herself headlong round the corner. Chunks of broken brickwork rained on to her as she landed in the disgusting pool.

The firing stopped. She pushed herself up, something awful crunching under one hand in the muck. Cockroaches slithered away from her. The tunnel sloped upwards again, the source of the daylight visible at its end. An opening into a larger chamber.

A way out.

Nina ran up the slope. Water trickled from above the opening. She reached the end—

And grabbed desperately at an overhead pipe as she almost fell down an open shaft.

She hung for a moment, one hand round the pipe and her toes clinging to the edge of the tunnel. Then, very carefully, she shifted her weight and leaned back, wobbling on the brink before regaining her balance.

The tall chamber she had entered was about ten feet across, some sort of sewer shaft. Pipes entered it at various heights and angles, spewing their contents into the void below. The daylight came through grubby glass bricks in the ceiling some forty feet above. As she watched, somebody walked over them, for a moment blotting out the sky.

Rusted rungs protruded from the wall, a ladder leading up to a manhole cover at street level . . .

A *locked* manhole cover. Even from this distance, she could see a padlock holding it shut.

She looked down. The rungs descended into the abyss below, but she couldn't even guess how deep it went. Not that it mattered. Whether she went up or down, the gunmen would reach the end of the tunnel long before she reached either end of the ladder.

But there was something on the other side of the shaft, another passage. The entrance was smaller than the one in which she was standing, but she could see the distant glimmer of a light within. Another way out.

If she could reach it. There was no bridge across the shaft, only the metal pipe above her head—

No choice.

Nina cradled the heavy book on her shoulder, squeezing it as firmly as she could between her cheek and her upper arm as she reached up and took hold of the pipe with her left hand. Then she stretched out her right hand, took a deep, fearful breath . . .

And swung out over the shaft.

The book wobbled, threatening to pitch forward. She pushed her face harder against the leather to keep it in place. If the book fell, the jolt when the chain pulled taut would tear her loose.

Gripping the pipe as tightly as she could, she slid her right hand forward by about a foot. Then she jerked her left hand along behind it, a couple of inches at a time, trying to keep the book in position. Its hard edge dug savagely into her shoulder. Another foot, another series of little jerks to catch up . . .

She heard splashing from the passage behind.

Nina let out a strained gasp as she tried to move faster. The book slipped again. She wrestled it between her head and arm, forcing it back into place. Another foot, then the frantic catch-up, right hand forward once more . . .

Halfway across. She had no idea when the gunmen would be able to see her hanging there, an unmissable target.

But if they shot her, she would fall into the unknown below, taking the book with her. If the shaft opened into a main sewer line, their prize would be swept away. That might deter them from firing.

Maybe . . .

Every move made her gasp now, panic rising. A line of pain seared through her shoulder as the book's brass frame ground into her muscles. Three feet, two, boots clattering up the sloping passage behind her . . .

Rancid water, and worse, spewed on to her from an outlet above, drenching her hair and clothing. The pipe was slick under her hands. Nina could feel the book shifting, sliding backwards this time. She pushed her cheek against it, trying to hold it in place, but it was moving towards the point of no return.

Less than a foot to go—

The book tipped. Leather rubbed against her face, then the cold edge of its frame.

And *gone*.

It fell, the chain snaking past her head just as she grabbed the edge of the passage with her right hand. Her fingers closed around metal. The sudden weight of the book wrenched her left hand from the pipe—

Her grip on the frame held. Just. Stifling a scream, Nina stretched out one leg and managed to get a toehold on the edge of the low tunnel. The book swung below her like a pendulum. It banged against the side of the shaft, the clasp that held it shut breaking. Every muscle on fire, she hauled herself on to the solid floor of the tunnel entrance, dragging the book with her.

One of the gunmen appeared at the end of the passage opposite, raised his weapon, and pulled the trigger—

Click.

Nothing happened. The Asian man tried again, then pulled out

122

the magazine to examine it and shouted what she was certain was an obscenity. Out of ammo.

The ponytailed man appeared behind him. He snapped out an order. The first man gave him a dubious look, then reached up to grab the overhead pipe.

Nina turned to run. The man swung out over the shaft—

The end of the pipe sheared off from the wall.

With a piercing scream, he plunged down the shaft and disappeared into the darkness, the pipe breaking loose at its other end and falling after him. The splash from below took longer to arrive than Nina expected.

She looked back at the ponytailed man, who seemed more annoyed than shocked by the death of his associate. His eyes locked on to hers. Apparently he too was out of ammo. With no way across the shaft, the chase was over.

'Say hi to the chuds for me!' said Nina, slamming the book closed and hurrying down the passage.

She got about ten feet before hearing movement behind her—

She looked round to see the man leap across the shaft, coat billowing like a cape. Arms outstretched, he slammed against the lip of the passage, grunting at the impact before gripping the metal frame and pulling himself up.

'Oh, *shit*!' She ran again, more terrified than ever. The dim maintenance lights whipped past just overhead. This passage, while more confined than the last, was at least dry, and she could hear something else ahead, a familiar sound – the rumble and clatter of a passing train. She was re-joining the subway tunnels.

Brighter lights ahead, the cold blue of fluorescents shining on concrete walls. She emerged in a rectangular chamber, more tunnels leading off in different directions. After the darkness of the passage, the glare of the lights was almost blinding. Bare walls, service access for the subway – with an open elevator.

Nina threw herself into the cramped car and hammered at the topmost button on the control panel, waiting for the doors to close. It took her a moment to realise that she had to close the old-fashioned cage gates herself. She grabbed the handles of the outer doors and dragged them together, the concertina-like metal framework clashing shut.

Fang burst out of the tunnel and ran straight at her. Something in his hands, a black cane, one hand whipping back—

She slammed the inner gate. A motor whined.

He thrust his hand at Nina, a silver line stabbing between the bars of the gate. She instinctively raised the book like a shield—

Tchink!

The sword blade went right through the book, effortlessly piercing leather and metal and glass and parchment.

And clothing.

And *flesh*.

Nina was slammed against the back wall of the little elevator, the book pressed against her chest. She let out an almost silent gasp, mouth open in a stunned O as she looked down.

The pointed tip of the sword blade was stuck in her chest, right over her heart . . .

But *only* the tip.

The book had taken the brunt of the blow, only a centimetre of sharpened metal making it all the way through to bury itself in her left breast.

Nina forced the book away from her body. The sword's tip slid free. A circle of blood swelled round the cut in her blouse, pain now searing through her shock.

Fang drew his sword hand back sharply, almost tearing the book from Nina's grip – she barely managed to keep hold with one hand. The text dropped heavily to the floor, more glass cracking. With the clasp broken, the book swung open as the blade withdrew.

The elevator started to ascend.

Fang snatched his sword clear and grasped the near edge of the open book with his free hand, standing the whole thing on its end and pulling it towards him. The two halves of the outer gate sprang apart, forced open by the book as it rose between them.

The chain round Nina's wrist pulled tight. Fang only needed to bring the book a few inches closer before it dropped over the edge of the elevator's floor and the chain was severed by the approaching ceiling—

Despite her pain, Nina grabbed the chain with both hands and hauled with all her strength. 'Screw – *you!*'

Still on its end, the book slid back just as it reached the ceiling—

The elevator continued relentlessly upwards, the edge of the ceiling slicing downwards through the metal spine of the book like a guillotine blade. With a crunch, the volume was ripped in two. Nina fell back and banged her head as her half broke free. The chamber below, and her enemy, disappeared from view.

Dizzy, she shoved herself into a sitting position. The patch of blood on her chest was about the size of her palm, slowly spreading through the sodden material. She pressed a hand against it, wincing. The wound hurt like hell, but didn't seem to be life-threatening.

Other things were, however. She might have briefly escaped her pursuer, but she still wasn't safe. There was a flight of stairs alongside the elevator – he was probably running up them already.

Nina scooped up the loose pieces of the book, then dragged herself to her feet as the upper floor slid into view. The elevator came to a stop. She threw the doors open and rushed out, hearing the ponytailed man pounding up the stairs.

Another door along the corridor, a fire exit . . .

She burst through it to find herself at the end of a subway platform. Canal Street, one stop north of Brooklyn Bridge station. She'd run much further than she realised, several blocks.

But she didn't care, because all that mattered was the train at the platform, doors open—

She ran into the nearest carriage, looking back at the fire door. Her attacker could appear at any moment.

The doors began to groan shut.

The fire door flew open. The ponytailed man barrelled on to the platform and ran at the train. His sword flashed again—

The doors slammed closed.

Nina jumped back with a shriek as the sword sliced through the rubber seal between the doors. But it wasn't thick enough to obstruct the mechanism. The train started moving. Fang ran alongside, glaring at Nina, then was forced to admit defeat and pull out his blade before the accelerating train tore it from his grip. A few seconds later, he vanished from sight as the train entered the tunnel.

She let out a long breath of relief, then turned to see that she had an audience. The other occupants of the carriage were staring at her. Even by the blasé standards of New Yorkers, a soaking, bloodied, slime-covered woman being chased on to a train by a man wielding a sword was hard to ignore.

'Hi,' Nina said wearily, holding up the book. 'Overdue. The guy didn't want to pay his fine.' A couple of people chuckled. She slumped into a seat, belatedly realising that the man next to her was her erstwhile Good Samaritan from the street near the Brotherhood's safe house. 'Oh, hey, you again,' she said to him, shaking something out from inside the sleeve of her ruined Armani jacket. 'Can you hold this for me?'

He looked at the cockroach she'd just deposited in his hands with utter horror, then threw it on to the floor and hurriedly found a new seat as far away from her as possible. Nina shot him a tired, sarcastic smile, then examined what was left of the book.

The front cover was missing, as were several folios. She quickly checked the remainder, splinters of cracked glass tinkling out as she turned the pages. She realised that her attacker now had the first four sheets of parchment, almost a fifth of the whole thing.

She had copies of the text, of course. But clearly there was something that could only be learned from the original, just as she'd thought – otherwise why go to such extreme lengths to steal it?

That was something she could figure out later, however. Right now, she needed to reach somewhere safe, where she could get first aid.

And have a very long shower.

Popadopoulos soundlessly opened and closed his mouth like a fish as Nina spread out what was left of the book containing the ancient dialogue of *Hermocrates* on her office desk. Pieces of broken glass spilled from the bent frames. 'This – this – this is a *catastrophe!*' he finally managed to say.

Nina scowled. 'I'm fine, thank you.' It was now evening, most of her day having been spent in a police station trying to explain the events that had left several men dead in a downtown office building, and three more burned, crushed or drowned in New York's subways and sewers. 'By the way, our ponytailed pal now has the first four pages.' She picked through the book to show him the missing section, more smashed glass crunching. 'I don't suppose you have any idea who he was or who he works for?'

'I was about to ask you that very question!' said the little historian, flustered. 'I have no idea! The only person I have dealt with directly about the *Hermocrates* parchments . . . is you.' He regarded her with sudden suspicion from behind his glasses. 'Perhaps this is all *your* doing, hmm? Hmm?'

Nina rubbed her temples in exasperation. 'Yeah, because whenever I hire a gang of psychos to steal ancient documents, I also ask them to try to *kill me*!'

'You survived.'

'So did you!' She regarded him quizzically, arching an eyebrow. 'Anyway, how *did* you survive? What happened to you?'

'Let us not speak of that,' Popadopoulos said hurriedly. He bent down, lowering Nina's desk lamp to illuminate one of the pages. 'Oh, no, no! Look! The parchment has been damaged!' He indicated the vertical slit made by the blade.

'It's like that on every page, I'm afraid. It got skewered by a sword.' Popadopoulos's eyes widened. Nina continued before he could express his outrage. 'And be glad it did, because if it *hadn't*, I'd be dead and our friend would have the entire thing.'

Popadopoulos's expression suggested he was weighing up the pros and cons of that particular scenario. 'None of this would have happened if you hadn't insisted on removing the text from my archive in Rome,' he finally said, turning the page over. The sheet of glass backing it broke into pieces and fell on to the desk. Nina gingerly lifted the shards away from the fragile parchment as he examined the blank side of the page for more signs of damage. 'Such a thing would never have happened there, no, no, no.'

Nina was about to ask if he were sure about that when Hector Amoros entered the office. 'Nina! Mr Popadopoulos! I'm glad you're both all right.'

'Thanks. One of us is too,' she replied. Popadopoulos pursed his lips in annoyance, then continued his careful survey of the pages beneath the lamp.

'How are you feeling?' Amoros asked.

'Like I've been stuck with about fifty injections of antibiotics. I think I'll live, though.'

'That's a relief. It turns out you're not the only member of the IHA who's been involved in an . . . *incident* today.' He looked at Popadopoulos. 'Mr Popadopoulos, could I ask you to wait outside, just for a moment? I need to discuss something with Dr Wilde in private.'

'Don't worry, I'm not going to jump out the window with it again,' Nina said, gesturing at the scattered pages on the desk. Popadopoulos harrumphed, then left the room. She looked back at Amoros. 'What do you mean?'

'I just got off the phone with Eddie.'

'What?' Nina said, suddenly concerned. She'd all but forgotten him in the chaos of the day. 'What happened? Is he okay?'

'He's fine. He's on his way back to New York right now; he

called from the plane. He's been trying to contact you all day, actually.'

Nina glanced at the phone on her desk, noticing for the first time that its message light was flashing. 'Oh . . . Well, I *did* kind of have other things on my mind.'

'Indeed.' Amoros rubbed a thumb through his salt-and-pepper beard thoughtfully. 'You said that the men who attacked you today were Chinese?'

'East Asian, certainly. I didn't have a chance to check their passports.' The link struck her. 'Wait, you think there's some connection between them and Eddie going to China?'

'Eddie went to Shanghai,' Amoros explained, 'because he said he had a lead regarding the sinking of the SBX rig at Atlantis three months ago.'

'What kind of lead?'

'Some classified IHA files were downloaded from the rig via its satellite link just before it capsized. Eddie says he has copies of those files. They included information about the lost Plato texts,' he nodded at the pages on the desk, 'and IHA personnel files. Eddie's . . . and *yours*.'

Nina felt a chill. 'You're saying the rig was *deliberately* sunk? And that it's got something to do with what just happened to me?'

'There might be a connection, yes. What, we don't know yet . . . but I assure you, we're going to do our damnedest to find out. If someone was willing to kill everybody aboard the rig just to cover up stealing our files, it must be for something big.'

'Jesus.' Nina went back to her desk and leaned against it, shaken. 'Where did Eddie get these files? Who had them?'

Amoros's face became more grim. 'According to Eddie, Richard

Yuen.'

'*What?*' She remembered him from the party aboard René Corvus's yacht. Arrogant, smug, cocky, overbearing . . . but she hadn't imagined he might also be a killer.

'We're going to get to the bottom of this, Nina, don't worry. But there's not much I can do until I see the files for myself.'

'So when will Eddie get back?'

'Sometime early in the morning, around five a.m. He's going to come straight here.'

'Right.' She remembered something Amoros had told her earlier. 'Wait, when you said he'd been involved in an *incident* . . .'

'The important thing is that he's fine,' Amoros quickly assured her. 'And so are you. And you still have the Plato text.'

'Most of it,' she reminded him glumly.

'What do you want to do with it?'

'I think Pops out there wants to bundle it up and jump straight on a plane back to Rome,' said Nina, gesturing at the door. 'But we need to keep it safe, until we can find out why Yuen's willing to kill to find out the location of the Tomb of Hercules.'

'We don't know for sure that it's Yuen behind this,' Amoros pointed out.

'Eddie seems to think so.'

'Let's wait until we get all the facts before we start making any accusations. Especially against one of the IHA's own directors.' He headed for the door. 'I'll go find Popadopoulos, try to convince him to let us keep hold of the text for now.'

'Thanks,' said Nina. He nodded, and left the room. She sighed, suddenly feeling more exhausted than ever. What the hell had Chase been up to in Shanghai?

She sniffed. There was an odd smell, and it wasn't her—

'Shit!' Nina whipped round to see that one of the pieces of parchment was still directly beneath the hood of her lamp, the leathery sheet beginning to shrivel under the heat from the bulb.

She snatched the lamp away, flapping a hand and blowing on the ancient document to cool it. Her heart raced in panic at the thought of the text going up in smoke right there on her desk, but to her enormous relief it had survived, if more crinkled than before. The smell wasn't burning . . .

So what *was* it?

The odour was faint but somehow familiar, a sharp, sour tang that some part of her mind immediately associated with the kitchen. Like vinegar, or lemon juice . . .

Nina clapped a hand to her mouth, muffling a 'Whoa!' as she realised the significance of the scent. She brought the lamp back down, warming the blank side of the parchment.

Faint brown marks slowly appeared. At a casual glance they seemed unremarkable, nothing more than random stains and scribbles. But Nina knew that the mere fact they had been hidden meant there was far more to them.

She picked up the parchment and shook off the remaining splinters of glass. Then she turned to the other pages . . .

Popadopoulos re-entered the office. 'Dr Wilde, I— Aah!' He froze, mouth goldfishing again as he saw Nina smashing open the frames and plucking the fragile pages from the broken glass. 'What are you *doing*? You, you – *lunatic vandal woman!*'

Nina held up a hand to signal him to shut up. 'The *backs* of the parchments,' she said, speaking as rapidly as her mind was working. 'Nobody ever examined them before, right?'

'There was nothing *to* examine! They are blank!'

'Oh, yeah?' She showed him the page on which the markings had appeared. His flustered horror suddenly became fascination. 'You agreed it was unusual that only one side of the parchment was used, right? But all the centuries that the Brotherhood had *Hermocrates* in its archives, nobody ever thought to ask *why*. Well, I'll tell you why.' All the pages now removed from the glass, Nina used the edge of a plastic binder to sweep the broken fragments aside before laying out the pieces of parchment on her desk, face down. 'Because Plato wanted to use the backs of the pages for something else! Look!' She lowered the lamp over a different part of the first page. More markings faded into view. 'He drew something in *invisible ink*!'

'My God!' Popadopoulos exclaimed, hunching down and staring intently at the page.

'Invisible ink,' Nina said again, with a slightly accusatory, mocking tone. 'One of the oldest tricks ever invented for concealing information ... and the Brotherhood never once thought to check for it in over two thousand years.'

'Our purpose was to keep knowledge of Atlantis out of the hands of others,' Popadopoulos sniffed, 'not go treasure-hunting for unrelated Greek myths.' He carefully moved the parchment around under the lamp, searching for more hidden markings. 'How long will the ink remain visible?'

'I don't know – it might be permanent, or it might fade again once it cools. Either way, I'll make sure everything's photographed.' She tipped her head to one side. 'That's odd.'

'What?'

'Whatever this is meant to show, it looks as though it's been cut off.' She pointed at a particular area near the centre of the page. 'See? All the marks suddenly stop along a straight line, as though . . . as though another page had been laid on top of it!' She slid the edge of another sheet of parchment over the first to demonstrate. 'We need more lights.'

Nina ran from the room, soon returning with two more lamps swiped from nearby offices. She plugged them in and placed them on her desk. 'Warm them all up. We need to see the markings on every page.'

It took several minutes, but with the help of Popadopoulos each of the parchments was given the same impromptu heat treatment as the first. They all turned out to have faint marks hidden on them. 'I can't tell what it is meant to represent,' Popadopoulos complained, stepping back to get an overview of the whole collection.

'I can,' Nina told him. 'Or at least, what it's *going* to be. Look at this.' She indicated a group of small symbols on one page. 'These are Greek letters – the bottom halves of Greek letters, at least. And the top halves are . . .' She searched the other pages, spotting more symbols along the edge of a different sheet. When they were brought together, the symbols matched up perfectly to form a word – βoθvó. *Mountain*. 'The whole thing's a *map*! It's like a jigsaw – all we have to do is put it together and it'll tell us how to find the Tomb of Hercules!'

Popadopoulos regarded the parchments in disbelief. 'But that would mean . . .'

'The clue was right there, all along! "For even a man who cannot see may know the path when he turns his empty face to the warmth of the sun"! Empty face – blank page! Critias must have told Plato how to find the Tomb, but for whatever reason they

wanted to obfuscate the details – maybe they didn't want Plato's
students to run off and raid the place. So when Plato dramatised
what he'd been told into the dialogue of *Hermocrates*, he put hints
on how to find the map within the text itself – and hid the actual
map right there on the master transcript!'

'Only for the ancient Brotherhood of Selasphoros to steal it,'
mused Popadopoulos. 'All they cared about was suppressing the
section of the dialogue concerning Atlantis, but they never realised
how much else was in it . . .'

'But now *we* do,' Nina reminded him. 'Let's put it all together.'

It took some time to assemble the puzzle, the faintness of the
markings and damage to parts of the pages obscuring details, but
eventually they succeeded. Mostly.

'Bollocks!' Nina burst out. Popadopoulos gave her a strange
look. She blushed. 'That's, er, something I picked up from my
boyfriend. He's English. But look, we're missing a whole section
of the map.'

The assemblage of pages looked almost random, sheets of
parchment overlaid upon each other at different angles, some
nearly hidden under two or three others. But the image that was
revealed was clear enough. It *was* a map, a path leading to a
representation of a mountain annotated with a single Greek word.

Ηρακλεφ. Heracles. *Hercules.*

The Tomb of Hercules. It existed, was an actual, physical place.
Nina felt a surge of adrenalin at the sight. She'd been *right*.

But it was impossible to reach . . .

'I see,' said Popadopoulos, examining the map. 'This river, it
curves and twists as it widens, as if it is about to reach the sea.
But . . . no sea.'

'The coastline,' Nina moaned. 'The map of the coastline's on the other pages, the ones we don't have. And if we don't have the coastline to use as a point of reference, there's no way we can find the Tomb!'

'There is one good thing, though, hmm?'

'What?'

'Whoever stole the other pages cannot find the Tomb either!'

'You have a point.' Nina looked back at the map. So close to finding what she was looking for, yet she couldn't take the very first step . . . 'I'll photograph this, make sure all the details are recorded.'

'Good! Then I can arrange for the return of what is left of the text to my archive, yes?' asked Popadopoulos hopefully.

Nina considered this. 'Not yet,' she said, ignoring the historian's glower. 'I still think there's more to it. There are other phrases in the text that Plato seems to have left as clues, like he did about the map. But I'm sure I'll need the original copy of the text to work them out.'

Popadopoulos growled in frustration. 'Very well, Dr Wilde, very well. The parchments are already so badly damaged they will be difficult to preserve . . . But I do not see how you will be able to find the Tomb even if you do decipher other clues. You are still missing several pages.'

'Then we have to get them back.' Nina set her jaw in determination. 'I already think I know who's got them. We go after him and get them back.'

'Assuming,' Popadopoulos warned, 'that he doesn't come after *you* first.'

8

'Come on in,' said Chase, opening the apartment door and leading Sophia inside. 'Nina? You home?' No reply. 'She must be at the office.' He gestured at the couch for Sophia to sit, then went to the kitchen area. 'Cuppa?'

'I'd love one. Thank you.' Sophia, now wearing nondescript casual clothes that Chase had bought at Pudong airport, perched on the edge of the couch. 'So this Nina . . . how did you meet?'

Chase put the kettle on the hob. 'I was her bodyguard.'

Sophia raised an eyebrow. 'That sounds rather familiar.'

He ignored the remark. 'After the job was over, we got together. That was about a year and a half ago.'

'And how have things been going since then?' Again, Chase didn't respond. 'I see.'

'There's nothing *to* see,' he said defensively.

'Hmm.' She looked round the room. 'So this is your place.'

'Yeah. Been living here for five or six months.'

'I have to say, it makes me think more of Dr Frasier Crane than of you. Well, except for *that*.' She glanced disdainfully at the Castro cigar-box holder on the counter. 'I remember that awful thing all too well.'

'Well, interior decorating was never really my thing, was it? A settee and a decent TV was pretty much all I was bothered about.'

'Yes, I know.' There was a hint of sharpness in her words. 'I take it she was in a different kind of job before she took on her position at the IHA.'

'I suppose,' Chase told her. 'Same line of work, archaeology, but she was at a university rather than the UN. Why?'

She shrugged airily. 'Oh, no reason.'

'No – I know that voice, there *is* a reason. What?'

Sophia looked mildly annoyed at being challenged. 'Oh, all right. It's just that this apartment, the decor, all the little accoutrements' – she waved at the rack of Henckel knives on the counter by Chase – 'they just come over as being rather . . . *nouveau*, if you know what I mean.'

'As in *nouveau riche*?' Chase's frown deepened. 'Well, I'm sorry our flat doesn't meet up to your standards, your ladyshipness.'

She jumped to her feet, apologetic. 'Eddie, I didn't mean it like—'

'Forget it.' They regarded each other in silence for a moment. Then the kettle began to whistle. Chase took it off the hob.

Sophia gave him a hesitant smile. 'Americans. They have a labour-saving gadget for absolutely every trivial task, yet they've never seemed to grasp the concept of the electric kettle. Ridiculous lot.'

Chase smiled back. 'Yeah, I know. And you try getting hold of Marmite over here! Nightmare!' They both laughed.

'Eddie?'

Chase looked across the room to see Nina standing in the

bedroom doorway, wrapped in a dressing gown and looking bleary and bedraggled. He had no idea how long she'd been there. 'Nina! I rang about five times. I thought you'd gone to work!' He hurried over to her.

'I was asleep, I had kind of a stressful day yesterday.'

'Yeah, Hector told me.' He hugged her, then sniffed her hair and jerked his head back sharply. 'Ugh!'

'*Don't*,' she snapped, in the tone of a first and only warning. Chase got the message. 'I've had three showers and I *still* can't get rid of the smell.' She looked past him at Sophia and lowered her voice. 'What's *she* doing here?'

Chase took a breath, bracing himself for trouble. 'Okay. Nina, you remember Sophia Blackwood, right? Sophia, Nina Wilde?'

'Hello again,' said Sophia politely.

Nina nodded in disinterested acknowledgement before turning back to Chase. 'What's going on?'

'Hector told you that I went to Shanghai to get some IHA files stolen from the rig that sank at Atlantis, right?'

'Yes. He said you thought they were stolen by Richard Yuen.' Nina looked back at Sophia, somewhat accusingly.

'That's right. The thing is, Sophia's the one who told me Yuen had the files in the first place. I went to China to get them – and also to rescue her.'

'*Rescue?* From what?'

'My husband's a very dangerous man,' Sophia said, stepping closer. 'I had no idea when I married him, of course, but since then I've learned some things about him that I wish I hadn't.'

'It's a good job you did, though,' Chase told her. 'Otherwise we'd never have found out that our rig was sunk deliberately. And whatever it is he's up to, he'd have been able to carry on doing it without anyone knowing.'

'So what *is* he doing?' asked Nina.

Sophia shook her head. 'I'm still not entirely sure. All I know is that he apparently had a lot of people killed to get hold of the IHA's files on the Tomb of Hercules – and from the sound of it, tried to kill you as well.'

'Think I'll have to have words with him,' Chase rumbled, one fist clenching.

Sophia put a hand on his arm. Nina blinked in surprise at the contact. 'Eddie, please don't rush into anything. You saw how much security my husband had in Shanghai, and now he'll have even more.'

Chase smiled mirthlessly. 'Trust me, it won't be enough. If I'd known what I know now when you gave me that note, I would have killed the bastard right there on the boat.'

Nina tapped his other arm. 'What note?'

'When we were at the party the other night, Sophia stuck a note in my jacket.'

'And why did she give the note to you in the first place?' Nina looked back and forth between Chase and Sophia. 'Y'know, I got the impression that there was some hostility between you. Which seems to have completely disappeared now, by the way!' Sophia withdrew her hand.

'Oh boy,' Chase said to himself, before facing Nina. 'Okay. Nina. This is the thing. Sophia and I, we know each other because . . . we used to be married.'

It took a couple of seconds before Nina managed a response. *'What!'*

'I'll go and make the tea while you discuss it,' Sophia said, quickly heading for the kettle.

'*She's* your ex-wife?' Nina flapped a disbelieving hand after her. '*Lady* Blackwood, I believe she was introduced as? You were married to – to – to *royalty*?'

'She's not royalty!' Chase corrected. 'Her dad was a lord, and after he died . . . Look, I don't know how it works. I never cared about that side of things!'

'But you didn't think it was worth *mentioning*? You know, maybe in passing?'

'What difference does it make? It didn't work out, we got divorced, I didn't see her again until the other night. I mean, I don't ask you about all your past boyfriends.'

'Those were *boyfriends*, Eddie. Not *husbands*. There is a difference. Especially when your ex is a member of the English aristocracy!'

'God!' Chase rubbed his forehead, exasperated. 'Okay, you want to know one reason why I never talked about it? In case exactly this happened! You Yanks, you keep going on about how great it was that you kicked out the Brits and now everybody's equal and all that, but one whiff of a title and you start cringing and fawning like you're still part of the bloody colonies!'

'We do *not!*' Nina protested.

'But I bet you're already comparing yourself to her, aren't you? You're thinking "She's *Lady* Blackwood, not *Ms* Blackwood or *Dr* Blackwood", like that automatically means she's better than you.'

'*She* is standing right here,' said Sophia in a chilly tone as she poured the tea.

Chase ignored her, looking deep into Nina's eyes. 'Tell me *honestly* that you haven't been comparing yourself to her, and I'll admit I was wrong not telling you about us.'

Nina looked away first, drawing her dressing gown more tightly round her. 'I need to get dressed,' she said sullenly, retreating into the bedroom and closing the door.

'Fuck,' Chase muttered under his breath.

'I don't mean to be rude, Eddie,' Sophia offered from across the room, 'but you really haven't got any better at defusing arguments since we were married.'

'Shut up. Sorry,' he added after a moment. 'Christ! Why the hell didn't I tell her? She already knew I'd been married before, so why didn't I just get the whole thing out into the open?' He slumped heavily on to the couch.

Sophia came out from behind the counter, bearing two cups of tea. She placed one on the table in front of him. 'Because you never expected it to become an issue. This whole thing is my fault. I'm sorry.'

Chase gave her a look as she sat next to him. 'Well, that's something *you've* got better at since we were married. You, apologising?'

'A lot of things have changed since then,' she said, sounding sad. 'Not all of them for the better.'

They sat in silence for a few minutes, sipping tea. Then they looked up as Nina emerged from the bedroom. She was dressed in unassuming jeans and a T-shirt, red hair tied back in a ponytail.

'Okay, Eddie,' she said with an all-business air, 'we can talk about this later, because right now we have more important things to worry about. Sophia, I apologise if I was rude to you just now.'

'That's all right,' said Sophia. 'I can understand that it must have been something of a shock. I'm sorry.'

'Thanks. So.' She sat in an armchair, facing them. 'I guess now we need to figure out why your husband is so interested in the Tomb of Hercules.'

The Atlantic at dawn was a beautiful shade of deep, almost iridescent blue far below the 747, but Nina was in no mood to appreciate the view from the porthole. Instead she flicked through the pages of *Hermocrates* – now sealed in plastic sheets clipped into a binder, a far cry from the solid and heavy Victorian album in which they had formerly been preserved – and checked her notes as she tried to ignore the conversation taking place on the opposite side of the first class cabin.

She, Chase and Sophia were the only passengers in the compartment; it seemed that the tourists making up most of the half-filled plane's passengers were already spending so much on their African safari vacations that the thousands of extra dollars required to go first class were an extravagance too far. They were an extravagance too far for the IHA as well, which had originally only paid for economy tickets to Botswana. Sophia had arranged for the upgrade, one phone call from Nina's apartment the previous day seeing a replacement black American Express card arrive via motorcycle courier within hours. Apparently Yuen hadn't thought to cancel his wife's credit cards.

Nina was grateful to her for that much at least, as the big reclining seat made working much easier than if she'd been jammed into economy ... but she still resented Sophia's mere presence. All the more so as she glanced surreptitiously across the cabin. Chase and Sophia were sitting together, talking quietly, easily. From the occasional snippets she could overhear, they were talking about their past.

The past Chase had never bothered to tell her about. She clenched her jaw at the thought and turned away from them as far as she could without its looking obvious that she was turning away, beginning another read-through of the ancient Greek text.

Chase, sitting by the opposite window, looked past Sophia to see Nina turning her back on them in a huff. Great. He sat back and sighed.

'Nina?' Sophia asked.

'Yeah. Oh, hell*fire*, this is a mess.'

'It's my fault. I'm sorry.'

Chase exhaled slowly. 'No, it's not. We were having problems before you showed up.'

'What kind of problems?'

'Same kind we had,' he said.

She looked puzzled. 'What do you mean?'

'Come on, she's a PhD – a scientist, an intellectual. She knows about art and literature and stuff; she can do the *New York Times* crossword in twenty minutes. I can barely manage the quick crossword in the *Sun!*'

'Maybe you should switch to sudoku,' Sophia suggested teasingly.

'You know what I mean. She's *different* from me. A *lot* different. We've got different backgrounds, different lines of work, like different music and films and telly . . . we're not even from the same *country*, for God's sake!'

'I suppose we at least had that much in common.'

'Not a lot else, though.' Chase looked away, gazing at the ocean below. 'But it's the same thing all over again, isn't it? I come in as the rescuer, the white knight who shoots the bad guys and saves the beautiful woman. Then when she gets to know me, the *real* me, she realises that I'm *not* the white knight, I'm not a superhero. I'm just some bloke from Yorkshire who's good with a gun and his fists . . . and not a lot else.'

Sophia said nothing. After a moment, Chase faced her again. 'Yeah,' he went on, 'that's what I thought. It just took you a while to realise, didn't it? Your dad knew it right from the start, though. He couldn't stand me. He thought I was just some squaddie yob, his daughter's bit of rough.'

'That's not fair,' said Sophia.

'No? Then how come all the time we were married he hardly spoke to you? Especially about his business. I mean, Christ, you saw what was coming, but he wouldn't listen to you even when he was ill because he was so pissed off about me!'

'And by the time he *did* listen, it was too late,' Sophia said, almost to herself.

'Too late for us by then as well, wasn't it? And you didn't waste any time moving on. There was that slimy ponce from the City, and—'

She gripped his arm. 'Eddie, *please* don't. I know what I did. I was just . . . I was angry with you, and I was angry with myself, and my father . . . I was lashing out. I wanted to hurt somebody. And you were the easiest person to hurt. Which I deeply, deeply regret. I'm so sorry.'

Chase remained still, not wanting to look at her. 'Just tell me one thing. Why did you lie to me about having an affair with Jason Starkman?'

'What do you mean?'

'I know that you two never did anything. He told me.'

Sophia seemed surprised. 'When?'

'Doesn't matter. He's dead now. But he said nothing ever happened between the two of you, and I believed him.' He fixed her with his gaze. 'Why'd you lie to me, Sophia? I mean, I already knew you'd had an affair. So why did you tell me you'd had one with Jason as well? One of my best friends?'

She took her hands off his arm and rested them in her lap, looking down at them shame-faced. 'As I said,' she began, voice barely above a whisper, 'I wanted to hurt you. Jason had already left, gone rogue or whatever it was he did; he couldn't contradict me. So . . . I lied. I wish I hadn't, but I can't change the past. I'm sorry, I really am.'

Chase regarded her silently, his face expressionless except for a brief twinge of sadness around his eyes. Then he turned away, operating the controls to recline his seat. 'You know, I'm knackered,' he said in a neutral voice. 'Done a lot of flying in the past few days. I'm a bit jet-lagged. There's still another four hours before we land, so I think I could use a kip.' He turned on his side, back to her, and lowered the blind over the port-hole.

'Okay,' Sophia said softly. 'I'll . . . I'll let you sleep.' She stood and walked to the rear of the cabin.

Across the aisle, Nina looked across at them, unsure what had happened – or how she felt about it.

★

About ten minutes later Nina was surprised when Sophia returned, bearing two drinks, and sat down in the empty seat next to her.

'It's just tonic water,' Sophia explained, handing her one of the cups. 'I thought alcohol might interfere with your work.'

'Thank you,' Nina said automatically as she took it.

Sophia nodded at the binder. 'Have you managed to find out anything new?'

'Not beyond the map, which isn't much use until we have the other pages. There are still some phrases within the text that I'm convinced are clues of some kind, but so far I haven't been able to work out what they mean.'

'Perhaps I can help?'

Nina regarded her dubiously. 'Can you read ancient Greek?'

'As I said at the party, it's not my speciality,' she replied with a thin smile. 'But ancient history is a hobby of mine. Blame Indiana Jones for that – I forced my father to pay for me to visit all kinds of ancient sites around the world looking for everything from the mines of Solomon to the Garden of Eden when I was younger!'

'Well, it's not a hobby to me,' Nina told her, trying not to sound too withering, 'it's my profession, just like it was for my parents. It's what I *do*.'

'I understand. But as I said, I'm not ignorant of the subject. And Plato's dialogues were required reading during my studies at Cambridge, of course.'

'Of course,' said Nina stiffly.

'Actually having the chance to read a previously undiscovered one is rather exciting. So, what have you found?'

Reluctantly, Nina turned to the appropriate page. 'The phrase I think is most significant comes here, when Critias is talking to Hermocrates. There's an earlier paragraph where Critias mentions the Tomb of Hercules, which is where the clue regarding the map was – he had a line about finding the path by turning an empty page to the heat of the sun. Then here, there's another line – "By these words we relive the Trials of Heracles; yet just as the wondrous erubescent glass of Egypt shows the world in startling new form, so too may the words of our friend Hermocrates reveal still other words within, and in so doing safely show the way as if through the Underworld." Which on its own doesn't stand out as anything unusual, but as a part of the rest of the paragraph doesn't feel quite right. The fact that Plato has Critias specifically mention the Tomb again just beforehand makes me think it's another clue.'

'But to what? If the map's already been found . . .'

'I don't know.' Nina leafed to the back of the binder and a glossy photo of the assembled map. She tapped on the symbol at the end of the path. 'There's definitely more to it, though. Maybe once you reach the Tomb, you still need to know how to open it, or something. I don't know. Yet,' she added quickly. 'I don't know *yet*. But I'm sure I'll figure it out. Then all we'll need is the missing part of the map.' She closed the binder and faced Sophia. 'Are you *sure* it's your husband who has the other pages?'

'I'm positive,' she replied. 'The files I found, the ones Eddie brought to Admiral Amoros, they prove that my husband is somehow connected to the sinking of your rig, and that he was after information on the Tomb. The first time we met you, on the yacht, he even brought it up. He already *knew* that you were studying the text of *Hermocrates* to find it.'

'Yeah, he must have,' Nina admitted, thinking back. 'Still doesn't explain how his men knew about the Brotherhood's safe house, though.'

'All sorts of ways. Your phones could have been bugged, your computer hacked; he could have had people following you, maybe even paid off someone within the IHA itself. Believe me,' Sophia sighed, 'he'll stop at nothing to gain the advantage in business. Or *any* part of his life. My husband always gets what he wants . . . and he wants the map to the Tomb of Hercules.'

'Unless we get the rest of the map off of *him* first. You think the guy who attacked me will have taken it to him in Botswana?'

Sophia nodded. 'Your description of him sounded an awful lot like a man who works for my husband, Fang Yi. He takes care of security problems – the *unofficial* kind of security problems. If he has the pages, he will have taken them straight to him – and since my husband is in Botswana right now, that's where Fang will have gone too.'

'So what's he doing in Botswana?' asked Nina. 'I remember he said he owns a diamond mine there . . .'

'It's not just *a* diamond mine,' Sophia said, 'it's *the* diamond mine, the biggest in the country as of . . . well, now. That's why he's there. The Botswanan government takes a cut from the sale of every diamond mined in the country, and my husband's mine has been *extremely* productive. There's going to be an official ceremony to mark its becoming the biggest mine – the President will be there, various other bigwigs. I was supposed to attend it with Richard, actually. In my role as the perfect wife.'

'You'll still be there,' Nina pointed out. 'Just not up on stage with the guest of honour.'

Sophia shifted in her seat. 'It's a risk, I know. But if we can get to him when he's not expecting it . . .' She looked across at Chase, seeming to brighten a little. 'Eddie can be extremely persuasive.'

'Yeah, I know.' Nina sat back, silently having an internal debate before finally coming out with the question that had been on her mind ever since she'd first spoken to the Englishwoman. 'So how did you meet Eddie?'

Sophia glanced at Chase again, as if to check that he was asleep. 'From what I gather, it was similar to the way you met him. He told me that he was hired as your bodyguard?'

'Yeah,' said Nina, wondering what else Chase had told her.

'He was my bodyguard as well – in a manner of speaking. He was still in the SAS at the time, about six years ago. I told you that my father paid for me to travel the world?' Nina nodded. 'One of the countries I went to visit was Cambodia, to see the ancient temples at Angkor Wat and other sites like it. Unfortunately, at that time an Islamic militant group, the Golden Way, was trying to gain attention. The method they chose was to kidnap and threaten to execute a group of British visitors unless their demands were met. I was a member of that group.'

Nina's eyes widened. 'My God . . .'

'At the time my father, Lord Blackwood, was a very important man. He was a member of the House of Lords, obviously, but he was also a former government minister and an influential businessman, with connections on both sides of the House of Commons. The kidnapping of his only child was something which was *not* going to be allowed to stand.'

'So the government sent in the SAS to get you? Including Eddie?'

'Yes. The Cambodians were dithering, they wanted to negotiate, but that fell apart when the Golden Way killed one of the hostages. So the SAS were secretly sent in. Their mission was simple: locate and rescue the hostages . . . and kill every one of the kidnappers.'

Nina suppressed a slight shiver. She knew enough about Chase's military career to be aware that he had seen combat in clandestine missions, and that he could – and would – kill to save the lives of those under his protection. But hearing such a blunt order was something new, and far from pleasant. 'Since you and Eddie are both sitting here, I kinda guess they succeeded!' she said with forced levity.

'They did. But . . .' Sophia looked over at Chase once more. 'The Golden Way had reinforcements nearby, and when the SAS withdrew with the hostages Eddie and I got cut off. We had to get away on our own, through the jungle. It took three days for us to reach safety, with the terrorists after us. Eddie protected me the whole time.' Her expression turned wistful, eyes focusing on something beyond the cabin walls. 'He was a hero. He was *my* hero. And by the time we got back to England, I was completely, utterly, head-over-heels in love with him. We were married within a month.'

'Wow.' Nina's mind was reeling; Chase had never even hinted at such an intense event in his past. She also couldn't help but feel a sting of jealousy. She and Chase had come through an equally dangerous adventure and also ended up together, but there had been no suggestion of marriage. 'So what happened?'

'My father, for one.' Sophia's face darkened. 'He was absolutely appalled that I would get married without consulting him. Especially since I was the daughter of a lord – you know, that sort of thing just isn't done!' A single, somewhat bitter, laugh. 'He was furious. And he *despised* Eddie. Never mind that he'd saved my life – he was just some lower-class nobody, a *commoner*. He wanted nothing to do with him. And because I was married to Eddie, and loved him, he all but cut me off too.'

Nina couldn't help but feel a rising anger at the criticism of Chase, even second-hand. 'Not meaning to be rude, but your dad sounds like kind of an asshole.'

Sophia bit back a harsh rejoinder, gathering her composure before speaking more calmly. 'He made mistakes; he was wrong about some things. But he was still my father, and he's no longer with us, so I never had the opportunity to set things straight between us. You didn't know him, so I'd prefer it if you didn't criticise him. I'm sure you feel the same about your parents.'

'I'm sorry,' said Nina, stung with guilt. Sophia was right – she would have reacted the same way.

Sophia closed her eyes and sighed. 'That's all right. My father passed away three years ago. Much as I try, I still feel some lingering resentment.' She opened her eyes again, resolute. 'But my father's attitude definitely put a strain on the marriage. And it didn't help when my initial euphoria started to wear off, and I started to see Eddie . . . as Eddie.'

'What do you mean?' But she already knew.

And Sophia knew that she knew, Nina seeing the understanding in her brown eyes. 'I married my hero,' Sophia said softly. 'But it didn't take me long to realise that behind the hero . . . was just a very ordinary man. It was absolutely heartbreaking. But it was also undeniable. And once I realised that, then . . .'

'It was over,' Nina finished for her.

'Yes.' Sophia looked away. 'Excuse me.' She got up and walked back down the aisle.

Nina remained still. She wanted to look across at Chase, but didn't dare.

In case the sight of him brought her to the same realisation as Sophia.

9

Botswana

'Well, hey,' said the towering African woman, arms folded sternly. 'If it isn't Edward Chase.'

'Tamara Defendé,' Chase replied as he walked up to her. They regarded each other with apparent mutual suspicion for a few moments . . . before she swept her arms around him.

'Eddie!' she cried, squeezing Chase tightly, creasing his leather jacket. 'Great to see you!'

'It's been a while,' Chase wheezed. 'Okay, TD, you can let go now. I need my lungs.'

Nina and Sophia exchanged glances. 'Was it like this for you too?' Nina whispered.

Sophia nodded. 'Mysterious women all over the world? Mm-hmm.'

'TD,' said Chase, making introductions, 'this is Dr Nina Wilde' – Nina couldn't help noticing that he had omitted any mention of their relationship – 'and Sophia Blackwood. Nina, Sophia, this is a good friend of mine, TD.'

TD's curious expression indicated that she knew of Sophia's past connection to Chase, but she didn't comment on it. Instead, she shook their hands, her grip strong. 'Good to meet you both.'

'How do you know Eddie?' Nina asked.

Chase shot her a warning look – more military secrets he wanted to keep, Nina guessed – but TD simply smirked at him before answering. 'I'm a pilot, I have my own plane. Eddie and his chums have hired me to fly them to . . .' She grinned again at Chase, who seemed to have developed a facial tic, before letting him off the hook. '. . . various *workplaces* around Africa. You know what his work is like, I'm sure!'

'Not so much now,' Chase cut in. 'I usually sit behind a desk these days.'

'Oh, what a shame!' TD's accent was a melodious melange of West African intonations, hints of French and Dutch blended in. 'I hope you're not getting rusty in your old age!'

'I'm keeping my hand in,' said Chase, not amused at the 'old age' remark. 'You got everything I asked for?'

'In my plane. Come on.' TD jerked a thumb at a battered open-top Land Rover waiting nearby. The temperature was warm, in the mid-seventies, but not oppressively hot. 'I got your parcel as well. I was impressed – I didn't know you could send handguns by courier flight!'

'Working for the UN has the occasional perk. Like customs waivers and "do not X-ray" stickers.'

They headed for the Land Rover, Nina at the rear of the little group. She looked TD up and down as they walked. She was not the first of Chase's helpful international 'girlfriends' Nina had met, and while it didn't seem that his relationships with any of them went beyond friendship, she couldn't help wondering what it was about him that inspired such loyalty. Especially when he could be so *infuriating* at times.

Maybe that was it, she thought. He never stayed around long enough to drive them mad.

TD certainly stood out among the others. She was easily over six feet tall, her height increased by a pair of chunky-heeled cowboy boots. And she dressed to draw the eye, wearing a pair of shorts that were only an inch of material away from qualifying as hotpants and a cut-off shirt that exposed her well-toned midriff. Her long hair was braided, the strands flowing down her back through a red baseball cap with its top cut out. Nina had no doubt that she attracted a lot of male attention – and also that she could handle it on her own terms. TD's sole piece of clothing which could be described as 'modest' was a faded denim jacket – under which, Nina was certain, was hidden a holstered gun.

They climbed into the Land Rover. TD drove them across Gaborone airport, her hair flapping in the wind. 'You didn't give me a lot of time to prepare for you,' she told Chase. 'Twenty-four hours – it was tough!'

'But you managed it, right?'

'Of course! Have I ever let you down?'

'Only romantically,' Chase said, smiling.

TD laughed. 'But the media passes, they were the hardest part,' she continued, serious again. 'I would never have been able to get them without the information you gave me – not without a much bigger bribe than I could have managed at such short notice, anyway. How did you get it?'

'That was my doing,' said Sophia. 'I still have friends within my husband's company, and some access to its computer network. I was able to set things up for you.'

'Well, thank you! I always like it when someone makes my life a little easier – especially on a job like this!'

They reached a hangar section, wind-blown old structures housing light aircraft. TD pulled into one of the buildings. 'This is my plane,' she said proudly.

Nina wasn't sure that the plane actually *was* anything to be proud of – the twin-engined aircraft, its fuselage painted a time-scoured taxicab yellow, looked at least forty years old. 'Oh, don't worry,' TD told her, correctly reading her expression, 'I take very good care of her, and in return she takes very good care of me!'

'Piper Twin Comanche,' Chase added. 'Small enough to land pretty much anywhere, even on bush strips – and big enough to carry a team and their gear. And this one's got a few extra tricks in case we need to make a quick getaway. Which after we have words with Yuen, I think we might need to.'

'Try not to kill President Molowe in the crossfire,' TD warned as she unlocked the plane's hatch. 'I voted for him.'

'Don't worry, I'll be careful. I've already got a death sentence on me in two African countries; I don't need another one.'

'You've got *what*?' Nina yelped.

'Nothing to worry about,' Chase quickly assured her.

She spotted something on the aircraft's wing. 'Is that – is that a *bullet hole?*'

'Nothing to worry about!'

TD flew them some four hundred and fifty miles north by northwest from Gaborone. Their course took them over the vast desert plains and dry bushlands of the Kalahari before they descended towards a private airstrip fifty miles west of the town of Maun.

Chase sat in the co-pilot's seat. Nina looked over his shoulder in amazement at the view to the north. Beyond the dusty desert was a vast swathe of vibrant greenery stretching over the horizon.

'The Okavango Delta,' TD piped up. 'Biggest inland delta in the world. And a huge wildlife reserve, as well. If you weren't here on business, I'd give you a tour!'

'Maybe later,' said Chase. 'Besides, you've seen one pissed-off hippo, you've seen 'em all.'

TD smiled, then spoke to somebody on the ground over her headset to receive final landing instructions. The plane banked, turning westwards. The distant beauty of the delta was replaced by . . .

'Bloody hell,' muttered Chase. 'That's an eyesore.'

'I'm afraid environmentalism and diamond mining don't mix,' Sophia said.

Nina couldn't agree more. Ahead, growing rapidly as the plane descended, was Yuen's diamond mine, a colossal crater gouged out of the earth. Nina could make out yellow vehicles moving up and down the long paths spiralling down to the base of the giant pit; she did a double take when she realised they were still miles from the hole. The trucks were enormous, in keeping with the terrifying scale of the mine itself.

Beyond the pit were numerous warehouse-like buildings and cylindrical towers, all on the same massive scale. The whole complex of pit and support buildings spanned over a mile, and the distant fences round the mine suggested plenty of room for expansion.

The Twin Comanche made a bumpy landing, taxiing to the end of the runway and being directed into a large parking area off to one side. There were already numerous other aircraft on the ground, ranging from small chartered props to corporate jets. It was clearly a major event.

With equally major security.

Chase, Nina and Sophia – TD remained in the plane – were met at a cordon by a group of unsmiling armed men. Private security, not Botswanan armed forces. It took Chase only a moment's observation to tell that they had military training, their stance, alertness and hold on their weapons a dead giveaway. As he approached, he deliberately relaxed his own stance, trying to look as undisciplined as possible as he shambled up to the checkpoint with two heavy bags of equipment.

One of the guards held up a hand, his companions subtly shifting position to cover the new arrivals. 'Good afternoon, welcome to the Ygem diamond mine,' he said mechanically. 'May I see your visitor passes and identification, please?'

Sophia spoke for them, aristocratic accent to full commanding effect. 'Good afternoon. I'm Sophia Black, from the CNB news bureau in Cape Town. This is Ed Case, my cameraman, and Nina Jones, my sound engineer.' She gave the guard the documents that TD had obtained.

He checked them against a list on a clipboard and made an approving noise. 'Thank you,' he said, returning the documents. Another man ran an electronic wand over their bodies, detecting innocuous items like keys and coins. The first man went through their luggage. 'Can you switch this on, please?' he asked of the bulky video camera he took from one of Chase's bags.

Chase obliged, the camera coming to life. The guard peered through the viewfinder to be sure, even opening the tape door to check inside. 'Camera, battery packs, spare tapes, boom mike, sandwiches,' Chase said, pointing out each item in turn. 'Hey, you mind if I get some footage of you guys? You know, for background colour?'

'Yes, I do mind,' the guard told him firmly. As Chase repacked his gear, the man looked through Nina's little backpack, finding only the binder. He flicked through the first few pages of her handwritten notes with no interest, then returned it and went on in a bored voice, 'It is the policy of the Ygem diamond mine to remind all visitors that diamond theft is an extremely serious offence, which will be punished by the full force of Botswanan criminal and civil law. Thank you, you can now enter. Please wait over there for the bus.' He pointed to some covered benches beside the nearby road, where other people were already sitting.

'Cheers, mate,' Chase said, picking up his bags. '*Ed Case?*' he hissed to Sophia as they walked away. 'Very bloody funny. Makes me sound like a nutter.'

'Just my little joke.'

'At least they got us in,' Nina said.

'Yeah, I suppose.' Chase put a hand on Sophia's shoulder. 'Good work.'

She smiled. 'Thank you.'

After a few minutes, a bus pulled up, and those waiting – all members of the international press corps – boarded. Chase took a seat near the back of the bus, and Sophia sat down next to him. Feeling slightly left out, Nina settled in the row behind. A few minutes later, another small group of people boarded, and the bus moved off.

Once he was sure that nobody was watching, Chase took the long tubular boom mike from his bag and prised it open to reveal that it was hollow, his disassembled Wildey pistol and its holster crammed inside. He quickly reassembled the big gun, then donned the holster, slipped the weapon into it and put his leather jacket back on to hide it.

'I thought you were trying to cut down on shooting people,' said Sophia.

'Well, it's kind of like a diet – you know, you stick at it for a while, then . . .' Chase joked, before his face hardened. 'And after what happened to Nina, somebody *deserves* to get shot.'

Nina said nothing, somewhat affronted that it had taken him this long to remember she was with him.

The bus slowed. Looking ahead, she saw they were approaching a checkpoint, a high corrugated metal fence topping a berm of bulldozed earth running off in each direction. But that wasn't what seized her attention. *'Tanks?'*

'Must be here as part of the presidential guard. Bit of a show of force to let everyone know how seriously they look after their diamond mines,' Chase observed. The two tanks in mottled brown desert camouflage flanking the gate were Leopards, a relatively old German design long since superseded in the West by more modern weapons, but still formidable.

'I'm not surprised,' said Sophia. 'Three-quarters of Botswana's export earnings come from diamonds.'

Chase grunted. 'Never saw the appeal myself. "Ooh, look, it's so

161

sparkly!" Yeah, that's well worth a month's pay. Might as well polish up a bit of glass.'

'Right,' Nina said sarcastically. 'Nothing says "I love you" like a *glass* ring.'

'I didn't know you were bothered about stuff like that. I didn't *think* you were, anyway.' Chase's tone was cutting.

'Eddie,' Sophia warned. Chase frowned and fell silent as the bus passed through the gate, Nina fuming behind him.

Inside the fence, the bus drove along a road skirting the side of the enormous pit. Nina could barely take in its sheer size – or its utter ugliness, countless millions of tons of earth just ripped away as the massive excavators dug ever deeper. Mine workers in vivid orange safety jackets directed the bus well clear of the other traffic using the road – giant dump trucks. Calling them *house-sized* wouldn't be an exaggeration, Nina decided.

Almost eight metres high and barely short of sixteen metres long, with a fully loaded weight of well over six hundred tons, the Liebherr T282B was the largest truck in the world, costing over three million dollars. And the Ygem mine had over thirty of them, a constantly moving convoy making its laborious way up the huge spiral path from the bottom of the mine to the processing plant at the top, then returning to be loaded up once more. In diamond mining, bigger was always better; the more raw earth and rock that could be moved in one go, the more diamonds could be extracted at a time – and the more money could be made.

Chase watched one of the empty juggernauts rumble past on its way back into the pit, moving surprisingly quickly for something so huge. 'Bloody hell. Better than a Tonka toy any day.'

The bus passed under a huge banner bearing the Botswanan

flag, the Ygem logo and the slogan 'The Biggest, The Best: United In Prosperity'. Beyond was their destination, a covered stage which had been erected close to the mine's administration buildings, faced by ranks of stadium-style seats. An enormous marquee stood off to the side, waiters and waitresses in white uniforms bustling in and out between it and several catering trucks parked alongside.

Chase checked his watch. 'What time's this whole thing supposed to kick off?'

'Two o'clock,' Sophia told him.

'So we've got about an hour to find Dick before he gets up on stage with the President, which is when it gets kind of hard for us to have a word in private. I'm guessing he won't be hanging about afterwards.'

'Hardly,' said Sophia. 'If I remember our original itinerary, my husband wanted to get out of Botswana so quickly that he even had a helicopter laid on just to get back to the runway and the company jet as soon as the official function ends.'

'Where were you due to go next?' Chase asked. 'I mean, if we miss him here we're probably buggered, but we might get a second shot.'

'Switzerland. But he may have changed his plans since I left.'

The bus stopped beside the marquee's main entrance. Chase picked up the bags. Leaving the vehicle, they were directed into the huge tent. Its walls were lined with large poster displays showing off the mine's technological prowess; the giant trucks, the even bigger excavators that filled them, the security systems monitoring and protecting the precious stones, even an airship used to survey the Okavango for more diamond veins. Around two hundred people were already inside, buffet tables set out and staff serving drinks. There was also a clear social division: two-thirds of the interior was occupied by the attending media and the apparently less influential attendees, with a smaller roped-off VIP area at the far end.

'Uh-oh,' Chase said quietly as they moved through the throng, lowering his head and gesturing for Sophia to do the same. 'You see who I see?'

'I do,' she replied. Nina looked down the tent and spotted Yuen through the crowd, standing laughing with a small group of men in the VIP section.

But it wasn't Yuen who caught her eye. 'Shit,' she whispered, lowering her own head and summoning Chase closer. 'That's him. That's the guy who took the other pages!'

Chase cautiously followed her gaze. 'The guy with the ponytail?'

'That's Fang,' said Sophia. 'Fang Yi, my husband's . . . I suppose *enforcer* would be the most accurate term.'

Nina tried to get a better look. Fang was standing slightly apart from Yuen, something about his body language suggesting suppressed impatience, waiting for his boss to finish his conversation. He had his black cane in one hand, and in his other was a briefcase – which, Nina saw with a sudden jolt of excitement, was handcuffed to his wrist. Exactly how the Brotherhood had brought the *Hermocrates* text to New York.

'Oh, my God,' she said quietly. 'I think he's got the pages in that briefcase.'

'He's got *something* important in there, that's for sure.' Chase surveyed the rest of the tent. 'Bollocks. I don't see an easy way to get to him. There's too many goons around.' The rope dividing the marquee was guarded by several security men, all with pistols on their belts.

'We might be able to catch Richard before the tour,' Sophia suggested. 'I know him: he'll want to take a few minutes to meditate and put on a clean shirt for his speech. He'll probably get changed in the administration building.'

'Which means we need to get out of here and into the admin block,' Chase said. 'Okay, let's check out the catering entrance over there, see if we can sneak out. Say we need to use the loo or something.'

'Subtle as ever,' said Sophia with amusement as Chase led the way across the tent. None of the other guests or staff seemed interested in them. He checked that nobody was watching, about to dart through the door—

'Wait, wait!' Nina said. 'Look!' She indicated the VIP area. Yuen had finally ended his conversation, and Fang was taking him off to one side. He held up the briefcase and opened it. Inside was . . .

Nina's breath caught as she watched Yuen carefully lift something out of the case, turning his back to shield it from the sight of the other people nearby. But she didn't need a good view to know what it was.

The missing section of the book. The stolen pages of Plato's *Hermocrates*.

The rest of the map that would lead her to the Tomb of Hercules.

'That's it, that's the book!' she said in a high-pitched whisper, barely able to contain herself. 'It's here, he brought it!'

'All right, calm down, you'll have an aneurysm,' Chase told her dismissively. She huffed, then looked back at Yuen and Fang. Yuen examined the pages, then returned them to the case and said something to his henchman. Fang nodded, closed the case and walked away. A guard stepped aside to let him through an exit at the rear of the marquee.

'We've got to go after him!' said Nina. 'We've got to get the other pages!'

Chase frowned. 'Wait, we came here to get *Yuen*, remember?'

'No, Eddie, she's absolutely right,' Sophia said. 'Fang has the book – and he *doesn't* have any guards. All the security will be concentrated around my husband, and the President when he arrives. We can get the book – and then we don't *need* to do anything else, except get back to the plane.'

Chase looked from Yuen to the exit through which Fang had departed, then let out a breath between his teeth. 'Okay, let's bag him. But we'll have to shift to catch him.' He put down the bags, then ducked through the door.

They emerged by the catering trucks. A couple of uniformed staff looked at them disinterestedly before carrying on with their food preparation. The reason for their lack of surprise soon became obvious. The marquee was a no-smoking area; from the number of cigarette butts on the ground, this was the only place where the media could grab a smoke.

Chase led the way along the side of the tent and peered round the corner. There was another security guard outside the exit through which Fang had left, but his back was to Chase as he watched a pair of men carrying a set of wooden steps into an open area marked by a circle of white tape. They were preparing for the arrival of a helicopter, presumably President Molowe's.

Chase spotted Fang, heading for a line of white Toyota Land

Cruisers alongside the nearby administration building. 'I see him,' he told the two women. 'Looks like he's going for a drive.'

'What if he's leaving already?' asked Nina, worried. 'If he drives back to the airfield—'

'Follow him,' Sophia said. Chase checked that the guard was preoccupied, then crossed the few yards to take cover behind a parked bulldozer at the end of a row of similar machines. Sophia and Nina quickly joined him.

Fang got into one of the Land Cruisers and reached up to slide the keys out from the sun visor. He started the 4x4, orange warning lights on its roof flashing.

Keeping low, Chase hurried along the row of earthmovers until he reached the last one. He leaned out from behind it to watch as Fang set off. The Land Cruiser skirted the landing area – there was a second helipad further away, occupied by a Jet Ranger sporting the Ygem logo – and passed out of sight behind the marquee.

Chase popped open the leather strap holding his Wildey in its holster, then gestured for Nina and Sophia to hurry to the nearest Land Cruiser. He kept his eyes on the guard as they crossed the gap, one hand on his gun, but the man's attention was still elsewhere. Once the women were in cover, he ran to join them.

'Okay,' he said, opening the driver's door, 'I'll drive.' Sophia went to the front passenger door, again leaving Nina to sit on the row behind. Once inside, Chase tipped down the sun visor, the keys dropping into his hand. 'Guess they don't have much of a chav problem around here. Do this in England, your car'd be gone in *six* seconds, never mind sixty.'

'We *are* twenty miles from the nearest town,' Sophia pointed out. Chase grinned and started the engine.

'Ahem,' said Nina. Chase and Sophia looked round to see her holding up two white hard hats. 'These might make us a bit less conspicuous.'

Sophia looked impressed. 'Good idea.' She donned one of the plastic helmets, Chase grunting as he tried to force the other on to his head. Nina took a third hard hat as Chase set off.

He was briefly worried that he might have lost track of Fang, but the other Land Cruiser came back into view once they were past the marquee and the neighbouring stage. They didn't seem to be attracting any undue attention from the mine workers they passed.

Chase followed Fang's vehicle, keeping down to the thirty-kilometre-per-hour speed limit and staying well clear of the passing dump trucks. When they approached the road leading to the airfield, he was surprised when Fang didn't turn on to it. 'Hello, where's he going?'

Nina followed the path of the road. 'Down into the mine, it looks like.'

Chase reduced speed slightly as he continued after Fang, not wanting to get too close. Not that it would be possible to hide that he was following him – apart from the giant trucks, there was little else in the way of traffic. He looked at Sophia. 'What's down here?'

'I have no idea,' she said. 'Wearing a hard hat doesn't make me an expert in diamond mining.'

They continued down the long spiral deeper into the pit. The dump trucks took the longest, shallowest route, but Fang guided his 4x4 down steeper inclines cutting between levels. Chase followed a few hundred yards behind. They were getting close to the bottom of the crater, which was a scene of constant mechanised activity.

Giant mobile excavators, dwarfing even the dump trucks, tore away at the walls of the pit with enormous rotating scoops resembling the blade of a circular saw. The rubble was transported back along conveyors to be collected in hoppers, which then spewed out hundreds of tons at a time into the back of each waiting truck. The noise was horrendous, and clouds of dust swirled in the vortex of wind caused by the crater itself. 'Jesus,' said Chase, carefully following Fang's path between the colossal machines. 'They should have these on *Robot Wars*.'

'Just don't get too close,' Nina said, cringing at the thump of rock on metal as a boulder larger than their Land Cruiser dropped into the back of one of the trucks. 'I don't want to end up as a red spot on somebody's wedding ring.'

'A literal blood diamond,' commented Sophia, making Chase laugh. Despite all her other concerns, Nina couldn't help feeling annoyed that she hadn't thought of the joke first.

It had been a while since she'd made him laugh . . .

All such thoughts vanished in an instant when Chase said, 'He's stopping.' She squinted through the patina of dirt now smearing the windscreen to see the other Land Cruiser pull up by a tunnel entrance at the muddy bottom of the pit, away from the roaring machines.

'A mineshaft,' said Sophia, puzzled. 'Why would there be a mineshaft? This is an open-cast mine.'

'I thought you weren't an expert,' Nina said, hardly concealing her sarcasm.

'I'm not, but I *do* know the definition of "open-cast".' Sophia's tone was similarly derisive. 'This shouldn't be here.'

'Well, it is,' Chase stated, 'and he's going into it.' They watched as Fang, still holding the briefcase, put on a hard hat and went quickly to the tunnel entrance, where he was met by another man. They exchanged words, then disappeared inside.

Chase stopped next to Fang's 4x4. 'So, what do we do? Wait for him to come out so we can grab the map, or go in after him?'

'We go in,' Sophia said firmly. 'Whatever's in there, it *must* be connected to whatever my husband's doing. It's too out of place to be a coincidence. And Fang might have gone in there to give the pages to someone else. If we lose track of them, we may never get them back.'

'All right. But you two should wait for me in here.'

'I don't think so,' Nina protested, pointing at the excavators. 'What if the foreman comes over to ask what we're doing? If someone calls for security, we're screwed – there's only one way out of this hole.'

Chase nodded begrudgingly. 'Okay, okay. Just . . . be careful. And if it looks like there's going to be any trouble, run right back to the car and get out of the pit.'

'What, and leave you behind?' said Nina.

He took out his gun and gave her a patronising look. 'I can take care of myself.'

'And I can't? Not that I had much choice the other day, seeing as you'd run off to the other side of the planet—'

'I don't think this is the appropriate time,' Sophia interrupted sharply. She opened her door and stepped out, forestalling any further discussion. Chase frowned at Nina, then got out himself.

Left alone, Nina banged her fists on her seat in exasperation before she too exited the Land Cruiser.

The tunnel entrance before her was about ten feet wide, an almost perfectly circular hole disappearing into the dusty brown earth. Faint, widely spaced lights hung from the ceiling. It brought back unpleasant memories of the tunnels beneath New York. She tensed at the thought.

'You all right?' Chase asked. He put a hand lightly on her arm.

'I'm fine,' she said, shrugging him away and shouldering her backpack. 'Come on. Let's get my map.'

10

Chase led the way, using the wooden props supporting the tunnel as cover to check ahead. Fang and the other man were already lost in the darkness.

The ceaseless noise of the excavators faded as they went deeper underground, but Nina heard more mechanical clamour ahead.

'At least nobody'll hear us coming,' Chase remarked. He could see lights in the distance, a larger space which was the source of the rumbling. Fang and his companion were briefly silhouetted against the electric glare, then they rounded the far end of the tunnel and passed out of sight. 'Okay, I think we can move now. But keep to the sides, just in case.'

He increased his pace to a jog, every so often looking back to make sure nobody had entered the tunnel behind them. It didn't take long for them to reach the other end.

Chase warily peered round the last prop to see a large rectangular chamber. Three more circular tunnels led in different directions deeper underground. How they had been dug was now obvious; a large boring machine squatted on caterpillar tracks near the chamber's centre, its complex array of interlocking conical drill-heads covered with jagged metal studs to rip apart the rock and earth.

But that wasn't the machine responsible for the noise.

Conveyor belts emerged from each of the three tunnels, depositing the clumps of rubble they carried on to a single, broader conveyor which ascended almost twenty feet in the air to feed a huge crusher below. The pulverised ore then entered what Chase took to be some kind of processor. He couldn't see what went on inside it, only that most of the ore was discarded, spat on to a large pile in one corner of the chamber. Whatever was being mined ended up in black metal drums, a number of which were arranged on a pallet.

Behind the whole affair were several portable cabins, stacked on two levels. A series of yellow-painted catwalks connected them to the crusher assembly.

'What the hell is this?' Chase wondered. 'Why would you hide a diamond mine *in* a diamond mine?'

'I don't think it has anything to do with diamonds,' said Nina. She crouched, using her thumb and forefinger to prise something out of the wall.

'Jesus,' Chase gasped. Nina held a stone about the size of a pea. It was rough, uncut . . . but unmistakable.

A diamond.

'I just saw it, right there.' She moved a few feet back down the tunnel, then pointed. 'And there's another one.'

'My husband always did brag about this being the richest mine in the country, maybe even the world,' said Sophia. 'If diamonds are that easy to find, it seems he wasn't joking.'

'But these have just been ignored,' Nina pointed out. 'Whatever they're mining in here, it must be more valuable than diamonds. But what *is*?'

Chase looked back at the metal drums by the processor. 'Let's find out.'

He hefted his gun and moved quickly towards the three-foot-high drums, keeping a careful eye on the cabins. Sophia followed. Nina hesitated, then shoved the uncut diamond into a pocket and ran after them.

Chase examined the unmarked drums. Their tops were firmly secured by wingnuts screwed on to protruding bolts. Judging from the distance of the bolts from the outer edge of the drums, the containers were at least two inches thick.

Thick enough to contain something dangerous . . . or *shield* it.

Already starting to get a nasty idea of the purpose of the processor, he looked round, seeing an operator's console and, below it, a toolbox. He opened the box and took out a monkey wrench. 'Keep an eye on the cabins,' he told Sophia and Nina as he holstered his gun, then clamped the wrench on to one of the nuts and pushed hard. After a few seconds of straining, the nut turned.

Chase unscrewed it as quickly as he could, then repeated the process on the other bolts. Finally, the lid was free. He had to strain again to lift it aside, the metal as solid as a manhole cover.

They looked inside, to find . . .

The barrel was full of crushed grey ore with a silvery sheen. 'Definitely not diamonds,' said Nina, about to pick up a piece.

Chase grabbed her wrist. '*Don't*.' The tone of warning in the single word chilled her to the bone.

'Do you know what it is?' she asked.

'Yes. I know.' His expression was hard, a look she hadn't seen on him for a long time. A stony, focused determination. Chase was now one hundred per cent business. 'It's uranium.'

Nina flinched back. 'Are you sure?'

'I've had some experience with WMDs, so yeah. I'm sure.' He shoved the lid of the barrel back into place. 'We need to leave. Now.'

'But what about the map?' Nina asked, looking up at the cabins.

'Fuck the map,' Chase said coldly. He screwed the nuts back on to the bolts. 'We've got to get out of here and contact the UN, warn them what we've found – and do it before anyone realises we were here. If we get caught, we're dead.'

Nina's anger at Chase was overcome by fear. 'But uranium's mined all over the world—'

'And every mine's monitored *really* closely,' he interrupted. 'The International Atomic Energy Agency knows exactly how much uranium's in circulation – and where it came from, and where it went for processing. If terrorists got hold of a nuke and set it off, there'd be slightly different radioactive traces depending on who made it, 'cause there are different ways to make weapons-grade uranium. So you can trace the bomb back to its source.' He tightened the final bolt. 'But if you've got a supply of uranium nobody knows about, that cuts the trail right at the start. And if you can process it as well . . .'

'My husband has industrial facilities all over the world,' Sophia said. 'If anyone has the resources to build a secret processing plant, he does.'

'Which means he could make nukes and sell them to terrorists or rogue states without anyone ever knowing about it – until one goes off.' Chase turned the final wingnut as far as he could, then tossed the wrench back into the toolbox. 'Come on, we've got to go.'

Nina didn't move. 'Wait—'

'No,' Chase snapped. 'Forget your map; it's not important any more.' He grabbed her arm.

'That's not what I mean! Don't you hear it?'

Realisation crossed his face, and he looked at one of the tunnels. A chugging came from it, getting louder—

A squat little truck burst from the tunnel mouth. Four men in dirty overalls and hard hats rode on top of it. One of them glanced across at the processor – and reacted with shock at the sight of the three unfamiliar people standing by it. He grabbed a walkie-talkie from his toolbelt and shouted into it as the driver swerved the truck towards the intruders.

'Fuck!' Chase whipped out his gun and fired. The man with the walkie-talkie flew off the back of the truck, blood gouting from his chest. The driver hurriedly changed direction, heading for the tunnel leading outside as the other two miners flung themselves off the vehicle and ran for cover.

An alarm honked furiously, adding to the racket from the machinery. The man's warning had been heard.

The cabin doors flew open, men running along the catwalks. Fang appeared in one of the windows.

He saw Nina . . .

And *smiled*.

'Run!' Chase yelled, shoving Nina towards the exit. Sophia was already sprinting ahead. He raised his gun again, aiming at the driver. If they could steal the truck, it would give them a head start down the tunnel—

Automatic weapons fire crackled behind them. The ground ahead of Sophia suddenly erupted into geysers of dirt and stone chips, blocking her path. She threw up a hand to protect her eyes from the stinging debris, having nowhere to go but back to the processor. Nina shrieked and ducked behind the machinery as more bullets hit near her feet.

Chase whirled and looked up at the cabins. Men were charging down the steps, and on the upper level the man he'd seen with Fang was now crouched with an MP-5 sub-machine gun, firing another burst.

He wasn't trying to kill the intruders. He was trying to *contain* them, prevent them from escaping.

Chase fired two shots, but the gunman rolled along the catwalk, the Magnum rounds punching holes in the wall of the cabin above him.

More MP-5 fire from another angle: Fang, joining the attack from the cabin door. Unlike the other man, he wasn't aiming to miss, tracking Chase as he threw himself headlong into the cover of the processor.

'Jesus!' Chase gasped as bullets clonked against the heavy machinery just behind him. Nina and Sophia were hunched against the crusher a few yards away. 'They want you alive!' he shouted.

'What about you?' Nina cried.

'Not so much!' He popped his head round the corner of the processor for a fraction of a second, the brief glimpse showing him what he needed to know. Fang was running down the catwalk towards the other end of the crusher, while the other man crouched with the MP-5 aimed down at his hiding place. He expected bullets to follow, and he was right, rounds ripping into the steel casing of the machinery—

The firing stopped.

Chase had been counting the shots almost on a subconscious level from the moment the first was fired. An MP-5 magazine held thirty rounds, and now they were gone, requiring a reload.

He didn't allow one, whipping out from cover and firing a single shot that exploded square in the centre of the gunman's chest as he fumbled for a new magazine. The man fell backwards, dead.

'*Eddie!*'

He whirled to see one of the mine workers round the crusher and grab Nina in a bear hug. She struggled and kicked, thrashing against her captor – meaning Chase couldn't risk taking a shot . . .

Sophia smashed the man on the back of his neck with a large wrench. The crack of bone could be heard even over the noise of the crusher. He instantly collapsed, but took Nina down with him, landing on top of her.

'Sophia!' Chase warned. Another man ran under the conveyor and lunged at her – only to spin back as Chase shot him. Sophia gave him a quick look of thanks.

Then her eyes flicked up to something above him—

Chase was slammed to the ground as a man jumped on to him from the catwalk above the processor, knocking the Wildey from his grip.

Sophia dragged the unmoving body of the mine worker off Nina and pulled her to her feet as another two men ducked under the conveyor belt towards them. With Chase disarmed, the two miners from the now departed truck had been emboldened and were running at them from the other direction.

Chase saw his attacker's knee flash at his groin and just barely managed to twist his hips away in time to turn an incapacitating blow into a merely eye-watering one. 'You fucker!' he spat, lashing out with his leg. He caught the man's shin, knocking his foot out from under him and dropping him face-first on to the ground. A blow of Chase's own elbow against the back of the miner's skull resulted in a satisfying splat of blood and teeth.

He looked for Nina and Sophia, seeing them racing up a set of stairs to the first level of the catwalk. A moment later, the four men running for them converged at the base of the steps. Two of them went after the women – the other pair charged at him.

No time to look for his gun. The first man was unarmed, the second wielding a steel pipe. Chase jumped up to face them, fists raised.

They moved apart to take him from two directions at once. The one with the pipe made the first move, savagely swinging it at Chase's chest and forcing him to jump back – into the reach of his companion.

He grabbed Chase from behind, trying to pin his arms down at his sides as the pipe pulled back for another strike . . .

Nina ran along the catwalk – then screeched to a halt as she saw another man coming round the far end, crossing above the base of the rising conveyor belt. 'Oh, crap!' The two men chasing them were now on the catwalk, the first raising his hands to seize Sophia as he rushed her. She brought up one arm in a seemingly futile attempt to block him.

The miner grabbed it – only for her to suddenly twist free and take hold of *him*. Before the startled man could react, she made a fast quarter-turn to her left to haul him closer, and with shocking force drove her right arm up directly beneath his elbow. There was a horrible crunch as his arm abruptly bent the wrong way at the joint.

His screech of agony was enough to halt the other two men on the catwalk in their tracks. Sophia released him, then grabbed the handrails like parallel bars to push herself up and slam both feet square into the squealing man's chest. He flew backwards, colliding with the mine worker behind him and sending them both tumbling.

Nina gaped at her. 'Eddie taught me that,' Sophia said by way of rapid explanation.

'He didn't teach *me* that!'

Chase was faring less well than either of his pupils. The guy pinning his arms was strong, and he couldn't break free. The pipe swung – as Chase bent *forward*, flipping his captor over his back. The pipe smashed against the man's skull below the protection of his hard hat with a ringing crack.

Chase rolled and threw the limp miner to the ground. Frozen by the horrified realisation of what he'd just done to his comrade, the second man had no time to respond as Chase tackled him to the ground and delivered three brutal punches that flattened his face into pulp.

Sophia shoved past Nina and grabbed a small fire extinguisher from a hook by a ladder. She advanced on the man ahead, brandishing the extinguisher like a club. He hesitated for a moment, then cautiously moved towards her.

'What are you *doing*?' wailed Nina. The man with the broken arm was still screaming, but the other guy was already getting his breath back, pulling himself up.

'Go! I can take him,' Sophia replied, not taking her eyes off the miner as they closed on each other.

'But I can't take this guy!' Nina looked round in desperation. There was nothing she could use as a weapon, and the recovering miner was between her and the stairs. No way down . . .

Which meant her only escape route was up.

She scrambled up the ladder, the dusty rungs clanking beneath her feet. It led to a small inspection platform at the very top of the conveyor belt, overlooking the crusher – and there was a second ladder on the other side, going back down.

The ladder shook. The man was climbing after her. Fear rising, she quickened her ascent.

Chase got up, searching for the two women. 'Oh, *fuck*,' he muttered, seeing Sophia facing off against one man near the far end of the catwalk as Nina scaled a ladder running up the support of the conveyor belt, a second man climbing after her.

Not good.

He spotted his gun lying under the metal framework supporting the processor, and ran for it.

Sophia was only a few feet from her adversary now. The man was watching her movements cautiously, trying to anticipate her next action. She gripped the extinguisher more tightly, waiting for the right moment.

Nina was almost at the top of the ladder. Its shaking increased, her pursuer getting closer.

Chase reached for his gun and snatched it up. Then he ran back into the open, aiming up at the man climbing the ladder—

A new noise echoed through the chamber, deep, fierce, booming. Twin plumes of greasy exhaust smoke spouted like devil horns from the drilling machine in the chamber's centre as its engine roared to life. With a crash of gears, it lurched forward on its tracks, moving frighteningly quickly . . .

Straight at Chase.

'*Shit!*' Spotlights between the clusters of drill-heads burst into life, pinning him in their beams as the massive machine advanced. He fired a shot, blowing out one of the lights. But neither the driller nor its operator were affected. As if angered by his attack, the drills began to rotate, showering fragments of crushed rock in all directions. He turned and ran for the processor.

'Eddie!' Sophia shouted, her voice drowned out by the noise of the driller. The miner took advantage of her distraction to make his move—

Nina reached the top of the ladder, looking back down from the vertiginous platform to see Chase running away from the boring machine, Sophia grappling with the mine worker – and her own adversary still climbing after her.

She gripped the single railing and crossed the platform. The conveyor belt rumbled past underneath her, the gaping maw of the crusher below its end. Her hand reached the hooped metal guardrail at the top of the second ladder . . .

And she saw another man below. He had emerged from one of the cabins, retrieving the MP-5 dropped by the man Chase had shot, taking aim – not at her, but at the processor, which Chase was about to run round!

'Eddie, *get back!*' she screamed.

Even over the racket of the driller, Chase heard his name and instantly assumed that whatever Nina was yelling, it was a warning. He threw himself back against the processor as bullets ripped past him. Another shooter on the catwalk. Pinning him down.

The driller rumbled round the processor behind him, turning on its treads like a tank with a shriek of grinding metal.

There wasn't enough room for Chase to double back between the drills and the processor. And if he tried to go round the other side of the driller, he'd be exposing his back to the waiting gunman . . .

Sophia struggled with the man on the catwalk, each trying to wrest the fire extinguisher from the other. She lashed out to kick him in the crotch, but he jerked sideways, catching the blow on his thigh. He gave her a sneering smile for trying such an obvious attack – and she clapped her hand down on the extinguisher's handle, blasting a jet of freezing carbon dioxide into his face.

The man gasped, only making matters worse as the choking vapour entered his throat. He let go of the extinguisher, and Sophia bashed its thick rounded end against his forehead with a dull clonk.

She jumped over him as he fell and ran round the corner of the catwalk—

And froze.

Fang stood in front of her, his MP-5 raised. 'Lady Sophia!' he said. 'Please, drop the extinguisher and come with me.'

With no choice, she tossed it over the railing on to the rising conveyor belt, where it was rapidly whisked away.

Nina saw Sophia surrender and swore before turning to descend the ladder. If she could get down to the next level, she might be able to distract the gunman so Chase could get out from where he was trapped—

A hand clamped round her right arm and yanked her back up as if she were a doll. The miner dragged her on to the platform and savagely twisted her arm behind her back, pinning her down against the metal grillework floor as he pressed one knee into the base of her spine.

She flailed her free arm at him, but to no effect. The dirty surface of the conveyor belt rolled past beneath her. He pushed her arm up higher, pain ripping through her straining tendons. She cried out—

The machine rolled ever closer to Chase, its lowermost drill-heads kicking up a blinding spray of mud and stones as they scraped along the chamber's floor. He looked round the side of the processor, only to flinch back as a bullet smacked into the machine. Heart racing, he loosed another shot at the driller in the desperate hope that he might get lucky and hit some vital component, but it just sparked uselessly against spinning metal.

He had only seconds to choose between being shot, or crushed, or both—

Flaring spots of pain danced in Nina's vision as the man's remorseless hold threatened to break her arm, but she saw something through them, rushing past below the grille.

She grabbed at it, not knowing or caring what it was, only that it was her last chance, and swung up her arm—

With a flat thud of metal against bone, the fire extinguisher smacked her tormentor squarely on the temple. Blood spurted from a deep gash as he lurched sideways, only to bounce off the handrail and topple off the open side of the platform . . .

Into the crusher.

It didn't even pause as the screaming man fell into its maw, the human body far less resistant than rock. There was a brief wet crunch, then it continued working as if nothing had happened, only now with its rollers and cogs streaked red. The grey rubble being spewed on to the pile turned pink.

Nina didn't have time to think about the horrific sight as she sat up, her left shoulder burning. She looked down at the processor. Chase was still trapped, the gunman pinning him down, and the drilling machine continuing its advance—

'Dr Wilde!'

The voice was huge, distorted, booming from loudspeakers. She didn't recognise it – but then she saw Fang on the walkway below speaking into a telephone handset. His gun was trained on Sophia, standing a few paces away.

'Dr Wilde!' he repeated. 'I know you have the rest of the map! Give it to me, or I'll kill Lady Sophia!'

'Not a chance!' Nina shouted back. Sophia looked affronted. 'Kill your boss's wife? I don't think that'd look too good at your next pay review!'

Even from a distance, she could tell from Fang's expression that she'd called his bluff. But then his face changed. Another malevolent smile. 'Then give me the map . . . or *Chase* dies!'

No bluffing this time. Filled with fear, Nina looked at the drilling machine. It had slowed its advance on Chase . . . but was still moving.

'Give me the map!' Fang shouted. 'Or he will die! *Give me the map!*'

'Nina, don't do it!' Chase yelled. Trapped against the processor, the driller only feet away, he raised his gun and readied himself for a final kill-or-be-killed exchange of fire. 'Don't give it to him!'

Nina tore off her backpack and held it out over the crusher. 'Let Eddie go, or I drop it! And *nobody* gets the map!'

Fang said nothing for a moment, engaged in some internal debate. 'Give me the map, and you will all live!' he decided. 'Otherwise, you all *die*! Your choice, Dr Wilde!'

Clinging to the railing with one hand, Nina extended her other arm as far over the crusher as it would reach. 'I swear, I'll drop it! Let him go!'

'If you drop the map, the Tomb of Hercules will be lost for ever! *Nobody* will ever find it! Is that what you want?'

'Nina!' Chase shouted. 'Drop it! Whatever Yuen wants it for, you can't let him get it!' He was backed as far as he could go along the metal face of the processor, the drill-heads still advancing, spattering him with dirt.

Nina shook the backpack. 'Let him go!'

'If you give me the map, you have my word that you will not be harmed!' Fang countered. 'Think about it! Is the Tomb of Hercules worth your lover's *life*?'

Chase prepared to spring out and fire. '*Drop it!*' Three, two, one—

'Okay!' Nina screamed at Fang, pulling the pack back over the platform. 'Okay, okay! I'll give you the map! Just let him go!'

'Stop the drill!' Fang ordered. The boring machine stopped moving, its lethal prow less than a foot from Chase. The clanking and screeching of the drills wound down. 'Chase, you can come out now. You will not be harmed . . . if you surrender.'

Chase balled his fists in anger, but cautiously looked round the corner as ordered. The gunman still had the MP-5 trained on him, but didn't fire. Raising his hands, he dropped his Wildey before walking into the open.

Fang's voice rolled around the chamber. 'You made a good decision, Dr Wilde.'

Nina slumped, trembling with sudden exhaustion as adrenalin and emotion crashed on to her. Even though she, Chase and Sophia were still alive, she knew that her decision would turn out to be anything but good.

11

Nina, Chase and Sophia were taken to the administration building by Fang and four of his men. Inside, they were brought to Yuen – who, as Sophia had predicted, had been meditating in a private room adjoining one of the executive offices.

Yuen rolled the uncut diamond between his fingers. 'Tsk, tsk, Dr Wilde. Didn't they tell you at the airfield about the seriousness of diamond theft?'

'Screw diamonds,' said Chase. 'What about running an illegal uranium mine, *Dick*? Who're you selling it to – Iran? North Korea?'

Yuen sighed and nodded to Fang, who smashed Chase on the back of the head with the butt of the Wildey. Chase gasped in pain and dropped to his knees.

'Eddie!' cried Nina. She tried to help him up, but one of the uniformed guards pulled her away.

'That was long overdue,' said Yuen with a satisfied smirk. He glanced at the Wildey. 'Ridiculously large gun, huh? Compensating for something, perhaps? No wonder Sophia left you.'

Chase staggered to his feet. 'Do that again and I'll rip your fucking head off,' he snarled at Fang, who just looked smugly unconcerned.

Yuen went to a desk, on which lay the trio's personal possessions, plus Nina's backpack and the briefcase Fang had been carrying. 'I gotta say,' he went on, almost laughing as he took the binder from the pack and flipped through the pages, 'I never thought you'd actually bring the rest of the map right to me! There I was, about to tell Fang to track you down, and boom! Here you are!' He put the binder in the briefcase with the bound section of the *Hermocrates* text. 'Although I guess my security arrangements need overhauling if you were able to get into the mine so easily. I assume my lovely wife had a hand in that.'

He walked over to Sophia and cupped her chin in his hand. 'And you, Sophia! My darling wife, the flower in my garden, the light of my life! What *am* I going to do with you?' She narrowed her eyes in a disdainful sneer. He lowered his hand and addressed one of the guards. 'Keep her somewhere out of sight until the speeches are over, then take her to my helicopter.'

The guard nodded and led Sophia from the room.

'Where are you taking her?' Chase demanded.

'Marriage counselling,' said Yuen. 'Now, President Molowe and his minister of trade have just arrived to give some very boring speeches. You should be grateful to me – I'm going to spare you from having to sit through them.' He turned to Fang. 'Take them to the processing plant and throw them into the crushers—'

Chase whirled, striking at the nearest guard. He wrested the gun from his hand—

Fang clubbed him again, harder. Chase dropped face-first on to the carpet, blood oozing down his neck. He groaned, moving weakly.

'You son of a bitch!' Nina shouted at Fang. 'You gave your word you wouldn't kill us!'

Yuen looked surprised. 'You did?'

Fang nodded, almost apologetically. 'I did.'

'Oh.'

'But,' Fang continued, a cruel smile spreading across his face as he toyed with his cane, 'I never specified for how long.'

'Well, that's all right then.' At Yuen's nod, Fang and the guards picked up Chase, then took him and Nina from the room. 'Oh, by the way,' Yuen called after them, the men pausing, 'give me his gun.' Fang tossed it to him. 'Cool souvenir.'

Nina kicked at her captors, but they were too strong for her, whisking her and the semi-conscious Chase out of the building.

To their deaths.

The diamond mine's processing plant was similar in function to the one in the secret uranium mine – only on a vastly larger scale.

The enormous trucks dumped their loads on to broad conveyors, which directed the hundreds of tons of rubble brought by each vehicle into a series of gargantuan crushers, each of which could swallow one of the house-sized trucks with room to spare. Stone was smashed into smaller and smaller fragments at each stage, washed and shaken through ever finer filters, until nothing was left but dust . . .

And diamonds. The hardest naturally occurring substance on earth was the only thing able to withstand the relentless pounding of the machines. Under constant security, the precious stones were taken into a closed section of the plant for grading.

There was security at the crushers too – raw diamonds could

simply be jolted loose from the rubble and drop on to the floor – but the guards normally on duty had been relieved on the direct orders of the mine's owner. Any questions were forestalled by the promise of a bonus in the next pay packet. Whatever went on inside the huge building for the next few minutes, it was no longer their business.

Fang led the way into an elevator cage, which took the group to a gantry overlooking the crushers. By the time it reached the top, Chase was recovering from the blow to his head, though still groggy. 'Are you okay?' Nina asked.

'I've been better.' He looked down as a truck tipped out the contents of its dumper, rocks and dirt rising up the conveyor before cascading into the jaws of the crusher. Car-sized boulders exploded under the relentless pressure of the machinery within. 'Going to feel a lot worse in a minute, though.'

Fang slipped his black cane under one arm as he took out a silenced pistol. 'You have two choices,' he said as the guards carrying Chase dumped him on the gantry floor. 'Either you can be shot in the head and then thrown into the crusher. Or,' he added as Nina helped Chase stand, 'you can do something stupid, be shot in the *stomach*, and then thrown into the crusher. While you're still alive.'

'How about option C?' Chase asked. 'Holiday for two in the Caribbean, and *not* being thrown into the crusher?'

Fang smiled. 'I'm afraid not. On your knees.'

The three other guards all had their guns at the ready, moving back just out of striking range. Chase woozily weighed up the odds. The only person he had a chance of reaching before being gunned down was Fang, and it might be worth it just to take the ponytailed bastard into the crusher with him . . .

But that would leave Nina alone. And he didn't want the last thing she saw to be his bullet-riddled corpse, the last emotions she felt to be grief and anguish.

He turned to her. 'Nina. I . . .' The words he had in his mind didn't want to emerge. 'It's been an experience,' was all that came out.

Nina shot him a disbelieving look. 'Is that all you've got to say? They're going to *kill* us, and the best you can manage is "It's been an experience"?'

'Well, what do you *want* me to say?' He knew, but for some reason couldn't speak the words.

Her eyes filled with sadness, even through the fear. 'Eddie . . .'

Fang moved to stand behind them. He raised his gun, aiming at the back of Chase's head. His finger tightened on the trigger—

The head of one of the guards *exploded*, spraying the man next to him with chunks of jagged bone and brain matter. A moment later, the unmistakable *crack!* of a high-powered rifle reached them, the bullet having reached its target at supersonic speed.

Fang spun to hunt for the origin of the shot, hunching down behind one of the other men—

The back of a second guard's head blew out in a pink mist as a bullet hit him precisely between the eyes.

Chase looked down the length of the huge building. No sign of the shooter.

A third shot. The man Fang was using as cover flew backwards, blood gouting from the wound which had blossomed over his heart. He tumbled over the railing to land in the crusher and burst apart like the pulverised rocks.

Realising he was exposed, Fang dropped and grabbed Nina round the neck. He pulled her up, turning so she was between him and the unseen sniper. 'Don't try anything, Chase,' he warned, stepping crabwise across the gantry, cane squeezed under his gun arm. 'Tell your friend to put down his gun, or I'll kill her.'

'I don't even know who he is!' Chase protested. He now had a good idea where the shots had come from, but still hadn't seen the shooter.

Fang jammed the gun into Nina's back. 'Tell him, now, or—'

Nina grabbed the head of his cane, pulled—

And stabbed the sword back into Fang's side.

Fang howled, reflexively writhing away from the pain as he pulled the trigger.

The bullet shot between Nina's arm and her torso, hot gas searing her skin. But despite the pain she was already moving, releasing the sword and twisting at the waist to smash her elbow into Fang's jaw. Dazed, spitting blood, he staggered back—

Chase punched him in the face. The blow was so hard that Fang's feet actually left the floor before he crashed against the guard rail. He teetered for a moment, almost falling over the edge, then collapsed on top of one of the dead guards.

'You okay?' Chase asked Nina, picking up a fallen pistol.

'Yeah, but . . .' She looked at the bodies. 'What the hell just *happened*?'

'Dunno, but I'm pretty fucking happy that it did!' He looked down the plant again, finally spotting the sniper silhouetted in a distant skylight. Tough angle, Chase realised – whoever he was, he was an outstanding shot.

The sniper moved. For a moment Chase got a look at him – a

tall, muscular black man, glints of reflected sunlight from a row of piercings on his bald head – then he was gone.

Nina rubbed her aching elbow. 'Ow. That move never hurt as much when we practised it . . .'

'I'm just glad you remembered how to do it. Come on.'

She quickly followed Chase to the elevator.

The sound of rifle fire had carried all the way to the area behind the stage, where Yuen was talking to President Molowe and Minister of Trade and Industry Kamletese. Soldiers immediately surrounded Molowe and pushed him down, while others spread out, weapons raised, searching for signs of danger. Yuen's own guards moved to shield their boss.

'What was that?' asked Kamletese, worried.

Yuen looked in the direction of the processing plant. 'Some people were caught earlier trying to breach security,' he said, thinking fast. 'I'd been told they were under arrest. Apparently, I was misinformed. Mr President, you should stay out of sight until they've been dealt with. I'll find out what's going on.'

Molowe nodded, then with a human cordon round him went back to the marquee as Yuen and two of his men raced for the administration building. The President paused at the entrance to the tent. 'Go with him, find out what's happening,' he ordered Kamletese.

The portly politician blinked. 'Me?'

'Yes, you! Go on!' Molowe disappeared inside the marquee, leaving the flustered Kamletese to stand there under the glares of the soldiers guarding the entrance before he hurried off in Yuen's wake.

★

'What do we do now?' Nina asked as she and Chase ran towards the open end of the processing plant.

'We've got to find Sophia. Then we get the fuck out of here!'

'Can't we, you know, do it the other way round?'

Chase frowned at her in disbelief. 'Are you fucking serious?'

'Yes! Yuen won't hurt her, I could tell. You can get her later!'

'I'm not leaving her with that twat,' Chase insisted. They emerged into daylight, squinting at the brightness. 'Okay, we need some wheels.'

'I can't see anything,' said Nina. There were no cars or 4x4s anywhere in sight.

'What, are you blind?' Chase pointed at the huge yellow Liebherr dump truck approaching the building. 'What do you call that?'

She blanched. 'A very bad and stupid idea?'

'My speciality. Come on.' Ignoring Nina's protests, he ran towards the truck, waving his arms for it to stop.

The driver, twenty feet off the ground in the cab, gestured furiously for him to get out of the way, but Chase stood his ground. Brakes squealing, the truck slowed but didn't stop, still coming right at him.

Chase began to think that Nina had been right. 'Oh. Oh, shit.' He hopped back a few steps, then started to run as the truck's angular shadow swept over him. 'Oh shit!'

The tumult of a massive diesel engine filled his ears, almost drowning out the piercing screech of the brakes. Nowhere else to run, Chase threw himself flat on the ground and covered his ears as the giant vehicle swept overhead . . .

And stopped. Chase let out a relieved breath. He was under the front of the truck – but, he realised almost with amusement, he had only needed to crouch to fit safely beneath it. He moved back into the open and headed for the steps leading to the cab.

Nina joined him. 'Idiot!' she snapped, hitting his arm.

'Ow! What was that for?' The steps – almost steep enough to qualify as a ladder – crossed the front of the radiator grille, which itself was the size of a panel truck. Chase hurried up them, Nina following.

The driver came down, jabbing an angry finger. 'What the hell are you doing? And why aren't you wearing a hard—'

'Sorry, mate,' said Chase, punching him in the groin. He let out a pathetic little groan and bent double, and Chase tossed him bodily over the railing.

'Why did you do that?' Nina said. 'You have a gun, you could have just told him to get out!'

'We're kind of in a rush,' Chase replied as he ran up the remaining steps into the cab. 'Anyway, he'll be okay. As long as I don't run him over.'

'Do you even have a clue how to drive one of these things?'

Chase took in the controls. Steering wheel, accelerator, brake pedal, a number of levers that he assumed controlled the dumper, and several monitor screens showing the view from video cameras all round the vehicle. Judging from the surprisingly car-like lever beside the driver's seat, the transmission was entirely automatic. 'I think I can manage.'

'How the hell did they escape?' Yuen demanded.

'They had help,' Fang said painfully on the other end of the phone line. 'Somebody shot my men. A sniper.'

'What? *Who?*'

'I don't know, I didn't see him. He got away.'

'Find them! And *kill* them! If any of these bastards get away and tell the UN about the uranium mine, we're all fucked!'

He slammed down the phone, looking up to see Kamletese flanked by two security guards in the office doorway, face full of bewilderment. 'Uranium mine?' asked the minister. '*What* uranium mine?'

Yuen pressed a palm to his forehead. 'Aw, hell,' he sighed. 'Minister, I don't suppose you'd be open to a very large bribe, by any chance?'

Kamletese boggled. 'What? No, of course not! What's this about a uranium—'

'I thought not.' Yuen picked up Chase's Wildey from the desk and shot him. 'You,' he said to one of the guards, who looked almost as surprised as the late government official, 'go give the President the tragic, *tragic* news. A pair of diamond thieves called Eddie Chase and Nina Wilde have just murdered the minister of trade!' When the guard didn't move immediately, he frowned and waved the smoking gun in his direction. 'Well, go on!'

'Yes, sir!' gulped the guard, stepping over the dead body and hurrying from the room.

Yuen wiped his fingerprints from the gun, then dropped it and took the briefcase containing the *Hermocrates* pages. 'Take me to my wife,' he ordered the other guard.

Figuring out the surprisingly simple controls for the mammoth T282B truck was one thing. Actually controlling it was something else entirely, Chase rapidly discovered. With its load bed filled with over four hundred tons of earth and rock it took a long time to build up speed – and just as long to lose it. One of the largest warning gauges on the dashboard showed the brake temperatures of each of the twelve-foot-diameter wheels, and every time he touched the brake pedal to slow for a turn, the needles shot up into the red.

But now the truck was on course for the administration building, and Sophia.

'We've got company,' Nina warned nervously, gesturing at one of the monitors. A Land Cruiser was coming up fast on the truck's left. One of its doors was partly open, a man's head protruding through the window. 'He's going to try to jump aboard!'

'Bloody fare-dodgers,' said Chase. He spun the steering wheel, sending the truck lurching to the left. The Land Cruiser hurriedly dropped away.

Nina grabbed the back of Chase's seat for support. Even though he'd straightened out, the contents of the giant dumper were still shifting, the truck rolling like a ship in rough waters. 'Jesus! I thought we were going to tip over!'

'We need to dump the load.' He indicated the levers on the control panel. 'See if you can work the tipper – Christ, he's trying again!' The Land Cruiser pulled alongside, a security guard reaching out for a handrail.

Chase turned again. This time, the Toyota's driver wasn't fast enough, and the truck's giant front wheel clipped the back of the 4x4. The entire rear quarter sheared away, the guard barely managing to throw himself back inside the vehicle as the door was ripped from its hinges and crushed as flat as tin foil. One wheel gone, the Land Cruiser flipped on to its side.

Chase grinned. 'Okay, next time I'm driving in London, I want one of these!'

Nina pointed ahead. 'Watch out!' Two more Land Cruisers charged down the dirt road at them, security men leaning out of the windows.

Guns in their hands—

'Duck!' Chase shouted, but Nina had already seen the danger and hunched down behind the seat. Shooting from a moving vehicle was a lot harder than Hollywood made it seem, but the T282B was not exactly a small target. Bullets clonked around the cab, one side of the windscreen crazing as a shot punched a hole through it and hit the back wall.

'Okay, you want it that way . . .' Chase growled. He pushed harder on the accelerator, the engine shrilling beneath him, and aimed the truck at the oncoming 4x4s. One of them immediately decided that survival outweighed orders and swung away, but the other kept coming. More bullets hit. A section of the windscreen shattered, chunks of laminated glass showering over the dash. Chase flinched, but held his course.

The Land Cruiser's driver finally realised that he was playing chicken with an opponent three hundred times his weight and tried to turn away, but too late. The Toyota disappeared from view below the base of the windscreen, but an explosive crunch of metal – and a very small bump – told Chase that he'd scored a hit. A moment later, the remains of the Land Cruiser appeared on one of the rear-view monitors, only the severed wheel bouncing away from the wreckage giving away that the flattened roadkill had once been a vehicle.

Chase winced. 'Ouch.'

The admin building was coming up ahead, the stage and marquee beyond it. He saw what he assumed was Yuen's helicopter on the pad in front of the building, rotors whirling, figures running for it—

'Shit!' One of the figures was very familiar. 'They're taking Sophia!'

'Wait, what are you doing?' Nina asked as he changed direction, heading straight for the helicopter.

'Stopping them taking off!'

'How? By *crashing into them*? You'll kill her!'

Chase knew she was right, but couldn't think of anything else to do. 'I'm not letting him take her!'

'You can't stop him!' The helicopter was already rising, dust swirling beneath its skids. 'We'll never get there in time!'

'We'd be going faster if you'd dumped the load when I told you!'

'Oh, don't you start blaming *me* for this!' Nina snarled.

Yuen's helicopter cleared the pad and wheeled round, nose dipping as it turned for the airfield. 'Shit!' said Chase, banging a fist on the wheel. He watched helplessly as the chopper gained height and flew over the marquee.

'Eddie!' Nina pointed. President Molowe's helicopter was parked in their path near the tent, its rotors building up speed, and in front of it was a line of soldiers.

Taking aim . . .

Chase didn't need to issue a warning for Nina to throw herself flat on the cab floor. He dropped too, leaning almost horizontally to shield himself behind the dashboard as rifle bullets ripped into the cab. The rest of the windscreen exploded, fragments cascading over the dash like a crystal wave. Shots punched through the cab's steel walls, one of the video monitors blowing apart. The accelerator pedal kicked beneath his foot, the mechanism hit somewhere, but the engine kept roaring at full power.

Unable to see, all he could do was hold the wheel steady and keep going—

The firing stopped, the soldiers breaking ranks and running as the truck surged towards them. The helicopter's main rotor hadn't quite reached takeoff speed – the aircraft's occupants jumped out of the cabin and fled in panic, a soldier practically dragging Molowe out of the juggernaut's path.

The rotor blades sliced into the front of the truck, ripping the stairs to pieces before striking the solid steel framework of the truck's body and shattering like glass.

An instant later, the Liebherr slammed into the helicopter.

The chopper flipped on to its side, the fuselage disintegrating and the long tail boom snapping off to cartwheel away. Fire bloomed inside the engine compartment. The crushed wreckage was bowled along by the bumper for a moment—

Then it exploded, a dull thump of igniting fuel followed almost instantly by a louder, sharper detonation as the engine blew apart. Debris showered the front of the truck.

'Bloody hell!' Chase gasped as a burning shard of metal bounced off the cab roof and hit his arm. He kept the accelerator pressed down. There was a jolt as one of the wheels ran over the remains of the chopper, then the crushed wreckage was strewn out in their wake. He sat up – and saw something large directly ahead. 'Oh, shit!'

Nina had just raised her head when the truck swayed violently, banging her against the cab door as Chase tried to avoid the marquee.

He wasn't successful. The giant vehicle swept through the VIP end of the tent, tables and champagne bottles shattering beneath the mighty wheels. Nina caught a brief glimpse of the marquee's interior, waiters fleeing for the exits at the far end, before the tent roof was ripped free and the whole thing collapsed.

Checking the remaining video monitors, Chase saw the crumpled marquee falling behind, and beyond it the burning wreckage of the helicopter. 'Great,' he moaned as he aimed the truck back towards the road, 'that's another African leader who wants me dead.' He squinted into the dry wind rushing through the broken windscreen. Yuen's helicopter was still in sight ahead, now descending at the end of its short flight.

Nina levered herself upright. 'He might still get the chance.'

'What do you mean?'

'He's got tanks at that checkpoint, remember?'

Chase made a dismissive noise. 'There's no way they'll be able to ready them this fast. Besides, they're just for show.' He brought the truck on to the road to the airfield, hitting the celebratory banner spanning it like a runner breaking the tape at the finishing line. The banner was ripped free of its support poles and snagged on the truck's cab-level walkway, ropes snaking from it as it flapped furiously in the wind.

He turned towards the gate – to see *both* of the Leopards moving to block the road beyond the checkpoint, turrets swivelling to bring their main guns to bear.

12

'Buggeration and fuckery!' Chase yelled.

'Just for show, huh?' Nina said sarcastically as she ducked back behind the seat.

He didn't reply, instead pulling frantically at the wheel to turn the truck off the road, trying to put the high fence and the raised dirt berm between himself and the tanks to block their line of fire. A single tank shell hitting the front of the truck would destroy the engine – but that would hardly matter, as both he and Nina would already be dead. He looked out of the side of the cab. One tank had disappeared behind the fence, but the other was still tracking him with its gun—

The shot didn't come. The tank crews might have been fast enough off the mark to block the road, but hadn't yet managed to load their guns.

It wouldn't take long, though.

Yuen's helicopter was now out of sight behind the corrugated fence. Either it had landed or was just about to, and considering the circumstances the pilot of Yuen's private jet was probably gearing up for a very fast takeoff. There didn't seem to be any way Chase could rescue Sophia.

But he still had to *try* . . .

'How are we going to get out?' Nina asked.

He nodded at the fence on the crest of the sloping wall of earth ahead. 'You ever seen *The Great Escape?*'

'Yes – *no*,' she gulped, realising what he had in mind. 'No, you're not seriously going to—'

Chase grimly set his jaw. 'Hope we do better than Steve McQueen. You know you think that pendant of yours is lucky?'

'Yes?'

'Now'd be a good time to use it. Hang on!'

He floored the accelerator.

The truck charged forward like a bull, moving at over thirty miles per hour and still gaining speed as it hit the bottom of the berm and shot upwards.

Clutching her pendant, Nina screamed—

The fence blew into fragments as the truck ploughed through it, over six hundred tons of metal and rubber and stone airborne as it jumped over the top of the obstacle . . .

Then it hit the ground, the force of the impact so huge that the foot-thick tyres *rippled*. A massive spray of dust erupted from beneath the wheels, the shockwave running like a mini-earthquake through the ground strong enough to knock soldiers and security guards off their feet and flip 4x4s parked at the gate on to their sides. Car-sized boulders were tossed out of the truck and smashed into the ground like meteorites.

Both Nina *and* Chase screamed as the front end of the truck bounced back up into the air. It crashed down again, throwing a choking wave of dust and broken stones over the front of the tipper and into the cab. Partially blinded, Chase battled to keep hold of the wheel, turning it in the general direction of the runway.

'Nina! Are you okay?'

'Oh, super fine,' came an angry voice from the floor behind his seat, 'except for my *shattered pelvis*!'

'You're okay.' The dust blew away as the truck picked up speed once more, the banner flapping in the wind. He could see the airfield ahead. There was TD's plane parked amongst the others—

And a sleek private jet, already moving into takeoff position.

Chase had no doubts whose plane it was. 'He's taking off!' Heat plumes flared and rippled from the jet's engines, dust kicking up behind it.

'You can't catch up!' Nina yelled. 'We're too far away, we'll never make it in time!'

'I've got to—'

She grabbed his shoulders and shook him, her mouth almost against his ear. 'Eddie! *You can't reach her*. You can't.'

Chase looked round into her eyes, not wanting to accept her words even as he knew they were true. 'You can't,' she repeated. Torn, he looked back at the runway. The plane raced away from him.

Too fast to catch.

He finally admitted defeat. '*Fuck!*'

Nina released him. 'We've got to get to TD's plane,' she said, 'and get the hell out of here before they—'

With a deafening boom, an explosion ripped a crater out of the ground just ahead. Sand showered into the cab.

The tank gunners had loaded their weapons.

Chase turned sharply away from the airfield, trying to keep the back of the truck to the tanks—

Something shot past, more *felt* than seen as a displaced wave of hot air blew into the cab. A second later, another shell hit the ground ahead of them, this time further away. The gunner in the first tank to fire had been aiming low, trying to take out one of the truck's wheels.

The second had been aiming higher, going for its driver.

'Shit!' Nina stared at the crater in disbelief. 'They're shooting at us, there are fucking *tanks* shooting at us!'

'Yeah, I noticed!' Chase looked at the video screens. In the view directly behind, he saw the two tanks turning to pursue them. Their turrets remained almost stationary, the gunners tracking the fleeing truck. That both tanks had missed suggested they lacked modern computerised targeting systems, but they wouldn't be aiming manually – at the very least, they would have laser rangefinders, meaning all they had to do was keep their sights on the truck and the automatics would do the rest.

The airfield – and TD's plane – were no longer options for escape. He'd been lucky with the first shot, turning just enough in the brief period of the shell's flight for it to miss. If he headed back to the runway, he'd be an easy target, broadside-on to the tanks' guns. Not even the massive tyres could withstand a 105mm shell.

'I need you to watch them,' he told Nina, jabbing at the screen, 'tell me what they're doing.'

'Well, right now they're *chasing* us!'

'Thanks for that, Dr Obvious. I mean, tell me when they fire!' Chase checked the landscape ahead. They were heading roughly north, the sweeping green marshlands of the Okavango Delta taking over from dusty desert on the horizon. The flat terrain they were currently traversing would start sloping down to the huge river system in a mile or so—

'They've fired!' Nina shrieked. On the screen, the gun of one of the tanks flared with a huge burst of orange flame.

Chase yanked at the wheel, spinning it to the right as hard as he could. The truck swayed, threatening to tip on to its side.

A shell whined past to their left, exploding about a hundred yards ahead. Struggling to stay upright as she watched the screen, Nina saw the second tank fire. 'Incoming!'

The truck swung back to the left as Chase spun the wheel again. But not fast enough—

The entire truck jolted as if slammed by a blow from a giant's hammer, the explosion ringing through every inch of metal. The side windows shattered. 'Oh my God!' Nina screamed. 'They got us!'

'We're okay, we're okay!' Chase checked one of the other monitors, the camera mounted above the tipper and looking down at its contents. A huge plume of dust trailed out behind them – the shell had impacted inside the load bed and blown one of the boulders to pieces. 'It hit the rocks in the back!'

He started a mental count. How good were the gunners? How long would they take to reload?

'I think they're catching up!' Nina warned. Chase glanced at the rear-view monitor. The tanks were in hot pursuit, larger on the screen than before. A Leopard could manage around forty miles per hour over flat terrain – faster than the truck.

Faster than the *laden* truck . . .

'Nina! These controls for the tipper—'

'For God's sake!' she interrupted in accusatory disbelief. 'You're *still* going on about *that?*'

'No, no! It's a good job you *didn't* empty it before! Tip it out, dump the load! We need to go faster, and it'll work like a smokescreen!'

Ten seconds had passed, and neither tank had fired again. An automated loader would have done the job by now. That meant the reloading was being carried out manually, which even for a highly skilled crew in a stationary tank was a cumbersome process, and the jolting of the vehicle over the stony ground would add another couple of seconds . . .

Nina braced herself against the control panel with one hand, the other hovering over the levers. She found the most likely candidate and pulled it down.

A warning buzzer rasped in time to the flashes of a red light on the panel – operating the tipping mechanism while the truck was in motion was not recommended.

But it wasn't prohibited either. A skirl of hydraulics came from behind the cab. Chase glanced at the screens. The camera looking down into the dumper was fixed relative to its subject, so the ground appeared to be tilting underneath it.

The rocks shifted—

'*Incoming!*'

Chase turned again, going right. Nina was thrown against him—

Another slamming impact, much harder than before, the crack of shattering rock beneath the boom of the explosion now joined by a screech of wounded metal. The dumper camera flickered, then came back to life, revealing a jagged hole at the bottom of the still rising tipper.

The gunners were refining their aim, trying to take out the rear wheels. The tipper had acted as a shield as the hydraulics pushed it into the air, its back end behind the fulcrum and partially covering the tyres. The shells could penetrate armour much thicker than the dumper bed; the rocks it was carrying had absorbed the full force of the explosion.

But the rocks wouldn't be there much longer, already shifting and sliding as the tipper rose . . .

Fourteen seconds, Chase counted. It took the Leopard crews fourteen seconds to reload after each shot. That was how much time he had to come up with a plan.

Assuming he survived the next shot from the *second* tank, which would come any moment.

He was already swinging the truck fiercely back to the left as Nina yelled a warning. With the dumper partly elevated, the Liebherr's centre of gravity was shifting, top-heavy. He could feel the massive vehicle shuddering, on the edge of control as it threatened to roll over—

Boom!

Part of the cab roof was ripped away as something punched through it. Not the shell – shrapnel, a chunk of steel torn from the front end of the dumper where the shell had blasted a hole straight through the metal.

He straightened the wheel, turning the truck's back to the tanks once more.

Fourteen seconds to reload . . .

The steering wheel shook in his hands as the earth in the dumper finally succumbed to gravity and slid free.

Four hundred tons of dirt and rubble and rock cascaded out of the back of the truck. A huge amount of dust was kicked up, an impenetrable cloud roiling out in all directions. Boulders bounced through it, tracing their own lines of dust through the air like comet tails. They smashed on to the desert ground, kicking up still more dirt before being swallowed by the boiling cloud.

Both tanks lost sight of the truck, lost sight of *everything* beyond the opaque brown mass. One turned to swerve round the obstruction; the other ploughed fearlessly into it. Big as the cloud was, it would still only take a matter of seconds for the speeding Leopard to pass through it, and the rubble the truck had strewn in a pathetic attempt to block it would do nothing more than make for a bumpy ride . . .

The driver saw something in his periscope, a huge dark shape suddenly looming through the swirling dust directly ahead of him, *over* him, but it was too late to stop—

The main gun was abruptly punched backwards into the turret as its muzzle slammed into a boulder as big as the tank itself. The gun's loader barely escaped decapitation as the barrel speared over him, passing right between the legs of the seated tank commander and smashing into the back of the turret with a deafening clash of metal against metal. A moment later the Leopard's prow hit the massive rock. The tank came to an extremely sudden stop.

'Did we get them?' Nina asked anxiously, watching the monitors. All she could see was dust, a trail still swirling from the now-vertical dumper.

Chase risked a look back from the side window. One of the Leopards emerged from behind the cloud, skirting it. 'One's still going,' he reported, leaning back to check the screens. Nothing emerged from the haze behind them. 'Think we got the other one, though!'

'Well, great! Too bad we don't have another truck full of rocks!'

Chase was about to shoot back a sarcastic comment when a thought struck him.

They didn't have another truck full of rocks. But they still had *the truck itself* . . .

He confirmed the position of the remaining tank, then steered directly away from it. 'Keep watching that screen,' he said. 'Shout the moment it fires.'

'We can't keep dodging it for ever!' said Nina.

The desert earth below became darker, the muddy remnants of a small river feeding into the delta discolouring the ground. 'We won't have to,' Chase told her, turning the wheel back and forth so that the truck began a snaking motion. 'One way or another.'

Nina grimaced. 'I don't like the way you put that – *aah!*'

Chase took that as a sign the tank had fired again and immediately jammed the truck into as hard a turn as possible. The horizon tilted ahead, its angle steepening as the truck began to overbalance. The steering wheel quivered, the wobble of the tyres feeding back to him as both wheels on the inside of the turn left the ground—

Boom!

An explosion, frighteningly close, but on the *far* side of the truck from the tank. The shell had gone right between the front and rear wheels, *under* the truck as it almost tipped over.

Chase twitched the wheel to drop the T282B back on to all four wheels, but kept turning.

Fourteen seconds . . .

'What are you doing?' Nina asked, confusion joined by fear as she realised he was heading back towards the tank.

'It takes them fourteen seconds to reload,' Chase said. 'If we can reach them in thirteen seconds, then we can squash 'em before they fire again!'

'And if it takes us fifteen seconds, they'll blow us up!' Nina objected. The Leopard swung into view ahead, Chase aiming right at it. 'How long have we got left?'

'Four seconds!' Truck and tank raced directly at each other, neither slowing. 'Any last words?'

'Shitshit*shit*!'

The main gun rose, aiming at the cab.

Chase released the wheel and yanked Nina down across his lap, throwing his upper body on to hers to protect her—

Collision!

The Leopard weighed forty tons – but even unloaded the T282B was over five times its weight, and far larger.

The tank's gun bent like a cardboard tube as it stabbed through the truck's bodywork to hit the unyielding diesel block within. An instant later, the truck rode up over the Leopard's sloping front, stamping the tank down into the soft earth up to the base of its turret. The gun was ripped away, crushed under the Liebherr's enormous tyres and left poking out of the ground in a mangled U-shape.

Over the obstacle, the truck bounced back down on to the ground, turning again as the steering wheel whipped round.

Nina opened one eye, finding herself lying over Chase's lap, her head in the footwell. She felt his weight on top of her, holding her in place. She couldn't tell if he was moving, or even breathing. 'Eddie?'

A long silence, then: 'I thought somebody with your education'd come up with better last words.'

She flapped at him with her hands. 'Get offa me!'

Chase sat up, letting her push herself upright before retaking the wheel. He immediately realised that the steering had been damaged; it felt slack, unresponsive. With some effort, he managed to straighten the vehicle, seeing through the broken windscreen that they were now heading north again, towards the delta.

He lifted his foot off the accelerator . . .

Nina ran her hands though her hair. 'Jesus! I really thought we were going to die back there.' She was about to begin a tirade against Chase's insane actions when she took in his expression. It was one she'd seen before.

And it was never a good sign. 'What?'

He pointed at the floor. 'See my foot?'

'Yes?'

'See how it's not on the accelerator?'

'But we're still going – oh my God!' She looked at the dashboard. Several of the instruments had been damaged by bullets, but the speedometer was still intact – and she instantly translated the reading of sixty-six kilometers per hour into imperial units. 'We're doing over forty!'

'The throttle's jammed,' said Chase. The pedal was stuck firmly against the floor; he'd already tried to lift it with his foot, but to no avail. 'Hold on to the seat; this might get bumpy.'

'*Get?*' But she obeyed, crouching behind him.

Chase pushed the brake. The truck shook, a deep grinding noise coming from the wheels below. He watched the brake temperature gauges. One was no longer working, but the other three rose with worrying speed towards the red zone.

The speedo dropped, but not by much.

He pushed harder. The cab rattled, what little glass remained in the windows finally falling free. The speedometer needle juddered, dropping in jerky steps as the brake gauges flicked higher . . .

A noise like scrap metal in a tumble dryer made them both cringe. There was a sharp bang, then something clattered against the wheel below them and fell away.

Nina looked out of the window. Smoke billowed from the wheel hub. 'What the hell was that?'

'The brakes!' One of the temperature needles had flicked instantly back down to zero. 'They've burned out!'

Nina reached over and grabbed the gear shifter, trying to force it into the neutral position. It refused to move. 'Dammit!'

Chase eased off slightly on the brakes in the hope that their temperature would fall while the truck still slowed, but all that happened was that the speedometer rose again – the temperature gauges remained in the red. 'Bollocks!' He changed tack and stamped on the brake pedal as hard as he could. The truck swayed violently, the steering wheel writhing in his grasp.

Something crunched unpleasantly, then there was a dull crack from under the dashboard and the wheel immediately became still.

The brake needles rose higher, but the truck was shedding speed . . .

Another disc blew apart, shards of red-hot steel banging around inside the wheel hub. The speedometer needle moved back up.

Chase kept his foot pressed down in the vain hope that the two remaining brakes would stay intact. They didn't. Within seconds of each other they exploded under the stress.

'No handbrake?' Nina asked, not sounding the least bit hopeful.

'Nope.' Chase narrowed his eyes against the wind and surveyed the landscape ahead. If there was a steep enough slope, he might be able to aim the truck up it and cause it to slow so they could jump off . . .

There was a potential candidate some distance to the right. But he realised that he wasn't going to reach it when he turned the steering wheel . . . and nothing happened. The wheel was no longer connected to anything – the steering column had broken.

Chase stared at it in horror. 'Buggeration and fuckery!'

'Oh, that's never good to hear,' Nina said, wincing.

Chase spun the useless control back and forth to no effect, then angrily set it whirling like a roulette wheel. 'Okay, so no brakes and no steering. I'm open to any ideas.'

'Could we jump off?'

'We're going too fast. I might be able to land okay, I've had training, but you haven't.'

'Well, I'm going to have to chance it, aren't I?' Nina opened the cab door and went on to the walkway, looking over the flapping banner still caught there at the stairs below. 'Or maybe not!'

'What is it?'

'No stairs! They must have got wrecked when you drove into that helicopter!'

'Oh, right, it's all *my* fault!'

Nina ignored him, an idea coming to her. She looked back at the raised tipper, then returned to the cab and worked the hydraulic controls. The huge load bed began to descend. 'Give me a hand!' she called.

'Doing what?'

'Help me with this!' She pointed at the banner.

Chase hesitated, then decided that since he had no control over the truck there was little point staying in the driver's seat, and joined her.

'It's catching the wind, look,' Nina explained, putting a hand against the banner where it bulged between the railings. She quickly pulled it over the guardrail, bundling it up.

'Yeah? So? Are you going to just float off the side of the truck with it? I don't care what Dan Brown says, you *can't* use a tarpaulin as a parachute!'

'I *know*,' she replied, a flare of anger in her eyes. 'But I wasn't thinking of using it to fly – all it has to do is slow us down!'

Chase made a sarcastic snort. 'Hate to tell you, but this thing's not going to slow down a two-hundred-ton truck!'

'I didn't mean the truck!' The flat front end of the tipper banged down into place above them to form a roof over the walkway, warped steel claws twisted round the hole made by the tank shell. 'I just meant us! Although I'm tempted to leave you behind,' she added, scowling.

He suddenly realised what she intended. 'You mean, use it like a drogue 'chute to pull us off the back of the truck?'

'Yes, exactly! It won't stop us – but it might slow us enough to survive the landing.' Nina pulled the end of the banner on to the walkway and checked the lines from which it had been suspended.

Nylon with a core of steel wire, strong enough to withstand the winds that blew across the mine.

'Not from the back of the truck, we won't – it's over twenty feet high.' Chase looked ahead – then stiffened. 'Although I think we should give it a try, right now!'

'Why?' Nina saw what he had just seen. 'Oh!'

Ahead of them, a line bisected the landscape: before it the dirt and stone of the edge of the Kalahari, beyond, the verdant sweep of the Okavango. It only took a moment for her to see a definite parallax shift, the desert seeming to move faster than the delta . . . because there was a height difference between the two sides.

They were heading straight for the edge of a cliff.

'Get up there, now!' Chase shouted, lifting Nina on to the railing and cupping his hands to give her a leg up on to the top of the dumper. She scrambled over the metal edge, then turned and peered back down at him, holding out her hands. Chase picked up the banner and hurriedly fed it up to her. 'Open it out a bit, but for Christ's sake don't let it blow away!'

Nina looked ahead. The cliff edge was approaching fast, the truck speeding uncontrollably towards destruction. 'What about you?'

'I'll be up in a second! Put your legs over the edge, and hang on!'

She hooked the backs of her knees against the forward edge of the dumper and did the best she could to unfurl the banner. The wind immediately snatched at it, trying to pull it from her grip.

Chase rushed into the cab and slammed down the lever controlling the hydraulic lifter, then ran back out and scaled the railing to climb on to the dumper about eight feet from Nina.

'Give me one of the ends!' he called, putting his own legs over the edge as the dumper began to rise.

She tossed a section of banner to him. He quickly wrapped the end of the line a few times round one wrist before grasping it in that hand, then used the other to drag more of the material to him.

Nina saw what he was doing and copied him. The pressure on her legs increased as the dumper tilted backwards, gravity pulling her down. She looked back over her shoulder and wished she hadn't. The ground was now at least thirty feet below her, and she was still rising.

Wind swirled over the front – now the top – of the dumper, catching the banner and inflating it. The sudden jolt almost pulled her from her perch.

'Not yet!' Chase yelled, leaning forward as far as he could. The cliff was coming up far too fast, but if they let go before the dumper reached a steep enough angle, they'd end up trapped inside it.

His leg muscles strained to hold him in place, the edge of the tipper digging painfully into his tendons. Just another few seconds . . .

The cliff passed out of sight behind the metal as the tipper kept rising, now at nearly a forty-five-degree angle—

'*Now!*'

Chase flung the flapping banner up into the air behind him, simultaneously straightening his legs and falling backwards. Nina did the same. The banner snapped open between them, the racing wind catching it and yanking them both back off the top of the dumper.

But it wasn't large enough to support their weight. They

immediately fell, landing painfully on the steepening metal slope of the tipper and skidding helplessly down it.

The banner held taut—

Nina and Chase shot off the back of the speeding truck, the swathe of material acting as a makeshift airbrake to cancel out some of their forward momentum.

But not all.

'*Roll!*' Chase screamed to Nina, more as a plea than an order as they hit the ground at twenty miles per hour.

She managed to tuck up her legs, free arm raised to protect her head as the other kept hold of the banner. Chase bounced alongside her, rolling like a log. They tumbled along, stones pounding them mercilessly at every impact before they finally came to a battered, dusty halt.

Head spinning, Chase looked up – just in time to see the truck shoot over the edge of the cliff and plunge out of sight. A couple of seconds later, there was a colossal crash that they felt through the ground, followed by more heavy booms and crunches as pieces of the shattered vehicle came to rest.

'Ow,' Nina said, shaking the line loose from her arm and making a feeble attempt to sit up. Chase fought past the pain he was feeling in seemingly every single part of his body to roll over and look at her. Her clothes were ripped, crimson stains visible through the dirt around several of the ragged holes, and an especially nasty-looking cut across her forehead just below the hairline was already leaking blood down her face.

'You're bleeding,' he grunted.

She looked at him, eyes widening in shock. 'So are you!'

He raised a hand to a particularly painful spot on his cheek, fingers coming away smeared with blood. There was a metallic taste in his mouth. Probing with his tongue, he realised that one of his back teeth had been jarred loose, held in place only by a few strands of tissue and rasping against its neighbours as he touched it.

'Shit,' Chase muttered, spitting out blood. 'I *hate* going to the dentist.' Nina tried to stand, holding in a gasp of pain as she put weight on her left foot. 'Are you okay? Is it broken?'

'No,' she said between her teeth, 'I just think it's – aah! – twisted. Ow, crap, oh.' She hesitantly lowered her foot again, wincing. 'I can walk. Or hop, anyway. What about you?'

He pushed himself on to his knees, then took a deep breath and stood up. His legs wobbled for a moment. It felt as though he'd been beaten all over with truncheons – but nothing seemed broken. He took a few experimental steps, then went to Nina. 'I'll live. Come on, we've got to keep moving. It won't take 'em long to catch up.'

Nina looked back at the plain they had just crossed. A plume of dust rose into the air in the distance where the truck had dropped its load, and there were much smaller clouds of drifting dirt on the horizon – other vehicles coming after them. 'Where do we go?' she asked, putting a hand to her head and cringing at the sudden sting of pain as she touched the bloody cut. 'We're never going to be able to get back to the airfield now.'

Supporting her, Chase moved closer to the cliff edge, looking out over the spectacular view before them. From here, the Okavango stretched as far as they could see, stretches of grassy savannah surrounded by dense marshes and broad, lazy rivers. Compared to the dusty desert behind them, the colours were almost overwhelmingly vivid. In the far distance was an aircraft, a white spot low and slow in the deep blue sky. 'First thing we need to do is find some transport.'

'Easier said than done.' Nina leaned cautiously over the edge to look down at the smoking wreckage of the truck, now lying on its back like a dead animal with all but one of its wheels missing.

'Oh, I dunno.' Chase sounded oddly enthusiastic, and she gave him a curious look. He pointed off to the right. The slope of the cliff became more shallow, a hill leading down to a lake – on the shore of which was a wooden building, a short jetty leading from it into the water. A boat was tied up at the end. 'You ever been on a river safari?'

13

'Aah! Slow down, slow down!' Nina gasped, her ankle throbbing painfully as Chase bustled her down the hill.

'Yeah, let's take it easy,' said Chase with a marked lack of sympathy. 'It's a nice day, we can take in the view, have a picnic. We've only got a bunch of hired killers and half the Botswanan army after us, so there's no rush!'

Nina scowled and drew in a deep breath through her nostrils, hoping to calm herself. The technique didn't work. 'You know, Eddie,' she began, voice flinty, 'I'm getting pretty fucking tired of your sarcasm.'

'Oh, is that a fact?' he replied. Sarcastically.

'Yes, it's a fact! You've been acting like a complete asshole for days – no, weeks, now I think about it. No, actually, *months*! What the hell's wrong with you?'

'There's nothing wrong with *me*,' said Chase. 'If anyone's acting like a complete arsehole, it's you.'

'*Me?*' she exclaimed, shocked and offended. 'What have *I* done wrong?'

Chase snorted. 'It's a long list.'

'Well, how about you tell me? I mean, it's obviously been

preying on your mind, so come on! Enlighten me!'

'You really want to know?'

'Yes! I do! Come on, tell me why I'm the worst person in the world compared to St Sophia!'

'Oh, it all comes out,' said Chase, a mocking smile curling his lips. 'This is what it's all about, isn't it? You think you don't want me any more 'cause I don't fit into your perfect world of fancy offices and poncy apartments and rubbing shoulders with the rich and powerful, but as soon as Sophia turns up you have a massive fit of jealousy!'

'When did I *ever* say that I didn't want you any more? When?' Chase didn't answer her. 'And Sophia didn't just "turn up". You disappeared and flew halfway around the world to get her – and brought her back into our home!'

'She was in trouble, she needed my help. She used to be my *wife*, for Christ's sake. What else was I going to do?'

Nina narrowed her eyes. 'How about, y'know, *not* running to do whatever she says when she clicks her fingers? She's your *ex*-wife, Eddie. *Ex*. As in *former*. And you don't owe her anything.'

Chase's posture stiffened, his tone becoming defensive. 'So being a historian makes you an expert on *my* past now, does it?'

'I know you never talk about it, but I do know some things. I know why you and Sophia broke up, for a start. Hugo told me.'

'Oh, he did, did he? He never could keep his bloody mouth shut.'

'Coming from you, that's ironic. He said that your wife had an affair. With Jason Starkman.'

'Ha!' Chase barked in angry triumph. 'Jason told me before he died that nothing happened between them, and she admitted it.'

'So you're happy that she *lied* to you in order to end your marriage?' Nina asked. He looked away. 'And I'm willing to bet that even if she did lie about Jason Starkman, there were others.'

'Woman's intuition?' he sneered.

'But I'm right, aren't I? She married you because you rescued her, and then after the euphoria wore off and her father made it clear what he thought of you, she decided she'd made a mistake and did everything she could to end things quickly. However much that meant hurting you.' Chase didn't reply, instead fixing his eyes on the distant hut. 'Eddie, I talked to her on the flight. She practically told me straight out that she cared more about her relationship with her father and his business than she did about you. I don't know why on earth you'd want to keep on defending her.'

Chase set his jaw, the tendons in his neck standing out. 'Maybe it's because I loved her,' he began, voice a low growl. 'And you know what? At least when I was with her, there was something there. There was some fucking *life*, and it was all about us.'

'Meaning *what*?'

'It means,' Chase said, getting louder, 'that Sophia actually *lives* life rather than just reading what some dead guy wrote about life thousands of years ago.'

'*I* live life!'

'Yeah? When was the last time you actually left your office and went out in the field? When did you last do anything spontaneous or romantic or sexy?'

'Oh, ho ho,' Nina said, laughing accusingly, '*now* we're getting down to it! It all comes down to sex, doesn't it? All that pent-up frustration you're feeling because now you're stuck in an office

224

instead of running around the world shooting people, and of course *I'm* to blame because I have a career with responsibilities rather than attending to your every sexual whim!' She clapped a theatrical hand to her chest. 'Oh, how *dare* I!'

'At least Sophia actually knew how to have a good time in bed,' Chase shot back. 'Yeah, I wasn't her first, and I wasn't her last, but you know what? Experience helps! She didn't need a copy of *The Dummies' Guide To Sex!*'

'Nor did I!' shrilled Nina, outraged.

'Oh, take it from me, you do. There *are* more than three positions! Now Sophia, she had positions that aren't even in the fucking *Kama Sutra*! You think that just because she's posh, she's all prim and proper? Oh, no. She was a fucking *animal* in bed.'

'If she's so great,' Nina seethed, 'then why don't you just marry her? Oh, wait – *you did*! And that turned out like a Harlequin romance, didn't it? Her ladyship and the soldier, new heir to the manor!'

'I never cared about any of that,' objected Chase.

Nina raised her eyebrows. 'Oh, really? Y'know, for someone who thinks he lives his life according to the lyrics of "Free Bird" you certainly change a lot whenever she's around.'

'Bollocks!'

'Oh, yeah. Everything about you! You stand up straighter, you swear less, even your accent changes! Whenever she's there, you sound like you're trying to be Hugh Grant! You might not admit it, but you so desperately, *desperately* want to be accepted by her as an equal because deep down you think she's *better* than you!'

Chase bared his teeth. 'Well, I'm fucking well fucking swearing now, aren't I, so what the fucking fuck does that fucking tell you?'

'I know what it tells me,' Nina said coldly. 'I've always known. It's a defence mechanism. That's something else Hugo told me about you. You get crude and offensive whenever you can't handle dealing with people emotionally and want to push them away. I guess it's about the only thing Sophia gave you from the divorce.'

'That's bullshit,' Chase spat. 'Absolute fucking crap.'

'Then how come I've been hearing a hell of a lot more of it from you recently? Eddie . . .' She looked at him, wanting him to look back at her, softening her voice slightly. 'You've fought in wars, faced terrorists, had so many people try to kill you that you've probably lost count . . . but the thing you're most afraid of is talking to me?'

He was silent for a moment. Then: 'I'm not afraid of anything. Fuck that, and fuck you too.' Before Nina could express her shock, he pressed on, a hint of quite deliberate cruelty in his voice that she'd never heard before. 'You know what? After I get us out of here, I'm going to go and rescue Sophia, and if I'm lucky then maybe she'll fall in love with me all over again. But even if she doesn't, at least I'll know that she's not going to waste her life afterwards on some bloody idiotic, empty obsession.'

'How *dare*—'

Chase stopped walking, pulling Nina to a halt and turning to face her. 'It's not even a real obsession! For fuck's sake, Nina! The only reason you ever gave a shit about this stupid fucking Tomb of Hercules in the first place was that you had a big hole in your life after you found Atlantis! This was just something to fill it! You had your new job, you had *me*, but that wasn't enough for you because you didn't have some great mythological *quest* any more. All your life you've been trying to be like your parents because

226

they had an obsession too, and look where they ended up because of it – dead in a fucking cave!'

Nina hit him. It wasn't a slap, but an actual punch to his face. Although it hurt, he was more startled by it than anything. 'Fuck you, Eddie,' she snarled, tears swelling in her eyes. 'Fuck you! You want Sophia? Have her, I don't care. Go and pretend to be something you're not with somebody who looks down on you. I don't care any more.' She turned away and limped down the slope, feeling pain shoot through her with each step but refusing to show it to Chase.

'Nina!' Chase called after her. '*Nina!* Shit.' He quickly caught up.

'Leave me alone, Eddie,' she said, angrily shaking him off when he tried to support her.

'I can't right now, can I? We're kind of in the middle of a situation. You remember, men with guns? Look, let's get out of here first, and then we can . . .' He realised he had no idea what his true feelings were, anger and confusion still boiling inside him. 'We can do . . . whatever.' He pointed at the hut. 'Come on, it's not far now.'

Nina stared at the building, refusing to look at him. She too was unable to resolve her feelings, a mixture of betrayal and humiliation failing to cover the true regret beneath. 'All right,' she finally said. Reluctantly, she let him take hold of her again to ease the load on her leg. 'Let's go.'

The hut turned out to be a ranger station, a workplace-cum-residence for one of the Okavango's game wardens. The vessel moored at the jetty was an airboat, a flat metal hull with an aircraft propeller mounted above its stern inside a protective metal grid, controlled from a spindly elevated seat in front of it. Chase had driven similar craft before; they were noisy and tricky to control, but their extremely shallow draught meant they could easily negotiate marshland that a conventional boat would find troublesome.

That the boat was there at all suggested the ranger station was occupied, which proved to be the case when Chase knocked on the door. An elderly, pot-bellied Botswanan wearing a khaki uniform of short-sleeved shirt and shorts opened it, looking surprised to have visitors, and more so as he took in their battered and bloodied state. 'Hello?' he said cautiously.

'Hi,' said Nina as Chase helped her limp into the room. A radio was playing music. 'We're so glad you're here! We had an accident, and we're kind of stranded. Is there any chance you could give us a ride out of here?'

'Are you hurt?' the ranger asked, a moment later rolling his eyes as if wondering whether he could have asked a question with a more obvious answer. 'Let me get the first-aid kit.'

'We're okay; it looks worse than it is,' Chase tried to assure him, but with no luck. The man opened a cabinet and took out a medical kit, gesturing for them to sit down.

'What happened to you?' he asked.

'Our truck rolled over,' Nina told him as she sat, being technically truthful. 'So, about that ride?'

The ranger opened the kit and took out a bottle of antiseptic and some bandages. 'The nearest place where you could get proper help is the diamond mine, about nine kilometres south of here.'

'Actually, we were sort of wanting to go the *other* way. As in, as far from the mine as possible.' The ranger gave her an odd look.

'Because, uh, we're very strongly ethically opposed to diamond mining. You know, cartels, price-fixing, blood diamonds, all that. Diamonds are, um, for *never*! Yeah.'

'I'll remember you said that,' Chase remarked quietly.

'Oh, shut up. Ow.' Nina winced as the ranger dabbed antiseptic on to the cut across her forehead.

'We do not have blood diamonds in Botswana,' said the ranger, offended.

Chase smirked. 'You see, Nina?' he said patronisingly. 'I *told* you we were in the wrong country to protest about blood diamonds, but would you listen? Women,' he added to the ranger, with a sigh and a shrug. The ranger nodded knowingly.

'Hey!' snapped Nina.

The ranger finished with the antiseptic, and carefully applied a sticking plaster over the cut. He was about to turn his attention to the wound on Chase's cheek when the music coming from the radio stopped and an announcer said, 'We interrupt this programme for some breaking news.' Nina and Chase exchanged glances.

A dramatic musical sting played, followed by a newsreader. 'An attempt has been made on the life of President Molowe, in an attack which also saw the murder of Minister of Trade and Industry Michael Kamletese. The President was attending a ceremony at a diamond mine in the North-West Province when the attack took place. The assassins are both white, a man and a woman in their thirties. They escaped the scene, but security sources have named them as Edward Chase and Nina Wilde—'

The ranger's mouth fell open as he realised the identities of his visitors, but Chase had already pulled out the gun he'd taken from the dead guard at the processing plant and aimed it at him. 'Okay, stay calm, mate.'

'What?' Nina spluttered. *'What?* We didn't assassinate the minister of trade, we didn't assassinate *anybody*! What the hell's going on?'

'We're being set up,' Chase told her, standing.

The ranger stared at the gun, wide-eyed. 'Now, ah, you're not going to do anything unreasonable, are you?'

'Not if you don't. Where're the keys to your airboat?'

'And I'm only twenty-nine,' Nina added indignantly.

'Media accuracy's not really our biggest worry right now,' Chase told her as the ranger nervously handed him a set of keys. 'You got a two-way radio?'

The ranger indicated a radio set at the rear of the room. Still keeping the gun aimed at him, Chase went to it and yanked its power cord from the wall before throwing it to the floor, putting his foot on the case and ripping out the other end of the lead. 'Okay, take a seat, mate. Nina, tie him to the chair.' He tossed the cord to her.

'Today just keeps getting better,' Nina grumbled as she tied the ranger's hands behind him, then knotted the other end round his ankles, pulling his feet back under the chair. 'First we're accused of murder, now we're assaulting a park ranger and committing grand theft . . . boat.' Once she'd finished, Chase checked the knots, tugging them tighter. The ranger winced.

'It won't hold him for long,' Chase told Nina as he led her from the hut, 'but we won't need long to get away from here. These airboats can shift.'

'Yeah, but where to?' she asked.

Chase thought for a moment, then ducked back into the cabin, returning with a tourist map of the Okavango Delta. 'Hey, it's better than nothing,' he said as he hopped on to the jetty to untie the airboat.

Nina stepped cautiously aboard, the flat hull rocking beneath her. With both the propeller and the driver's seat raised high above the metal deck, the vessel looked horribly top-heavy. 'Is this thing safe?'

'Safe as any other vehicle we ever get into.'

She buried her face in her hands. 'Oh, God . . .'

Chase threw the mooring rope aboard and climbed into the boat, examining the engine. He inserted the key and turned it. 'Okay, this is going to get loud!' The propeller growled into a blur behind the protective metal grille. He clambered up into the driver's seat and buckled himself in, resting his feet on the pedals and taking hold of the two long levers that controlled the steering vanes behind the propeller before revving the engine. The airboat slid from the jetty, then accelerated away.

Nina and Chase barely exchanged ten words in as many minutes as the airboat sped north, and it wasn't because the noise of the propeller made conversation difficult. She barely even looked back at him, instead watched the vibrant wetlands glide past. In return, the inhabitants of the Okavango watched them as they headed along the winding river. Buffalo and wildebeest warily observed their passage from the muddy banks, shoals of glittering fish darting out of the airboat's path beneath the clear water.

There were other, less timid creatures in the water as well.

Crocodiles occasionally surfaced to investigate the noise, while Chase made a point of giving larger animals like elephants and hippos a wide berth. A small group of leopards on the shore tracked the boat with unblinking stares as it passed.

Nina gazed back at the silent predators, her awe at their surroundings numbed by the aftermath of her fight with Chase, muddled feelings sitting in her stomach like a stone. Finally, she looked back at him. 'Where are we going?'

He slowed the engine, the propeller's rasp falling. 'There was a village on the map to the north that had an airstrip. Somebody'll have a phone – we can call TD and get her to pick us up.' He looked round to get his bearings, noticing that the aircraft he'd seen earlier was now closer, circling slowly off to the northeast, and tossed the folded map down to her. 'Actually, check the route, make sure we're going the right way.'

Nina opened the map, which flapped in the breeze. 'Where are we?'

'Find Ranger Station 12; that's where we were. Bottom left corner.'

She scanned the map. 'Got it.' Running her finger up the page, she found a village with the symbol of an aircraft next to it. 'Did you mean Nagembe?'

'Is there an airfield there?'

'Yes.'

'Then yeah. How far is it?'

Nina checked the map's scale. About forty kilometres. 'Twenty-five miles.'

'Be there in less than an hour, then. Doddle.' Chase noticed Nina's face fall as she saw something behind him. 'Or not . . .'

232

He looked round through the grille of the propeller – to see three speedboats racing along the river behind them.

Closing fast.

Even from a distance, Chase picked out Fang in one of the boats, his ponytail streaming in the wind behind him.

'Great, a killer with a grudge!' he said as he jammed the airboat to full power.

14

'How fast can this thing go?' Nina shouted.

Chase looked back at the other boats, which were eating up the distance between them. 'Not as fast as them!' The airboat relied for its speed on its shallow draught to lower the water resistance, but its square bow was far from hydrodynamic.

He looked ahead again. There was no way to outrun the boats on the open river. They would catch up very quickly.

Which meant he had to get *off* the open river . . .

He tossed the gun to Nina. 'Use it if they get too close,' he told her, steering the airboat towards a vast field of tall reeds. 'Tell me what they're doing!'

'Coming after us . . . *Still* coming after us . . . You get the idea!'

Chase shot her an annoyed look, then concentrated on steering the airboat. The water ahead became more murky.

Shallower, mudbanks rising beneath the surface—

A shot cracked behind them. Chase looked back. A man in one of the boats had a rifle in his hands. The way his craft was bouncing through the water, he had almost no chance of scoring a hit – but sometimes a person got lucky.

He hoped that Nina's pendant would live up to her belief in it.

The speedboats were under a hundred yards behind now, and the airboat was going flat out. The river still wasn't shallow enough to impede their pursuers, but the edge of the swathe of reeds was coming up fast—

More gunfire, this time from automatic weapons as men on two of the boats let rip with MP-5s. Their aim was still off, but with the number of bullets they were spraying they had much more chance of scoring a hit.

'Stay down!' he shouted to Nina. But there was no way he could take cover himself, elevated and isolated on the high seat.

Nina dived to the deck. Chase ducked as low as he could as bullets clanged around him. Part of the protective grillework broke loose and dropped on to the propeller, instantly shredding into thousands of metal splinters. He risked a glance back. Almost half the prop was now exposed, a lethal blur right behind him.

A bullet twanged off the engine casing. The other boats were only fifty yards away, closing fast.

Nina raised her head just as the airboat reached the edge of the reeds, a wall of green rising as high as ten feet out of the water. The boat's flat prow mowed them down, carving a path. She covered her eyes as fragments of leaves and stalks whipped down around her. A huge commotion erupted off to one side; for a moment she thought it was an explosion, before she realised it was *birds*, thousands of them leaping from their perches on the tops of the reeds and taking to the air in fright, wings cracking.

The reeds were higher even than Chase on his raised seat, his vision ahead filled with nothing but vertical lines of green. Swaying stalks thrashed at him, but he couldn't shield his face –

he needed both hands to steer. He kept the power on and turned the airboat deeper into the bizarre forest, the exposed propeller slashing the plants to shreds.

The speedboats followed, roaring outboards and intermittent bursts of gunfire behind him—

There was a loud thump and the note of one of the engines changed abruptly, the propeller over-revving as it breached the surface of the lake. The boat had run on to a mudbank under the shallow water.

But it had only slowed the boat, not stopped it. It quickly cleared the obstruction.

And the other two boats were still slicing through the reeds. One on each side, trying to flank them.

Nina looked for the nearest boat. Hunched low, her head little more than a foot above the waterline, she could see only the occasional flash of white hull. The reeds were so dense that anything more than ten feet away was practically invisible. But she could hear it all too clearly, its engine roaring and the towering stalks crashing and snapping before it.

Suddenly the blizzard of broken leaves ceased. The airboat shot out of the reed bed, entering a stagnant marshy lake semi-isolated from the river by mudbanks. A few seconds later, the first powerboat burst from the reeds some fifty feet to starboard.

Nina instantly recognised Fang as one of the three men in the boat. He spotted her, and gave her a nasty smile. The smile vanished as she whipped up the gun and fired off the remaining rounds at him. The boat's driver ducked and turned the vessel sharply away from her.

'Son of a bitch!' Nina snarled as the gun clicked empty. The speedboat swung back round. Fang jabbed an angry finger at her. She displayed a finger of her own, which served only to infuriate him even more.

He brought up an MP-5, as did the other passenger in the back seat, both men aiming at the airboat—

'Shit!' Chase yelled as the second boat drew level on the port side. A man inside it was also aiming a weapon – but this was no sub-machine gun. It was an American M72 rocket launcher. '*RPG!*'

Nina didn't need to know what the initials stood for to realise that they were in serious trouble – the warning in Chase's voice was enough. She dropped as low as she could into the airboat's hull, arms covering her head.

The man with the tubular launcher lined up the sight on Chase, braced himself for the recoil . . .

And fired.

Chase pulled savagely on the steering levers and spun the airboat a full 360 degrees as it skimmed over the turgid water, the rocket missing him by inches as he was whipped out of its path. Its smoke trail streaked past – and hit the security guard in the back of the other speedboat square in his chest.

He was hurled over the side of the boat, the missile's rocket motor still burning as he hit the water – then it exploded, a bright red waterspout gushing fifty feet into the air, pieces of body spinning within it.

The speedboat's driver stared slackly at Fang, in shock at his near miss. Chase swerved the airboat sharply to starboard, aiming at their vessel. Fang shouted a warning, but too late.

Chase slammed his craft broadside-on against the speedboat.

The driver and Fang were both knocked from their seats, the latter's MP-5 whirling over the side of the boat and disappearing into the churned-up, bloody water.

The second boat turned to follow as Chase accelerated away. Some distance beyond it, the third boat finally broke through the wall of reeds and re-joined the chase.

Nina lifted her head. 'What happened?'

'One-nil to us!'

'One boat?'

'One guy.'

'Is that *all*?'

Chase scowled. 'Okay, let's not keep score.' He rapidly checked the surrounding area. More reeds on the other side of the lake, and a long, thin island rising slightly above the water, a few twisted trees along its length . . .

And something else *in* the water, in front of the island.

He aimed the airboat at the dark objects lurking just under the surface. 'What are you doing?' Nina asked. 'You're heading straight for that island!'

'I know!'

'Shouldn't you, maybe, go *around* it?'

'Short cut!' Chase yelled. He could now make out more of the shapes, even the smallest of them as big as the airboat.

Nina saw them too. 'What are those?' she demanded anxiously.

'Hippos!'

'*What?*'

It was indeed a herd of hippos, wallowing in the still waters of the lake, only their eyes and nostrils exposed. Fully grown, an adult hippopotamus weighed over four tons – and despite its almost comical appearance, possessed a vicious temper. Even the slightest provocation could rile a hippo to a lethal anger.

Which was exactly what Chase needed.

He checked the positions of the other boats. The nearest was twenty yards behind, the late arrival over a hundred yards further back. Fang and his driver had only just recovered from the collision, their speedboat coming back to life with a surge of froth from its stern.

'I know I keep saying this,' he shouted to Nina, 'but hold on tight!'

She hugged her arms tightly round one of the bench seats. 'Why are you driving at hippos? Are you *insane?*'

Chase couldn't hold back a smile as he remembered being asked that same question by another woman only a few days before. 'It's been suggested!' He looked for a hippo that was more or less lengthways-on to him, found one, steered the airboat at it—

The enormous animal was only a few inches below the water, less than the airboat's draught. There was a hollow bang as the prow rode up the hippo's rump and over its back. Roaring in surprise and fury, the hippo thrust its huge head upwards – just as the airboat's flat bottom skidded over it. The speeding vessel was thrown out of the water.

Only for a moment, only by inches – but it was just enough for it to clear the lip of the bank. The airboat skidded on its belly across the island, scraping over tree roots and rocks before splashing back down into the river on the other side.

Nina and Chase looked back.

The entire herd had been roused to instant collective rage by their passage, the calm waters erupting as furious hippos burst from their torpor to find a target for their anger.

The lead speedboat, its driver already committed to following Chase and Nina over the crest of the little island, fitted the bill perfectly.

A fifteen-foot bull hippo exploded from the water directly beneath the speedboat and batted it into the air as if it were a plastic toy. One of the three men in the boat flew out and plunged screaming into the midst of the rampage to be instantly crushed to death.

His two companions fared no better, the vessel flipping end over end and smashing into a tree. It sheared in two, the forward half shattering against the gnarled trunk along with its occupant, the rear section cartwheeling along the ground – and blowing to pieces in a huge ball of flame.

'*Now* it's one-nil!' Chase whooped, pumping a fist.

The two other boats hurriedly changed direction, splitting up to avoid the hippos and pass round each end of the island.

Nina looked ahead as Chase revved the engine and powered away from the island, hoping to take advantage of their brief lead over the speedboats. She couldn't see much except the deeper water of the river off to the left, and another thick bank of reeds to the right. 'Which way do we go now?'

Chase was asking himself the same question. The speedboats could still outpace them on open water, which left him no alternative but to head into the reeds and try to lose them.

But then what? Fang must have worked out by now that they were heading north, so even if they did manage to shake them off by hiding in the mass of vegetation, his two boats could just break off, go upriver and wait for their prey.

Which meant . . . they had to get rid of Fang and his men. Take out their pursuers. Go on the offensive.

Something of a problem, considering their lack of weapons.

Chase took a moment to survey the contents of the airboat from his vantage position. An oar secured to one side of the hull, the mooring rope, a hook at its end . . .

An idea came to him. He made a sharp right turn, heading back at the nearer speedboat. 'Chuck me that rope!'

'You're going *towards* them!' Nina protested.

'I know! The rope, chuck it up here!'

She did, then dropped as low as she could in the hull as Chase caught the rope and hefted the hook in one hand. The speedboat was approaching rapidly, the three men aboard barely able to believe their luck as their quarry came straight to them.

Chase worked the steering levers to sway the airboat, trying to make himself a harder target. The men on the powerboat realised that he was charging right for them in a suicide run and opened fire. Chase hunched down as bullets whipped past, the boat taking hits. Another piece of grillework was blown off.

Collision course—

The driver of the speedboat swerved first, throwing off the aim of the other men.

Just as Chase had hoped.

He hurled the hook at the speedboat. It hit its bow with a bang as the two vessels passed. The rope whipped out behind it.

The hook shot back across the bow—

And caught on the handrail, snapping taut.

The gunmen were just recovering their aim when the nose of

their craft suddenly flew up into the air, the speedboat flipping upside down as the airboat yanked it backwards.

All three men were flung from the boat, splashing into the muddy water. A moment later, the inverted speedboat landed on top of them and slammed them into oblivion.

The airboat lurched as it dragged the speedboat behind it. Chase pointed at the metal ring where the mooring rope was tied to the hull. Nina clambered over to it and, after some fumbling, unfastened the knot. The rope shot free and disappeared behind them, the airboat surging forward as the weight of the capsized speedboat was released.

Chase looked up to get a bearing on the sun, then turned north-wards. There was still one more boat chasing them, its engine revving.

There was another noise too, a distant rumble somewhere off to the northeast.

Rapids.

But Chase didn't have time to think about it. More small islands lay ahead, knots of earth and rock and trees with narrow water-ways winding between them. A pair of gazelles looked round in fright at the noise of the boat, then fled, leaping from one island to the next.

Envying them their speed, he turned left, hoping to get back on to the river leading to Nagembe—

'Eddie!' Nina yelled, pointing back. Chase saw Fang's boat only twenty yards to port, angling after them.

Fang stood in the passenger seat, holding the top of the wind-screen. He had something in one hand, sunlight flashing from it—

'Jesus!' Nina gasped. 'That crazy bastard's still got his sword!'

242

Chase could imagine only one reason why Fang would have that particular weapon at the ready. 'He's going to jump aboard!'

'Oh my God! What does he think this is, *Pirates of the* frickin' *Caribbean?*'

'Get up here!' Chase yelled. 'You drive the boat – I'll take care of him!'

'Are you *serious?*'

Chase flashed her a crooked grin as he awkwardly got out of the seat to let Nina climb up. 'Stand by to repel boarders!' He jumped down to the deck as Nina took the controls.

The speedboat was level with them now, closing fast. 'Go between the islands!' Chase told Nina as he picked up the oar, indicating the twisting channel ahead.

'It's too narrow! This thing steers worse than an SUV!'

'Just pretend you're trying to swerve through the potholes on Fifth Avenue!' Chase gripped the metal frame supporting the chair with one hand as he faced the speedboat—

It slammed into the side of his vessel, kicking up a wall of water and almost throwing Nina from her perch. Chase staggered, only his hold on the seat keeping him from being knocked flat on his back.

With a yell, Fang leapt from the speedboat.

He landed in the empty bow of the airboat and immediately dropped into a fighting stance with his sword held out before him, legs spread wide for balance as Nina clumsily guided the vessel into the channel between the islands. It was too narrow for both boats to enter side by side; the speedboat slowed abruptly and swerved in behind her, the tip of its bow only a few feet from the airboat's stern.

Chase quickly assessed his opponent. The sword-cane wasn't just an affectation – Fang clearly knew how to wield the blade in anger.

And all he had as a weapon was an oar . . .

Fang sprang forward, the sword slashing at Chase's head. Chase whipped up the oar to deflect it.

Crack!

The oar broke in two as the sword sliced cleanly through it. Dismayed, Chase ducked, then dropped the clumsy paddle end as Fang drew back and attacked again, this time stabbing at his chest. He swung the other piece of the oar like a club, trying to hit Fang's sword arm as he twisted away from the thrust.

Fang saw the move coming – and changed targets.

The sword sliced through the sleeve of Chase's leather jacket and into his right bicep. Chase roared in pain, dropping the oar and grabbing the wound with his left hand as his adversary drew the bloodied sword back for another strike—

The airboat shook violently, the edge of its hull scraping along the steep bank of the channel as Nina's turn went wide. Fang lurched, throwing his arms out for balance.

Chase dived at him.

He rammed the top of his head into Fang's ribcage like a charging bull, following with a punch from his left hand into his stomach. Air whooshed explosively from Fang's mouth and he fell back on to one of the bench seats.

Chase straightened and grabbed Fang's sword arm with his left hand, fiercely gouging his thumb into the tendons in his wrist. If he could make him drop the sword—

Pain exploded in his wounded arm. Fang was doing the same to

244

him – but his thumb was digging into the bloody cut in his bicep!

Chase screamed, the pain almost overwhelming him. He released Fang's wrist and wrenched himself free of the other man's grip, in the process stumbling over a seat and falling on his back.

Fang stood and raised his sword, about to plunge it down like a steel stake into Chase's heart—

Nina slammed the airboat against the other bank of the channel, this time on purpose. Dust and stones showered its occupants. She hauled at the controls, the craft rocking drunkenly across the confined waterway.

Staggering from the impact, Fang fell, the blade still pointing down at Chase—

Chase saw the flash of silver descending and snapped up both his legs, catching Fang's torso on the soles of his boots and flinging him over his head to crash down in front of the driver's seat.

Another bank loomed ahead. Nina pulled on the control levers, the airboat slewing sideways round the curve and just barely avoiding impaling itself on the rocky shore before sweeping out of the channel and back on to another river, now heading downstream. The speedboat followed, gaining speed and moving alongside.

Its driver took out a gun.

Chase rolled and jumped to his feet, wincing at another searing stab of pain from his arm. Fang seemed dazed, but he was still holding the sword.

If Chase could kick it out of his hand . . .

He leapt over the bench seat—

Nina saw the gun pointing at her. 'Shit!' She swerved the airboat – not away from the other vessel, but towards it.

The deck shifted beneath Chase as he landed, his boot just missing Fang's hand. He wobbled, unbalanced.

The other boat swung away, its driver sawing frantically at the wheel to avoid a collision, his gun momentarily forgotten.

Fang's arm sliced up.

The blade chopped through Chase's jeans and bit into his calf in a spurt of blood.

The agony was so great that Chase almost passed out. He collapsed on to one of the seats. Fang got to his feet, ponytail whipping in the wind. Chase could see Nina in the driver's seat behind him, a look of helpless horror on her face.

He pressed his left hand over the wound, a new wave of pain rolling through his leg. Fang sneered down at him, lifting the sword again. The bloodied tip danced like an insect in front of Chase's eyes, about to make a killing thrust—

Fang's head suddenly snapped forward as Nina smashed her boot heel into the back of his skull.

He staggered—

And came within reach of Chase's uninjured leg.

Chase drove his foot hard against Fang's kneecap. It crunched horribly, Fang's face contorting in pain as he hobbled backwards. Nina swung her arm and delivered a backhand punch into his face as he drew level with her, knocking him back still further—

His ponytail caught in the propeller.

Before he even had time to scream, Fang was snatched off his feet and dragged head-first into the unprotected blades. A huge spray of gore spewed out from the airboat's rear like a psychopath's lawn sprinker, the wet crunch as his skull disintegrated audible even over the noise of the engine. His headless body dropped to the deck beside the driver's seat, still clutching the sword in its twitching hand.

Nina had no time to react to the awful sight, because she had two other things to worry about. The driver of the speedboat, though looking just as shocked and disgusted by the death of his boss as she was, had got over his loss very quickly and turned back towards her, gun in hand.

And the river itself was becoming rougher, the formerly placid waters starting to churn and froth as they picked up speed, rapids flowing towards a—

'*Waterfall!*' she screamed.

Ahead, the river swept over the edge of a vast bowl, a depression caused by the geological rifts that cut through the Okavango Delta. The cliff wasn't high, the drop of the falls no more than twenty feet, but it would be more than enough to wreck the airboat and probably kill its occupants on the rocks below.

Either the driver of the speedboat hadn't seen the approaching falls, or he had but was angry enough not to care. He powered towards the airboat—

'Hang on!' Nina yelled to Chase, just as the two vessels collided. 'Jesus!'

She clung tightly to the control levers, all too aware that she hadn't had time to fasten herself into the chair, and used them to redirect the vanes behind the propeller. The airboat swung round, slithering along the water's surface like a stone on ice. If she had enough space, she might be able to bring the craft about in a long sweeping turn before it reached the edge of the falls—

Another collision, harder, almost throwing her from the seat. Fang's sword fell from his nerveless hand and clanged on to the deck. Chase dragged himself towards it, crawling painfully over the seats.

Nina held her turn, the airboat finally starting to respond as the blast from the propeller pushed it round. She looked at the speedboat.

The driver was aiming his gun at her—

She ducked. The bullet burned the air just above her.

Chase heard the shot, glanced across at the new threat, and kept crawling.

The speedboat closed in once more, bouncing through the choppy waters. The cliff was coming up fast, fifty metres, the thunder of the falls rising.

The driver fired again. The shot hit the airboat's engine with a loud *spang*. The engine immediately coughed and rasped as a fine spray of oil jetted from a crack in its casing. Smoke billowed from the exhausts, streaming out behind the propeller.

Nina cringed as the man lined up a last shot—

Chase grabbed the sword and flung it at the speedboat.

It stabbed into the driver's shoulder, sticking out like an oversized dart. He wailed and dropped the gun, fumbling to pull the blade out of his flesh as his boat curled away from the airboat.

Nina pulled at the control levers, slewing the airboat round. The engine struggled behind her – but still had just enough power finally to bring the vessel into a turn, skipping over the surging water as it hurtled towards the edge of the cliff, now only ten metres away, five . . .

The airboat skimmed through the mist of spray along the edge of the falls, parallel to the drop for a moment before turning away and sweeping towards the bank.

The speedboat wasn't so lucky. The driver spun the wheel in a desperate attempt to turn away, but with only one hand he couldn't bring it about fast enough. The boat shot over the edge and smashed into the rocks beneath the stormy water. It blew apart in a splintered shower of wood and fibreglass and steel.

Fighting the controls, Nina as much *willed* as guided the airboat towards the shore. The engine was on fire now, thick black smoke gouting from it. She braced herself as rocks scraped the underside of the hull, the river shallowing to nothing—

The airboat skidded out of the water on to the muddy bank, then banged against a steeper grass-covered slope and came to an abrupt halt. Nina jumped from the driver's seat just before the crash. She hit the ground with a thud, bouncing once before coming to rest in a patch of tall dry grass.

She sat up, head spinning. The airboat's engine had stalled, a column of oily black smoke rising from it.

Where was Chase?

'Eddie!' she cried, slithering down the slope, her twisted ankle throbbing. Fang's decapitated corpse lay in a broken heap over one of the seats, but Chase was nowhere in sight.

'Down here,' came the wheezing reply in a familiar Yorkshire accent. Chase's hand rose up from behind the other side of the boat and waved weakly at her before its owner levered himself into a sitting position. He indicated the body. 'Used Shorty here as a cushion. Not exactly an airbag, but it worked, sort of.'

Nina came round the boat to help him. 'How badly are you hurt?'

'Well, I got stabbed in the arm and had my leg cut like he was trying to carve a turkey, so take a guess.'

She kneeled to examine the wound in his calf. His jeans were soaked with blood. 'Jesus. This'll need stitches.'

'If you've got a needle and thread on you, go for it.'

'All I've got's an empty gun. Can you MacGyver anything from that?'

'Only if I bang myself on the head with it until the pain goes away.' Chase tried to stand up, but grimaced sharply when he moved his leg. 'Oh, *fuck*! That hurts. That really fucking hurts.'

'Just keep still. I'll see where we are.' Nina climbed back up the grassy slope, hoping to see some sign of civilisation.

All she saw was water. They'd landed on an island, rapids rushing over the falls on both sides.

'I think we have a slight problem!' she called back to Chase.

'No change there, then,' he said with a sardonic smile. 'What's wrong?'

'We're stranded! This is an island.'

'You're joking.' Nina shook her head. 'Buggeration—'

'And fuckery, I know.'

'Right.' Chase twisted to get a better look at the airboat's engine, wondering if there might be a chance of restarting it, but the smoke pouring from a crack in the metal block immediately told him that its working days were over. 'Well, this is fucking marvellous. They're bound to get a chopper or a plane into the air to look for us before too long, and this' – he jerked a thumb at the pillar of smoke – 'is going to lead 'em right to us!'

'Not if somebody else sees us first!' said Nina, suddenly waving her arms above her head.

Chase looked at her incredulously. 'What the bloody hell are you doing?'

She pointed into the sky. 'Look!'

He turned his head to look back out over the falls . . . and saw something completely unexpected.

It was the aircraft he'd noticed in the distance earlier – but it was something much more exotic than he'd thought.

Descending towards them was an *airship*. Its fat cigar-shaped hull was emblazoned with several company logos, but the largest read 'GemQuest', the G represented as a stylised diamond. It approached with a spooky silence for something so large, the whine of its three vectoring propellers only becoming audible over the noise of the falls when it was less than a hundred metres away. The two props protruding from the lower sides of the hull above the gondola cabin tilted upwards, slowing its descent.

'Okay,' said Chase, 'I'm impressed.'

The mooring lines dangling from the 75-metre-long Zeppelin's nose dragged over the island as it eased into position, blotting out the sun. The propellers shrilled, holding it in a hover with the gondola about twenty feet above the ground. A door in the cabin slid open and a blond man in a broad-brimmed safari hat leaned out. 'Ahoy there!' he shouted, his accent South African. 'We saw your smoke – you need a hand?'

Chase had a sarcastic rejoinder lined up, but Nina spoke first. 'We've got an injured man here! Can you get him to a hospital?' Chase mouthed 'hospital?' to her – the last place they needed to go while wanted for murder was any kind of state facility – but she shook her head very slightly, indicating that he should keep quiet.

The man exchanged words with the pilot, then looked back

down at them. 'We surely can, miss! Just give us a minute to come a bit lower. This is the tricky part! Can your friend stand up?'

Nina hobbled back to Chase and carefully helped him up. He groaned at the pain from his calf when he straightened his leg. 'How bad is it?' she asked, worried.

'SAS one-to-ten pain scale? About a five,' he said, wincing.

'And on a normal person's pain scale?'

'Somewhere in the *aargh–Christ–kill–me–now* range.'

Nina assisting him as best she could with her own sore ankle, they made their way up to the top of the slope. The Zeppelin was now hovering unsteadily about four feet from the ground.

'Okay, let's get you aboard,' said the man, jumping down from the door. His weight gone, the airship rose a foot before the engines reduced speed slightly and the gondola dropped again. He made a face when he saw the bloodstains on Chase's tattered clothing. 'Jesus, man, what happened to you?'

'Boating accident,' Chase deadpanned. He reached into the cabin with his left arm, Nina and the South African lifting him inside. The back of the cabin was mostly occupied by electronic equipment, including a screen showing what he recognised as a ground-penetrating radar image. The Zeppelin was being used to conduct an airborne geological survey, hunting for diamonds. The pilot revved the propellers to hold the aircraft steady, increasing power as first Nina and then the crewman climbed aboard.

'Have you got everything from your boat?' the man asked, looking down at the smoking airboat. He did a sudden double take as he saw Fang's body. 'God's balls! What happened to *him*? Where's his head?'

Chase flopped into a seat. 'In the river, on the propeller, on my jacket . . .'

The South African looked shocked. 'This was no boating accident! What's going on?' He fell silent when Nina pointed her gun at him. The pilot looked round, eyes bulging in surprise.

'I'm sorry to have to do this,' she said, 'but I've had a *really* shitty day – several days, in fact – and I need you to take us to . . . what was the name of that village?'

'Nagembe,' Chase answered.

'What he said. I know it's not far, so if you could just take us there as fast as possible, I'd be very grateful. How about it?'

Hands half raised, the South African nervously backed up and sat in the empty copilot's seat. 'I think we can manage that for you, miss. Can't we, Ted?' The pilot nodded repeatedly in confirmation.

'Great.' Nina sat in the chair next to the survey equipment, noticing something in a tray on the desk. 'Eddie, here,' she said, tossing him a phone. 'Call TD, get her to meet us when we arrive. How long will it take to reach the village?' she asked as Chase started to dial.

'About thirty minutes,' the South African told her. He paused, then gave her an incredulous look. 'Are you *really* hijacking a Zeppelin?'

Nina managed a tired grin as the engine noise increased, the airship rising and turning north. 'You know what's weird? That's not even the craziest thing I've done today.'

'That's one hell of a story,' said TD.

Chase stretched his neck, working out a crick. 'Tell me about it.'

TD had hurriedly taken off from the airfield shortly after Yuen's jet departed; the sight of one of the mine's massive trucks smashing through the fence and heading off across the desert with tanks in hot pursuit had been something that, as she put it, 'had Eddie Chase written all over it'. Still airborne when she got Chase's call, she changed course for the airstrip at Nagembe and arrived a few minutes before the airship. At the prompting of Nina's gun, the pilot brought the Zeppelin down next to the Piper. A quick hobble between the two aircraft saw Nina and Chase aboard TD's plane in time for a rapid takeoff, watched by a group of surprised locals who had come to find out why a gleaming airship had made an unscheduled stop at their little village.

Now, they were across the border in Namibia, sitting in a darkened room in an abandoned bush farmhouse. As TD gave Nina and Chase first aid, including stitching up the wound in Chase's leg, they told her about the afternoon's events. 'I knew political assassinations weren't your style, Eddie,' TD said with relief.

'But how are we going to prove it?' Nina wondered miserably.

'That's not your biggest worry just now,' said TD. 'It won't take long for the story to get out of Botswana and into its neighbours. A lot of people will be looking for you – you need to get out of here before that happens. And I don't just mean out of Namibia. I mean out of Africa.'

Nina ran her hands back through her dishevelled hair. 'How are we going to do that? We've got no passports, no money – and we're wanted for the murder of a senior government official! There'll be pictures of us at every airport on the continent!'

Chase looked thoughtful, but also somewhat troubled. 'I might be able to sort something out . . . but it'll mean calling in a big favour.' He frowned. 'Maybe *too* big. Mac probably won't go for it.'

'Mac?' asked TD, surprised. 'You want to ask Mac for a favour?' A sly smile crept on to her face. 'In that case, I might be able to help. He was down here on business last year, and now he owes *me* a favour. Well, several favours.'

'Who's Mac?' Nina wanted to know.

'Old friend,' Chase said, giving TD a suspicious look. 'Why does Mac owe you a favour?'

'Several favours.' She waggled her eyebrows suggestively.

Chase was appalled. 'He's twice your age!'

'He has lots of experience,' TD countered.

'He's only got one leg!'

'Which opens up all kinds of new poss—'

He threw up his hands in horror. 'Don't! Don't say another bloody word!'

'*Possibilities*,' TD finished with a toothy grin.

Chase made a pained face. 'Oh, why'd you have to tell me that? You and Mac? Ee-hew.' He shuddered.

TD folded her arms and pouted. 'Do you want me to help or not?'

'Yes, *very* much,' Nina cut in before Chase could reply. 'Who's Mac?'

'He's somebody who can get you and Eddie to England,' TD told her. 'It might take a day or so, but he has the connections to arrange travel for people even without passports.'

'How?'

'Mac's got friends in high places,' said Chase. 'Or low places. Depends how you look at it.'

'Either way, I'm sure he'll help you,' TD said. She smiled at Chase as she took out her phone. 'Do you want to talk to him, or shall I?'

'You have a word,' Chase said. He put a hand to his forehead and sighed. 'Or several.'

15

London

'Look who it is,' said the bearded Scotsman in a soft burr, a mischievous twinkle in his eye. 'Eddie Chase, international assassin.'

Chase smiled humourlessly. 'Mac, I'm grateful for your help and everything, but seriously – sod off.'

'Good to see you again too.' He grinned, opening the door wider to admit Chase and Nina to the hall of the terraced Victorian townhouse. 'And you must be Dr Wilde. Welcome to London – my name's Jim. But my friends call me Mac.' He shook Nina's hand.

'Call me Nina. Glad to meet you,' she said. Mac was, she guessed, about sixty, six feet tall with bristling grey hair. Despite his age, he was still craggily handsome and in good physical shape. After Chase's comment in Namibia she couldn't help glancing down at his legs, but was unable to tell which one was artificial. 'How do you know Eddie?'

Mac arched an eyebrow. 'He didn't tell you?'

'He's very secretive about his past,' she said acidly.

He closed the door behind them, and Nina took a moment to look around. The hall was actually more of an atrium, two floors of balcony landings running round it above them, topped by a pair of beautiful old stained-glass skylights. Like its owner, the house had a crisp, spartan air, the few examples of ornamentation she could see clearly valuable antiques.

Mac ushered them into an adjoining living room. 'I used to be Eddie's commanding officer,' he explained. 'Colonel Jim McCrimmon of Her Majesty's Special Air Service. Retired now, of course. But I still work as a consultant for . . . certain agencies.'

'He means MI6,' Chase said with a disapproving sneer. 'Bunch of tossers.'

Mac chuckled. 'Eddie has a very low opinion of the Secret Intelligence Service, I'm afraid. But they're not all bad – by spook standards, at least. You wouldn't be here now if some of them hadn't arranged a black bag flight to get you out of Namibia. Please, take a seat.'

Although there was a sofa in the room, Nina and Chase sat on separate armchairs. Mac noted this with a twitch of his eyebrow, but didn't comment. 'So,' he began, voice becoming more serious, 'you both made it in one piece, more or less. Now, perhaps you'd care to explain why I just pulled an awful lot of strings to get you here?'

Chase did most of the talking, Nina occasionally chipping in to add information, or to correct him. The presence of his former commander seemed to temper his responses to her, though they still had a distinct sarcastic edge. It took some time for the full story to be explained, and when it was, Mac leaned back in his chair with an expression of concern.

'So, this man Yuen has a secret uranium mine . . .' he rumbled, steepling his fingers.

'And he's kidnapped Sophia,' Chase reminded him.

'She *is* his wife. I don't know if kidnapping is technically the correct term in the circumstances. But it's the uranium mine that's the most important issue here.' He frowned. 'Though you do realise that I can't act on what you've just told me?'

Chase was confused. 'Why not? Just get the UN involved, they can send inspectors into the mine—'

'It's not the mine, Eddie. It's *you*! You've been accused of assassinating a government minister, for God's sake! And I fully believe that you're innocent,' he continued, waving a finger to forestall Chase's objections, 'but I can't go to the head of SIS with a bizarre story about uranium mines and ancient parchments, and ask him to authorise an investigation when the source of the story is wanted for the murder of a minister of state! The man was even shot with that ridiculous hand cannon of yours!'

'We do have kind of a credibility problem,' Nina was forced to admit.

Chase was undeterred. 'It won't matter once somebody sees that mine. All it'll take is one piece of uranium ore and Yuen's up shit creek.' He leaned forward, hands open pleadingly. 'Come on, Mac. I'm not asking you to go direct to the Prime Minister, but I know you can at least nudge things in the right direction. Get someone to check out the mine, and everything'll snowball from there.'

'Hrmm.' Mac appeared to be agonising over a decision. 'Oh,

what the hell,' he finally said. 'I'm already in this up to my waist by getting you out of the country. Might as well go all the way to my neck, eh?'

Chase grinned. 'That's the spirit.'

'It could take a few days, though. I used up a lot of favours arranging your extraction, so I'll need to take a softly, softly approach. But yes, one way or another, we'll get somebody into that mine, and then we can take a closer look at this Yuen fellow.'

'Great.' Chase sat back. 'And speaking of Yuen, I need to use your computer to do some Googling. Sophia told me that after he left Botswana he was going to Switzerland – I'm hoping he stuck to his plan. Once I find out where he is, I can catch him before he leaves with Sophia.'

'Wait, what?' Nina said in surprise. 'You're still going after her?'

His voice turned stony. 'I promised I'd help her. I always see the job through.'

'This isn't your job any more, Eddie! Let other people handle it.'

'That's not my style.' Chase stood. 'Computer still in the study upstairs, is it?' he asked Mac, who nodded, the subtlest hint of warning in his eyes. Chase ignored it and headed for the door.

'Eddie!' Nina shouted, standing up. 'Don't do this, don't be stupid!'

He rounded on her, angry. 'Oh, is that what you really think of me, *Doctor*? That I'm stupid?'

'I didn't mean it like that,' Nina backtracked, regretting her poor choice of words, but Chase pressed on.

'You think just because I don't have a bunch of letters after my name that I'm an idiot? This is exactly the sort of crap I've been putting up with ever since you let your job title go to your head and started thinking you were better than me. No, I take that back – you *always* thought you were better than me, you just stopped hiding it!'

'That's not true!'

'At least I knew where I stood with Sophia,' he growled. They regarded each other in silence for a moment before Chase dismissively turned away.

'Eddie,' Nina said, fighting to maintain a façade of reason and calm, 'you work for the IHA now, you're not a freelancer. What you want to do, it's got nothing to do with the sinking of the rig or recovering the *Hermocrates* text. It's a personal vendetta! You can't do that, not as a member of the IHA.'

Chase kept his broad back to her for some seconds before he finally half turned, not quite looking at her. 'Then I quit,' he said bluntly, and left the room.

Nina stared after him, paralysed by the turmoil of her emotions. Somehow she knew that Chase hadn't merely been talking about his job; that he had walked out on her in more than a literal sense. She tried to call after him, but her throat had clenched shut, lips trembling.

She heard Mac stand up behind her, suddenly filled with shame and embarrassment that he had witnessed the fight. 'I – I'm sorry,' she managed to whisper.

'No need to apologise,' he said softly. After a moment, he put a reassuring hand on her arm. She looked round, and saw his sympathetic gaze. 'I know that Eddie sometimes makes . . . rash decisions. But he usually comes to his senses.'

'It's not just him, though,' Nina told him. 'He's not – he wasn't wrong about me. I *did* let my job go to my head. I . . .' Even thinking of the confession was painful, never mind actually giving voice to it. 'I stopped being an archaeologist, and started being a bureaucrat. No, worse than that – I started being a *politician*. It all became about playing power games to get what I wanted. And the worst thing was, I enjoyed it.' She looked away from Mac, drawing in a long breath as a deeper shame demanded admission. 'No, the worst thing was . . . I really *did* think I was better than Eddie, just because of my job title. I hurt him without even realising it.' Blinking away tears, she looked back into Mac's eyes. 'Oh, my God, I've wrecked everything.'

'Perhaps you should tell him,' Mac suggested quietly.

'I can't. Not when he's . . . you know what he's like. He won't listen, he'll just try to twist it so that he can claim victory.'

'Hrmm. Maybe he does need to cool off first,' Mac conceded. He took his hand off Nina, straightening purposefully. 'I have a suggestion. You look as though you've had rather a rough few days.'

Nina managed a sad laugh. 'You could say that.'

'In that case, why don't you take a bath? A nice long hot soak, get yourself cleaned up, ease all your aches and pains. It always works for me!'

'I don't know,' said Nina . . . but the idea *did* sound appealing.

'Trust me, it'll help. And it'll give you and Eddie some extra time to think things over as well.'

'Okay,' she said, defences finally crumbling. 'A hot bath it is.'

Chase looked up from the computer as Mac entered the study. 'I've found where Yuen's gone – he's got a microchip factory in the Swiss Alps. I need to use your phone to get in touch with

Mitzi. And I'll need another favour from you – I've got to get there, as fast as possible.'

'I see.' Mac sat in a high-backed armchair, taking a book from a little round table next to it and opening it. He settled back as if about to start a long read.

Chase glared at him and waved impatiently. 'Earth to Mac. Did you hear me?'

'Oh, I heard you,' said the Scotsman unhurriedly, not looking up from his book.

'So can you do it?'

'Well, of course I can do it. The question is, *should* I?' Mac's eyes flicked up towards Chase, steel in his gaze. 'You know as well as I do that when you embark on a mission, you need to have an absolutely crystal-clear objective. And to be honest, I don't believe you do.'

'It couldn't *be* any clearer,' Chase said, annoyed. 'I'm going to rescue Sophia. That's it.'

'But *why* are you going to rescue her? And more to the point, what are you going to do with her afterwards?'

'What do you mean?'

Mac lowered the book. 'I had a talk with Nina.'

'Oh, great.' Chase snorted. 'Let me guess, she told you all about how I've turned into a pain in the arse because I feel stifled by my job, I show her up when she's trying to network with all her new bigshot friends, blah blah blah.'

'Quite the contrary. You know, she's an extremely intelligent and perceptive young woman.' A pointed look. 'You really should try talking to her once in a while.'

'Why, what did she say?'

'It's not for me to comment. But you might want to consider doing so before you go rushing off across Europe after your ex-wife.'

Chase couldn't help noticing a certain emphasis on the word *ex*. 'There isn't time,' he said defensively. 'And whatever Nina says, this *isn't* a personal vendetta. Yuen's mining uranium, which means he's selling it, which means some nasty little bastards are *buying* it. If I can get to Yuen . . .' He gave Mac a small, cold smile. 'He'll tell me all about it.'

His former commanding officer fixed him with a piercing stare, the trained lie-detector gaze of a practised interrogator. 'Are you absolutely sure that's your *only* objective, Eddie?'

'Yes,' Chase said, after a moment.

Mac's eyes didn't waver for several long seconds, but then he finally nodded. 'Very well. If you absolutely insist on going through with this lunacy, I'm sure I can have a new passport waiting for you by the time you get to the airport. Whatever you may think of them, MI6 are actually rather efficient. In some areas.'

'Thanks, Mac. I owe you one.'

'You owe me *more* than one,' Mac reminded him as he put down the book and stood. Chase grinned and turned back to the computer.

'Sophia won't take you back, you know,' Mac said quietly from the doorway.

Chase's grin vanished. 'I . . . never thought that she might.'

'Hrmm.' The little noise was a more damning accusation than any words could have been. 'Eddie, you remember what I taught you in the Regiment, about fighting to the end?'

'Yeah, of course. You went on about it so much, I started using "Fight To The End" as a motto instead of "Who Dares, Wins".'

For a moment Mac seemed amused, then his lined face took on an expression that Chase had never seen on him before. Sadness. 'There's only been one fight in my entire life that I didn't see through until the end. At the time, I didn't think it was worth the effort. But now, it's the thing that I most regret.'

'What was it?' Chase asked. But he already knew.

'I'm an old man in an empty house, Eddie,' Mac said with a sigh. 'But I wouldn't be alone if I'd fought harder to save my marriage. Don't let pride stop you from fighting for what you have. For what you *both* have.' He turned away. 'Call whoever you need. I'll take care of the arrangements.'

Chase watched him leave, but didn't really see him go, too deep in thought. It was some time before he managed to compose himself and pick up the phone.

Nina awoke with a start, bathwater rippling around her. Lulled into a state of deep relaxation by a long soak in the steaming water – which was now on the brink of tepidity – she had dozed off. Briefly disoriented by the unfamiliar surroundings, she stood and took a towel from the rail, wrapping it round herself before stepping from the bath. It was an impressive piece of work, a free-standing giant of thick enamel and metal, standing on four cast-iron feet that looked like a lion's paws. It wouldn't exactly go with her New York apartment, but she had to admit it had its charms.

Drying herself, Nina checked her watch and was staggered to find she had been in the bath for over two hours. She wrapped the towel round her head and donned the dressing gown Mac had provided so that her dirty clothes could be put in the wash. Considering their tattered state, though, she doubted they would be fit to wear again even clean. The five-hundred-dollar hairstyle was long past salvation; it looked as if she'd be going back to her traditional ponytail for the foreseeable future.

She let the water out of the bath and padded on to the landing. The bathroom, the larger of the two in the house, was on the top floor. She took a closer look at the ornate skylights, their colours dappled by clouds moving across the late afternoon sun, before hearing voices from below and peering over the balcony railing.

Chase and Mac were in the hall, talking. Nina stiffened, dismay and anger rising when she saw that Chase had a bag at his feet, ready to leave. Mac stood between him and the front door, his stance suggesting that he would prefer him not to go, but not enough to make an issue of it. She strained to listen.

'So you keep saying,' Chase said irritably, 'but I'm still going.'

'You're not even going to do her the simple courtesy of telling her that you're leaving?' asked Mac, disapproval clear in his voice even from two floors up.

'Christ, Mac, I *want* to talk to her, I really do. I appreciate what you said earlier, and you're right, I know you are. But I've *got* to do this, and if I talk to her now it'll only confuse things. I'll talk to her when I get back, tell her how I feel.'

'Do you even know how you feel?' Chase didn't answer, his silence hurting Nina all the more. 'Hrmm. Well, you're a grown man, even if you don't always act like one, so it's your decision. I just hope you're not throwing everything away.'

Chase said something Nina couldn't hear, two quiet words. They *could* have been 'Me too' ... but they could have been something else. 'Oh, and one more thing,' he said, more loudly. 'Any chance you could give me your exit code?'

'You know I can't,' Mac told him firmly.

'I might need a quick getaway, especially if I've got Sophia with me. And it's not like you need it any more.'

'I *do* still travel on business, you know.'

'Yeah, I heard you were in Africa last year.' Chase raised his voice in only partially mock agitation. 'You and TD! What were you thinking? No, I can guess what you were thinking. What was *she* thinking?'

Mac sounded almost wistful. 'What can I say? She's a lovely girl. Very strong . . .'

'I don't want to know,' Chase moaned. 'Come on, Mac. Odds are I won't need it, and nobody'll ever know you told me. But if I get proof of what Yuen's doing . . .'

'All right,' said Mac, conflicted. 'Why not? I could only be any deeper in this mess if I'd gone to Botswana and shot the silly sod myself.' Nina couldn't make out what he then said, but Chase nodded.

'Got it. Thanks.'

'Don't thank me. I still think this is a very bad idea.'

'People keep telling me that,' Chase said, picking up the bag. 'This bloke'll have everything I need at the airport?'

'He'll be there.' Mac held out his hand. 'Good luck, Eddie. Fight to the end.'

Chase shook it. 'Look, about that . . . tell Nina that I want to talk to her, I *do* want to sort things out. But it'll have to wait until after I get back. I *have* to do this.'

'I'll tell her,' said Mac.

'I'll be back in no time,' Chase assured him as he opened the front door and walked out. It closed behind him with a dull funereal thump.

Mac regarded the door for a moment, then spoke. 'You can come down now, Nina.'

Surprised, she leaned over the railing. 'You knew I was listening?'

'I know every sound in this house – I heard the bathroom door creak.' He looked up at her. 'I'm sorry. I thought I might be able to persuade him not to go.'

'You could have just not helped him,' she pointed out sharply.

'In which case he would have gone anyway, and probably ended up being arrested trying to get through customs. Which, in the circumstances, you have to admit would be an even worse alternative.'

Nina was forced to agree. 'God damn it!' she wailed. 'Why does he have to be so *stubborn*?'

Mac let out a muted laugh. 'I've known Eddie for a long time, and that's one thing about him that's never changed.'

'You mean there are other things that he actually *is* willing to change?' It was intended as a rhetorical question, with more than a hint of bitterness, and she was rather taken aback to get an answer.

'You'd be surprised. I've seen quite a lot of changes in Eddie in the years I've known him.'

'Really?'

'Really. But,' he went on, 'if you want to talk about them, I think it would be better – certainly for my neck! – if we didn't discuss them over a balcony like Romeo and Juliet, eh?' He indicated the door leading to the kitchen at the back of the house. 'Come downstairs and I'll get you something to eat. Then, if you'd like, we can talk about young Mr Chase.'

The sun had set on London, buildings silhouetted against the dying glow of the western sky. Streetlights illuminated the Belgravia terraces with a salmon-pink cast.

That same light fell on a white van as it pulled up opposite Mac's house. Ignoring the double yellow lines, its flashing hazard lights came on, the traditional cloaking device of any British driver wanting to park where it was prohibited.

There were three men in the front of the van, and four more in the back. All were young, large, trained, and dressed entirely in black. They were also armed, six of them equipped with ultra-compact Brügger & Thomet MP9 sub-machine guns, and other weapons besides.

The seventh man lacked an MP9, but in some ways he had the most powerful weapon of all. On his knees was a laptop computer, and connected to it by a cable was an unassuming white box attached to a makeshift frame bolted to the side of the van.

'Switching on,' he said. The laptop's screen came to life, a random swirl of greys and whites against a blood-red background quickly taking on form.

The interior of Mac's house.

The white box was the antenna for a millimetre-wave radar, working on a frequency capable of penetrating Victorian brickwork with ease. The operator used a small joystick to direct the antenna, slowly panning and tilting through the house, looking for signs of life . . .

'Got them,' he announced.

★

Nina looked more closely at the photograph. 'Oh my God, is that Eddie?'

'That's him,' Mac confirmed. After they'd eaten and Nina had changed into one of his shirts, which came almost to her knees, and a pair of slippers while she waited for her own clothes to dry, he had taken her on a brief tour of the house, ending up in a library on the top floor – though it was as much a private exhibition of the Scotsman's past as a repository for books. One wall was filled with framed pictures from different periods of his military career.

'He's got hair!' Despite Chase's military crop in the photo, he still had more follicular coverage than his present-day counterpart. 'How old was he in this?'

'That was taken ten years ago, so he'd be about twenty-five.' As well as Chase, Mac himself was in the picture, as were several other men in desert camouflage posing for the camera. 'I think it was his third year in the SAS.'

Nina moved on to the next picture, which looked as though it had been taken in a restaurant or a pub. A group of men round a table all cheerfully toasted the cameraman, whom she assumed to be Mac himself. 'Oh, wow! Is that Hugo?'

Mac peered at the picture, which included Chase and Hugo Castille, the latter sporting a very unflattering droopy moustache. 'So it is. Took it just after we got back from a NATO joint op in the Balkans. You knew him?' Nina nodded. 'Good man. Obsessed with fruit, though.'

'Yes, I remember.' Also in the picture was someone she recalled much less fondly. 'Oh. And that's Jason Starkman.'

'Yes,' said Mac disapprovingly, 'shame about him. Having an affair with a fellow soldier's wife, that's the sort of thing a man should be horsewhipped for.'

'Actually . . .' Nina began, before pausing, not sure if she wanted to discuss the topic. Mac's quizzical look encouraged her to press on. 'Eddie told me that Starkman *didn't* have an affair with Sophia. She made it up to hurt him.'

Mac nodded almost imperceptibly. 'You know, that doesn't surprise me. I always thought Sophia had rather a cruel streak. She had an inflated sense of entitlement, and got quite nasty if anything wasn't exactly how she wanted it. Not that Eddie noticed it until it was too late, the poor sod.'

'Didn't you or Hugo think to, y'know, drop a hint?'

'What could we say? He was in love with a rich, cultured and very beautiful young woman. I don't think there's anything we could have done to change what he thought about her. Only *she* could do that . . . and it still took a long time for him to admit it to himself. The whole experience changed him quite a bit, unfortunately.'

So Chase wasn't as immutable as he claimed, Nina thought. 'Hugo once told me that Eddie used to be . . . chivalrous?'

Mac laughed. 'Oh, good God, yes! A true knight in shining body armour. Went out of his way to help women in need, and never asked for anything in return. That's the kind of behaviour that wins a man a lot of admirers.'

'He does seem to have rather a lot of, ah, *lady friends* around the world,' Nina said.

'And with good reason. A lot of people owe Eddie their lives. But he was also enough of a gentleman to see that they were *just* friends – until Sophia. Then after that, while he still always tried to help people, he'd also developed a rather tiresomely crass attitude.'

'A defence mechanism.'

'I suppose.' Mac gave Nina a look. 'But somebody was clearly able to break through it.'

'For what it was worth,' she said unhappily.

'You've been together for, what, eighteen months now?'

'More or less.'

'Which is longer than Eddie was with Sophia.' He left Nina to consider that as he crossed the library, a dividing beam on the ceiling showing where two smaller rooms had been knocked together into one, and reached up to brush a speck of dust off a set of bagpipes mounted on a large shield-shaped plaque of dark wood.

'Can you play them?' she asked, taking the opportunity to change the subject.

Mac smiled wryly. 'Not a note. My family actually left Edinburgh when I was ten and moved to Chingford. But soldiers are rather unimaginative when they buy retirement presents. Either that, or they take the piss. I'm not really sure which case this was. But it's the feeling behind it that counts.'

He smiled again, more warmly, then left the bagpipes and went into an adjoining room. Nina followed, finding herself in a games room, a full-sized snooker table occupying most of the space. Mac picked up a white cardboard box from the green baize, snooker balls rattling inside it. He toyed with it for a moment as if about to lay the balls out for a game, then turned to face Nina.

'The thing with Eddie,' he said, 'is that yes, he can be . . . let's be generous and say *annoying*. Even before Sophia left him, there were times when I thought a bullet in the head would be the only way to get him to shut up.'

'He does kind of go on,' Nina admitted, half smiling.

'But at the same time, he's quite possibly the most loyal, courageous and downright indomitable man I ever served with.' He took a cue from the table and tapped it against his left shin. There was a clack of plastic and metal against the wood. 'Got this in Afghanistan. It was the reason I had to retire from active duty and go into spook work. Blown clean off below the knee by RPG shrapnel.'

'My God,' said Nina, wide-eyed.

'It was Eddie who got me out of there. Not only did he run into enemy fire to pull me out of a burning Land Rover, and then pick me right up over his shoulder – well, I *was* a leg lighter, I suppose – but he also took out the men firing at us while he was running back into cover with me. That's the kind of man he is. When it comes to protecting the people he cares about, he's determined and fearless, and will go to any lengths to do it. From what you said over dinner about how you met, I got the impression you know that from first-hand experience.'

'Yeah, I do,' she said, remembering how Chase had boarded a plane – *while it was taking off* – to rescue her.

'He's a man of action,' said Mac, returning the cue to the table, 'which unfortunately sometimes means that he acts without thinking. And *speaks* without thinking. I suppose for the people close to him, it's a matter of balancing the negatives against the positives . . . and dealing with the negatives.'

'People like me, you mean?'

He gave her an innocent look. 'Perhaps.'

She smiled. 'You know, I never really thought of SAS men as relationship counsellors.'

'Not every battlefield is out of doors,' he said, returning the smile—

A very faint noise came from above, a brief scrape. Nina barely registered it, but Mac's head snapped up to search for the source, his smile instantly vanishing.

'What is it?' she asked.

'Come with me. Quickly.' His voice was commanding, all business. He headed through the door on to the landing and hurried down the stairs to the first floor, Nina right behind him. 'We've got to get to the study.'

'What is it? What's wrong?'

'There's somebody on the roof. I heard a footstep on one of the slates.' They reached the study. Mac dropped to a crouch, for the first time showing signs of awkwardness on his false leg. 'Keep your head down. They might be watching the window.'

Nina ducked and followed him across the room to a cabinet. He opened it and took out a sinister black pump-action shotgun, which became even more menacing as he racked the slide. *Ka-chack*. The sound alone sent a chill down Nina's spine.

'You make enemies in the SAS,' Mac offered by way of curt explanation. 'Some of them have been known to make house calls.' The gun held in one hand, he kept low and made his way to the desk to pick up the phone.

Another noise, a dull *whump* from the street outside.

Mac instantly dropped the phone and dived at Nina, tackling her to the ground to protect her with his body.

The window broke, a neat round two-inch hole punched through it—

'Cover your ears!' Mac shouted. Nina just barely managed to bring her hands up to her head—

The stun grenade exploded with a deafening bang.

16

Nina's ears were ringing as Mac dragged her to her feet and pulled her on to the first floor landing, the shirt flapping around her legs. There was a loud crash from below, and she looked down to see two armed men, dressed all in black and wearing balaclavas, burst through the front door. Another bang of splintering wood came from the kitchen as the back door was simultaneously smashed open.

The two intruders already knew where she and Mac were, immediately looking up at the balcony. Mac aimed his shotgun at them—

Stained glass suddenly rained down from above as both skylights shattered. Mac ducked back as jagged shards showered on to the landing.

Two black nylon ropes dropped through the holes in the ceiling, uncoiling as they fell all the way to the floor of the hall. A moment later, two more men rapidly started descending the ropes.

Boom!

Mac's shotgun went off almost as loudly as the stun grenade. One of the hanging men flew backwards as the full force of the blast hit him in the chest, swinging from his rope over the balustrade. He smashed against the wall of the top floor landing and dropped to the floor.

But there had been no blood. The attackers were all wearing body armour. The man Mac had hit was dazed, but he was still alive, still a threat.

The wooden banister burst into splinters as the men below opened fire. Nina threw up her arms to protect her face. Next to her, Mac pumped his shotgun and raised it again as the other man above twisted to aim his MP9—

Mac fired first. But not at the armoured man. Instead, he aimed *above* him, red-hot shotgun pellets shredding his rope. The man plunged downwards, his scream abruptly cut short by a crack of breaking bones.

The firing from below stopped. Nina's hope that the two gunmen in the hall might be helping their fallen comrade was dashed when she realised they were running for the stairs.

'Upstairs!' Mac yelled, grabbing her arm and racing up to the top floor. His left foot made a metallic thud each time it hit the carpet, but the Scotsman was barely slowed by the prosthetic.

'There's still one of them up here!' Nina warned him. The rappeller Mac had blasted in the chest was on the other side of the landing across the atrium, groggily lifting himself to his knees.

'And there's *four* of them down there!' There was another crash from the ground floor as a door was kicked open, the men who had entered via the kitchen advancing through the house. 'The library – there's a passage to the back staircase!'

He pushed Nina ahead of him as they reached the top of the

stairs. The library was at the rear of the landing, the door of the games room open to one side as they ran—

Automatic fire from the rappeller's gun raked the wall ahead of Nina, shattered plaster and lath fountaining out. She screamed and dived into the games room, skidding across the wooden floor to end up at the head of the snooker table.

Mac ran through the door behind her. The MP9 chattered again – and a stream of bullets tore into his left leg above the ankle. Ripped cloth and shredded plastic flew in all directions as his foot was blown off.

Mac fell heavily to the floor. The shotgun was jolted from his grip and bounced away across the room.

Nina jumped up, adrenalin overcoming the resurgent pain from her ankle. Mac was sprawled on his front a few feet inside the door, the jagged metal 'bone' of his severed artificial leg poking into the air above his bent knee. She looked for the shotgun. It was at the far end of the room against the wall. It would take her a couple of seconds to run round the table, more to pick up the gun and bring it about.

And the gunman was charging across the landing, almost at the door—

She grabbed the box of snooker balls and whipped it round. A cascade of brightly coloured spheres flew over the fallen Mac to bang down on the floor and skitter towards the door just as the black-clad intruder ran through it, gun raised—

His foot shot out from under him as he slipped on the balls, falling forward.

On to Mac's upraised leg.

Mac's yell of pain as the remains of the prosthesis crunched against his stump was nothing compared to the startled gasp of the gunman as the sharp metal spike burst through his ribcage into his heart. He convulsed for a moment, then slumped over Mac's legs, a circle of dark blood rapidly swelling across the floor beneath him. Several snooker balls rolled through it, leaving thin red trails in their wake.

Nina only had a moment to stare before the sound of feet pounding up the stairs yanked her back to the remaining dangers. She grabbed the dead man's gun, then ran to the end of the room to retrieve Mac's shotgun.

'Get to the back stairs!' Mac ordered, twisting to kick off the impaled corpse.

'But you—'

'They want to *catch* you, not *kill* you! Go! I'll hold them off !'

Nina hesitated, then gave him his gun and ran to the door. She glanced out. Two men were halfway up the second flight of stairs, another pair having just entered the hall. She gave a last look back at Mac, who frowned at her for still being there, then turned and ran through the connecting door to the library.

Another deafening retort from Mac's shotgun blew a chunk of the balcony rail to smithereens as the first man ran past the door. But the shot was a fraction of a second too late to catch him. The second man jerked to a standstill just before reaching the door, the *ka-chack* of another shell being chambered deterring him from crossing in front of it.

'Get her!' he yelled to his companion. 'I'll nail the old bastard!'

He pointed his MP9 round the door frame, unleashing a devastating spray of fire into the room. Wood cracked and baize shredded as bullets ripped into the snooker table, the slate bed beneath the green surface splintering under the onslaught.

Already ejecting his spent magazine and reloading, the gunman jerked his head round the edge of the door for the briefest moment, not so much to see the results of his assault as to draw any fire, making his target waste both a round and the time it took to reload. The room remained silent. More confident now, the intruder swung round the door with his gun at the ready.

No sign of the old man, just one of the other members of the snatch team dead on the floor and a battle-scarred snooker table—

The shotgun blast from under the table ripped his thighs into bloody mince. Screaming in agony, the man staggered back – and toppled through the hole blown in the railing. He fell, still wailing, to land with a neck-breaking crunch beside the first of his dead compatriots.

Mac bumped an appreciative fist against the underside of the slate that had protected him as effectively as any armour, then crawled out from beneath it.

Nina ran across the library to the nearer of the two doors at its rear, throwing it open to find herself in a narrow passage that vanished into darkness in either direction. Only then did it occur to her that she didn't know whether to go left or right to reach the stairs.

Her pursuer entered the library from the landing . . .

She went left. The light from behind her provided just enough illumination to pick out the door to the other half of the library as she passed it, then another door directly ahead. She grabbed the handle and threw it open, expecting to see the promised stairs – only to find a cupboard, dusty suitcases squatting on its shelves.

'Shit!'

The level of illumination plunged. She whirled, seeing the man standing in the open doorway, blocking the light. The gun was a menacing black shape in his hand.

The gun—

She had one of her own!

Nina snapped up the stolen MP9 and yelled a battle cry of pure fury as she hosed the passage with the entire contents of the clip. Spent shell casings pinged off the wall and sizzled past her as she swung the gun back and forth, almost blinded by the muzzle flash.

The hail of fire ceased abruptly as the magazine ran dry. Her shout died as she tried to blink away the wafting after-images of flame, hoping to see the man lying dead on the floor . . .

He wasn't. He wasn't even in sight. He must have flung himself back into the library just as she started shooting—

The second, nearer library door opened, more light filling the passage. The man stepped through it, gun raised. Through the hole in his black balaclava, his mouth twisted into an unpleasant smile.

'Ooh, out of bullets,' he said in a patronising tone. 'Never mind, I've still got plenty.'

'You won't shoot me,' said Nina, faking defiance. 'You need me alive.'

The gun tilted down to aim at her bare legs beneath the long shirt. 'You can shoot someone and not kill them, you know.' He advanced on her. 'Just give me an excuse—'

There was a discordant squeal from the other end of the passage as something flew through the far door and hit the wall before dropping to the floor. The startled gunman whirled, gun blazing – and blew Mac's wailing bagpipes to shreds.

He stepped forward. 'What the fu—'

The shotgun boomed from the library, blowing the man's knees to a gruesome pulp. He fell, howling in agony.

Mac hobbled over with a snooker cue wedged under his arm as a makeshift crutch. 'Oh, shut up,' he growled at the screaming man, slamming the butt of his shotgun against his head. The noise stopped immediately. 'Are you okay?'

'Yeah,' Nina said.

'Get to the stairs. Go!'

She didn't hesitate this time, running for the far end of the corridor to find another door. To her relief, there were stairs beyond this one. She started to run down them – only to stop at a noise from below. Someone was running *up* them!

She turned back, re-entering the library. 'They've cut us off!'

Mac muttered a curse. 'On to the landing!'

'But they'll be coming up the stairs—'

'Come on!' The tip of the cue banging against the floor, he staggered to the door. Nina followed.

Another man was on the landing below. Mac loosed a shotgun blast at him, forcing him to dive back behind a support pillar for cover.

The intact rope still hung from the broken skylight. 'Can you climb a rope?' Mac asked, swinging the barrel of his gun to snag it.

'I can *hang on to* a rope,' Nina said nervously, realising what he had in mind, 'but that's not the same thing!'

'It's your only way down! Just get out of the front door, and run!' He thrust the black line into her hands, then pumped another round and fired again at the man on the floor below. Plaster spat from the pillar. 'Go!'

'Oh, God!' Nina wailed as she gripped the rope as tightly as she could . . .

And swung out from the landing over empty space.

If she hadn't trained with Chase, she would have lost her grip. Shirt billowing in the breeze, one slipper falling from her foot, she lowered herself hand over hand as quickly as she dared.

It wasn't quickly enough. Even as she heard Mac reloading, the man leaned out from behind the pillar and saw her. He jerked his gun towards her, then hesitated, remembering his orders to take her alive. He ducked back as Mac fired again, pellets cratering the walls. 'She's going down on her own!' the man yelled, Nina for the first time seeing the line of a radio microphone curving in front of his mouth.

She increased her pace, dropping faster. Her hands, damp with sweat and fear, started to slip on the rope, friction burning her palms—

'Fire in the hole!' The man, now level with her, swung out of cover to throw something up at Mac's position.

A grenade—

Mac saw it arc through the air towards him. He turned and dived into the bathroom.

Nina loosened her grip and slid down the rope, barely able to control her descent. Her hands seared. Above, she heard a clack as the grenade landed just outside the bathroom.

Mac dropped his gun and the makeshift crutch, using his one good leg to propel himself over the rim of the bath—

The grenade detonated.

This was no stun grenade, but a lethal explosive.

The balustrade was blasted to pieces, shattered wood spinning through the air into the hall below. The blast ripped through the open door of the bathroom, the window blowing out.

The rope shuddered in Nina's hands, then went slack, severed. She was still over ten feet above the unforgiving marble floor, and unprepared for the fall. She plummeted—

And landed on the body of the man Mac had shot in the thighs. The impact knocked the breath from her, her ankle flaring with pain, but she was otherwise unhurt.

Gasping, she looked up as the echo of the explosion died away. The man who had thrown the grenade was running back down the stairs after her. On the top floor, she saw another black-clad figure toss something considerably larger than a grenade on to the floor outside the bathroom, then run like hell back into the library, slamming the door behind him.

Covered in broken pieces of wood and plaster and tile, Mac sat up. The thick sides of the old bath had shielded him from the direct blast of the grenade. Dust and smoke swirled through the room, but he could still see clearly enough to make out something outside the broken doorway, a squat cylinder lying on its side on the smouldering carpet . . .

'Bastards!' he hissed.

He knew what it was. He'd used similar devices in his own career.

It was a fuel-air explosive charge. An anti-terrorist weapon, designed to clear large but confined spaces like cave systems by releasing a cloud of highly flammable vapour and then detonating, creating a massive fireball that raced outwards to fill every nook and cranny, consuming whatever lay in its path.

And it would work just as well in a London house as an Afghan cavern.

A grey mist spewed from the cylinder.

'Nina!' he yelled as he stood. 'Get out of the house! *Get out!*'

The desperate urgency in his voice spurred Nina to action even more than the sight of the gunman racing down the stairs. She jumped up, fear overcoming the pain as fragments of stained glass stabbed into her bare foot, and sprinted for the front door.

The man charged after her, rapidly closing the gap—

A small electrical arc cracked across the nozzle of the explosive cylinder.

A millisecond later, the vapour cloud ignited, expanding at near-supersonic speed into a ball of liquid fire which incinerated everything it touched as it swept outwards to fill the bathroom, the upper landing, the entire hall—

Nina cleared the front door and ran down the stone steps as the bomb detonated. She threw herself flat.

The house's windows exploded in rapid floor-by-floor succession, huge jets of flame bursting through them and boiling skywards. Another gout of fire erupted from the front door as the gunman hurtled through it, the blast propelling him over Nina to land in the street. He yelled and rolled frantically on to his back, trying to smother his burning clothes.

Nina looked up. One of her attackers was occupied with his own survival, the other had escaped through the back of the house and would have to run round the block to reach her – this was her chance to flee and find help.

She stood—

And a metal dart thudded into her thigh.

There was a white van parked across the street, another man climbing out of its side door with an odd-looking gun in his hand.

'Son of a *bitch* . . .' Nina just had time to mumble before blackness swallowed her senses.

17

Switzerland

Chase panned the binoculars up the length of the valley. The moon was high in the night sky, the snowy mountains bathed in a vivid ghost-light – a spectacular sight.

But natural beauty was the last thing on his mind. Instead, he focused on something man-made and charmlessly utilitarian.

'So Yuen's in there?' he asked, breath steaming in the cold air as he surveyed the factory complex sprawled across the valley floor below.

'As far as I know,' said his companion. Mitzi Fontana was a long-haired and pretty Swiss blonde in her early twenties. 'He's been there a few hours. I persuaded one of the staff to tell me when he left the hotel.'

Chase took a moment to glance at the low-cut blouse beneath her partly fastened coat. 'I won't ask how.'

She smiled. 'Oh, *Eddie*! They had no luggage with them, so they haven't checked out. This is the only place they could have gone.'

'Unless they wanted some quiet time on the piste, but somehow I don't think Yuen came here for the skiing. Any chance he left before we got here?'

'My friend at the hotel promised to call me if he came back. So far, he hasn't.'

'Could be en route, but . . .' There was no sign of any traffic travelling down the road to the nearest town, two miles away. Chase raised the binoculars to confirm that there was no other way out; about half a mile beyond the factory, the valley was abruptly truncated by a sheer wall of concrete, a hydro-electric dam. The generating station at its base was lit up as brightly as Yuen's facility.

More lights at the top of the dam caught his attention, a building right at the edge of the sheer valley side. 'What's that up there?'

'A cable car station,' Mitzi told him.

Chase perked up. 'A cable car?' Now that he knew what to look for, he picked out a seemingly gossamer-thin line catching the moonlight, running from the building down to a similar station within the factory's boundary fence.

'Please, Eddie,' she sighed, 'don't start talking about *Where Eagles Dare*.'

'Aw, come on, it's one of my favourite films – and the scenery's perfect for it.' He laughed briefly, before returning to business. 'What's up there?'

'There's an airstrip about a kilometre from the dam.'

He frowned. 'So Yuen could have left that way?'

'No, I checked. There is a private jet at the airstrip, and it has not left yet.'

'That's something, then.' He turned the binoculars back to the factory. Security looked tight; tighter than he would have expected for just a microchip manufacturing facility. 'What about Sophia? Is she with him?'

'According to my friend at the hotel, there was a woman with him, but he did not get a good look at her – she was taken straight from the suite to the car by two bodyguards.'

'It has to be her. Do you know what kind of car it was?'

'A black Mercedes. I'm afraid I don't know the model.'

'Whatever's the most expensive, I bet.' Chase lowered the binoculars. 'Thanks for helping me with this, Mitzi. I know it was short notice.'

'And rather pricey!' She nodded at the bundles in the back seat of her SUV. 'My sky diving club were rather surprised that I needed a parachute so urgently. And somehow I suspect I won't be able to return it for a refund . . .'

'I'll pay you back,' Chase assured her.

She patted his arm. 'I'm joking, Eddie. I already owe you much more than the price of a parachute.'

He shook his head. 'You don't owe me anything. I'll take care of it when I get back.'

'*If* you get back,' Mitzi said hesitantly. 'Eddie, don't you think you're rushing into this?'

'If I didn't rush into things, you and your mother wouldn't be alive,' he snapped, more harshly than he'd meant to. 'Sorry. But Sophia's down there, and I'm going to get her out. That's all there is to it.'

'In that case, all I can do is wish you good luck and help you on your way,' she said resignedly.

'Thanks.'

'And Eddie, please don't blow up the dam. My grandparents live down the valley.'

He grinned. 'I'll try not to.'

Mitzi laughed, then suddenly fixed him with a stern stare. 'Really. Don't.'

'I dunno where I got this reputation,' Chase said with a nonchalant shrug, then opened the car's rear door and moved the parachute aside. He nodded approvingly as he saw a gun and a hand grenade.

'Where did you get these?'

'I go rock climbing as well. One of my instructors used to be in the Army. He kept a few souvenirs.'

Chase grinned. 'Sky diving, rock climbing . . . you're turning into a right action girl.'

'All because of you, Eddie,' Mitzi told him, beaming.

Slightly embarrassed by her attention, Chase picked up another bundle which he unrolled and spread out on the ground. Then he took an aerosol can and shook it before kneeling to spray part of the material with black paint. 'See? I thought far enough ahead for this. These things are *supposed* to be high-visibility, which is exactly what I don't need.'

Mitzi stood back from the reeking mist, wrinkling her nose. 'I see that's something else I won't be able to get a refund for . . .'

A few minutes later, Mitzi pulled her Porsche Cayenne out of the scenic vantage point from where she and Chase had surveyed the valley on to a four-lane highway slicing through the mountains. At the height of the skiing season it would be packed with holidaymakers, but now, in the middle of the night, it was deserted.

Ahead, stretching across the valley in the direction of Bern, was a bridge, an elegant span with a single central support rising over five hundred feet above the valley floor. Mitzi checked that the road was clear, then accelerated towards it. 'Are you ready?' she shouted to Chase.

He wasn't in the SUV with her – he was on top of it, crouched on the roof with one hand holding the roof rack. 'Go for it!' he yelled, extending his other arm out behind him for balance. The one-piece garment he was wearing over his clothes rippled as the wind rapidly increased, the car passing forty, fifty miles per hour as it reached the bridge.

Mitzi gingerly drifted the Cayenne almost to the barriers at the centre of the highway, still accelerating. Sixty, and they were coming up to the centre of the bridge, its highest point—

'*Now!*' Chase bellowed.

Mitzi swerved the car hard across both lanes, seemingly on a suicidal course to plough straight through the concrete wall – then at the last possible moment swung back into line, the whole vehicle swaying—

Giving Chase an extra boost as he leapt from the roof into empty space.

He threw his arms and legs wide into a star shape, the triangles of fabric stretching between his wrists and waist snapping open like the wings of a bat. Another nylon wedge between his legs filled with air as he fell.

The wingsuit couldn't stop his descent – the amount of extra lift the material provided was far too small – but it could slow it.

And let him *direct* it.

Chase tilted his outstretched arms to bring himself into a turn. The lights of the microchip plant wheeled into view below.

Not as far below as they had been just seconds before. Although he was now gliding up the valley at an ever-increasing pace, his rate of vertical descent was practically pure freefall.

Icy wind slashed at his face. He had already dropped below three hundred and fifty feet, three hundred—

He tore at the ripcord.

The parachute erupted from its pack like a slow-motion explosion, black as the night sky. Chase braced himself, swinging to an upright position as the straps yanked tight, and grabbed the control lines.

The barbed-wire top of the high perimeter fence swept past below. The black paint he had sprayed over the vivid yellow panels of the wingsuit would reduce the chance of his being seen, but if some guard had heard the thump of the parachute opening and recognised its cause, he could still be spotted, highlighted by the glow of the moon . . .

He shot over the roof of a building. If he descended any further he would come down in the middle of a brightly lit area—

Chase tugged the lines to collapse the 'chute, legs out ahead of him as he slammed on to the roof and rolled to absorb the impact. Pain bit at the stitches in his calf. He gritted his teeth, trying to suppress it.

Even as he shrugged off the parachute he had already drawn the black Steyr GB pistol. He turned in a fast circle, hunting for exits from the roof.

The top of a ladder rose above one corner. He aimed the gun at it, listening for movement below. If he heard the clang of ascending feet, what he'd hoped would be a stealth mission would turn into a battle . . .

No clanging, no footsteps. The only noise was the faint rush of the wind and the whine of electrical equipment.

He relaxed, slightly, and unzipped the wingsuit, stepping out of it to reveal nothing but black beneath; black jeans, black polo neck, his battered leather jacket. After bundling up the parachute, he trod quietly across to the ladder and looked down.

The building below contained offices, all but a few of the windows dark. Across the broad road was a large white two-storey structure. Its windowless walls suggested industrial use, and from the large number of air conditioning units on the flat roof Chase guessed it was a chip fabrication facility. The most expensive microchips could be rendered utterly worthless by the tiniest speck of dust introduced during the manufacturing process, so the air had to be filtered to be as pure as possible.

He looked for signs of life. At the far end of the road to the right was a high chain-link fence, beyond it the river running from the dam. A white SUV drove past, then disappeared behind another building. A security patrol, checking the perimeter. Chase grinned. They obviously hadn't expected anyone to drop in from above.

He turned and slid down the ladder, then brought up his gun again. Still no sign of anyone. He raced across the road to the corner of the industrial building and darted into a long alley.

Chase knew the factory's general layout from a printout of an aerial photo Mitzi had taken from the Internet. He reached the end of the alley. There should be another, larger complex of buildings ahead . . .

He was right; there were more of the anonymous structures across another road. And something else – a black Mercedes S600 parked in front of one of the buildings, a bored-looking chauffeur at the wheel.

'Good to see you again, *Dick*,' Chase whispered. He looked back at the building. Unlike the one he was flanking, this had windows on its upper floor, only one of them illuminated. There was a set of large glass doors close to the Mercedes, but there was also a security guard visible in a reception area beyond *and* a video camera staring down at the doors. That entrance was not an option, then.

But there was a ladder running up the side of the building, away from any cameras . . .

He checked the road again, then sprinted across it to the ladder, pausing briefly to check that there was still no activity behind him before starting a rapid ascent.

The roof was a metal forest of air conditioning ducts and rumbling filtration units. There were no skylights or other possible access points that he could see, so instead he went to the front of the building and, lying flat, looked down over the edge. A darkened window was directly beneath him.

Chase inched forward until his waist was level with the edge of the building, then carefully leaned down and peered through the window. The glare from the streetlights was enough to let him see that it was an office, screensavers drifting on idle computers.

The nearest lit window was several rooms away. Hopefully nobody would hear him . . .

He pressed one hand flat against the glass. Then with the other he sharply rapped the butt of his gun against the window to punch a jagged hole by the side of the frame. The glass beneath his palm shuddered and cracked, but he had absorbed most of the vibration, preventing the whole pane from shattering and dropping noisily to the ground.

He carefully reached through the hole and fumbled with the handle. The window swung open. Chase extracted his hand, then quickly lowered himself through the gap. Feet thumping on to the floor, he shut the window and drew his gun again.

Still nothing. He was clear – for now.

A glance out of the window to make sure Yuen's Mercedes was still outside, then he moved to the office door and opened it a crack. The corridor outside was lit by cold compact-fluorescent lights. Nobody was in sight.

He advanced quickly along the corridor, gun in hand. At the end, a flight of stairs led downwards, and opposite it were doors to male and female lavatories.

He looked down the stairs. At the bottom, a corridor led away to one side, presumably to the lobby. There was another door directly opposite the foot of the stairs, but Chase instantly saw that it had an electronic lock. A card reader. If he wanted to get on to the factory floor, he would need somebody's ID.

'Bollocks,' he muttered.

He opened the door next to the stairs and entered an office. The overhead lights were off – but there was still plenty of illumination. One whole wall was glass, overlooking the building's interior.

Chase crouched and moved closer to the window, using a chair as cover as he looked out over a huge space. Rows of brilliant lights in the ceiling lit every corner with an intense, even whiteness. A central aisle led from one end of the enormous room to the other, but to each side of it were dozens of rectangular chambers, their walls and ceilings all glass.

Clean rooms. Each unit had an airlock at one end, and pipes leading up to the filters on the roof. Inside, newly manufactured silicon wafers – each containing dozens or even hundreds of chips – were being carefully examined and tested for flaws.

Tested by humans, not machines. To Chase's dismay, the night shift at the plant was busy; he could see at least two dozen people, all covered head to toe in white 'bunny suits', their faces hidden behind filter masks, working within the clean rooms. So much for sneaking through the building . . .

The thought was instantly dismissed from his mind as he saw someone else. *Yuen.*

He was in another glass-walled room on the first floor at the far end of the factory, some kind of executive conference chamber to judge from the large circular table and black leather high-backed chairs. He appeared to be engaged in a discussion with two other men, one suited and the other in a white lab coat. There were two more men in black suits on the far side of the table, apparently not involved in the conversation – Yuen's bodyguards, he guessed – and seated between them—

His heart pounded.

Sophia!

He backed away from the window. He was sure he could handle the two bodyguards flanking Sophia, and he doubted either of the other men with Yuen would pose a threat, especially with a gun waved in their faces. As for Yuen himself, he was going to get a proper kicking, whether he offered any resistance or not.

But he had to get to them first . . .

His attention was caught by a technician walking along the factory floor towards the stairs. He was wearing a bunny suit, but had pulled down the hood and was in the process of taking off his mask. As Chase watched, he fiddled with a card attached to a reel on his suit by a thin wire.

Chase moved back across the dimly lit room and out into the corridor. He heard a chime come from the bottom of the stairs, followed by a buzz as the electronic lock was released. As he ducked into the gents, he heard the man coming up the stairs.

The technician opened the door and entered, yawning – then stopped in confusion as he saw the unfamiliar figure waiting for him.

'Ay up,' said Chase with a disarming smile. 'Come to read the meter.' He pointed off to one side. The technician instinctively glanced in that direction—

And took Chase's mighty fist square in his face. He made an almost comical little squeak, then slumped backwards, eyes rolled up into his head. Chase caught him before he hit the floor.

'Sorry about that.' He unzipped the white suit. 'Now, don't get the wrong idea . . .'

Three minutes later, Chase – wearing the technician's bunny suit, his face almost totally obscured by the mask and hood – stepped on to the factory floor. The keycard snapped back to the reel as he released it.

There was nowhere to hide his gun in the suit, so he'd been forced to holster it under his jacket. It would take a few seconds to tear down the zip and draw it. He just hoped he wouldn't need the weapon in a hurry.

He made his way through the huge room, trying to look purposeful without appearing too urgent. None of the technicians seemed to be paying any attention to him, just another figure in white. A casual glance up at the conference room to check on his target—

Shit!

The room was now dark, a cold glow from the far side revealing that it had windows on two walls, looking out across another section of the factory. Yuen had gone – and so had Sophia.

He increased his pace, no longer concerned about fitting in. He needed to catch Yuen and his companions when they were alone, away from any workers who might raise the alarm—

The door at the far end of the central aisle opened. Yuen stepped through, marching straight towards him.

Chase made a sharp turn to stand at the airlock of the nearest clean room. Yuen was accompanied by the suited, goatee-bearded man he'd been talking to in the conference room and a uniformed security guard. An *armed* security guard, a holstered pistol at his side. Of the man in the lab coat, the two bodyguards and Sophia there was no sign.

Yuen was approaching fast, eyes sweeping from side to side as he surveyed his domain. He glanced at Chase – and his gaze locked on to him.

Chase tensed, lifting a hand towards his suit's zip . . .

But there was no shock of recognition in Yuen's face, no barked orders to the guard. Chase realised why he had drawn his attention – Yuen was wondering why one of his employees was standing around rather than working.

Chase ran the card through the reader beside the airlock door, not even knowing if the man from whom he'd stolen it had access to this particular chamber. Green light. The door buzzed. Chase gratefully pulled it open and stepped inside, pretending to fumble with his card as Yuen walked past—

'*You!*'

Chase looked round at the shout, audible even through the glass walls. Yuen had stopped, and was pointing an accusing finger at him. His companions stopped as well, the security guard's hand hovering over his gun.

Caught, knowing he could never draw his own gun fast enough to beat the guard, Chase did the only thing he could think of – act innocent. He pointed a gloved finger uncertainly at himself, raising his eyebrows in surprise.

'Yes, you!' Yuen repeated, looking irate. He glared at Chase for a long and uncomfortable moment, then indicated the matting on the floor. '*Wipe your feet!* Every time you track dust in there, it costs me half a million dollars in ruined silicon wafers!'

Chase offered an apologetic nod, then made a show of carefully wiping his covered feet on the mat. Yuen jerked his head in exasperation, then strode away, the two other men in tow.

Relieved, Chase watched surreptitiously until they turned from the central aisle and headed for an enclosed cabin at one side of the room, then swiped his card to leave the airlock. He resumed his course for the door at the far end of the factory. There was another card reader next to it; he slid his stolen ID through it—

Red light, and a harsh warning rasp. *Access denied.* The technician he was impersonating didn't have clearance to enter this part of the facility.

He looked back at the nearby clean rooms, suddenly nervous. If any of the other workers wondered why he was trying to enter a restricted area, they could raise the alarm at any moment . . .

A chime. Chase whipped round to see that the light on the card reader had turned green, the door buzzing as it unlocked. He opened it and hurried through.

Instantly suspicious. There was no way the computer controlling the lock would deny him access, then change its mind several seconds later without another swipe of the keycard. Someone had *let* him in.

He was in a hallway. Directly ahead was another security door, leading into the next section of the factory. Corridors headed off to each side, but the stairs up to the next floor were his first priority. If he had to search for Sophia, it made sense to begin from where he'd last seen her. He pulled off the overalls and shoved the keycard into a pocket, then drew his gun.

Chase ascended the stairs, rapidly swinging the Steyr in both directions at the top in case anybody was waiting for him, then jogged to the door of the conference room.

He burst through it, gun sweeping the darkened room. Empty. To his left was the window overlooking the huge chip fabrication room he'd just exited. Knowing Sophia wasn't there, he instead went to the window on his right and looked at the industrial facility that lay below.

It wasn't making microchips.

Chase recognised several barrels as being the same kind that he'd seen in the mine in Botswana. Barrels filled with uranium ore.

They were lined up on a conveyor belt that led into a very large and solid-looking machine. Some kind of furnace; even though it was fully enclosed, the air above it shimmered with heat haze, banks of air conditioners on the ceiling providing cooling. A heavy pipe led off to one side into a thick steel container, seemingly for waste; other pipes went into a second furnace. Although it was smaller than the first, the fact that it was practically buried inside cooling equipment suggested it was far hotter.

From there, more pipes – thick, carrying high-pressure gas – passed into several condenser chambers, light rapidly pulsing through little inspection portholes of six-inch-thick leaded glass. Laser light, the blue flashes pure and unvarying. At the front of each chamber was another steel compartment, where the end result of the process was collected.

Chase knew what the process was; what it made. He'd been briefed on it by the SAS as preparation for a secret mission in Iran, partly so that if he encountered it he could identify it . . . but mostly so that he could sabotage it.

It was an AVLIS system – Atomic Vapour Laser Isotope Separation – and it had only one purpose: to take uranium ore, vaporise it, and pass the resulting superheated gas through a powerful laser beam of a very specific wavelength. The science had been way over Chase's head – he was a soldier, not an atomic physicist – but he knew what the laser separated out inside the collection chambers. *Enriched* uranium, weapons grade, produced faster, more safely and with greater purity than in traditional gas centrifuge systems.

And as Chase surveyed the rest of the factory, he saw the uranium's destination.

An assembly line had been set up, a row of at least twenty gleaming stainless steel cases in progressive stages of completion spaced out along it.

Bomb cases.

'Buggeration and fuckery . . .' he whispered. What he saw below was advanced technology, beyond the capabilities of most nations seeking to join the nuclear club.

But Yuen had it – his own *personal* nuclear bomb factory, built in secret with the billions of dollars his high-tech companies had brought him.

Everything had changed. This was no longer just a rescue mission, and Yuen's dealings were now more than selling uranium on the black market. He was building – *had built*, Chase realised, as he saw the completed last bomb on the line – nuclear weapons. Whatever Yuen's intentions, the factory had to be shut down. *Now.*

He looked over the plant again, looking for weak spots. According to his SAS briefing, the lasers were the key, the most complex and expensive part of the entire process. If they were destroyed, or even damaged, the whole system would be rendered utterly useless.

And he knew that if there was one thing he was good at, it was damaging and destroying things.

There were five condenser chambers, though at the moment only four were active. Two men, wearing not the white bunny suits found in the innocuous chip fabrication plant but yellow hazard suits with full face masks, were working on the fifth, a panel open and what Chase guessed was the laser partially removed. That meant he could take care of one of the lasers just by knocking it on the floor, but the others would present more of a problem.

The lights in the conference room suddenly flicked on.

Chase whirled, gun flashing up at the door as it opened—

Sophia!

She stood in the doorway, terrified. Behind her was Yuen, pressing a gun against her head. Behind *him* were two uniformed security guards and the two black-suited bodyguards, all with their guns raised.

Pointing at Chase.

'I *told* you to wipe your feet.' Smirking, Yuen advanced into the room, shoving Sophia before him. His men followed, spreading out two to each side. 'Now, drop your gun or your ex-wife becomes your *really* ex-wife.'

'You won't hurt her, *Dick*,' growled Chase, concentrating more on the other men than on Yuen. While the billionaire was gloating, he was distracted – but his guards were silent and completely focused, weapons unwavering. 'Not after the trouble you went through to get her back.'

'Oh, you mean the way you dropped my dear trophy wife right back into my lap, without my even having to lift a finger?' Yuen laughed, and ground the gun against the side of Sophia's face. She whimpered. 'Do it,' he snapped, voice hardening. 'Or she dies. I can get another wife. But you won't get another warning.'

Left with no choice, Chase held up his hands and dropped the gun. The guards immediately rushed forward, grabbing his arms and searching him.

Yuen stepped out from behind Sophia. He lowered his gun . . .

And handed it to his wife.

Sickening disbelief rose in Chase's stomach as Sophia flicked her hair and gave him a smile of fake apology. 'Sorry, Eddie,' she said. 'But you never were terribly bright, were you?'

18

'What the fuck is *this*, Sophia?' Chase demanded as the guards tossed his belongings on to the circular table and shoved him back against the wall, guns pressed against his chest.

'This,' said Yuen smugly, 'is what marriage is all about. Two equals working together in perfect harmony to get what they want.' He kissed Sophia on the cheek. She smiled. Chase's stomach churned at the full realisation of her betrayal – and his complete gullibility.

Yuen went to the window, opening his arms wide as if to embrace the machinery of death below. 'So, what do you think of my little toy factory? Looks good, doesn't it?'

'It'll look even better as a smoking crater,' Chase replied defiantly.

'Oh, let me guess,' said Yuen. 'You're thinking that even if something happens to you, your friend Mac knows where you went and will use his influence with MI6 to start an investigation?' His mouth curled into another smirk. 'Sorry, but he had a slight accident. His house kind of . . . blew up.'

Mac's house – *Nina*.

Chase erupted in rage, trying to tear free of the men holding him to rip out Yuen's throat with his bare hands, but the guards kept their grip and shoved him painfully back against the wall. 'You *bastard*! I'll fucking kill you!'

'No, you won't.' Yuen nodded to his men. 'Kill him and get rid of the body.'

One of the security guards moved his gun over Chase's heart—

'Aren't you even going to tell him *why* you're making the bombs?' Sophia asked in a seductive voice, running a finger up Yuen's arm. The guards paused.

Yuen looked askance at her. 'What am I, a Bond villain? Maybe after I tell him my entire plan I can put him in a tank of sharks with frickin' laser beams on their heads.'

'Oh, go on,' she purred, draping herself over him. 'Do it for me. I just want to see the look on his face. And *then* you can kill him.'

Yuen paused, taking in the scent of Sophia's perfume, then relented. 'Aw, why not?' he said, stepping forward. 'Although you're probably going to be disappointed, Chase. I don't have some insane scheme for world domination. It's just about money.'

'So being a billionaire isn't enough for you?' Chase sneered.

'There's no such thing as too much money.' Yuen looked down at the assembly line. 'I have twenty-four nuclear bombs – okay, I soon *will* have twenty-four nuclear bombs, as only the first one's fully assembled. But they'll be made available through various black-market channels to the highest bidders. I think a hundred million dollars would be a fair starting point per bomb.'

'No bulk discount?' asked Chase sarcastically.

'You know, I hadn't thought of that. Maybe I could sell them in six-packs.' Yuen gave him a mocking grin. 'But the point is, now anyone can become a nuclear power, whether they be a country, a terrorist organisation or even just a rich guy who really, really wants to keep the neighbourhood kids off his lawn. All they need is the money.' He took another step towards Chase. 'So, for the price of a couple of fighter jets, you can have a fifteen-kiloton nuclear device that's so simple and rugged any illiterate peasant can operate it, can be disassembled and carried by two guys, or even one if he puts his back into it, and has a design that's absolutely foolproof. Your own personal Hiroshima, for a very reasonable price. Pretty cool, huh?'

'That'll only get you two point four billion dollars,' Chase pointed out. 'You won't exactly knock Bill Gates off the rich list.'

Yuen smirked again. 'You're not thinking of the big picture – which is why I'm a billionaire, and you're a loser with thirty seconds left to live. Think of the paranoia when the major governments realise there are nukes running loose! They could be anywhere – they could even be in their capital cities right now! That means a massive spending boost for the military, homeland security, intelligence services . . . and all the corporations that contract for them. Like mine. It's the gift that keeps on giving.' He glanced over his shoulder at Sophia. 'Is that the look you wanted?'

The look on Chase's face was actually as blank a mask as he could manage as he tried to conceal his thoughts. This was his last chance, the only remaining moment for him to break free . . .

But he knew he couldn't succeed. Each of the four men pinning him against the wall was as strong as he was, and if even one of them pulled their trigger in the split second it would take him to move, he would be dead.

Not that it would stop him trying. He tensed his muscles, about to make a final desperate attempt to throw off his captors . . . when something occurred to him.

It was a trivial thought, a question, in the circumstances totally irrelevant. But even as it entered his mind, Chase realised that he *had* to know the answer.

'Wait,' he said, as Yuen opened his mouth to order Chase's death. 'The map Nina found – what's it got to do with the nukes? Why do you want to find the Tomb of Hercules?'

Yuen seemed genuinely surprised. 'The Tomb of Hercules? I don't give a rat's ass about it – the only reason I pretended to was because Sophia asked me.'

'That's quite enough of that, dear,' said Sophia from behind him—

A bullet exploded from a messy exit wound in his chest as Sophia shot him. Yuen's mouth opened in a silent scream, then he collapsed to the floor.

Before anyone had a chance to react, Sophia turned and shot one of the uniformed security guards in the head, blood splattering the wall behind him. The other security guard managed to bring his gun round – only for one of the bodyguards to shoot him in the stomach. He dropped to the floor, writhing in agony – and Sophia fired another shot into his back. The man instantly fell still.

For a moment, hope rose inside Chase – Sophia had just been playing along with Yuen, waiting for the right time to help him . . .

The hope was crushed as she lifted her gun again, aiming at *him*. The two bodyguards stepped away, keeping their weapons trained on his chest.

'So,' said Chase, recovering from his shock, 'I guess couples counselling didn't work out.'

'Show some tact, Eddie,' Sophia said in a clipped tone of mock offence. 'I'm recently bereaved! I need some time to grieve for my late husband.' She looked down at Yuen's corpse for half a second, then back at Chase. 'There, that should do. Thank you, boys,' she told the bodyguards, who nodded respectfully.

Chase regarded the two men warily. 'So what now? You going to kill me too?'

'Don't be absurd. I never discard something I need. If I'd wanted you dead I would have had you shot while you were still dangling from your parachute. Yes, I knew you were coming,' she added on seeing Chase's expression. 'I hid a tracking device in that awful leather jacket of yours while we were on the flight to Botswana. I knew you'd keep wearing it.'

Chase cautiously lifted his hands to search his pockets. 'Outside chest pocket, left side,' Sophia told him. 'Where you used to keep your cigarettes before you stopped smoking. You never used that pocket for anything else, so I knew you wouldn't check it.'

His fingertips touched metal and plastic, and he took a small rectangular device from the pocket before tossing it in disgust to the floor. 'The question still stands, Sophia,' he said. 'What do *you* want with the Tomb of Hercules?'

She smiled coldly. 'You'll see. But for now, I need to collect my own personal Hiroshima.'

'Why?'

'As I said, you'll see.'

Chase looked towards the window and the assembly line below. 'There's only one completed bomb.'

'I only need one.' Sophia addressed one of the bodyguards.

'Philippe, you stay here and watch Eddie until we're ready to leave. If he tries anything, shoot him in the legs, but try not to kill him. For now.' She gave Chase a little grin, which he didn't return, before turning to the larger man of the two. 'Eduardo, come with me. I need you to carry something to the plane.'

'Yes, ma'am,' said Eduardo. With a final triumphant glance back at Chase, Sophia strode from the room, the hulking bodyguard following her.

The other man, Philippe, waved his gun, directing Chase to take a seat at the circular table. 'So, *Philippe*,' he said as he reluctantly obeyed, 'on first-name terms with Sophia, are you?'

Philippe said nothing, moving round the table, out of his reach.

' 'Cause I know that she doesn't normally get too familiar with the help,' Chase went on. 'Unless . . . you're something more than that?' He noticed a very slight twitch around the bodyguard's eyes, an involuntary response to the comment. 'Or you think you're *going* to be. Is that it? You think that if you help her, you'll get to shag her?'

'Shut up,' said Philippe, annoyed.

'Yeah, I thought so. You know, she's crap in bed. Just lies there like a dead fish.'

Philippe stepped forward and struck Chase painfully on the base of the neck with the butt of his Glock-19 pistol. 'I told you to shut up! Talk again and I will shoot you!'

Chase stayed silent, rubbing his neck, but knew he'd found a potential weakness. Sophia almost certainly *had* promised the bodyguard favours, including sex, if he helped her. The question was, how could he turn this to his advantage?

A couple of minutes passed, neither man speaking. Chase slowly turned his swivel chair to get a better view over the bomb factory, and with dismay saw the other bodyguard pushing a cart bearing the completed weapon towards the far end of the chamber, Sophia strutting ahead of him. There was presumably another exit, hidden from view by the machinery. Neither wore a hazard suit, suggesting radiation levels in the room were safe for short exposures.

They passed out of sight behind the furnace. Chase frowned. He couldn't let her leave with the bomb . . .

'She'll betray you,' he said.

Philippe was unprepared for the comment. 'What?'

'Sophia. She'll betray you, same as she did to me . . . and Yuen.' He pointed at the corpse on the floor. 'Once she's got what she wants from you, she'll dump you – and if she thinks you might cause trouble, she'll *kill* you.'

'I told you to be quiet.'

Chase turned the chair, his back to the bodyguard. 'I mean, do you seriously think she'd be interested in a bloke like you? You're just a bit of rough, mate. Soon as she gets bored with you, you're gone! She's like one of those insects that bites off the poor bastard's head once they're done—'

Philippe stepped forward again. 'Shut *up!*' The gun whistled down – and Chase's hands snapped up, locking round Philippe's hand and arresting the blow millimetres above its target. The bodyguard froze, confused for the briefest moment, and Chase pulled forward with all his strength. Philippe slammed into the high back of the chair.

The bodyguard's head was above Chase's left shoulder. He smashed his right fist into Philippe's face three times, knuckles coming away bloodied. His left hand closed round the gun, trying to tear it from his opponent's grip.

Philippe's free hand clamped round Chase's face, fingers stabbing for his eyes. Chase punched him again, hearing something crunch – his nose or a tooth – then grabbed the bodyguard's forefinger before it could plunge into his eye socket and bent it back as hard as he could. Faced with the choice of releasing his grip on Chase's head or having a finger broken, Philippe chose the former, letting out an anguished screech.

Chase jumped up, trying to break the other man's elbow over his shoulder. Philippe managed to twist his arm just in time and smashed the point of his elbow hard against Chase's ear, making the Englishman roar with pain.

The chair still trapped between them, both men struggled for control of the gun, reeling away from the table in a brutal waltz. They spun faster, the room whirling around them. Chase had the disadvantage, the edge of the seat digging into the backs of his knees, restricting his ability to move and bending him into an increasingly awkward position.

Philippe's shuddering left hand moved nearer to Chase's eyes despite his grip on its forefinger, the other digits curled into claws, getting closer, *closer* . . .

Chase dropped heavily on to the seat. The sudden movement pulled Philippe off balance and over the top of the chair's back, his feet leaving the ground.

Chase kicked out, heels hitting the floor and propelling the chair backwards on its castors across the conference room. The gun slipped from the grip of both combatants, but it was too late for either of them to act upon that fact—

The chair and its occupants crashed through the window and fell into the bomb factory. Philippe was on the bottom, having just enough time to begin a horrified scream before it was abruptly cut off as he hit the floor and the combined weight of Chase and the chair crushed his ribcage flat.

The impact flung Chase from the chair. He slammed down on his side, broken glass showering all around him. A stinging pain burned across the side of his head – he'd been cut. Shaking off fragments, he got to his feet and looked round.

The two men in hazard suits stood about fifty feet away, regarding him with astonishment. Then one of them dashed to the nearest wall, hand flailing at a panel, and a warbling alarm burst from loudspeakers around the chamber. The two men ran as best they could in their bulky suits for the exit.

If the technicians got through the door and it closed before Chase reached it, without a keycard he'd be trapped in the factory with no weapon, easy prey for the security force when they arrived.

Chase broke into a sprint, chasing the yellow figures. They were at the door, one of them already swiping his keycard. He passed the exposed laser they'd been working on, running faster as the door opened and they threw themselves through it. It swung shut behind them.

Twenty feet, ten, his arm outstretched—

The lock clunked.

Chase reached the door a moment too late. 'Fuck!' He pulled the handle, but it didn't budge.

He turned to see where Sophia had gone. At the far end of the chamber was another door, identical to the one beside him. Undoubtedly with an identical clearance level.

312

He was trapped. And despite the fact that he was in a room where devastating weapons were being built, there was nothing he could use to defend himself.

Unless . . .

He ran back to the condenser chamber on which the technicians had been working. The laser, inside a steel tube about the length of his arm and ten centimetres in diameter, had been pulled out of the end of the chamber on a metal rail, heavy-duty electrical cable still connected to its side. Attached to it by a ribbon connector was some kind of calibration device, a box festooned with buttons and gauges.

But only two controls caught his attention. One was a large dial with the stylised symbol of a lightning bolt above it, the other a red button.

An electronic chime sounded.

The door burst open, security guards pouring into the room. Guns raised and ready.

They saw him—

Chase grabbed the laser and swung it round, supporting it with his right arm as his left whirled the dial to full power and stabbed at the button.

There was a blue flash and a noise like a muffled gunshot. For a moment Chase thought the laser had overloaded . . . then every single one of the guards keeled over dead, smoke billowing from neat holes in their chests. The fully powered laser beam, invisible in the filtered air of the factory, had burned straight through the line of men in a millisecond, leaving a smouldering dark spot on the far wall behind them.

'Oh, I *like* this!' Chase crowed, experiencing an incongruous moment of elation at his new toy before remembering what he had to do. He turned back round, taking aim at the protruding cabinet housing the laser of the farthest condenser chamber. Another touch of the button, and he saw the briefest flicker of intense blue light on the cabinet before the access hatch blew out with a huge bang and a cloud of smoke. Warning lights flashed red on the control panel.

One down. He lined up the laser on the next condenser and fired again, getting another satisfying explosion as the assembly blew apart. Two more shots took care of the remaining condensers.

Another chime, more distant. The door at the other end of the room had opened, and he could hear more men shouting as they ran into the factory. Chase brought the laser round to take aim, but couldn't see them from his position, blocked by the furnace.

Time to leave.

He hunted for an escape route. The broken window of the conference room was too high to reach, and there was nothing nearby he could climb on to.

But there were pipes above it, conduits for the air conditioning and filtration system . . .

He pushed the red button again, this time keeping his finger firmly on it as he swept the laser across the suspended pipes, the blue spot of the beam burning with supernova fury and slicing through the metal. The severed conduits swung down like a giant hinge and hit the floor with an echoing crash.

Chase threw down the laser to break it, and ran up the fallen pipework. Momentum alone carried him most of the way up the steep slope before he started to lose his footing, the metal buckling beneath his feet.

More shouts, a gunshot—

He flung himself through the hole in the window as if performing a high jump, clearing the lower sill by an inch. He thumped on to the carpet and rolled to a stop, then sprang up to find the Glock that Philippe had dropped. He grabbed it, then rushed round the table to retrieve his possessions. The grenade he shoved into a pocket, then he hefted his pistol.

A gun in each hand, he turned to face the door.

Charging footsteps outside—

Chase whipped back round to the window overlooking the chip fabrication plant and raised both guns, squeezed the triggers, then *ran*—

The window shattered just before he reached it and leapt out. He arced towards one of the clean rooms, about to crash down on to its glass ceiling.

He fired again, guns aimed downwards. The ceiling exploded, a razor-edged monsoon cascading into the clean room below. Chase's feet thudded bone-jarringly on to a workbench, the pain of his leg wound flaring back to life. He ignored it and threw himself into a forward roll, racks of fragile silicon wafers tumbling and crunching beneath him, and flew off the end of the bench to land on both feet.

His jacket was covered with the broken remains of glinting microprocessors. 'Chips with everything,' he muttered as he got his bearings. He had landed near one side of the huge room, the door through which he'd originally entered in the centre of the far wall. A warren of glass lay between himself and the exit.

Shouting from above – the guards had entered the conference room and realised where he had gone. And more were spilling through the entrance off to his left, with a clear line of fire up the central aisle.

But the shortest distance between two points was a straight line . . .

Both guns raised in front of him, Chase ran again, heading directly for the far exit. That the route was blocked by clean rooms didn't stop him – he kept firing, glass walls bursting apart in his path as terrified technicians dived for cover. He sprinted through the transparent maze as it parted in his path, shimmering fragments spraying around his pumping legs like breaking waves.

Philippe's gun clicked empty. Without a moment of hesitation Chase dropped it, still firing with his own automatic at the last clean room. One bullet took out both walls – he ran faster through the debris, free hand pulling out the keycard as he charged for the door.

Guards were running after him. He fired a single shot into the throng, as much to force them to seek cover as to kill. They scattered.

Swipe—

Green light. Chime. *Go!*

He ran through and immediately turned down the corridor leading to the lobby. A security guard stood in his path, but Chase blew him away with a single shot before the man even had time to take aim.

Into the lobby, an anonymous corporate space with murals of microcircuitry on the walls. No more guards. Chase turned again, running for the double doors. Yuen's Mercedes was still parked outside, the driver now standing outside the car, waiting anxiously for his boss.

Chase didn't waste the second it would have taken to open the doors. Instead he simply fired a shot both to shatter the glass and to warn the driver to get the hell out of his way, and vaulted through the empty frame to land by the car's open door. The driver had taken the hint, already making good time towards Bern.

He jumped into the Mercedes, finding the engine running; the driver had been prepared to get his employer to safety as quickly as possible. But Chase didn't intend to head for safety as he floored the accelerator, the car fishtailing away from the microchip factory in a trail of smoking rubber.

He had to stop Sophia from getting away with the nuke. No matter what.

19

Chase knew where Sophia was heading. To get the bomb to her plane, she would have to take the cable car up to the top of the dam.

The lower cable-car station was at the facility's northwestern corner. He made a screeching turn on to the road running parallel to the river and powered towards it. The station was easily distinguishable from the industrial units, a tower with a high sloping roof.

A white van was parked in front of it. Its rear doors gaped open, the interior empty. The nuke had already been transferred.

Chase's gaze flicked to the cable stretching away to the upper station. There were no cars moving along it. Sophia hadn't set off yet. There was still a chance to stop her.

Headlights flashed behind him, an SUV skidding round a corner in pursuit. A few hundred yards back, but it wouldn't take long to catch up once Chase stopped the Mercedes.

And now movement ahead – the second bodyguard, Eduardo, appeared in the station's entrance.

Chase ducked as a shot smacked into the windscreen, spiderweb cracks instantly obscuring his view. The bullet zipped past him and hit the back seat with a whump of tearing leather.

A second bullet blasted the rear-view mirror from its stalk with a tinkle of broken glass. Seven years' bad luck, thought Chase, but one of them would run out of luck in considerably less time, well under seven *seconds*—

He swerved the Mercedes, charging at the ramp up to the entrance.

Eduardo fired two more shots, one gouging a hole in the bonnet, the other shattering the windscreen.

A freezing gale hit Chase. He braced himself.

Engine screaming, the Mercedes ploughed up the ramp. Eduardo was trapped in the doorway, nowhere to go—

The car rammed into him, folding him over the bonnet as the Mercedes hit the doors and crashed into the interior of the cable-car station.

Chase stamped on the brake, but the car was already swerving uncontrollably towards a wall—

It hit at an angle, the left front wing crushed to scrap in an instant. Eduardo flew from the bonnet and bounced off the wall in a spray of blood.

The airbags all inflated simultaneously with rifle-shot bangs of expanding gas. Chase felt as though he'd been punched in the face by the Michelin Man. Even over the crunch of the collision, he heard cartilage crackle inside his nose.

The car spun to a standstill. The airbag deflated and Chase sat up. His nose throbbed. It wasn't a break – he knew *that* painful sensation all too well – but it felt like a hairline split that would be sore for some time.

But if he didn't get out of the car fast, an aching nose would be the least of his worries. The pursuing guards would be here in thirty seconds, less . . .

He snatched up his gun and scrambled from the wrecked Mercedes. The white-painted interior of the cable-car station was bland and functional, the only colour a literal splash of red where Eduardo's body had been flung against the wall. No sign of Sophia – or the bomb – but a flight of stairs led upwards.

Chase ran up them, emerging in a large and chilly open-ended room – the terminus for the cable cars. It was technically a 'gondola lift' rather than a traditional cable-car system, the gondolas able to detach from the line so passengers could board and disembark while other cars on the cable kept moving. Two boxy enclosed gondolas sat stationary, waiting to re-join the line.

A third was in motion.

Sophia stood at its rear window. She smiled at Chase, waving as the gondola swept from the brightly lit terminus and out into the moonlit night.

Chase whipped up his gun, aiming it at her head. She didn't move.

And neither did he. He couldn't pull the trigger. Whatever she'd done, whatever she was planning to do, she had still once been his lover, his *wife*—

'Shit!' Chase snarled, angry as much at himself as at her. The gondola ascended, Sophia now just a silhouette in the window. The moving cable sang over the rumble of the machinery driving it.

The SUV squealed to a stop outside. Chase jumped into the first of the waiting cars and found a control panel by the front window. A large red button was marked 'Starten'.

He hit it.

Chains and gears rattled. The gondola lurched along its track round the huge horizontal wheel at the end of the cable, then jolted as it slipped back on to the line. Ratchets clunked above him, and the gondola locked on to the steel cable to begin its ascent.

Sophia's car was about a hundred feet ahead. They would reach the top station at most twenty seconds apart – meaning Sophia would barely have time to get clear of the gondola before he arrived, never mind transfer the bomb to another vehicle.

She looked back at Chase. He gave her a wave that was considerably less cheery than the one she'd given him. Sophia cocked her head in a once familiar expression of annoyance. Then she raised a hand, not waving this time but pointing at something in his gondola.

Or, he realised, *behind* it.

Chase rushed to the rear window. Another gondola had just mounted the cable. He could see three security guards aboard.

Armed guards.

And not just armed with handguns. They were carrying Steyr AUG A3 carbines – and were already opening the windows of their car, preparing to fire up the cable at him and turn his own gondola into Swiss cheese!

Chase knew from its weight alone that his own gun only had one bullet left. The grenade was a hard, cold bulge in his jacket pocket, but even if he lobbed it perfectly through the other car's open window they would still have time to cut him to pieces.

He checked the view ahead. His car was about a quarter of the way along the cable, ascending quickly. It would only take another two minutes to reach the top.

Whether he could survive for two minutes was another matter entirely . . .

The gondola had room for about twelve people, padded bench seats running round the interior. The bench beneath the rear window acted as the top cover for a compartment beneath containing rescue equipment.

Chase smashed the overhead fluorescent light with the butt of his pistol to mask himself in darkness, then seized the top of the rear seat and ripped it loose. He dropped it on its long edge against the front of the compartment and threw himself on to the floor beside it—

The rear windows blew apart as streams of bullets spat through them, the guards firing their AUGs on full auto. The rapid-fire *clank-clank-clank* of more shots puncturing the sheet-steel skin of the gondola sounded like a hailstorm.

'Jesus fucking *Christ*!' Chase yelled, arms raised to protect his face from the blizzard of glass as the other windows were smashed by the onslaught. Behind him, the contents of the emergency compartment were ripped to pieces by gunfire, the bullets smacking through the metal side of the box and the padding of the bench seat – before embedding in the sturdy wood of the bench itself.

The seat kicked with each impact, but Chase knew that the chances of an AUG bullet's passing through *five* layers of protection – the skin of the gondola, the coils of rope and chain escape ladders, the side of the emergency compartment, the seat padding and the wooden bench – were low enough to give him a hope of survival.

A slim hope – but he would take whatever he could get.

His attackers sprayed the gondola with burst after burst. Every window was already destroyed, holes erupting in the walls, the ceiling, even the floor. A lump of wood blew off the corner of the bench inches from his head. The makeshift barricade wouldn't last much longer.

A brief pause in the barrage. The guards were reloading. But that would only take a few seconds. And there wasn't much he could do in that time.

Except—

Chase jumped up and grabbed the bottom rung of the emergency ladder running along the gondola's ceiling, swinging it down. He dropped back to the floor as the firing began again. Each new hit felt like a pickaxe blow against the bench, and at any moment a bullet could rip through the wood and bury itself in his back . . .

The entire car suddenly jolted, swinging like a pendulum from the cable. Tortured metal groaned and creaked.

Chase risked opening his eyes as shrapnel sprayed through the gondola. His vision was adjusting to the darkness, the interior lit by the unearthly blue-white glow of the moon – and in the half-light he saw the perforated ceiling *flex*, crumple lines radiating out from the centre like strained kitchen foil.

The gondola was tearing loose from its support arm!

The metal was giving way, the bullet holes weakening it so much that it could no longer support its own weight—

And more holes appeared every second.

Chase looked at the emergency ladder. He hadn't intended to go into the open to jump from the car until the last possible moment

– but if he didn't do so within the next few seconds, the only direction he would go was several hundred feet straight down.

Wood splintered behind him, broken pieces hitting his legs.

Metal screeched, and the back end of the gondola dropped a few inches. There was a rip in the ceiling, a gash torn across it behind the base of the suspension arm.

It was going to fall—

The firing stopped.

Reloading—

Chase hared up the ladder and flung open the top hatch. He jumped on to the roof, throwing himself against the bulky steel suspension arm.

With an almost human scream, the metal roof tore apart. The pockmarked gondola dropped away, tumbling towards the valley floor far below and smashing on to the rocks with a bang that echoed off the towering face of the dam.

The suspension arm swung madly, the entire cable whipping with the sudden loss of weight. Chase clung desperately to the cold metal, fighting for a foothold on the mangled remains of the roof. He saw the gondola behind juddering as well, one of the gunmen falling to the floor.

He strained to look over his shoulder at the car ahead. Maybe Sophia had been pitched out of a window as her gondola shook. No such luck. Bracing herself on a handrail, she glared back at him, having seen that he'd escaped the falling cabin.

The shuddering eased, though the suspension arm was still swinging. Chase tried to get a better handhold, but there was nothing.

He looked round again, not at Sophia but at the top station beyond her. Over two-thirds of the way there now—

Gunfire!

Bullets from the lower car flew past him with *fwips* of seared air, hammer-clangs striking against the suspension arm.

The metal Chase was pressed against was a foot wide at most. He was somewhat broader. He twisted, turning sideways to shield as much of his body as possible.

But his hands and upper arms were still exposed, reaching round the sides. If a bullet even clipped him, he would lose his grip and fall to his death.

Sophia's car was approaching the upper station. What was left of Chase's would reach it in thirty seconds—

A bullet struck the suspension arm just above his left hand, shockwaves buzzing through the metal. His fingers slipped on the grimy surface. He clawed for grip, feeling his other hand sliding, the remains of the roof beneath his feet bending under his weight . . .

His fingertips caught protruding metal: a bolt.

Arms burning, he pulled himself up by a couple of inches, just enough to stop the roof from giving way.

Another flurry of shots spanged against the suspension arm.

Sophia was nearly at the station, its lights washing over her gondola. Chase could see the building clearly now, another open-ended concrete structure, perched almost on the edge of the cliff.

Almost.

There was a steep rocky ledge, just a few feet across, between the thick foundation of the terminus and the sheer drop away to the valley floor.

Something hard nudged his side, caught between his body and the suspension arm.

The grenade . . .

The cable vibrated as Sophia's car detached.

More gunfire. Shots cracked against the cliff face.

Ten seconds, less.

The guards kept firing.

With a yell, Chase let go of the support with one hand, pain slicing through the fingertips of the other as they took his entire weight. The metal beneath his feet buckled. Flailing, he managed to reach into his jacket and pull out the grenade.

The cliff was just feet away.

Chase pulled himself up, teeth clamping round the ring attached to the grenade's pin to tug it out. The curved metal spoon sprang away and disappeared into the darkness below.

Four second fuse—

'Going down!'

He thrust the grenade upwards, jamming it into the runner hooking the gondola on to the cable. Then he threw himself on to the rocky ledge.

Loose pebbles skittered and slithered beneath him. He scrabbled for grip as if swimming up a waterfall of stones—

The suspension arm passed overhead into the station.

The guards took aim—

The grenade exploded.

The blast severed the main cable. The suspension arm dropped, smashing on to the station's concrete floor before being yanked backwards with tremendous force. It shot over Chase's head like a giant anchor as the full weight of the line and the third gondola snatched it into the valley.

The terrified screams of the security guards faded to nothing as they plunged hundreds of feet to splatter on the rocks far below.

Chase was still sliding down the scree, grasping for anything that might stop him from following them. His legs went over the lip of the cliff, his waist . . .

One hand locked round a rock.

Chase brought up his other hand. The rock held firm. He pulled himself back up, managing to get a foothold. Another few seconds, and he was on the ledge proper, feeling his whole body shivering with the adrenalin aftershock.

But he couldn't stop. Not yet. He still had to reach Sophia.

He clambered up the ledge to the foot of the building, spotting metal rungs set into the concrete nearby. He began a rapid ascent, pausing just below the final rung to draw his gun. Ready . . .

Go!

He whipped up and swept his gun across the station, locking on to a target.

'Don't move!' he shouted.

Sophia was kneeling near the back of the room, frozen by his command. She had realised what Chase had done with the grenade just in time to throw herself into cover behind one of the stationary gondolas, and was only now recovering from the ear-splitting shock of an explosion in a confined concrete space.

'Eddie,' she said, scowling as he climbed up and walked towards her, the gun never wavering. 'I suppose I shouldn't be surprised. You never could take a hint that you weren't wanted.'

'Where's the bomb, Sophia?' Chase demanded.

'Still in the cable car.' She smiled thinly. 'It's a little heavy for me to carry. Would you mind getting it out for me?'

'Shut up!' She was taken aback by his shout, her defiant expression faltering as she saw that he was deadly serious. Still keeping his gun locked on to her, Chase walked to the gondola and peered inside. The bomb rested in the centre of the floor.

It was his first opportunity to take a proper look at the device. A truncated cone of shining steel acted as a base, three metal rails rising from a hole in its centre to a squat, overhanging cylindrical cap of the same polished metal. A slot in the base looked as though it would house the arming system, but it was currently empty. Standing close to three feet tall, the bomb appeared to weigh at least a hundred pounds – but with its uranium core, it would be considerably more than that.

The design was unusual, but Chase knew enough about the basics of nuclear weapons to recognise the type. It was a 'gun' device, the simplest and crudest kind of nuke – but also the easiest to build, transport and maintain. Other types of nuclear devices were precision instruments, engineered to minuscule tolerances and requiring every part to function perfectly in a sequence of events measured in microseconds to achieve a proper detonation.

Gun bombs, on the other hand, were blunt instruments needing little more than raw force to work. Take two pieces of enriched uranium-235 of a certain combined total mass. Smash them together, hard. Critical mass is reached, and a nuclear explosion results. The type's name came from the first example of the kind, the bomb dropped on Hiroshima; it literally was a length of gun barrel, a uranium slug fired from one end into a larger piece at the other.

Yuen's bomb was smaller and more refined, but the principle was exactly the same. Chase guessed that the slug was in the base

328

– an explosive charge beneath it would fire it up the guide rails like a bullet and into the uranium target inside the steel cap. Simple, crude . . . but effective.

And deadly. If Yuen's boast had been accurate, the bomb had a fifteen-kiloton yield – slightly more powerful than Hiroshima, and enough to level the heart of any city and cause a firestorm that would raze buildings for miles around, to say nothing of the radioactive fallout that would be produced.

He looked back at Sophia. 'What do you want with a nuke, Sophia?'

She narrowed her eyes. 'My dry-cleaner ruined my Prada skirt, so I wanted to show my disapproval.'

He strode over to her, snapping the gun up almost against her forehead. 'Tell me!'

'You won't hurt me,' she said quietly. Chase just stared at her stonily. The gun didn't waver by so much as a millimetre, rock steady. Uncertainty crept into her eyes. 'Eddie . . .'

'This is over, Sophia,' Chase told her. 'Give me your phone. I'm going to contact the authorities, then—'

The gun was smashed out of his grip and spun away across the room. A moment later, the sound of a supersonic rifle shot reached him from outside the open end of the station.

Clutching his hand, Chase looked for the shooter. No sign of anyone, just the dam stretching away across the valley. He threw himself into a roll to make himself a more difficult target, diving for his fallen gun.

Even before he reached it, he saw that it was a pointless move. A hole had been blown straight through the Steyr just above the trigger, severing the linkage to the hammer and rendering the

THE TOMB OF HERCULES

weapon completely useless. Whoever had shot the gun from his hand was either unbelievably lucky – or an almost supernaturally skilled sniper.

Chase changed tactics. He had no weapons – and there was only one thing in the station that could protect him from a high-velocity rifle bullet.

He leapt back the way he had come – and landed behind the kneeling Sophia. Right hand going numb from the shock of impact, he clamped his left round her throat. 'Get up!' he snarled, pulling her to her feet.

'Eddie!' she shrieked, genuine fear in her voice.

'Whoever's out there, tell him to stand down!' Chase ordered, dragging her round to act as a human shield. 'I know he can see you – tell him!'

'If you hurt me, he'll kill you!'

'If he doesn't stand down, *I'll* kill *you!*'

Neither of them moved, statue still for an eternal two seconds. Then: 'You won't,' said Sophia, voice choked but recovering her former arrogance. 'You couldn't. I know you too well—'

Chase squeezed her throat tighter, cutting her off. 'You killed Mac. You killed *Nina*. Give me one good reason why I should let you live.'

'Didn't – kill – Nina,' she rasped.

'What?' He eased his grip, very slightly.

'She's not dead. Yet.'

His hand tightened again. 'Nor are you. *Yet.*'

'Phone,' Sophia managed to whisper, reaching into a pocket. 'Show – you . . .'

Chase's right hand still had enough sensation left in it for him to tell that she was indeed taking out a phone rather than a knife or a gun. He eased the pressure on her throat a little. 'Go on.'

She held up the phone and thumbed the touchscreen, which lit up. Another couple of pushes, and she entered the photo album. There was only one stored image.

Even from the little thumbnail of the picture Chase knew who it was, but that didn't stop a horrible chill of fear hitting him when Sophia zoomed it to fill the screen.

Nina.

Face grazed, mouth stuffed with a gag, eyes wide in fear. She was lying on her back, red hair strewn out across the floor like a splatter of blood.

'If anything happens to me,' Sophia hissed, 'she dies. Don't imagine for a moment that I won't do it. I just killed my own *husband* – your parvenue ginger fuck-toy means nothing to me. Now, let go.' Chase didn't move. 'Let *go*, Eddie. You fought to the end – but this *is* the end. The fight's over. You lost.'

With a snarl of fury and anguish, Chase pulled his hand from her neck. Sophia stepped away, giving him a sour sneer of triumph as she rubbed her throat. 'Kneel down, Eddie. Hands behind your head. We don't want to give my friend out there a reason to blow off a limb or two, do we?'

Chase reluctantly got to his knees, looking across the dam – and for the first time saw the sniper. Despite himself, he couldn't help but be impressed by his enemy's shooting skills. The man, a silhouette against the pale grey of the dam, stood on a viewing platform halfway across the structure, at least four hundred yards away. Just scoring a hit on a person at that distance was an achievement in itself for most; hitting a pinpoint target on that person was the stuff of a world-class marksman.

Sophia dialled a number and raised her phone. 'I have it,' she said. 'I need someone to come and pick me up, though – there's been a spot of bother with my ex-husband.' She listened to a surprised question from the other end of the line, then smiled. 'No, the other one. Don't worry, Joe's got him covered. Just get the car here. Quick as you can, thank you.'

She disconnected, then walked to Chase, taking care not to cross the line of fire. 'This actually works out rather well,' she said. 'I wasn't sure how I was going to make that whiny little Yank tart do what I need her to do, but now that I've got you, well . . .'

'I dunno,' said Chase, forcing himself to stay calm and not rise to her bait. 'The way things were between us when I left her, she'll probably be glad to see the back of me.'

Sophia smirked. 'Nice try. But I could tell how she really felt about you – and how you felt about her. I knew you wouldn't risk anything happening to her. She'll do the same for you. Just because somebody drives you mad doesn't mean you don't care deeply for them.'

'What would you know about caring for *anybody*?' Chase demanded. The jab worked, her face hardening. She turned and walked away, leaving Chase pinned in the sniper's sights until a car pulled up outside and more of her men entered the station.

20

France

L ying on a bench, Chase looked up at the sound of approaching footsteps. The cellar he was in wasn't precisely a cell, but it was windowless, the thick door was securely locked, and he knew from the brief occasions over the past day when they had opened it to give him food and water that there were at least two of Sophia's men on guard outside.

One of the sets of footsteps belonged to Sophia. The click of her high heels, the strutting, impatient pace . . . he remembered them well. So he wasn't the least bit surprised when the door opened to reveal her, with an armed man at her side. It was the sniper from the dam, a dark-skinned, muscular giant wearing a black leather waistcoat, rows of silver piercings running back over his bald head.

'Hello, Eddie,' said Sophia. Sultry, confident, back in command.

'Hi, bitch-face.'

She pouted. 'Really, Eddie. There's no need to be childish. Not when I'm about to reunite you with your beloved.'

He sat up. 'Is she all right?'

'Of course she is! I need her to do something for me, something which requires a clear head, so it would be counterproductive to hurt her. For now, anyway.' She smiled a little at the implied threat; her companion, on the other hand, treated Chase to a malevolent beaming grin, revealing a diamond set into one of his teeth. 'By the way, I don't believe I've introduced my friend. Eddie, this is Joe Komosa. My guardian angel, so to speak. And yours too.'

'I've been watching you for some time,' said Komosa, flashing his glinting smile again.

'You were the guy in Botswana,' Chase said, remembering the figure he'd briefly seen through the skylight. 'At the crusher, you shot the guards.'

'I couldn't very well let Nina die when I still needed her, could I?' explained Sophia. 'And I needed you to get her out of the mine safely. I didn't expect you to get all the way to London, though! As for parachuting into the factory . . . It's a good job I'd planted that tracker on you, or we would never have known you were coming. Still, it all worked out for the best.'

'Except for Dick,' Chase said sarcastically.

'Not all marriages have a fairytale ending. As you know. But on the bright side, he left everything to me in his will.'

'I think that you *murdering* him might sort of invalidate it.'

Sophia laughed. 'But *I* didn't kill him, Eddie! You did!'

Chase stood up sharply, prompting Komosa to raise his gun. 'What?'

'In a fit of jealous rage. It's quite romantic, actually, in a twisted way. You were so overcome with fury when you found out I'd married Richard that you chased him to two different countries in an attempt to kill him and win me back. At least, that's what the witnesses to his death will say, once I choose them. And of course, it'll be a huge embarrassment to the IHA, especially after you assassinated that Botswanan minister. Which,' she added, 'was entirely Richard's doing. I had no part in that . . . but again, it worked out for the best. After losing that rig at Atlantis as well, I wouldn't be surprised if the UN decides to cut its losses and disband the entire agency.'

'Leaving you free to look for the Tomb of Hercules without anyone knowing, I suppose.'

Sophia raised a patronising eyebrow. 'Well done, Eddie. I honestly wasn't sure if you'd figure it out.'

'I've had all day to think about it.'

'Yes, I'm sorry about that. The owner of this château – well, co-owner now, I suppose,' she gave him a sly smile, 'couldn't get here immediately, and then we had something to take care of during the day. But now you have our undivided attention.' She stepped back through the door, Komosa gesturing with his gun for Chase to follow. He saw for the first time that the hulking man was bare-chested beneath his waistcoat, more lines of piercings running down his chest into the waistband of his leather jeans, a huge silver ring through each of his nipples. 'Come along.'

'Do they go all the way down, Sophia?' Chase asked, pointing a thumb at the glinting studs.

'Why are you asking me?'

'I just get the feeling you know from personal experience.'

Sophia merely smirked suggestively and walked away. Komosa

raised his gun towards Chase's face as he passed. 'Show her ladyship the respect she deserves, hey?'

'I *was* doing,' Chase said, grinning coldly.

Komosa smacked him on the side of his skull with the butt of his pistol. Chase staggered, clutching his head. 'Now, boys,' Sophia called back to them, 'let's not have any unpleasantness on this special day, shall we?'

Chase glared at Komosa, jabbing a finger at the ring piercing his left nipple. 'When you least expect it, mate, I'm going to rip that thing right off and pull your fucking heart out with it.' The Nigerian just gave him a sarcastic smile and followed him out of the room. 'And what do you mean, "special day"?'

Sophia didn't reply, leading the way up a flight of stairs to a large and ornate hall. More men lurked at the sides of the room, hands resting on their holstered guns, but Chase lost all interest in them when he saw—

'Eddie!' cried Nina, wearing jeans and a khaki shirt, from the opposite end of the hall. She tried to run to him, but the guards flanking her pulled her back.

Relief flooded through Chase. 'Oh my God, you're all right, you're okay!' The image of Nina from Sophia's phone, her frozen face of fear, had haunted him the entire time since leaving Switzerland.

'Well, now that we've got the reunion out of the way,' said Sophia, hands on her hips, 'we can get down to business. Nina, Eddie's alive and well; Eddie, Nina's alive and well. If you want that situation to be maintained, you'll do as I say.'

'Find the Tomb of Hercules for you, you mean,' said Nina, shooting Sophia a look of utter hatred.

'What do you *want* with it?' asked Chase. 'You've already got Yuen's money *and* a nuclear bomb – what else is there in the Tomb that you could want?'

'A nuclear *what*?' Nina yelped.

'Actually,' said a new voice from above, 'it's what *I* want.'

Nina and Chase looked up. Curving staircases swept upwards on each side of the hall to a balcony above. Standing imperiously at its centre was . . .

'Well, well,' said Nina coldly. 'René Corvus.'

The billionaire descended the stairs. 'Everything that has happened has been according to my design,' he said, moving to join Sophia. 'The sinking of the SBX rig, your discovery of the uranium mine, even Sophia's marriage to Yuen. All part of my plan.'

Chase was shocked. 'Wait, *you* sank the SBX?'

'I built it,' said Corvus, 'or rather, one of my companies did. It seemed only fitting that I should destroy it.'

Sophia nodded at Komosa. 'Actually, Joe did the hands-on work.' Komosa smiled his diamond smile.

'There were over seventy people on that rig!' Nina shouted.

'Regrettable, but necessary,' said Corvus. 'As a non-executive director of the IHA I knew you were using the *Hermocrates* text to find the Tomb of Hercules, but I had no access to the IHA's classified servers. Using the rig's direct satellite link allowed my people to get that access – and the sinking of the rig then removed all evidence of the intrusion.'

'Then you set Yuen up to make it look like he was responsible,' Chase said. 'And set *me* up to make it look like I killed him.'

'He'd served his purpose,' Sophia remarked, as casually as if she'd killed a fly. 'Now all of his businesses belong to me.'

'Which means they also belong to me,' Corvus said, smiling.

Nina frowned. 'What?'

Sophia held up her left hand. For a moment, Nina thought she was flipping her the bird – until she realised that Sophia was holding up her ring finger.

Which had a new and very large diamond ring on it.

'Well?' said Sophia. 'Aren't you going to congratulate the new bride?'

'You fucking *married* him?' Chase spluttered.

'About an hour ago,' Sophia told him. 'A little civil ceremony, nothing gaudy.'

Corvus slipped an arm round Sophia's waist. 'A perfect union, a merger of both personal and business interests. Yuen's companies will now become part of the Corvus empire. And Sophia,' he beamed at her, 'will at last be with me. I've waited a long time for this day. You have no idea how hard I found it to see her married to another man, even if it was necessary.' He paused. 'Well, perhaps you know, Mr Chase.'

'*Au contraire*, mate,' Chase growled, folding his arms. 'Far as I'm concerned, you can fucking have her. Word of advice, though.'

'And what would that be?'

'Don't turn your back on her. She's got a habit of screwing over her husbands.'

Corvus sniffed dismissively as Sophia wrapped her arms round him. 'Bitterness doesn't suit you, Eddie,' she said. 'Now, Nina, this is where you come in. A wedding isn't a wedding without a honeymoon. The thing is, we simply don't know where to go. I'd like you to help us find a destination.' Her voice became pointed. 'Somewhere with a lot of *history* . . .'

★

Nina carefully aligned the pieces of ancient parchment, matching up the faint brown markings, then leaned back to take in the entire image. For the first time in over two and a half thousand years, the map concealed on the pages of Plato's *Hermocrates* was complete.

She gave Chase a nervous glance. The Englishman sat in a chair in a corner of the château's library, hands cuffed behind his back, Komosa and another guard flanking him. It had been made very clear to Nina that any delay or mistake in assembling the map would result in Chase's suffering severe pain. As emphasis, Komosa had lined up various implements on a little table nearby, ranging from a cosh through pliers to an electric masonry drill.

Chase returned the look. He knew as well as Nina that once the Tomb was found, their usefulness to Corvus and Sophia would be at an end. All they could do for the moment was play along and look for any opportunity to escape . . .

'Well?' Sophia asked impatiently, striding across the room to look at the map. 'Where is it?'

'Jesus, give me a chance,' Nina complained as she opened an atlas. 'I don't have every coastline in the world memorised.'

She did, however, have a reasonably good idea of where to start looking. One of the previously missing pages featured a compass rose, so now she knew the coastline was at the southern edge of a sea. Considering the limits of exploration for the ancient Greeks, it was almost certainly the Mediterranean, placing the Tomb in North Africa.

Which made sense, she realised. According to legend, Hercules had spent much time travelling through ancient Libya – a far greater expanse than the boundaries of the modern country of that name. The Tomb could well be located at the site of some great deed from those years.

It only took a brief examination of the atlas to narrow down the list of possible locations. The coastline ran roughly southeast to northwest, but at its northern end it made a sharp turn to head almost directly northeast. Given the scale of the ancient map, just one area matched that description.

Nina's finger fell upon the coast of Tunisia, the Gulf of Gabès. 'Is that it?' Sophia demanded.

'It matches, yes,' said Nina, looking back and forth between the two maps. 'River mouths here and here, this island just off the coast to the east . . .'

Corvus stepped up to the table. 'Tunisia?'

'Maybe not,' Sophia told him, tracing the route over the parchment from the coast to the site of the Tomb. 'The scale doesn't—'

'Do you mind?' snapped Nina, academic annoyance at being second-guessed overcoming any worries about retribution. 'Let's see, this lake off to the west must be this one here on the modern map, which is about fifty miles from the coast. Even taking inaccuracies of scale into account, it's roughly a third of the way from the coast to the end of the route, so the Tomb must be about a hundred and fifty miles inland, southwest of Gabès. Which would place it in—'

'Algeria,' Chase announced from across the room. 'Know it well.'

'Oh, yes,' said Sophia with a disparaging sigh, 'stargazing in the Grand Erg, the most incredible sky you've ever seen, how many times did I hear *that* story?'

'Photograph it,' Corvus ordered one of his men, who clambered on to a stool to take pictures of the completed map from above. 'Thank you, Dr Wilde. Now that you have located the Tomb of Hercules, I believe my people will be able to take things from here.'

'Let me guess,' said Nina, eyeing him defiantly. 'You're going to fly us back to New York in your private jet?'

'Hardly.' He turned to Komosa. 'Dispose of them.'

'No.' The authority in Sophia's voice surprised even Corvus; an absolute command. 'We still need them.'

'Why, my dear?' Corvus asked slowly.

'Because, *my dear*, Dr Wilde hasn't told us everything.' She grabbed Nina's ponytail and pulled her head back. Nina gasped in pain. 'Have you, Nina?'

'Don't know what you mean,' Nina said through her teeth.

'Oh, but you do. Remember on the flight to Botswana, you told me how you thought there were more clues hidden within the text of *Hermocrates*, clues that didn't just concern the *location* of the Tomb, but also how to get *inside* it?' Sophia twisted her wrist, pulling Nina's hair still harder. 'I think you're holding back, that you're hoping that even if we find the Tomb we won't be able to gain entry – or even fall victim to booby traps.'

'Booby traps wouldn't still be working after thousands of years,' Nina growled. 'This isn't a game of *Tomb Raider*.'

Chase cleared his throat. 'Er, actually, there were some in Tibet that still worked. Sort of. They nearly killed me and Jason on the way out.' Despite her pain, Nina glared at him. 'Yeah, I know. Should have told you about that. Sorry.'

'This is why your relationship isn't working,' said Sophia to

Nina. 'Lack of communication.' She let go of her hair. 'So, enlighten us. How do we get in?'

'I don't know,' Nina told her truthfully.

Sophia nodded to Komosa, who swept down his huge fist to punch Chase in the stomach. He whooped for breath. 'How do we get in?' she asked again.

'Jesus!' said Nina, horrified. 'I don't know!'

Another nod, and Komosa took the cosh and smacked it viciously down on to Chase's neck. He let out a cry of agony as he fell from the chair, banging his head on the library's hard wooden floor.

Sophia stared down coldly at him. 'How do we get in?'

'You fucking bitch!' Nina screamed. 'I told you, I don't know! Leave him alone!'

Sophia didn't need to nod this time for Komosa to turn to the little table and pick up the masonry drill. He pumped the trigger twice, the device making a sinister robotic whine each time, then bent down and placed the tip against Chase's shoulder blade. Before Nina could say a word, he squeezed the trigger.

Chase screamed as the heavy-duty drill bit tore into his flesh. Blood sprayed out, spattering the floor. Even Corvus seemed shocked.

'Stop!' Nina wailed, begging Sophia. 'Stop, stop it! I don't know, I don't fucking *know*! But I'll find out, I'll tell you, just please *stop*!'

Sophia considered for a moment, then flicked a finger back at the little table. Looking disappointed, Komosa returned the drill to its place, blood dripping from the tip.

Not caring if anyone tried to stop her, Nina ran to Chase. The wound in his back was about a centimetre wide, a torn hole running with blood, so much that she couldn't see how deeply the drill had penetrated. Chase shivered, face twisted with mute pain. She knelt and pressed one palm over the brimming gash, feeling hot liquid ooze between her fingers as she looked up at Sophia. 'For God's sake, help him! I'll do what you want, I'll work out how to get into the Tomb!'

'Fix him up,' ordered Sophia, accepting her surrender. Komosa pulled Nina away from Chase. She protested and struggled, but then two more men lifted up the barely conscious Chase and took him from the room.

'Glad to have you aboard,' Sophia told her with frosty triumph. 'Get to work – you have until we find the Tomb to decipher the text. Otherwise Eddie will need more than a few bandages to fix what Joe does to him.' She started across the room as if to follow the men carrying Chase, then suddenly stopped and kicked Nina hard in the side with the pointed toe of her boot. Nina doubled over in agony. 'And if you ever call me a bitch again, I'll cut out your fucking tongue.' With that, she turned on her high heels and left the library.

'Get up, Dr Wilde,' ordered Corvus. 'You have work to do. I shall arrange for an expedition to Algeria as soon as possible.' He too left the library, pausing at the door. 'By the way, go and wash. I don't want you to ruin the parchments.'

With that he exited, leaving Nina to stare at the blood on her hands.

21

Algeria

The three helicopters thundered over the desert, nothing in sight below but mile after mile of gnarled, shimmering sand dunes. In the shade, the temperature would have been around eighty-five degrees Fahrenheit . . . but there *was* no shade, the merciless glare of the sun baking everything with an extra twenty degrees of sickening heat.

The cabin of the lead helicopter, a large Sikorsky S-92 transporter, was air conditioned, but neither Nina nor Chase took any comfort from the fact. It had been two days since they were reunited, but in that time Nina had come no nearer to uncovering the final secrets hidden within the *Hermocrates* text.

And her time was rapidly running out.

'Ten minutes,' announced Sophia. She and Komosa were in the rear section of the cabin with Chase and Nina, Corvus riding in the co-pilot's seat up front. 'I hope you have a brainwave soon, Nina.'

'These aren't exactly ideal conditions,' Nina complained. Her hands were cuffed, in front of her so she could still work with the parchments. Chase's hands were locked behind his back. The wound to his shoulder had been treated and bandaged, but he was still in considerable pain. For no apparent reason other than her own sadistic amusement, Sophia had given him back his leather jacket – which because of the handcuffs he could now not take off, sweating even under the cooling breeze from the air-con.

The same breeze ruffled the pages Nina was holding, to her irritation. But the distraction was a minor one, her mind focused as fully as it could be on her task.

She was more convinced than ever that there was a clue within Plato's words, a cryptic linguistic key that would unlock the puzzle. With each new reading of the ancient Greek text, that key seemed to come a tantalising step closer.

But not close enough for her to turn it. She frowned.

'No joy?' asked Chase. Compared to his usual self, he had been distinctly muted since his injury.

She shook her head. 'All I can think of is that there's some kind of cipher code which is used to find the relevant words describing how to get into the Tomb – like if word three, line six, page one is "turn", word seven of line twelve is "key", and so on. I mean, it flat-out says that there are words hidden amongst other words! But I can't find anything that could be the cipher itself. There needs to be a starting point, a way to know where to begin and how to proceed, otherwise it would be impossible even for the intended recipient to work it out. Only . . . there isn't one.'

'There's nothing else on the paper?' Chase asked. 'Hidden messages or anything?'

'What you see is what you get,' said Sophia. 'Something as simple as invisible ink was the equivalent of quantum encryption in Plato's time, so there's nothing else to uncover. The clues must be in the words themselves.' She checked her watch. 'Which you now have six minutes to find.'

Nina turned her attention back to the parchments, scanning through the text as quickly as she could. Words hidden within words . . . but which words? She read faster, the ancient, mottled ink almost becoming a blur as her eyes sped over each page.

But she knew she would find nothing that she hadn't already discovered. If there was a cipher, its key was not contained within the text of *Hermocrates*. Either it was to be found in some other source not in her possession, in which case she had absolutely no chance of working it out . . . or there *was* no cipher.

'I know that face,' said Chase, for the first time in a while sounding hopeful.

Nina looked up at him. 'Hmm?'

'That's your crossword face, when you've just cracked a clue. What've you found?'

'Yes, what *have* you found?' said Sophia, taking a new interest. Corvus turned in his seat, watching Nina closely.

'I . . . I'm not sure yet. But I think I've been looking at the problem from the wrong angle. The reference to words being hidden within other words, I just assumed it was a cipher – specific individual words from the text combining to form a message.' She shuffled through the parchments to the first page. 'But what if it's not? The clue to finding the map on the back was quite literal – so maybe this is too. "The words of our friend

346

Hermocrates reveal still other words within" . . . And "erubescent glass" . . . erubescent, red glass, *coloured* glass . . .'

She looked up at the cabin roof. Above the front seats were windows in the ceiling, there to give the pilot a clear view of the rotor blades. They were tinted green to act as a sunscreen. Nina leaned forward and held out the page so the light of the sun overhead fell upon it. The entire page changed colour to a garish emerald shade, the muddy tones of the ink becoming a darker brown.

Nina practically jumped from her seat. 'I've got it, I've got it!'

'Got what?' Chase asked, confused.

'I need something *red*, red plastic or glass.' Nina looked round the cabin. 'Come on, come on!' she snapped at Sophia. 'Make yourself useful, find something!'

Sophia frowned, but did as she was asked. 'Joe, hand me my bag. The blue one.' Komosa reached behind her seat, lifted out a holdall and passed it to her. She searched through the contents. 'Here,' she said, handing Nina a binder. 'Will this do?'

'Perfect,' said Nina, snatching it from her. The binder contained pages bearing translations of *Hermocrates* from Greek to English, but she discarded them. The binder itself, with a cover of transparent red plastic, was what she wanted.

She placed the first sheet of parchment inside the binder, then held it by one of the windows, trying to get as much direct light on to it as possible. Beneath the plastic, the reddish-brown text almost vanished, its colour absorbed by the red filter to leave nothing but a faint shadow.

But something else suddenly leapt from the page in perfect clarity.

Within the ghost words of the original text, individual letters stood out, what had previously seemed like discoloured ink turning almost black . . .

'That's what the line about seeing the world through erubescent glass meant,' Nina said, awed. 'I thought the darker spots were just impurities in the ink – but they must have been added *after* the main text was written. Red glass was *incredibly* rare and valuable in Plato's time, so very few people would have been able to find the hidden text. Somebody traced over the letters with a watered-down blue ink to hide a message, words within words. It could have been octopus ink, I suppose, or maybe—'

'They could have done it in Biro for all I care,' said Sophia impatiently. 'What does it *say*?'

'Notebook, notebook.' Nina snapped her fingers. Chase couldn't help but smile slightly at Sophia's aggrieved expression as she passed Nina a notebook and pen. 'Okay, let's see . . .'

Somewhat awkwardly thanks to the handcuffs, she wrote down each highlighted letter in turn, a sentence in ancient Greek characters gradually taking form. 'Well, that's a promising start,' she said, translating it in her head. 'It says the entrance faces the dawn.'

'Land by the eastern face of the mountain,' Corvus told the pilot. 'What else?'

'I don't know, that's all I've got so far,' Nina told him testily. 'I'll need to keep working on it.'

'You'll have to do it on the move,' Sophia said. 'We're here.'

Everyone looked ahead. Before them was a small rocky hill, a darker mound against the unending pale greys and browns of the dunes.

'That's not exactly a mountain,' observed Chase, sounding let down. 'It's more like a zit. I thought Hercules would have something a bit more impressive.'

'Unlike some men, I doubt Hercules would feel any need to overcompensate,' said Sophia dryly. 'Besides, I'm sure that the contents of the Tomb itself will be rather more impressive.'

The helicopter moved into a hover at the bottom of the hill's eastern face, landing in a vortex of dust and grit. The other choppers followed it down.

'Spread out,' Corvus ordered over the radio. 'There is an entrance somewhere – find it.' Armed men in desert camouflage jumped from the helicopters to begin the hunt. He turned back to Nina. 'Dr Wilde, keep working. I want as much information as possible about the interior of the Tomb by the time the entrance is located. Once it is found, I'm afraid you will have to work on the move.'

'Why the rush?' Chase asked. 'It's not like this is a race – nobody else even knows where the thing is.'

'I doubt that you would understand, Chase,' said Corvus, voice full of scorn. 'You are a small man, with small and insignificant dreams. But when you have a dream like mine, and stand on the verge of seeing it become a reality . . . you too would not want to wait.'

'Hey, I have dreams that I want to see come true an' all,' Chase told him. 'Had one last night, in fact. You were in it. And so were you,' he added, nodding to Sophia, 'and Joe Ring-Tits there.' He smiled coldly. 'And I had a baseball bat. With nails in it.'

'Oh, *do* be quiet, Eddie,' Sophia huffed. She turned to Nina. 'This is one of the reasons why I left him. He would never shut up. I'm sure you've noticed.'

'If *everyone* would shut up, I might be able to concentrate,' said Nina, annoyed.

With the power off, the temperature in the cabin rose quickly. Nina was the only one who didn't notice, focused entirely on picking out the letters hidden amongst the text. She was on the ninth page of parchment when a call came in from one of Corvus's men over the cabin speaker.

'Sir, this is Bertillon,' he said excitedly. 'We found it, about two hundred metres to the north behind the tall rock.' Everyone looked to see a weather-worn stone pillar protruding from the hillside.

'Excellent,' said Corvus, stepping out of the cabin and donning a wide-brimmed sunhat. Komosa climbed through the rear door and held it open for Sophia, then dragged Chase from his seat and threw him on to the hot sand. Nina reluctantly followed, clutching the *Hermocrates* manuscript.

She squinted at the surrounding landscape, the glare of the sun against the ground dazzling her. Stinging sweat beaded around her eyes. Apart from the rolling dunes, which stretched to the horizon in every direction, the low hill was the only landmark to be seen.

The nearest town, Nina knew from the satellite images used at Corvus's château to pinpoint the location of the Tomb, was almost a hundred miles away. Nobody came out here without a very good reason. While it was not the hottest desert on earth, the Grand Erg was still desolate and unforgiving.

A good place to hide a great treasure . . .

Corvus's men returned to the helicopters to collect more equipment as their leader headed for the distinctive rock, the others following. Nina found herself drenched in sweat in barely a minute. She asked Sophia to let the sweltering Chase take off his

350

jacket, but as she'd expected, the request was rejected – with a degree of pleasure.

They reached the rock, and found a smaller boulder lying half buried next to it. The gap between them formed a passage some four feet wide, which led deeper into the hillside. Corvus's man, Bertillon, peered out of the shadows within as the group arrived. 'It goes back quite a way, sir. And there's something you should see. We're not the first people to come here.'

Lighting torches, they entered the tunnel mouth. 'Not very impressive,' sniffed Sophia as she shone her torch round the chamber inside.

'There's more back here, ma'am,' said Bertillon, moving deeper. An archway marked the entrance to a second chamber, the air cool and still. Nina immediately identified the architecture as ancient Athenian in design, still elegant despite the wear of millennia. They were almost certainly in the right place, then, but what else would they find?

'Oh, wow,' she gasped as she saw the awesome sight for herself.

Sophia stopped next to her, playing her torch beam over the huge object. 'All right, I admit – *that's* impressive.'

It was a statue, a stylised representation of a lion close to twelve feet high and almost as wide, blocking the end of the chamber. Its mouth was open in a silent roar, one clawed paw raised as if to strike, the other flat on the stone floor.

Beneath that paw was a body.

'Dead a long time,' Nina said, kneeling for a better look. The crushed corpse was little more than a dusty skeleton, desiccated scraps of skin clinging to it. 'A thousand years, at least. Maybe even longer.'

'What happened to him?' asked Corvus, shining his torch at the lion's mouth, which was almost eight feet off the ground. While the statue itself was stone, its teeth were tarnished bronze . . . with faint stains of blood still visible on them, more having gushed down the lion's jaw as if it had bitten somebody's arm off.

'Isn't it obvious?' said Chase, nodding at the heavy stone paw that had flattened the luckless explorer. 'Clarence here squashed him. The thing's a booby trap.'

Everyone quickly stepped back to a respectful distance from the statue, and all eyes turned to Nina. 'I think it's time you told us what else you've found in your translations,' Sophia said, resting a hand on her holstered gun.

Nina flicked back through her notebook. 'I guess this is the Nemean Lion – the first of the ten trials of Hercules.'

'Ten?' Sophia raised a dubious eyebrow. 'I thought there were twelve.'

'It depends which version of the legend you read. In the earliest tellings from ancient Greece, Hercules only had ten trials, and the order in which they took place varied according to who was telling the story. The only constants were that the first task was always slaying the Nemean Lion, the hide of which Hercules used to make his impenetrable cloak, and the second was killing the Lernaean Hydra, where he obtained the poison for his arrows. The final task was always the same as well – defeating Cerberus, the guardian of the Underworld.'

'So to get into Herc's tomb, you've got to re-enact his challenges?' asked Chase. Everyone looked at him. 'What? I'm right, aren't I, Nina?'

'He is,' Nina confirmed, nodding. 'That's what was hidden in the text of *Hermocrates* – it tells you what the challenges are, and also which direction to go through the labyrinth, which is supposed to represent the Underworld, to reach them.'

Sophia regarded her with suspicion. 'But not how to beat them?'

'It wouldn't need to. The trials of Hercules were as familiar to every ancient Greek as the stories of Cinderella or Robin Hood or . . . or *Star Wars* are to us. Any self-respecting Athenian would already know how to beat them.' Nina indicated the lion's mouth. 'Hercules defeated the Nemean Lion by reaching into its mouth and pulling out its insides. My guess would be that there's some kind of trigger in there that you have to release to open the way into the next chamber.'

Komosa tentatively clambered up on one of the lion's paws and shone a torch into its mouth. Close up, it was clear that the lower jaw was separate from the main body of the statue itself, able to hinge open and shut. 'She's right,' he said after a moment. 'There's a lever in here, looks like bronze.' He leaned back, directing the light into the gap between the two paws. 'And there's another passage down here.'

'Whoever tried to enter the Tomb obviously got past the first challenge, then,' said Nina. 'But not all of them survived.' She glanced at the crushed skeleton. 'This guy got stomped, and judging from those stains somebody else lost an arm trying to reach into the lion's mouth.'

Corvus gave her an incredulous look. 'Are you saying that the statue *moved*?'

'Yeah. You set off a trap somewhere, and the lion rolls up the passage, the mouth bites, and the paws go up and down to try to gore or crush you. In fact . . .' She backed up, running a toe over the floor of the chamber until she found a section that was slightly lower than those around it. It shifted under her touch. 'Here. See? This is loose – it's probably what sprung the trap. Step on this, and you get shut in, with the only way out being . . .'

'. . . to beat the challenge in the same way that Hercules did,' said Sophia thoughtfully. 'Assuming they haven't all been beaten, could any of the traps still be functioning?'

'I don't know. I would have said no, until Eddie told me about the one in Tibet, which would have been much older than these. If the mechanisms were made of stone and metal rather than wood and rope, then maybe . . .'

Sophia shone her torch into Nina's face. 'Well, it's a good job you're here to guide us through them. How far have you got?'

'I've reached the sixth trial, and got the directions through the labyrinth up to that point as well,' Nina said, blinking in irritation. 'I'd be able to work faster if, y'know, you took these damn things off of me.' She held up both hands, tugging the chain of the handcuffs taut between them.

Sophia considered for a moment. 'Release her,' she ordered at last.

'Are you sure?' asked Corvus.

Sophia smiled and walked over to Chase, running a hand along the shoulders of his leather jacket. 'She won't do anything stupid as long as we have him.'

Corvus nodded. 'Very well.' One of his men unlocked Nina's cuffs. She rubbed her wrists where the metal had dug grooves into her flesh. 'Now, let us proceed.'

One by one, the expedition members slipped through the narrow gap between the lion's paws.

The passages beyond were indeed a labyrinth, a tight, dusty maze. Nina had already written down the directions, however, and progression was a simple matter of following the correct choice of left or right at each junction.

The question had occurred to her of what would happen if the wrong path were taken, but she decided not to bring it up in case Sophia or Corvus decided to make Chase be the one to investigate.

They encountered other tasks along the way, more stylised statues frozen mid-attack when the release switch was found by past tomb raiders, or jammed against the end of each chamber having killed those who had tried – and failed – to pass them. With nobody to reset the traps, they were rendered harmless once triggered . . . but that didn't stop the party from negotiating each challenge with the utmost caution. Just in case.

The Lernaean Hydra: seven snake-like heads that had once shot poisoned darts taking the lives of three intruders, their skeletons twisted on the ground in the agonised contortions of death. The stone heads now lay broken on the floor, the statue decapitated. Not a literal interpretation of the myth, Nina knew, but she doubted that the Tomb's builders could make metal and stone spontaneously regenerate.

The Ceryneian Hind: one robber had been impaled on its imposing spiked iron antlers, but his companions had remembered how Hercules had hobbled the animal by shooting it in the leg. One of the statue's legs was indeed hinged to act as the escape trigger – though the robbers' tactic of pelting it with rocks until one scored a hit was not quite as impressive as the single arrow of legend.

The Augean Stables: according to myth, Hercules had diverted a river to clean out the stables, and the ancient map on the backs of the parchments had shown a small river running by the hill. This trial was one of intelligence rather than physical prowess, requiring floodgates to be opened in a certain order to direct water down particular channels. Make a mistake, and those opening the gates would be swept away by the deluge – a pair of broken bodies crushed against a grille at the end of one channel showed the penalty for failure. But with the river long dried up, the expedition was able to traverse the room with no difficulty.

The Stymphalian Birds: a narrow passage sloped steeply upwards, tracks in the ceiling sending brass statues of giant hawks hurtling down to the bottom, talons and sharp beaks extended to gore anyone in their path. Two birds had reached the foot of the slope, hitting with such force that their beaks were embedded in the wall – one having first punched straight through the chest of an unlucky robber. Another hawk lay a third of the way up the corridor, its supporting hook shot out by an arrow. Even Komosa was impressed by the marksmanship.

The Cretan Bull: a giant with the crudest method of attack so far, having simply advanced down a tight passage to crush anyone in its path. It had been defeated by lassooing its horns and pulling down its head, a few bone-dry strands of rope still hanging from them.

Two more had fallen victim to this last trap, having slipped and fallen under the huge rollers acting as the bull's 'feet' as they tried to pull down the head. Nina paused to examine them more closely. 'These are more recent,' she realised. 'The clothing, what's left of it, I'd say was fifteenth- or sixteenth-century European. Even a failed attempt to get through the traps clears the way for the next set of robbers.'

'So the next task should have been triggered as well?' Corvus asked as he clambered on to the bull to reach the exit passage behind its head.

'Not necessarily,' Sophia said as she followed him. 'We know the way through the maze. They didn't. Even if they got past each challenge, there might still have been other traps that killed them.' As she emerged on the other side of the statue, she looked calculatingly at Chase. 'Maybe we should find out.'

'There isn't time,' said Corvus, brushing dust from his clothes. Sophia seemed disappointed, but still gave Chase a look that suggested her idea wasn't going to go away. 'What is the next trial?' he asked Nina as she caught up.

She checked her notes. 'The Mares of Diomedes.'

'Horses, eh?' said Chase. 'I bet in the legend they weren't exactly My Little Ponies.'

'Not really. There are different versions of the story, but in all of them the horses are man-eaters.'

'Sounds like someone I know,' Chase muttered, glaring at Sophia.

'We should stop here for a while,' Nina told Corvus. 'I need to keep working on the translation – I haven't got very far past the next challenge.'

'No,' he replied. 'Work on the move. We are so close now, I will not wait. Concentrate on guiding us through the maze – even if any of the trials are still working, my men have weapons and explosives. We can take care of them.'

Nina made a disbelieving face, then shrugged. 'Whatever,' she said, concealing her concern – and also her hope. If any of the remaining trials actually were still functional, they could pose a genuine threat to Corvus's men – and give herself and Chase a chance to escape.

Once the entire party had gathered, they set off again, Nina directing them through the darkened twists of the labyrinth. Before long they reached the entrance to another chamber.

Bertillon, leading the way, shone his torch inside. 'I see no bodies,' he reported. 'I don't think this one has been sprung.' He switched the torch to his other hand as he unshouldered his gun, a sleek and futuristic Fabrique Nationale F2000 assault rifle with a 40mm grenade launcher fitted beneath the barrel. Two of his companions did the same.

Komosa joined them, torchlight glinting from his piercings as he looked into the long chamber. Nina peered past him to see what lay inside. At the far end were four oversized statues of horses, even more forcefully stylised than the previous creatures they had encountered. Their long, sharp teeth were bared, legs raised as if frozen mid-gallop . . . and ready to resume at any moment. The hooves were elongated, narrowed, more like blades than feet – making Nina think uncomfortably of some kind of agricultural threshing machine. The animals' legs ran the full width of the passage.

'Christ,' said Chase, standing beside her to see for himself. 'Teeth on those things look like the bloody Alien Queen.'

'We must go through,' said Corvus. He turned to Nina. 'How did Hercules defeat them?'

Nina paused, thinking – and exchanged the briefest of knowing glances with Chase. 'His task was to steal the horses from Diomedes, who kept them chained to a bronze manger,' she recounted after a moment. Corvus looked at the statues, which had bronze chains hanging from their necks, and nodded. 'Once he freed them, he drove them on to a peninsula and dug a trench to make it into an island so they couldn't escape.'

Bertillon aimed his torch at the floor of the chamber. 'Perhaps we are supposed to dig up the floor so the horses cannot get across, hey?' He switched off the torch and pocketed it, then raised his gun and activated its spotlight before loading the grenade launcher. 'I know a quick way to do that.'

Another man, an American, examined the chamber's entrance. 'There's a slot in the top of the arch here,' he announced. 'I guess a gate drops down when the trap goes off so you can't get out. We've got some titanium jacks – we can wedge them in so that it can't fall.'

'Do it,' ordered Corvus.

The jacks were quickly set in place, an inverted V blocking the slot above the entrance while still allowing room to pass underneath. Bertillon, Komosa and the two other men who had unshouldered their F2000s entered the chamber and cautiously advanced on the statues. The others watched from the entrance, Corvus using a radio so the team could communicate via headsets without shouting.

'Is there any sign of a spot where you might be supposed to dig up the floor?' he asked.

'Nothing so far,' Bertillon replied, carefully stepping forward. 'Perhaps we should use grenades to destroy the statues before they—'

Crunch.

A dull grind of shifting stone came from beneath his foot, clearly audible even to those waiting outside the entrance.

And then the entrance slammed shut, a metal portcullis dropping down – not from the slot which had been blocked by the jacks, but beyond it, on the far side of the arch. The slot was just a decoy, the real trap suspended a foot away.

With a screech of metal and rasp of stone the statues burst into life, moving for the first time in thousands of years. Their jaws snapped and their legs churned up and down, sharp hooves slicing the air and clanging cacophonously against the stone floor as they advanced.

Corvus's men outside the chamber ran to the gate and tried to lift it, but it refused to move, locked down.

Nina cringed and put her hands over her ears as Bertillon fired his grenade launcher. The echoing shotgun-like thud was nothing compared to the explosive crack that shook the chamber a moment later as the grenade hit one of the statues. Lumps of stone showered the room as a chunk was blown from the horse's chest, but the relentless advance continued.

Another man fired. The grenade shot between the stamping legs of the horses and into the exit tunnel behind them, detonating with a bang followed by the crunch of falling rocks.

'Stop!' Corvus shouted. 'You'll block the tunnel!' Bertillon and Komosa looked back at him in disbelief. 'Use bullets, not grenades! Destroy the legs!'

The three men with rifles exchanged glances, then did as they were ordered and switched their attack. Bullets blazed from the weapons, chipping and cratering the statues and spraying debris in all directions. The sharp metal hoof was blown from one of the pounding legs, but the jagged spear of stone that remained appeared just as lethal.

Komosa took out a large pistol as the others backed towards the entrance. 'What are their weak spots?' he demanded over the radio. 'How do we stop them?'

Sophia drew her own gun and pressed it against Nina's head. 'Well? Answer him! How did Hercules kill them?'

'He *didn't* kill them—' Nina began, before being interrupted by a scream from the chamber.

A bullet had ricocheted off the statues and hit Bertillon in his right thigh, dropping him bloodily to the floor. One of the other men went to drag him away, but jumped back as shrapnel from the third man's shots scythed past his face. By the time he recovered, the horses had reached the fallen man—

Bertillon screamed again, his agonised howl cut off within moments as the stamping feet trampled over him and tore him to pieces, the statues turning red with splattered blood. Nina looked away in horror, and even Chase was repulsed. Lumps of shredded flesh were flung into the air to slap down before the remaining three men.

Sophia aimed her gun at Chase. 'How did he stop them?' she yelled at Nina. 'In the *other* version of the legend? Tell me or Eddie dies!'

Nina gave Chase a despairing look, then acquiesced. 'He killed Diomedes and fed him to his own horses. Once they'd been fed, they calmed down and Hercules was able to take them!'

Sophia turned to the entrance, where Komosa and the two other men had their backs to the portcullis – the horses were only fifteen feet away and still coming. 'Joe! It's the mouths – you have to feed them with something!'

'Like what?' Komosa demanded.

'There's plenty of meat in there!'

Komosa was puzzled, then realised what she meant. With a disgusted look, he picked up Bertillon's left forearm, the hand flopping as he lifted it.

The mouths of the horses kept chomping, sharp teeth glistening in the torchlight. Every time they opened, they revealed a hole beyond, a channel curving down inside each statue.

Komosa pulled back his arm to make a throw, hesitating to get the timing right – then flung the severed limb into the mouth of the nearest horse.

It caught on the teeth, hanging for a moment as the mouth snapped shut – then dropped out of sight into the hole as the jaw opened again. Komosa and the others backed against the wall. The horses kept advancing . . . then slowed, the thundering gallop of their legs falling to a canter before stopping, barely four feet from the portcullis. Something rattled overhead. One of Corvus's men tried to lift the gate, and this time found that it moved.

Sophia whirled on Nina and punched her hard in the face, knocking her to the floor. Enraged, Chase stepped forward, but found guns thrust against his chest. 'If you hold *anything* back again,' Sophia snarled down at Nina, 'I won't just kill Eddie. I'll cut him apart, piece by piece, and make you watch every second of it. Am I clear?'

Nina spat out blood. 'Crystal,' she groaned.

'Good. Now get up. There are three more trials.' Sophia paused thoughtfully, then looked across at Chase. A malevolent smile grew on her face. 'Uncuff him,' she ordered one of the men.

'Are you sure that's wise?' asked Corvus.

Sophia's smile widened. 'He's going to need his hands free.'

Nina stood, a hand pressed against her cut lip. 'What are you doing?'

'I'm giving you an incentive to work as quickly and accurately as possible,' Sophia told her. 'Because Eddie's going to be leading the way. If you make a mistake . . . he dies.'

22

'Which way?' Chase said into his headset. The winding tunnel had reached another junction. 'Left or right?'

'Left,' said Nina through the earpiece after a moment.

'You sure?'

'Will you stop asking me that? Yes, I'm sure.'

'Just checking.' He took a step down the left passage, then looked back. Komosa watched him from about twenty feet behind, a silver Browning longslide pistol with a laser sight in one hand. Past him, Chase could see the torch beams of the rest of the party.

Komosa waved the gun for him to keep moving. Chase shot him a foul look, then continued down the next passage.

It didn't take long before his torch picked out something new. 'Okay, looks like another trial,' he reported. 'What's next on the list?'

Another pause from Nina. 'The Apples of the Hesperides.'

Chase rolled his eyes. 'What, I'm going to be attacked by giant apples?'

'There's only one way to find out, Eddie,' Sophia cut in mockingly. 'In you go.'

He glanced back to see the smiling Komosa pointing the gun at him. Huffing, Chase entered the chamber.

Unlike the long rooms which had housed the previous trials, this one was square. The floor was laid out in a grid of light and dark tiles like a chessboard, each tile around five feet to a side. The grid itself measured nine squares by nine, a light tile in each corner. Four stone columns carved to resemble trees, a squat metal cage at the top of each, rose to chest height on the light tiles halfway between the centre of the grid and the corners. At the far side of the room beyond the chessboard was a figure whom even Chase, with his limited knowledge of mythology, recognised as Atlas, holding the heavens on his shoulders. In this case, the heavens were represented by a large globe of copper or bronze. A pair of rails curved down from behind the statue's shoulders to the floor.

'Eddie, what do you see?' Nina asked.

Chase described the scene. 'I don't see any apples, though. How does the story go?'

'Atlas guarded the Garden of the Hesperides. Hercules wasn't able to reach the apples himself, so he offered to take the weight of the heavens for a while so Atlas could get them for him. Once Atlas got the apples, he decided to deliver them himself for a reward, but Hercules tricked him into taking back the heavens by saying that he wanted to adjust his cloak to get more comfortable, so if Atlas could just hold them for a moment . . .'

'So Atlas was thick as shit, then.' Chase scanned the room again. 'The globe looks like it moves, so . . . ah, I get it. I'm supposed to shove the globe off his shoulders so Atlas gets the apples somehow, then I have to roll it back up the rails on to his shoulders again to get out.'

'I doubt that the statue's going to come to life and collect the apples for you,' Sophia said. 'There must be more to it.'

'I'm still working on the text,' Nina told him. 'It's like the description of the Augean Stables – it's a puzzle, a test of wits rather than fighting skills, so it's more involved than the others. I just need time to transcribe and translate it.'

'Time is in short supply, Dr Wilde,' said Corvus impatiently. 'Chase, go to one of the columns, see if the apples are inside it.'

'I'd rather wait,' Chase said testily. He looked back at the entrance, seeing Komosa signalling with the Browning for him to go on. 'But I guess that's not an option, is it? Oh well, let's grab some Golden Delicious.'

He moved towards the first column on the left side of the room, stepping on to a dark tile—

'*Eddie, stay still!*' Nina shrieked through the headset, but too late.

The tile dropped out from under him. It was hinged along one edge, swinging away to pitch him into a black void below—

Chase threw out his arms, his torch spinning down into the darkness as he caught the side of the hole with one hand. Pain searing through the wound in his back, he swung helplessly for a moment before struggling to bring up his other arm. With a groan, he finally managed to secure himself.

Nina screamed his name through the headset. 'I'm okay, I'm okay!' he gasped. 'Well, technically.'

'What happened?' Sophia asked, sounding more professionally curious than concerned.

'The tile was hinged; it gave way when I stepped on it.' Chase turned his head to examine the side of the hole opposite the hinge. Metal strips supporting the tile from beneath had bent under his weight.

'I always said you could stand to lose a few pounds, Eddie,' said Sophia.

'Yeah, ho fucking ho. Get me out of here.'

Her voice became patronising. 'I'm disappointed in you. Can't you climb out on your own?'

'I would've if some bastard hadn't stuck a drill in my shoulder!' Chase twisted round to see Komosa still lurking in the entrance. 'Oi, Silvernips! Give me a hand, for fuck's sake.'

Komosa smirked, making no effort to move. Behind him, the other members of the expedition arrived, Nina leading. 'Help him, then!' she cried.

Corvus directed his torch at the dangling Chase. 'He fell in the hole, let him get out of it. Why should we help?'

Nina fixed him with a cold, determined stare. 'Because if he dies, you might as well kill me too, because there's no way in hell I'm going to translate another word of this.' She held up the parchments, thumb tightening. Part of one page tore. 'Oops.'

Sophia brought up her gun, but Corvus raised his hands. 'All right, Dr Wilde.' He nodded to Komosa. 'Get him out.' Annoyed, Komosa entered the room and pulled Chase from the hole.

'Cheers, mate,' Chase said sarcastically, kneeling on the solid light tile that he'd grabbed. He peered into the hole to see his torch lying on the ground ten feet below – surrounded by a nest of jagged metal spikes. 'Jesus. You'd need more than a tetanus shot if you landed on those.'

'How do we get across safely?' Sophia asked, looking at the

transcribed Greek text in Nina's notebook. 'Are all the dark squares booby-trapped?'

'Yes, but so are some of the light ones too,' said Nina, defensively turning the book away from her. 'Let me see . . . oh, Christ, this is complicated.' She frowned as she read through the text. 'Okay, I think I've got it. Every second light-coloured tile in the first row, the one along the left side of the room, is booby-trapped. Then in the second row, the *third* light tile is trapped. The third row, all the light tiles are safe. Then the pattern repeats – every second one, every third. All the others should be safe.'

'*Should* be safe?' Chase remarked dubiously.

Sophia pointed her gun at him. 'Only one way to find out.'

Cursing under his breath, Chase banged a heel down hard on the next light tile in the adjoining row. It didn't move. He warily stepped on to it, then with a little more confidence hopped diagonally to the light tile on which the column stood. 'Okay. Any chance of another torch?'

Komosa tossed him his. Chase caught it and examined the metal cage on top of the column. 'Yeah, we've got an apple in here.' He tugged at the cage, but it held firm. 'Better roll the ball, I suppose. You're absolutely sure about which tiles are booby-trapped?' he asked Nina.

Nina was working as quickly as she could, holding the red plastic sheet over one of the parchment pages and shining a light on it to spot each hidden letter in turn, then scrawling them into her notebook. 'As far as I can tell.'

'Well, if you're sure, that's good enough for me. Which way do I go?'

There was a short pause while Nina worked out the pattern. 'Okay, if I'm right, the light square diagonally to the right is trapped.'

Chase tested it with his heel. It dropped fractionally. 'Yep, you're right.'

'Okay, go left.' He moved cautiously; this light tile was solid. 'Now go right, right again and left to get to the second column, then go left, then right, and you'll be at the statue.'

Chase followed her directions, arms half raised ready to grab the sides if another hole opened up beneath him. Nothing happened. He reached the statue of Atlas, which stood seven feet tall, and looked up at the giant ball. There was some kind of mechanism beneath it, set between Atlas's shoulders. 'So I push this off, and then . . .' he muttered, as much to himself as to Nina, as he looked round. 'Oh, here we go. There are some holes in the wall. Three guesses what fruit they're shaped like.'

'You must have to put the apples in them, then push the ball back into place,' Nina suggested.

'Yeah, I guessed that. It's like a psycho version of *The Crystal Maze*.' Chase turned back to the statue and reached up to push the ball. Even though it was hollow, it still look a fair amount of effort before it started to move. 'Go on, you bugger!'

With an echoing rumble, the ball came free and rolled down the rails, picking up speed before reaching the steeper upward curve at the bottom. It trundled back and forth a few times, then finally came to rest.

Chase retraced his steps to the nearest of the four columns. This time, the metal cage rose easily. He reached inside and carefully lifted out the bronze apple. There was a square protrusion at its base, which he realised matched an indentation in one of the holes in the wall behind Atlas – a primitive key.

He returned to the statue and placed the apple in the indentation, experimentally turning it. It made a quarter-turn clockwise, then stopped. 'Okay, it seems to work.'

'Get the other three,' ordered Sophia.

Chase made an annoyed grunt and turned back to face the grid, standing before the central light square. 'Okay, Nina, is this one safe?'

A brief pause, then: 'Yes. Then go right.'

He took the step—

'No no no, stop, wait!' Nina shrieked. Chase flung himself back just as the tile fell away with a bang.

'Jesus!' he gasped. 'What happened? I thought you had this all worked out!'

'Sorry, sorry! We're facing in opposite directions – I meant, go to *my* right. Your left.'

A half-laugh escaped Chase's mouth. 'All those brains, but you still can't tell left from right?'

'Yeah, okay, sorry,' Nina said sheepishly. 'So, you need to go *left*, then left again to get to the next column.'

'Sure?'

'*Yes.*'

'Like I said, just checking.'

Under Nina's guidance, he gingerly picked his way back round the board to collect the three other apples before returning to the statue of Atlas and the keyholes behind it. He inserted the apples one by one. As he turned the final one, he heard some hidden mechanism click: a lock opening.

All that remained now was to push the heavy ball back up the rails and on to Atlas's shoulders. It took considerably more effort than it did to move it in the first place, but after a couple of minutes the ball rolled back into place on to the switch in the statue's shoulders. With a loud thump, one of the lighter tiles at the back of the room fell open.

'How do you like *them* apples?' Chase called triumphantly across the room as the rest of the party followed the safe route to the far side.

'One down,' said Sophia, unimpressed. 'Two to go. Get moving.'

'This is just what she was like when we were married,' Chase said into the headset for Nina's benefit, even though he knew full well that Sophia could also hear him. ' 'Cept for the cold-blooded murder, I mean.' Nina almost smiled.

'Let's keep the stupid comments to a minimum, Eddie,' Sophia said in a clipped tone. Chase shrugged and dropped through the newly opened hole, Komosa waiting for him to advance before jumping down after him.

Another series of junctions through the maze at Nina's guidance, and Chase found himself at the entrance to a new chamber. He aimed his torch inside. 'Okay, I see lots and lots of sharp pointy things. What's the story here?'

Nina completed the next translation. 'This must be . . . the Girdle of Hippolyta. Hercules had to get the magical belt of Hippolyta, the leader of the Amazons. But he knew that if he tried to take it by force, the other Amazons would kill him before he could escape, so he had to come up with another method. What do you see?'

Chase cautiously stepped into the chamber. 'Well, what we've got here is a round room about twenty-five feet across, and all round the outside are statues of women holding spears and arrows.' He took a closer look at the nearest statue, noting that the spear it held continued back into a hole in the wall. He reached out a finger. 'I don't know if they're work—'

He only gave it the lightest touch, but the spear suddenly sprang from the statue's hand and hurtled across the room to smash against the wall opposite, its sharp flint head shattering on impact.

At the same moment, an arrow shot with a twang from the other side of the room, coming straight at him.

Chase just barely flinched out of its way, but it still sliced a nick in his jacket's sleeve. 'Shit! Take that back, I *do* know if they're working,' he said, quickly stepping back. The traps were interlinked, to deter anyone from simply setting them off one by one.

He noticed other arrows and spears lying broken on the floor; presumably they had gone off of their own accord over time. But if all the remaining weapons fired at once, anybody inside the room would be turned into a pincushion.

He turned his attention to the statue standing alone in the centre of the chamber. 'So how did Herc get the belt? There's another statue here which must be Hippo Legs, and yeah, she's got a belt on, or at least part of one.' The sculpted woman stood almost as tall as the statue of Atlas, feet apart and hands on her hips in a stance of unmistakable dominance. Around her waist was a bronze and silver band, part of which could clearly be detached from the statue.

But Chase had no intention of simply pulling it loose, keeping a wary eye on the weapons all around him. He described the statue to Nina. 'So, what do I do?'

'There are different versions of the story,' she told him, 'but the most common one is that Hercules persuaded Hippolyta to *give* him the girdle of her own free will. Basically, he told her why he needed it, and she agreed to let him have it – either to avoid a fight that would end badly for both sides, or because she fell in love with him. Again, there are different versions.' She thought for a moment. 'Did you say the statue was in a dominant stance?'

'Yeah, hands on hips. Kind of like the way you stand when I'm watching telly and you want me to move furniture.'

'Cute. But is there anything on the floor around her feet, or on the feet themselves?'

Chase turned the torch downwards, and saw that her guess was correct. 'Looks like part of the feet move, like they're trigger stones or something.' He cast a nervous look up at the spears and arrows. 'Wait, what if they fire everything?'

'I don't think they will. The story is about *submission*; to get what he needed, Hercules had to grovel to Hippolyta. I think that's what has to be done here.'

'You mean . . .'

'Get down on your knees, Eddie,' said Sophia over the radio with unconcealed amusement. Outside the doorway, Komosa stifled a laugh. 'You finally take your rightful place in front of a woman. Wait a second, though – I have to see this.'

'Glad you're having fun,' Chase grumbled as she skipped up the tunnel to peer round the entrance. He kneeled down, real-ising there was a third trigger set into the floor beneath his knees – simply standing on the statue's feet wouldn't work.

He leaned forward, bending into an embarrassingly submissive position in order to place both hands on the stone feet. 'All right,' he sighed as he pushed down, 'let's get this over with.'

'I really think you should call her Mistress,' Sophia called from the door, but he ignored her, instead looking up as a soft clink of metal sounded above his head. The belt had moved slightly. He rose and gingerly touched it, more than half expecting a fusillade of spears to impale him . . .

They didn't. But in the quiet of the chamber, his ears picked up a faint but distinct creak, like a bowstring tensing. He looked round. A thin line of dust slowly drifted down from one of the nearby spearheads, shaken loose by a very slight vibration.

The trap was still primed.

Chase warily took in the dozens of other sharpened points also aimed at him, belatedly realising his mouth had gone dry. He swallowed, then turned his attention back to the belt, carefully placing the fingertips of both hands against it.

No sounds, no missiles flying to impale him. He applied more pressure, slowly pulling the metal band towards him. Metal scraped against stone. There were protrusions on the back of the belt, catching the statue—

Creak.

Chase froze. The sound had come from his left. Not even breathing, he eased his grip on the belt and cautiously turned his head. More dust wafted down from the head of an arrow pointing straight at his face.

He leaned back out of its path, then set his jaw. He'd done everything he was supposed to do – if the trap was going to fire, there didn't seem to be any way he could prevent it. One eye on the arrow, he took hold of the belt again, and pulled.

The curved metal band slid free. The weapons surrounding him remained still. Chase blew out a relieved breath and stood.

He had already noticed a recess in the closed door on the far side of the circular chamber, and was not surprised to find that it matched the shape of the belt. Slots accepted pegs on the back of the ancient bronze piece, and he heard a lock clunk as he pushed it into place. Another, harder push, and the door swung open to reveal a black tunnel beyond.

Komosa came into the room, Sophia behind him. 'Only one more task to accomplish, Eddie,' she said. 'Get to it.'

'And then what happens?' Chase wanted to know. 'You going to kill us as soon as we get into the Tomb?'

Sophia didn't reply, but there was something in her smile that gave Chase pause. At that moment, he knew that she wasn't simply going to kill Nina and himself. She had something else in mind. He doubted he would like it. Whatever it was, Komosa seemed to be in on it, sharing a similar look of expectant sadism.

He left the circular room for the new tunnel just as Nina entered from the other side. She took in the surrounding statues, but Corvus urged her along when she stopped for a closer look.

Nina stood her ground, the rest of Corvus's men bunching up behind them. 'The least you can do is let me *look* at them. This is an incredible archaeological find.'

'I am not interested in the past,' Corvus said sniffily. 'Only the future. Go on,' he told his men. They shuffled round the statue of Hippolyta.

Nina's voice filled with sarcastic contempt. 'Don't you know that those who don't learn from the past are doomed to—'

Thwack!

They both jumped at a sudden blur of movement, which was followed by an anguished gurgle as one of the men slumped to his knees. He had accidentally brushed a spear as he passed it, and the trap had fired, shooting the weapon deep into his ribcage – and an arrow from across the room into his chest. With a final dying gasp, he flopped forward, driving the arrow even further into his body.

Nina looked away from the body, at Corvus. 'Case in point. Eddie learned not to do that five minutes ago.'

The other men nervously turned to Corvus, one of them bending to retrieve the dead man's equipment and gun. 'Leave him,' Corvus ordered. 'We'll collect him on the way out.' Now taking much greater care to stay well clear of the poised weapons, the group moved on.

Chase led the way, waiting at each junction for Nina's instructions as she transcribed the hidden letters on the fly. What dangers lay down the paths not taken he had no idea, but he stopped thinking about them as the tunnel reached the entrance to another chamber.

The last Trial of Hercules. Cerberus, the guardian of the Underworld.

This trap appeared similar in design to the Mares of Diomedes, but in this case there was only a single statue waiting to advance, a juggernaut filling the entire width of the passage. That wasn't what caught Chase's attention, though, nor was it the pair of huge paws which he suspected would pound up and down to crush anyone who got too close.

It was the heads – plural. Cerberus looked like a particularly savage Rottweiler, but its broad shoulders supported no fewer than three snarling heads, each over two feet across. Unlike those of the Mares of Diomedes, the jaws seemed sculpted to remain fully open.

'Bloody hell, it's Fluffy,' Chase said into the headset. 'So what's the trick to dealing with giant three-headed dogs?'

'Hercules had to wrestle Cerberus,' Nina told him. 'His task was to bring the dog out of the Underworld, which he did basically by putting a headlock on the middle head and dragging it out with him.'

'I think this mutt's a bit big to drag anywhere, and Hagrid's never around when you need him. So, I'm going to have to give it a bit of Hulk Hogan, am I?' If the paws did indeed move up and down, they seemed far too massive to do so at the same speed as the legs of the horses that had killed Bertillon. If he could jump on to one of them, he should then be able to grab the central head when it lifted him up . . . 'Okay, then. Walkies.'

He entered the passage, advancing step by step and bracing himself for the moment when a footfall would bring the statue to 'life' . . .

Clunk.

A stone slab dropped half an inch beneath his foot. Faint rattles came from beneath the floor, a chain reaction working its way towards the statue to knock out whatever final pin held the mechanism in check.

Cerberus lurched forward, each huge paw rising five feet into the air in turn before smashing back down on to the ground with enough force to crack the slabs beneath. Behind Chase, a gate slammed down to block his exit. The statue was moving more slowly than the Mares of Diomedes, but it would still crush him against the back wall in little over a minute.

Each paw had claws curving out from it like scimitars. One more thing to worry about. Holding the torch in his left hand, he moved towards the giant statue, waiting for the precise moment to—

Jump!

Chase vaulted on to the statue's left paw as it hit the ground in a cloud of dust. After a moment, it rose again, lifting him towards the heads. He braced himself, ready to grab the middle head and twist it round. This was easier than he'd expected . . .

A new noise came from the head above him, sounding oddly like clanking crockery.

Instantly on alert, Chase looked up. A sealed earthenware pot about the size of a grapefruit dropped from a hole at the back of the dog's mouth on to the gaping lower jaw.

Chase leapt from the left paw on to the right—

The pot smashed on impact, the liquid inside spraying everywhere. He felt some of it splatter on to the back of his leather jacket. A sharp smell stung his nostrils.

Hissing fumes rose from the dust-covered stone, from his back.

Acid!

'Jesus!' He shone the light over his shoulder, seeing that the corrosive liquid had already burned the topmost layer of leather from black to an ugly mottled brown, and was rapidly eating through what lay beneath.

And with his weight now on the other paw as it rose, he heard more clinking sounds from above, another container about to drop from the right-hand head—

'What is it, what's going on?' Nina shouted in his ear.

'It's spraying fucking *acid* at me!' Chase yelled, jumping back on to the left paw just as a second pot smashed, froth pouring from the mouth.

'His spit's poisonous in the legend!'

'You could have told me that before!' The right paw crashed down on to the floor, pieces of broken paving scattering around it. The left paw began to ascend again. Chase looked up. It was his extra weight on the moving stone that was triggering the acid trap, which meant another would be released at any moment.

The mouth above him was still dripping, fumes burning his eyes and nostrils. He coughed. The statue had already covered half the length of the passage . . .

Cerberus's central head sneered down at him. Unlike its outlying companions it was a separate piece from the rest of the statue, its neck fitting into a circular hole.

Another clay pot skittered from the hole at the back of the dog's throat—

Chase threw himself at the middle head. The pot burst open, a liquid limb sluicing after him.

He grabbed the statue, feeling the acid splash against his arm and side. Pinprick splashes burned his left hand and scalp as he pressed his face against the stone head for what little protection it offered, but he knew they would be nothing compared to what he would feel when the searing corrosive ate away the leather and started on his flesh.

And now he had no footholds, dangling with both arms wrapped round Cerberus's neck.

He twisted, kicking against the statue's chest as he got a grip on one of the ears and wrenched at it with all his weight.

It didn't move.

'Shit!' His sleeve was smoking, the fumes so strong that he could barely breathe.

Ten feet away from the back wall of the passage, nine . . .

He kicked again, swinging into a new position to grip the top of the statue's head with his left arm and turn it anticlockwise. Stray drops of acid seared his cheek as he raised his arm over his head.

Fingers closed round the other stone ear. The wall was six feet away.

Last chance—

Roaring, Chase pulled at the head, feet scrabbling against the dog's chest for every ounce of leverage.

Four feet, three . . .

The head turned.

Both the giant paws fell to the floor with enormous force, one of the scimitar claws breaking loose and clashing against the portcullis gate. Cerberus juddered to a halt.

Chase dropped from the head, tearing off his jacket and throwing it to the ground. Swirls of smoke billowed from it, holes eaten through the left sleeve and the back. He wiped frantically at the burns on his head and hands with the material of his T-shirt. 'Fuck! Fucking hell, that hurts!'

Komosa and another man lifted the gate. Beneath the central head, a stone slab moved slightly. Komosa shoved past Chase and kicked it open to reveal the exit. 'We're through,' he announced to Sophia and Corvus as they arrived.

Chase looked mournfully down at the smouldering leather at

his feet. 'Lost my jacket, lost my gun,' he complained. 'This hasn't been a good week.' But his expression lifted – slightly – when he saw Nina behind Sophia. 'Haven't lost everything, though,' he told her. She didn't quite smile, but her relief at seeing him again was plain.

Corvus turned to Nina. 'Is this it? Was that the last obstacle?'

'I've still got one more page to translate. But yes, that was the last trial. The Tomb of Hercules is through there.' She indicated the new opening.

Corvus stepped eagerly towards it, but Sophia held his arm. 'I think we should send Yorkshire Jones in first. Just in case.'

Komosa prodded Chase with his gun. Wearily, Chase moved to the hole.

'Wait,' said Nina. 'Send me instead.'

Sophia snorted mockingly. 'I don't think so.'

Nina turned to Corvus. 'This is *my* discovery. You wouldn't be here without me. You wouldn't even know this place *existed* without me. At least let me be the first to see it.'

After a moment, Corvus nodded. Sophia shot him a warning frown. 'René . . .'

'If she tries anything, kill Chase,' he ordered Komosa. The Nigerian gave Chase an expectant grin as he handed his torch to Nina.

'Good luck,' Chase told her as she bent down and clambered through the hole.

The low passage ran under the statue before opening out in the chamber behind it, the cogs and chains and counterweights that had driven Cerberus now still and silent. She ignored them, her torch beam falling upon another archway at the far end.

Much larger than the previous exits, this one was far more ornate, decorated in silver and gold and precious stones.

Nina walked to it, shining the torch through the opening. More treasures glinted back at her.

'I think this is it,' she called as she reached the opening – and stepped through.

With that, Nina became the first person in thousands of years to enter the Tomb of Hercules.

23

'Wow,' Nina whispered.

The tomb was square, a hundred and fifty feet to a side with a ceiling rising to form a flattened dome that topped out thirty feet above the centre of the huge chamber. Four broad pillars round a central plinth supported it; sloping walls rose diagonally from the foot of each pillar up to the base of the dome at each corner, great stone wedges dividing the room.

But the architecture wasn't at the forefront of Nina's mind. It was what lay round it, literally piled head-high against the tomb walls.

Gold.

And more besides – other precious metals gleamed as she panned her torch round the chamber. Silver, platinum, even the reddish hue of orichalcum, the gold-copper alloy favoured by the Atlanteans. Some was in the form of ingots, but much had been worked into what seemed to Nina like an almost infinite variety of treasures, large and small – statues, cups, shields, bracelets, crowns, plates, ceremonial pieces even she struggled to name . . .

Amongst it all glittered precious stones of every colour imaginable, scattered like snowflakes. While the tomb was smaller, the value of the treasures within outshone by far the Temple of Poseidon that Nina had discovered a year and a half earlier. She couldn't begin to work out how much it would all be worth. Billions of dollars, easily.

Footsteps echoed behind her. She turned to see Sophia and Corvus leading the group into the tomb, their expressions turning to utter astonishment as they took in the sight.

'My God,' breathed Corvus, 'it's more than I ever imagined. Look at it!'

Even Sophia, for once, seemed overawed. 'Real treasure,' she said softly, moving for a closer look at a nearby golden pile. 'Real *wealth*.'

'Nina!' Chase pushed past Komosa and ran to Nina. She threw her arms round him. Chase returned the gesture, holding her tightly. Komosa regarded them coldly and looked to Sophia, but she was too engrossed by the riches of the tomb to care what her ex-husband was doing.

'My God, oh, my God!' said Nina. 'Are you okay?'

'Bit burned, but that doesn't matter,' Chase told her. 'Main thing is, you're all right.'

Sill holding him, Nina took another look round the tomb's interior as Corvus's remaining men spread out, torchlight dancing over the golden hoard. Her eyes widened in amazement as still more treasures were revealed. 'Jesus, this is incredible!' She released Chase and turned to take in the entire space, almost skipping with excitement. 'My God, look at this! This . . . this practically *rewrites* ancient history! The Tomb of Hercules, almost completely intact. And look at all this treasure! This is probably the biggest find *ever*!'

'You can't take it with you,' Chase said, 'but Herc had a bloody good try.'

'He might not even have known about it. This is all tribute, gifts from a grateful people to honour their hero.' She raised her flashlight and led him to one of the ramp-like sloping walls. Komosa followed a few steps behind, gun in hand. Running along the wall was an elaborate frieze made from thousands of small coloured tiles, forming a series of pictures. 'See, these are all scenes celebrating his life and his adventures.'

Chase examined them. 'So we've got Hercules killing some bloke, Hercules killing *several* blokes and a couple of dogs, Hercules in . . . an orgy.' He looked more closely and raised an eyebrow. 'Kind of a *gay* orgy.'

'Hercules had as many male lovers as female,' Nina pointed out. 'And yes, he did kill an awful lot of people, often quite casually. He also played a major part in the sacking of Troy and the massacre of its inhabitants, and that was just one of his campaigns. One civilisation's legendary hero is another's marauding psychopath.'

'Funny how they didn't show any of that in the Disney version, isn't it?'

'So where is Hercules himself?' Corvus asked, finally tearing his gaze away from the treasures around him to address Nina. 'If this is his tomb, then where is he?'

Nina pointed to the plinth between the four pillars. 'There, would be my guess.'

On the plinth was a golden sarcophagus; at its head a statue, again in gold, of a man.

Hercules.

The mythological hero in physical form, tall and muscular, head raised in triumph. In one hand he held a large club, and draped from his shoulders was a cloak. At his side was a quiver of arrows. All three golden accessories were inset with thousands of gemstones, on the club lined up to resemble grained wood, on the cloak more randomly like the rawness of animal hide, each arrowhead made from a single large gem cut to a sharp point.

Nina also noticed that they were separate entities, removable from the statue itself . . .

She looked up at the sloping wall. At its top was a dark alcove in the corner of the ceiling, an object lurking inside. The outer edges of the ramp were raised, as if to guide something down it.

'Eddie, look up there,' she whispered, aiming the torch upwards. The circle of light briefly passed over the alcove before moving on, Nina not wanting to draw attention to her discovery. Within it was a thick stone disc, easily weighing several tons, balanced on its edge.

'Booby trap?' Chase whispered back. Nina nodded slightly, pretending to examine the gilded decorations on the ceiling while actually illuminating each of the ramps in turn. They all had discs poised at their tops.

As Corvus walked towards the sarcophagus, Nina placed the final page of *Hermocrates* under the red plastic sheet and scribbled down the last letters that were revealed. Her eyes widened slightly as she read the words, then she whispered to Chase, 'Get ready.'

He nodded, taking in the positions of everyone else in the tomb.

'Those are representations of Hercules' cloak, arrows and club,' Nina said loudly when Corvus reached the plinth. Everyone turned to her as she walked towards him, Chase gradually falling behind as she continued her lecture. 'As much as his physical strength, they were the symbols of his power. The cloak could fend off any blow, the arrows penetrate any hide or armour, and the club crush any enemy. I'd imagine that of all the treasures in the tomb, those three have the highest individual monetary values in terms of the craftsmanship that went into them and the materials used. If you take their value in a historical context into account as well, each of them could be worth more than the Mona Lisa or the mask of Tutankhamun.' She stopped near Corvus, Chase now several feet behind and not far from Komosa. 'Imagine holding something that valuable in your hand. It must be an incredible feeling.'

The greed in Corvus's eyes was plain. 'It must,' he agreed. He climbed up on to the plinth and walked round the sarcophagus, gazing up into the face of the statue for a moment before reaching out to take one of the arrows—

Sophia's sharp command of 'Stop!' and the click of her gun as she thumbed back the hammer and pressed it against the side of Nina's head came simultaneously. Corvus froze.

With her other hand, Sophia took Nina's notebook. 'Nice try,' Sophia told her coldly. 'But just because I said ancient Greek wasn't my speciality doesn't mean that I didn't pass it. I can translate the word *trap*.'

Corvus flinched back as if he'd received an electric shock. 'What?'

Sophia stepped away from Nina, keeping the gun trained on her. 'She's absolutely right that those are the most valuable items in the entire tomb – which makes them the perfect final trap. No thief would be able to resist them . . . but taking them triggers the last booby trap and brings down the entire tomb! Look at the top of the ramps.' Torches snapped up to light the alcoves. 'If those stones roll down, they'll smash the support pillars and the roof will collapse.'

Corvus wiped his brow. 'My God! She would have killed us all!'

'Oh, I think she was more hoping that we'd be distracted long enough for them to run for the exit. Look at how Eddie was trying to sidle close enough to Joe to take a swing at him.' Komosa looked at Chase, then whipped up his gun and jumped back with an almost outraged expression.

Chase shrugged nonchalantly. 'Ah well. Gave it our best shot.'

'I think "shot" is the right word,' said Corvus angrily. 'Kill them!'

His men raised their guns—

'Oh, really, René,' Sophia said with a mischievous smile, waving at the gunmen to stand down. They paused mid-motion, weapons raised but not aimed. 'Aren't you at least going to tell them why you've gone to all this trouble to find the Tomb of Hercules? It would be terribly disappointing if they died thinking it was merely about money.'

Corvus frowned. 'I am not Dr No or Blofeld, Sophia,' he said. 'I am not going to waste time telling them my plans before I have them killed.'

Sophia climbed on to the plinth and slunk seductively over to him, running her hands round his waist and placing her chin teasingly on his shoulder. 'Oh, come on. I know you're dying to tell *somebody*. Go on, impress them with your vision of the new world order.' Her voice dropped to a breathy near-whisper. 'I know it impressed *me*.'

Chase made a gagging sound, but Corvus smiled. 'Very well. But first, we should get things moving.' He looked down at one of his men at the foot of the plinth. 'Have you got our precise location?'

The man checked the screen of a tablet computer. 'According to the inertial mapper, we've travelled one hundred and seventy-six metres west from the entrance.'

Corvus looked surprised. 'That would take us right under the other side of the hill!'

'It's not a hill,' Nina explained. 'The tomb, the labyrinth, all the trials – the builders constructed them first, and then they buried them. The whole hill is man-made – that's why it doesn't fit the topography of the region.'

Corvus looked up at the ceiling. 'You mean everything above us is artificial?'

'Yeah. As ancient feats of engineering go, it's not that impressive – all they needed to do was pile up enough rubble. It wasn't like building the Pyramids. But it's what was beneath it that was important.'

Corvus addressed the man with the computer again. 'Contact the team outside, have them fly to directly above this location. How deep underground are we?'

The man tapped a stylus on the screen, making calculations. 'There should be no more than a metre between the ceiling of the tomb and the ground above. Perhaps even less.'

'Easy to blast through, then. We can open a hole in the roof and use the winch platform to lift the gold to the surface.' The billion-aire tipped back his head to examine the ceiling again. 'Make the arrangements. We will transport as much as the helicopters can carry, then return with more heavy-lift aircraft for the rest.'

'So, Auric, what *do* you want with the gold?' Chase taunted.

Corvus apparently didn't understand the *Goldfinger* reference, but still took up position at the edge of the plinth, staring down at Chase and Nina. Sophia stood behind his left shoulder. 'Sophia was correct – I want to establish a new world order. One where men like myself, the elite of humanity, are able to create wealth and exercise our power without hindrance from small-minded bureaucrats and petty populist vote-grubbers. I am going to establish . . .' He paused, raising his voice grandly. 'A new Atlantis.'

Nina and Chase shared a look. 'Been, seen, done,' said Nina, unimpressed.

Corvus smirked. 'This is not some insane plan to ethnically cleanse the world, Dr Wilde. What use is a business empire when three-quarters of your potential customers and labour force are dead? No, my Atlantis will be something else. The new capital of the world.'

'Sorry,' said Nina, shaking her head, 'but New York's not gonna give up the title without a fight.'

'London,' Chase corrected her.

'New York!'

'Atlantis,' said Corvus, looking slightly irritated by their distraction, '*will* rule the world. An entirely new city, a home to the world's wealthiest and most powerful people – subject to my personal invitation. A city from where their global empires can be run free from interference from governments, free of taxes, free to do business as business should be done.'

'There's nowhere on earth that'll let you set up your own little free state on their territory,' Nina pointed out. 'Or were you just planning to buy an entire country with all this?' She waved a hand at the treasures around them.

'My Atlantis will be built where the name suggests,' said Corvus. 'In the Atlantic. Or, more precisely, *beneath* it. The technology has already been proved with my home in the Bahamas, and with my underwater hotel in Dubai. It is merely a matter of scaling it up to create a city capable of supporting thousands of people. It will be the coming together of the most powerful group of men in human history.'

'Oh, so you're not Goldfinger,' said Chase. 'You're Stromberg.'

'It won't work,' Nina scoffed. 'You seriously think the world's governments are going to let their richest citizens swan off to some self-proclaimed new city-state so they can play Masters of the Universe without paying any taxes? The first visitor you'll get will be the US Navy, and your housewarming gift will be a ton of depth charges!'

'The independence of Atlantis will be quickly granted by the United Nations,' Corvus said smugly. 'I have an incentive. Yuen's atomic bombs, which now belong to me. Nothing ensures international concessions, particularly from the United States, more quickly than a nuclear deterrent.'

Chase grinned. 'Except you've only got one bomb. I fucked up the factory in Switzerland.'

'You destroyed the *lasers*, Chase. Not the factory. The lasers are just components, nothing more. They have already been replaced.'

Chase's face fell. 'Oh. Buggeration and fuckery.'

'So why would the world's richest men need the treasure from the Tomb of Hercules?' Nina asked.

'As a guarantee of financial independence,' explained Corvus. 'The world's major currencies are now backed by little more than government promises – the days when every paper dollar issued by the US government was matched by a dollar's worth of gold are long gone. So not only is the entire global economy nothing more than a bubble supported by faith in those currencies, but governments can – and do – use their power over currency and the stock markets to attack corporations. If the Securities and Exchange Commission suspends a company's stocks, then that company and its shareholders are wiped out in a moment by nothing more than loss of faith, billions of dollars reduced to zero.' He swept out his arms, taking in the unimaginable riches surrounding him. 'But all of this . . . this will be the base for Atlantis's currency. It will be backed up by *physical* wealth, by gold, which retains its value even if the world economy collapses.'

Nina looked sickened. 'So you find the greatest archaeological treasure in human history, and all you want it for is *bullion*?' She frowned. 'That means you and your billionaire buddies could make yourself even richer if you *deliberately* triggered an economic crash by selling all your stocks – the value of your physical assets would increase in relative terms as the markets fell. Then you could use those assets as collateral to buy up the fallen stock at a massively reduced price – it'd be the biggest bear market of all time!'

Chase looked pained. 'I have no idea what you just said, but it sounds bad.'

'It is. It's "the rich get richer and the poor get poorer" taken to the extreme – the only people who wouldn't be completely destroyed by the crash are Corvus and whoever else he invites to his little undersea kingdom.'

'That will not happen,' said Corvus, shaking his head. 'I am a businessman, after all. It is in the interests of myself and those I intend to invite to join me in my new Atlantis to see a healthy and growing world economy from which we can all profit. I would not do such a thing.'

'But I would,' said Sophia from behind him.

Surprised, Corvus looked round at her – as a gory bullet hole exploded in his chest.

24

Nina shrieked as Corvus toppled from the plinth and hit the stone floor face-first. Sophia raised her gun to her lips and blew away the smoke. 'I've been waiting *such* a long time to do that. Pompous old bastard.'

'Well, I did warn him not to turn his back on you,' said Chase. He noticed that none of the other men had done anything more than flinch at the sudden gunshot. They weren't Corvus's people, but *Sophia's*, knowing about her plan all along. 'Two dead husbands in one week? That's got to be a record.'

'It'll be three soon enough, Eddie,' Sophia told him pointedly.

An eager smile appeared on Komosa's face, his diamond-studded tooth glinting as much as the treasures of the tomb. 'Does that mean I can kill them now?'

Sophia shook her head. 'I think it's only fair to Eddie that I be the one who kills him. For old times' sake. Business before pleasure, though – we need to start moving the gold. Eddie, Nina, sit down. This may take some time.' She hopped from the plinth. 'Joe, keep an eye on them.'

Komosa's smile disappeared, but he did as he was told, directing Chase and Nina to sit with their backs against the ramp next to one of the piles of treasure. 'So what do *you* want with all of this?' Chase asked Sophia.

'René was a megalomaniac idealist,' said Sophia, with a disdainful glance at her husband's corpse, 'which is a rather deluded combination. His plan would never have worked, anyway – putting that many arrogant, ultra-ambitious, ruthlessly competitive people into the same confined space would be a recipe for disaster. My plan is somewhat more realistic.'

'And what *is* your plan?' Nina asked.

Sophia smiled. 'To paraphrase my two late husbands, I'm not a James Bond villain. So I'm not going to tell you.' She walked to the man with the tablet computer, who was talking into his radio. 'What's the situation?'

'The helicopters are just landing, ma'am,' he told her. 'Once they're down, they can take a ground sonar reading to find the best penetration point.'

'Good,' said Sophia. She addressed the other men. 'Start collecting the gold. Get the ingots first; they'll be the easiest to handle.' They moved to obey.

'Well, this didn't turn out too well,' said Chase, watching as the men stacked up the gold bars in a section of open floor near the plinth.

'We're not dead yet,' Nina reminded him, picking up a large golden bowl and reading the Greek letters inscribed round its side. ' "In honour of the mighty Heracles, our saviour and friend." Huh. Shame he can't help us now.' She put the bowl down next to Chase and picked up a diamond. She was no expert, but from its size alone guessed it had to be at least five carats, worth tens of thousands of dollars. 'It's amazing. He really existed, even if his achievements were mythologised over time. And he must have been incredibly highly thought of, for people to have paid him this much tribute. This is as big an archaeological discovery as Atlantis.'

'Yeah, but you're not going to get to tell anyone about finding this either,' Chase told her ruefully. She closed her fist round the diamond and leaned against him, holding his hand.

It wasn't long before they heard a muffled thump from overhead: a small explosive cartridge being fired into the ground to act as a sonar source, reflected sound waves telling those above the thickness of the sand and rock covering the roof of the tomb. Within minutes, the results were relayed to Sophia, the man with the computer pacing to a spot several yards to one side of the plinth.

'Clear that area,' she ordered. Her men quickly moved the nearby treasure aside to leave an open space. Everyone moved well clear. A few minutes later, there was a much louder detonation. Large chunks of stone dropped from the roof and smashed on the floor, sand streaming down through a hole in the ceiling. A spear of blinding daylight lanced into the tomb, the gold lighting up as if aflame.

There was a wait while the team on the surface used their sonar device again to check the ceiling's structural integrity; then, satisfied that it was safe, they widened the hole with picks and mallets, causing more stones to fall into the chamber. Before long, an opening some ten feet by six had been knocked through the ceiling. Another wait, shadows dancing through the beam of daylight as men worked above to set up a heavy-duty winch system, and then a metal platform was lowered into the tomb.

'Good work, boys,' said Sophia. 'Start loading the gold. How much will the choppers be able to carry? Bearing in mind that there'll be five fewer passengers on the return trip, of course.'

'About five thousand four hundred kilos per helicopter,' said the man with the computer after a few seconds of calculations. 'It will take the platform . . . twenty-three trips to carry that much.'

'Then we'd better get started.' She watched as ingots were loaded on to the platform, until a shout from above told the men that it had reached its weight limit. With a strained electric whine, it slowly rose to the ceiling, blotting out the light when it reached the top. The men in the tomb began moving more bars into place ready for the next trip as their counterparts above unloaded the cargo for transport to the helicopters.

'That was really quite a sight,' said Sophia to Chase as she stood next to Komosa. 'Twenty million dollars in gold, all fitted on to one little platform. And that was only the first load.'

'You should have brought red, white and blue Mini Coopers instead of choppers,' Chase said unenthusiastically. 'So, now what? Is this it? You going to kill us?'

Sophia drew her gun. 'I think it's about time, yes. Get up.' Chase started to stand, but she waved him back down. 'No, no. Her first.'

Nina stood, fists clenched. 'Nina, don't,' Chase said.

'It's okay, Eddie,' she told him, fixing Sophia with a defiant glare. 'There's no way I'm going to die on my knees. Not in front of this bitch.'

Sophia's eyes narrowed. 'I *told* you what I'd do to you if you called me a bitch again.'

'Yeah? Bring it on, *bitch!*'

The whirr of the descending platform came from the other side of the ramp, unnoticed, as Sophia turned angrily to Komosa. 'Joe, give me your knife.'

Nina's gaze flicked down to meet Chase's, just for a moment – but it was all the time they needed to communicate. Chase shifted position, very slightly.

Komosa looked away from his prisoners down to the sheathed knife on his belt as he reached for it. Sophia impatiently held out her left hand, her gun shifting slightly away from Nina – and Nina lashed out, slicing a gash across Sophia's cheek with the sharp tip of the diamond she had pushed out between her clenched fingers. Sophia gasped in pain, clapping her free hand against her face. Anger flared in her eyes, momentarily overpowering reason, the gun forgotten.

But Komosa hadn't forgotten *his* gun. He snapped round to shoot Nina—

Chase jumped up and hurled the heavy golden bowl like a discus.

Not at Sophia or Komosa, but over the end of the ramp, at the statue of Hercules.

It struck the golden club with a sound like a ringing gong and spun away, dented. The club wobbled . . . then fell from the statue's hand.

And all hell broke loose.

The dull clanks made by the wedges restraining the heavy carved discs as they dropped down into their sockets were drowned out by the crunch of stone against stone. The discs began to roll inexorably down the ramps, rapidly picking up speed.

Nina and Chase barged Sophia and Komosa aside and sprinted

for the exit from the tomb. Behind them, one of the discs hit a weighty chunk of ceiling debris that had fallen on the ramp and tipped over the edge, smashing on to the tomb floor like a stone bomb.

But the other three stayed on course for the pillars surrounding the sarcophagus—

The bases of two of the pillars were pulverised, immediately collapsing. The third suffered a more glancing blow, a section knocked sideways so that it still barely held up the column above.

But it would not hold for long.

An entire section of roof on the far side of the plinth plummeted downwards, the stone slabs of the ceiling and the tons of loose rock and sand covering it hitting the floor with earth-shaking force. Cracks radiated outwards, widening the jagged gap, more spears of daylight stabbing into the tomb as smaller holes ripped open in their wake.

Komosa recovered from his shocked paralysis and turned to aim at Chase and Nina as they fled – only to see Sophia hurdling the bottom of the ramp, running as fast as she could for the winch platform. Eyes widening as he realised he was being abandoned, he raced after her.

Weaving through the meteor storm of falling stones, Nina and Chase kept running.

Sophia rushed past her men, most of whom had dived to the floor to avoid the broken disc as it came off the ramp, and leapt on to the platform. Several bars of gold had already been loaded, but she ignored them and hit the green button to start the winch.

The platform began to ascend. A second later, Komosa vaulted one of the bewildered men and landed beside her. He gave her a dirty look, which she ignored, instead throwing one of the ingots from the platform. Komosa got the idea and did the same, the heavy ringing thud of the soft metal bars hitting the floor joining the clash of more falling stones.

Another man tried to jump on to the platform as it rose, slamming into it at chest height and scrabbling for a handhold. Sophia and Komosa exchanged glances, then as one kicked him in the face. He screamed as he fell back to the ground. The extra weight gone, the platform picked up speed.

The exit was a dark rectangle ahead of Nina. Chase was right beside her.

Stone above splintered like breaking bone. Another section of roof tore loose, slabs crashing down in a solid wave behind them.

The damaged pillar finally collapsed. The ceiling above it held for a moment, then succumbed to gravity.

Even before the platform reached the surface, Sophia and Komosa threw themselves from it and raced desperately away across the stony hill as the holes behind them widened and merged, gaping mouths in the ground swallowing everything up.

The platform disappeared back into the earth from which it had just emerged, the winch following. One of the helicopters was consumed as well, teetering on the edge of the expanding sinkhole before being pitched nose-first into the maelstrom of churning rubble and dust below.

All support gone, what remained of the tomb's ceiling gave way at once, a square a hundred and fifty feet across suddenly collapsing with an impact so huge that one of the other helicopters was thrown on its side, rotor blades snapping like dry sticks.

Chase and Nina dived at the archway as the roof dropped, all light abruptly blotted out by hundreds of tons of stone—

Sophia sat up, panting, and squinted through the dust cloud. Inches from her feet was the edge of a crater. Komosa's diving escape had been even narrower, his shins actually over the rim of the great hole.

'Jesus Christ!' Sophia gasped, her normal composure shaken. 'That . . . that fucking *maniac!*' She staggered to her feet and moved to a safer distance from the angular crater before surveying the scene. The tail of one of the helicopters poked up from the rubble below. On the far side of the hole, the handful of her men who had managed to get clear of the collapse milled in confusion around the surviving chopper.

Komosa joined her, wiping dust from his face and bald head. 'Now what do we do?'

Sophia took a long breath to settle herself. 'Well, we'll need some more helicopters, for a start,' she finally said, voice returning to her usual clipped, even tones. 'But this can still be excavated and the gold recovered; it'll just take a little more time. And I don't actually need the gold to be in my possession – as long as I know where it is and can still get to it, that's what's important. But we'll need to get a trustworthy team of diggers out here as soon as possible. I don't want to delay the plan.'

Komosa peered down into the pit. Broken slabs of roof jutted out of the rubble like the bones of some vast animal carcass. 'And what about . . . *them?* Do you think they could have survived?'

Sophia frowned. 'Even if they survived, which I very much hope they didn't, and even if they manage to get back through the maze . . . they'll be stuck in the desert a hundred miles from anywhere with no food, no water and no survival equipment. Eddie's good, but he's not *that* good.' She looked back at the destroyed helicopters. 'Just to be safe, as well as recovering the gold, have everything that could be used for survival stripped out of the wrecked choppers.'

Komosa nodded, then set off round the edge of the hole. Sophia remained still for a moment, gazing into the crater. 'Goodbye, Eddie,' she said, before turning away to follow the Nigerian.

25

Chase opened his eyes . . . to see nothing but blackness.

He knew he wasn't dead, though. The stitches in his leg ached too much.

The collapsing roof had felt like a bomb exploding behind him, a shockwave of displaced air blasting him through the gilded archway into the passage beyond. Ears still ringing, he got to his knees. The air was full of dust; he coughed, putting a hand over his mouth and nose to filter the worst of it.

Eyes adjusting, he saw a feeble scrap of daylight making it through the stone and sand now blocking the archway, dust swirling through the soft glow.

That was the end of the Tomb of Hercules, he thought. Anything inside would have been hammered flat as the ceiling collapsed. Nina wouldn't be happy . . .

'Nina!'

The name burst from him, shocking him back to full awareness. She had been beside him just before they reached the exit – where was she now?

He groped blindly through the rubble on the floor of the passage, feeling nothing but hard stone, the dry and gritty rasp of sand. The faint light didn't even provide enough illumination for him to make out his own fingers.

A fear rose inside him, the cold horror of loss. He'd felt it before, in combat, the growing certainty that somebody from his unit wasn't coming back.

But this wasn't combat. And Nina was more than any comrade in arms . . .

'*Nina!*' A scream this time, but still unanswered. His hands clawed harder through the smashed stones, scattering them aside in an increasingly desperate search for anything that wasn't unyielding and cold—

His fingers brushed soft cloth. Nina's shirt.

Under a lump of stone.

'Shit!' Chase pulled the fractured slab off her, throwing it aside. He still couldn't see, but felt her lying on her back.

Unmoving.

'Oh, fuck,' he gasped, reaching for her neck, searching for a pulse. 'Shit, come on, come on . . .'

Nothing—

'Come *on!*'

A pulsation beneath his fingertip, weak but definitely there.

Relief exploded within him. 'Oh, Jesus, *yes!*' he cried, clearing the rest of the rubble from her. 'Nina, come on, wake up . . .'

Chase hurriedly checked her for the wetness of blood or the jagged bulge of a broken bone beneath the skin. Not finding either, he bent to feel for her breath against his cheek.

Nothing.

Without light, there was no way for him to tell why she was unresponsive. He didn't even know how long she had been unconscious, having lost track of time while he'd been dazed. It could have been just seconds, or over a minute . . .

He began CPR. Heel of his hand on Nina's chest, pushing down firmly. Thirty compressions. Then he tilted back her head and pinched shut her nose with one hand, delivering two breaths into her open mouth.

No response.

The fear returning, he started a second round of chest compressions, fighting not to rush. Ten, twenty, thirty. Tipping her head back again, another two breaths, anxiously waiting for any kind of reaction—

She convulsed, gasping hoarsely. Chase squeezed her hand. 'Nina! Can you hear me? Are you okay?'

Nina took in several deep, whooping breaths, Chase feeling her pulse racing as he held her hand more tightly. 'Eddie . . .' she finally managed to wheeze.

'Are you okay?'

'You know something?' she whispered.

'What?'

'That's the first time we've kissed in ages.'

Even though Chase couldn't see her face, he could tell she was smiling. 'Well, this is the second,' he said, lowering his head.

'Are you all right?' she asked when they finally moved apart.

'Fine as I can be,' he said. 'Hold on, I'm going to get up. Can you stand?'

She cautiously moved her limbs. 'I think so.'

Chase stood. The dust had settled somewhat, but the faint illumination from the ruined tomb was no brighter than before.

He took her hand. 'Ready?' On her vaguely positive response, he straightened, bringing her up with him.

'Ow, shit!' she complained. 'God damn it, son of a *bitch*! Oh, God, my ankle hurts again. Shit!'

'Lean against me,' Chase told her, putting an arm round her waist to take her weight.

'Thanks,' Nina gasped. 'Oh, that bitch. I'm *so* going to kick her ass.' She looked around, seeing nothing but the weak light in the blackness. 'Where are we? Is that daylight?'

'Yeah,' said Chase, 'but there's about a hundred tons of rock in front of it. We're in the room with the dog statue.'

'Then only the actual tomb collapsed, not the whole thing?'

'Far as I can tell.'

Excitement entered Nina's voice. 'Then we can still get out! All we have to do is backtrack through the labyrinth!'

'Well, that'd be dead easy if we could actually *see* anything. Unless you've got some night-vision goggles hidden in your knickers.'

She batted a hand lightly on his chest. 'Don't start. We only have to get to the room with Hippolyta, and then we can get a flashlight. One of Corvus's men had a little accident after you left. They didn't pick up his gear. Once we've got a light, we can work back through the maze just by following the tracks we made coming in.'

Now it was Chase's turn to sound excited. 'Did he have a radio?'

'I think so. But it'll only be short range, surely? Unless you were planning to ask Sophia for a ride in her helicopter.'

'Don't worry about that,' Chase assured her. 'You just try to remember how to get us back through the maze. I don't want to survive all this only to make a wrong turn and fall down some bloody pit . . .'

To Chase's relief, Nina was able to guide them back through the labyrinth.

By the time they finally emerged from the tomb, the sun was low on the horizon behind the hill. The temperature was still searingly hot, however, heat haze rippling the endless dunes.

Nina stayed in the shade of the rock passage as Chase warily emerged with the F2000 rifle he'd taken from the dead man in the chamber of Hippolyta, in case Sophia had left anyone lying in wait for them. But there was no sign of life other than flitting insects.

'So now what do we do?' Nina asked. 'It's a long way to the nearest town, and this' – she held up the man's half-litre water bottle – 'isn't exactly going to see us through. Unless you know some kind of super SAS desert survival techniques?'

'I know something even better,' said Chase with a sly grin, switching on the radio and setting it to a particular channel. He looked skywards as he pushed the transmit key and spoke into it, Nina becoming more puzzled with each word. 'Bravo, Romeo, Delta, Sierra, Whisky, Romeo, Delta. The pipes are calling. I say again . . .' He repeated the bizarre message twice more.

Nina's eyebrows rose in utter incredulity. 'What the *hell* was that?'

'That,' said Chase, 'was Mac's MI6 exit code. Every spook's got one, it's a sort of absolute last resort, "I'm in deep shit, get me the fuck out of here!" message. Soon as MI6 hears one, they do whatever they can to extract whoever sent it. And since we're not in the middle of a war zone or in some country with massive border defences, hopefully they shouldn't have too much trouble getting to us.'

Nina pointed at the walkie-talkie. 'But how are they going to hear it on that little Radio Shack piece of crap?'

'They won't. But the National Security Agency in the States *will*. American spooks are usually even bigger dickheads than British ones, but their technology's bloody amazing – they can hear a sparrow fart on the other side of the Atlantic. They'll have pinpointed where it was sent from by satellite, and they'll know it's an exit code, so they'll pass it right on to their poodles at Vauxhall Cross.' He squinted up at the deep blue sky as if expecting to see one of the satellites passing overhead. 'I'll repeat it every hour, but they'll have got it already. We just need to sit tight and wait for 'em to show up.'

'I'll remember that the next time I don't have money for a cab ride home,' said Nina.

'Well, not with that code – they're a one-shot deal. But it's useful to know.' He returned to the shade, sitting down next to Nina. 'So, we've got a bit of time to kill. Anything you want to talk about?'

'I think there's something we both need to talk about,' Nina said. They looked at each other for a long moment.

'Actually,' said Chase, 'I don't think you need to say anything. I do, though. About how I've been acting like a complete twat for the past few months.'

'I wouldn't say *complete* . . .' Another exchange of looks, and they both smiled. 'But I haven't exactly been the model of understanding either. I got so obsessed with finding the Tomb of Hercules that I wasn't paying any attention to anything – or any*one*

– else. And it was purely for my own gratification, as well. Just because I couldn't go public about finding Atlantis, I ended up fixating on something that I *could* brag to the world about discovering. And look where it got us.'

'You did find it, though,' Chase reminded her.

'For what it's worth. You were right, I was putting it above everything else. And I'm sorry. And not just for the whole evil-ex-wife-steals-gold-and-nukes thing, either.'

Chase sighed. 'Yeah, well, I'm sorry too. This whole bloody mess is my fault. If I hadn't gone running off to help Sophia . . . Christ.' He banged his head against the rock. 'All this 'cause I thought my girlfriend wasn't paying enough attention to me. Any normal bloke'd just go to a strip club with his mates, but no, *I* have to start World War fucking Three.'

'Sophia was right,' Nina said sadly, prompting Chase to look questioningly at her. 'We *weren't* communicating. I was obsessing, you had cabin fever . . . and it wasn't that we didn't tell each other. We just didn't *listen*.'

'Well, I'm listening now. Just hope it's not too late to make a difference.'

Her tone became hopeful. 'I don't think it is. What about you?'

'I think . . .' His voice filled with barely contained emotion. 'There was a moment back there, after the roof fell in, that I thought I'd lost you. And . . . I think that was the worst moment in my entire life.'

'Really?'

He nodded. 'We've had some problems, but fuck it. Once we get out of this, I want to fix them. Whatever it takes.'

She rested her head on his shoulder. 'Me too. Whatever it takes. I don't want to lose you again either.'

He kissed her forehead. 'Great. Then we're in agreement.'

'It's been a while.'

'Too long. So let's keep it this way.'

'I agree.'

Chase managed a tired laugh, stroking her arm. 'Now all we've got to do actually *is* get out of this. Just hope MI6 are more reliable than last time.'

Nina looked up at him. 'Last time?'

He grinned. 'Long story.'

She smiled back. 'I think you've got time to tell it.'

Night had fallen.

Nina and Chase huddled together between the rocks, out of the wind. The stars overhead shone with an almost unnatural brilliance, sparkling like the gems strewn throughout the Tomb of Hercules. Nina shifted position to gaze up at the spectacle. 'You were right.'

'About what?'

'Stargazing in the Grand Erg. It really *is* amazing.'

Chase chuckled, putting his arm around her. 'I love you.'

Nina gave him a look of delighted surprise. 'Where did *that* come from?'

'Thought I owed it to you. Should have said it a long time ago.'

She hugged him. 'Better late than never. And I love you too.'

'Glad to hear it.' Chase smiled, then rubbed his bare arms. The heat of the day was gone, the temperature having plunged enough to give him goose pimples. 'God, I really miss my jacket,' he grumbled. 'Went through all kinds of stuff in it. Never thought it'd be melted by acid.'

'I'll get you a new one,' Nina assured him.

'It won't be the same.'

'It'll be better, I promise.'

He smiled. 'Is that like a metaphor or something?'

'Could be . . .' Suddenly, she felt him tense. 'What is it?'

'I can hear something.' They both stood, Chase picking up the rifle, and stepped out of the stone passage.

Nina could now hear it too, a distant rumble. 'Chopper?'

'Sounds like it. Can't tell from where, though.' He pointed to the south. 'See if you can see any nav lights.'

Nina scanned the horizon, but saw nothing except stars. 'What if it's Sophia?'

He hefted the F2000. 'Then I've got twenty bullets with her name on them. And ten spares for that body-pierced bastard.'

After a minute, Nina called out to Chase, who was watching the sky to the north. 'Over here!'

He ran to her, seeing flashing lights low over the horizon to the southeast. 'Coming right at us, whoever it is.' He looked thoughtfully at the approaching helicopter, then switched on the rifle's spotlight and aimed it at the aircraft.

'You sure that's a good idea? If it's Sophia, you're leading her right to us.'

'I don't think it's a Sikorsky. Too small. But wait in the tunnel entrance, just in case.'

The next minute passed with rising anxiety as the helicopter closed in. When it was four hundred yards away, it slowed to a hover and turned sideways-on to them, whipping up sand in its downwash. Chase locked the crosshairs on to the pilot, but nobody within the craft was aiming weapons back at him. The helicopter only had two people aboard, neither of whom was Sophia or Komosa. In the co-pilot's seat, he saw a man staring at him through binoculars.

Chase lowered the rifle and waved. The chopper drifted closer. 'Looks promising,' he called to Nina, 'but stay out of sight for now.'

The helicopter set down two hundred feet away, Chase shielding his eyes against the blowing grit. A man jumped from the cabin. Head low until he was clear of the spinning blades, he jogged towards the tomb entrance. 'Mac!' he shouted. 'Mac, is that you?'

'Oh, Christ,' Chase muttered. He thought he knew the voice, and a glance through the sights – during which time he was very tempted to pull the trigger – confirmed his suspicions. 'Hold it, Alderley! Of all the fucking people they could send, it *would* be you, wouldn't it?'

The man froze. 'Well, blimey. Eddie Chase.' His right hand slipped into his jacket.

'Don't even think about it,' Chase told him, raising the gun and shining its spotlight to reveal a thin-faced, middle-aged man sporting what Chase could only think of as a 1970s porn star's moustache.

Alderley hurriedly raised his hands. 'You know, Chase, misuse of an SIS extraction code is a pretty serious offence. Unless Mac's hiding back there somewhere, you're in a lot of trouble.'

'Nothing new there. And Mac's dead.'

'What?' Alderley seemed genuinely unsettled for a moment,

before suspicion crept on to his face. '*You* didn't kill him, did you?'

'Of course I bloody didn't! The people who stranded us here did, though.'

'Who's "us"?' Alderley asked, looking round.

'Nina!' Chase called. Nina cautiously emerged from the tomb. 'Alderley, this is Dr Nina Wilde, Director of Operations for the UN's International Heritage Agency. Nina, this is Peter Alderley, MI6 spook and absolute bell-end.'

'Hi,' said Nina, waving politely. Alderley half-heartedly returned the gesture with one of his raised hands. 'Eddie, are you really going to keep pointing the gun at the guy who's come to rescue us?'

'I came to rescue *Mac*,' said Alderley. 'Not some sanctimonious ex-squaddie. I ought to just leave you here, Chase. Freelancers aren't any of my business. But ...' He looked at Nina. 'I can't really leave a lady in distress, can I?'

'Thank you,' said Nina. 'I'm very grateful. And so is Eddie,' she added. Chase grunted.

'All right.' Alderley sighed. 'This is entirely against protocol, but since I'm out here anyway, I may as well do my good deed for the day. Just get rid of the rifle, Chase. I don't want you sitting with a live weapon aimed at my back for the whole trip.'

Reluctantly, Chase tossed the F2000 aside. For a moment, Alderley hesitated as if about to draw his own gun, but then he lowered his arms. 'What *are* you doing out here, anyway?' he asked. 'This is supposed to be nothing but open desert, but when I checked the latest satellite image before setting off, there was a bloody huge smoking crater with a helicopter sticking out of it!'

'There was an ancient tomb under the hill,' Nina said, 'but it collapsed.'

Alderley gestured at Chase. 'And I imagine he was the cause of that?'

Chase gave the MI6 agent a nasty look. 'At least when I blow stuff up I try to minimise the collateral damage!'

'Two minutes,' said Alderley, rolling his eyes. 'I'm amazed it took so long for that to come up.'

Chase took an angry step towards him, but Nina took hold of his arm. 'Whatever problem you two have, could you maybe put it on hold? Until we're, y'know, not *stranded in the desert*?'

'I *suppose*,' Chase said irritably.

'Good. So, Mr Alderley? Can we go now?'

Alderley's base of operations was across the border in southern Tunisia, a small drilling rig in a bleak region of rocky desert.

'Natural gas exploration,' Alderley explained after they had landed and he had taken Nina and Chase to the cabin housing his office. 'It's really a cover so we can keep an eye on what's going on next door in Libya, but the funny thing is that it's actually been quite successful. Always nice to have an intelligence operation that turns a profit.'

'Great,' said Chase, unimpressed. 'You'll be able to buy another crappy old Ford Capri with it.'

'The Mark One 3000GT is a classic!' protested Alderley in what seemed to Nina to be automatic defensiveness, before he composed himself and sat at his desk to log on to his computer. 'Okay. Now, let me check what you told me on the flight . . .' He hunched forward, pecking at the keys with two fingers.

Nina and Chase sat on a small, worn couch. 'So, what's your problem with this guy?' Nina asked quietly.

Chase glared at Alderley. 'SAS and MI6 sometimes do joint ops, with a spook as a sort of overseer. We went after some al-Qaeda wanker who was hiding out in a village in Pakistan – it was a secret op since Pakistan's supposed to be an ally. Went in and bagged the guy without any trouble, but then this twat' – he jabbed a finger at Alderley – 'decides to cover our tracks by blowing up half the fucking village!'

'It was an entirely normal false flag operation so we could blame al-Qaeda for making bombs in a civilian area and lose them Pakistani support,' said Alderley patronisingly, barely looking up from the computer. 'And it was hardly half the village, it was three houses at most, and they were probably terrorist sympathisers anyway. You were the only person in the unit who objected.'

'Yeah, and I bet your nose still hurts.'

Alderley self-consciously rubbed the bridge of his nose, which Nina noticed for the first time had a prominent bump, the relic of an old break. 'Anyway,' he said, 'I have some news for you.'

Chase sat up. 'Let me guess. Good kind and bad kind?'

'Actually, yes. The good news is that Mac isn't dead.'

'He's okay?' Nina asked excitedly.

'That depends on your definition of okay. Apparently he jumped out of a window just before his entire house blew up. He's in a coma.'

Nina gripped Chase's hand. 'Oh, no . . .'

'And the bad news, for you two at least, is that as soon as I put your names into the system all kinds of warnings came up.' He leaned back in his chair, resting his right hand across his chest –

just an inch from the shoulder holster now visible beneath his jacket. 'You've been busy. Diamond theft, assassinating the Botswanan minister of trade . . . Mac must have pulled some very long strings just to get you back to England. And then you follow that by blowing up his house and murdering a Chinese–American billionaire!'

'We didn't kill anybody!' Nina cried, before thinking about it. 'Okay, maybe a few,' she corrected. 'But they were all bad guys!'

'Sophia Blackwood's behind the whole thing,' Chase said.

Alderley gave him a dubious frown. 'You mean *Lady* Sophia Blackwood?'

'Yep.'

'Your ex-wife?'

'And Richard Yuen's ex-wife as well. *And* René Corvus's, seeing as he was just shot through the heart, and she's to blame. Although I bet she hasn't made that public yet. Having two billionaire husbands die in four days might make people a bit suspicious.'

Alderley checked the computer, raising his eyebrows. 'You're right – it says here that she married this Corvus chap the day after the other one was killed. Nothing about him dying, though.'

'She did it to gain control of both their companies,' Nina told him. 'Yuen was using uranium he was secretly mining in Botswana to make atomic bombs that he planned to sell to terrorists. Sophia killed him so she could marry Corvus and he could start up his own little nuclear-armed fantasy island . . . but then she killed him too!'

'And now she's got a nuke,' Chase continued. 'Problem is, we don't know where she's taken it or what she wants to do with it.'

'Something to do with the financial markets,' said Nina. 'That's why Corvus wanted the contents of the Tomb of Hercules, to act as security. Presumably Sophia wants it for the same purpose – but a different motive.'

'The Tomb of Hercules, hmm?' Alderley said, pursing his lips dubiously. 'As in the Greek god?'

'Well, technically just a *demi*god, as he didn't actually ascend to divine status until after he died—'

'I don't think he wants a history lesson,' said Chase.

Alderley tapped a finger on his chin. 'This all sounds, ah, quite insane, actually. Uranium mines? Nuclear bombs? Ancient tombs? Hercules?' He turned to Chase. 'And you're saying that your ex-wife is behind it all?'

'Mac believed us,' said Chase firmly. 'He was going to persuade MI6 to check out the uranium mine.'

'Too bad he's not in any condition to confirm that. Or maybe that's a good thing, from your perspective.' The MI6 agent's right hand slid towards his holster again.

'He believed us enough to get us out of Africa,' Nina said. 'And enough to get Eddie the documents he needed to go to Switzerland. I'm sure you'll be able to confirm that much.'

With a wary eye on Chase, Alderley worked the computer. 'So he did. And he must have used up a few favours to pull it off so fast . . .'

'Mac trusted us,' Nina pleaded. 'If you can too, then we have a chance of stopping whatever Sophia intends to do. Before she sets off her nuke.'

Alderley looked conflicted, but also exasperated. 'It's your word against hers,' he said. 'And to be honest, she has a lot more credibility than you do. She's titled, she's a member of the establishment – and you're both wanted for murder!'

'Having a title doesn't stop you from being dodgy,' Chase reminded him. 'There's a couple of lords who've ended up in the slammer.'

'Even if I believe you, and I'm not making any promises, I don't see what I can do. If I tell MI6 that I have you, they'll just order me to arrest you both.'

'Then don't tell 'em,' said Chase. 'Just say you've found out something that means MI6 need to check into what Sophia's been doing in Botswana and Switzerland.'

'I can't do that without telling them *how* I found out,' Alderley insisted, 'and as soon as I do, they'll order me to arrest you and we'll be back where we started!'

'There must be *some* way you can help us,' Nina said.

'Not without proof of what you've told me.'

Chase snorted. 'Big smoking crater not enough for you?'

'If there isn't a nuclear weapon at the bottom of it, then no. Just because Mac believed you doesn't mean anyone else will, and so far all I've had from you are accusations. That isn't proof.'

'What if we could get you proof?' asked Nina thoughtfully.

Alderley leaned back. 'Considering your current lack of credibility, the kind of proof I'd need to show MI6 would more or less have to be a nuclear bomb with his ex-wife's fingerprints all over it, tied up with a pretty bow.'

'We'll get it.'

Chase looked at her. 'We will?'

'Okay, maybe not the pretty bow. But if we find Sophia, we'll find the bomb. And if we find the bomb, then Mr Alderley can do what he needs to do.'

'How will she be travelling?' asked Alderley.

'In one of Corvus's private jets.'

He nodded. 'Shouldn't be any problem to track down.'

Nina waved a hand at the computer. 'Please, be my guest!'

'It's in the air,' Alderley reported a few minutes later. 'Took off about an hour ago.'

'Where's it headed?' Chase asked.

'Flight plan says . . . Marsh Harbour. The Bahamas.'

'The Bahamas?' Chase's expression became more intense. 'That's where Corvus was testing his underwater city stuff.'

Alderley checked the computer again. 'Nearly all of Corvus's merchant ships are registered in the Bahamas.' More clicking. 'And it's listed as his primary country of residence for tax purposes.'

'If he's got a home there, it's probably where Sophia's going,' Chase realised. 'She sure as fuck won't be expecting to see us again. If we could catch her there . . .'

'Can you get us to the Bahamas?' Nina asked Alderley.

He blinked at her in momentary bewilderment before sitting upright. 'Er, *what*? Are you serious?'

'Perfectly. Whatever Sophia's doing in the Bahamas, I'm sure it isn't to work on her tan.'

'She tried to kill Mac,' Chase reminded him. 'Nearly succeeded, as well.'

Alderley scratched his moustache, thinking. 'If it wasn't for Mac, I wouldn't even be considering this,' he said at last. 'But I'll see what I can do. I don't know how much that'll be, though.'

'Well, Mac managed to get me a fake passport, plane tickets and a wad of cash in about four hours flat, and he wasn't even a full-time member of MI6, just a consultant,' Chase remarked.

'I get the point,' said Alderley, looking mildly stung. 'But you're seriously going to owe me for this, Chase. And if anything goes wrong, I'll just say that you forced me into it somehow. I'm sure they're more likely to believe me than the people who assassinated the Botswanan minister of trade.'

'We *didn't*!' Nina moaned.

Chase shrugged. 'Just sort things out for us, and I'll get you all the Ford Capri parts you'll ever need.'

Alderley actually smiled. 'I might hold you to that, Chase. They're surprisingly expensive these days ... All right, I'll do what I can. But you won't be able to fly out until tomorrow no matter what I do, so you'll have to spend the night here. Oh, and that sofa is the only spare bed in the place, so make yourselves comfortable.'

'I'm disappointed in you,' said Chase with a crooked grin. 'You're going to make a lady sleep on the settee while your own bed's going empty? You'll be in here for a while yet fixing everything up.'

Beaten, Alderley gestured at a door in the office's back wall. 'All right, Dr Wilde, my bed's through there.'

'Thank you,' Nina said, smiling as she stood.

He seemed mollified by her gratitude, though his expression changed when Chase stood up as well. 'And where do you think you're going?'

'Like I said,' Chase told him, grinning again, 'you're going to be working for a while yet. And me and my *girlfriend* need to make up for lost time.' He put his arms round Nina's waist.

420

She brushed him off. 'He's just kidding,' she assured the mortified Alderley.

'Yeah, right,' said Chase, trying to take hold of her again.

'No, really! This isn't the right time or place.'

'It couldn't be a *better* time!'

'Eddie! Besides, Mr Alderley might need to ask you more questions.'

'Oh, all bloody right,' Chase said, returning to the sofa and trying to ignore Alderley's smug look. 'So what *is* the right time?'

'Let's see – how about after we've cleared our names, found the bomb, caught Sophia and stopped whatever the hell insane plan she's trying to carry out?'

Chase cracked his knuckles and smiled wolfishly at Nina. 'Always good to have an incentive.'

'So,' she said, 'when we get to the Bahamas, do you have any lady friends there who can help us?'

'I've got a *friend*,' he told her. 'Not one I want to see in a miniskirt, mind . . .'

26

The Bahamas

Matt Trulli leaned back on his bar stool and regarded Chase and Nina uncertainly. 'So . . . you're telling me that my billionaire boss was actually some kind of crackpot megalomaniac?'

Chase nodded. 'Afraid so,' said Nina.

'Aw, what?' Trulli said in dismay, taking a gulp from his drink. 'Two for two?'

'Maybe you should come and work for the IHA,' Nina suggested. 'The pay might not be as good, but I don't think any world domination plots have ever come up in meetings.'

'And he's dead now?' Trulli asked.

'Yeah,' said Chase. 'My ex-wife shot him in the back.'

'Wow. Good job you never pissed her off that much, mate.'

'Oh, she'll be plenty pissed when she realises we're not dead,' said Nina. 'And even more so when we find her nuke.'

Trulli almost choked on his lager. '*Nuke?*' he gasped.

'Keep it down,' Chase said in a warning tone, glancing round the bar. Fortunately, none of the evening patrons were taking any interest in them. 'Yeah, she's got a nuke. So now we need to find her, so we can find *it*. Any idea where she might be?'

'We think she might be at Corvus's house,' Nina added.

Trulli smiled. 'Well, I know where *that* is!'

'You've been there?'

'I *built* it! It's the test bed for an underwater habitat – it was what René hired me for. He wanted a scalable, modular underwater habitat that could work at least thirty metres deep. Well, that kind of thing's been at the back of every marine engineer's mind ever since they drew their first submarine in crayon as a kid, you know? And it was a no-expense-spared deal that he wanted done as soon as possible, so I got right down to it, no worries. We had the prototype built and working within a year.' His pride became more tempered. 'Mind you, if I'd realised what he wanted it for, I might not have been in such a rush.'

'I need to get inside it,' Chase said. 'Soon. As in tonight. Can you help us?'

Trulli made a pained face. 'Your ex-missus doesn't sound like the kind of girl who cares about experimental submarines, so whatever happens I'm probably out of a job. And I don't really like the idea of nukes going off, so . . .' He took a quick gulp from his drink. 'Sure. What do you need?'

'A boat, and scuba gear. And a way inside that thing.'

Trulli smiled. 'Got all three, mate.'

Trulli's boat was a far cry from Corvus's cruiser when it came to size and luxury, but the Australian's fifteen-foot motor launch took them from one of the quays of Marsh Harbour up the coast of the island of Grand Abaco efficiently enough.

The habitat was two miles offshore, a man-made island amongst the myriad natural ones of the Bahamas. Like an iceberg, most of it was underwater, the section rising above the surface resembling a high-tech mushroom. Its brightly spotlit top was flattened to serve as a landing pad for helicopters – or, as Chase saw through a pair of binoculars, more exotic aircraft. 'Well, bugger me.'

Nina tapped his arm, wanting to see for herself. He gave her the binoculars. 'What *is* that thing?' she asked.

'Tilt-rotor,' said Chase. Hunched over the pad was a Bell 609 in Corvus's blue and red corporate livery. Although its fuselage looked like a regular plane's, the resemblance ended at the wings. On each wingtip was a bulbous pivoting engine nacelle, at the moment in the vertical position, above which rose an almost comically oversized propeller. 'Civvie version of the Osprey, like a cross between a plane and a chopper. The props point up so it can do vertical takeoffs and landings, then when it's in the air they tip forward so it can fly like a regular plane.'

Nina handed the binoculars back to him. 'Well, if it's there, presumably Sophia is too. Question is, for how long?'

'Weeks, if she wanted,' Trulli told her. 'It's got its own generators – wind and wave power that we were testing, plus diesels – and water purifiers. She could stay there for as long as she's got food.'

'I don't think she's planning on staying long,' said Chase, tightening the harness of the aqualung. 'Whatever she's doing, she wants to do it soon.'

'You sure?' Nina asked.

'I was married to her. I know when she wants to get something over with.' Nina and Trulli shared a suggestive look, then laughed. 'No, not like that, you cheeky bastards!' But Chase was smiling himself, at least until he looked ahead. His expression became entirely serious as he watched the distant habitat.

Nina sat beside him. 'Are you okay?'

'Yeah, I'm fine. Shoulder still hurts, but it won't be a problem.'

'No, I meant . . .' She took his hand. 'About Sophia. You might meet her in there.'

Chase smiled coldly. 'I'm looking forward to it.'

'No.' Nina shook her head. 'You're not. I know you're not. Eddie, you might . . . you might have to *kill* her to stop her.'

'She's tried to kill me. She tried to kill *you*.' Chase slipped a diving knife out of its sheath, examining the blade in the moonlight. 'That makes her a hostile.' The knife made a nasty slicing sound as he thrust it back into the sheath. 'Either she surrenders, or . . .'

'She's not just some goon with a gun,' Nina reminded him softly. 'Are you sure you'd be able to do it?'

Chase looked away from her, not answering. Nina was about to speak again when the burble of the outboard died down. They both looked round at Trulli.

'What's up?' Chase asked.

'Safer not to get any closer,' Trulli replied. 'We're half a kilometre away – any nearer, they might get nosy.'

Chase nodded and donned his diving mask, then took a breath of air from the scuba tank's mouthpiece to test that it was working. Satisfied, he moved to the side of the boat.

'It looks a long way,' said Nina, handing him an underwater digital camera. 'Will you be okay?'

'Half a klick? No problem.'

'Eddie, I . . .' She tailed off.

'Hey.' He touched her cheek. 'I'll be right back.'

'You'd better be. Or I'm coming after you.' She pulled him to her, kissing him deeply before eventually releasing him, screwing up her mouth.

'What's up?' Chase asked.

'You taste of rubber.'

He grinned, then popped in the mouthpiece and waved as he rolled backwards over the side of the boat and splashed into the sea. After taking a moment to orient himself, he swam away, quickly disappearing beneath the shallow waves.

'See you soon,' said Nina quietly after him.

Even in his battered state, it didn't take Chase long to cover the five hundred metres, swimming only a few feet deep. He surfaced briefly when he was about a hundred metres short to check his bearing, then descended.

The seabed on which the habitat had been built, according to Trulli, was about twenty-five metres down. The Australian had sketched the experimental outpost for him: a hefty anchoring base of steel and concrete made up the lowest five metres, a central shaft housing an elevator, a stairwell and trunks for all the electrical and life-support systems rising vertically from it to the landing platform.

There were three more levels below the surface. On Trulli's sketch they resembled doughnuts, a trio of tori making the habitat look to Chase more like some kind of space station than an underwater base. The upper and lower levels were the same size,

426

the central one somewhat larger in circumference, but the basic designs were identical. Each was made up from four habitation sections shaped like swollen crescents, linked into a circle by another four connecting modules running outwards from the central core like spokes.

These levels weren't Chase's immediate concern, however. It was the concrete base that was his first destination. While some of the modules on the second circular deck had airlocks, they were controlled by computers; being intended for use by tourists, the system had been designed to be as near foolproof as humanly possible so that, as Trulli had put it, 'Some drongo can't go "What does this button do?" and flood the place.' Trying to open one of the locks would raise an alarm.

But there was another airlock, a maintenance hatch leading into the habitat's base. And according to Trulli, it was manually operated. An unmonitored entrance.

Chase continued his descent amongst swirling shoals of fish as he neared the structure. Glowing ovals like blank eyes grew in brightness as he approached. He couldn't help but be impressed as he got close enough to make out details. Trulli's tourist-friendly design included lots of large acrylic resin windows set into the modules and smaller domes on their ceilings, through which he could make out the rooms inside.

He saw a figure moving in one of them. Caution and curiosity blending, he swam closer and peered down through one of the ceiling domes.

It was a control room. A man sat at a computer terminal; another walked back to another station with a cup in his hand. Chase carefully moved round the dome for a better look. As far as he could tell, there didn't appear to be security monitors. All the displays were concerned only with the facility's vital systems: tracking power consumption, checking the air. No CCTV cameras. One less thing to worry about once he got inside.

It occurred to him that he had the perfect opportunity to recce the habitat. He turned and swam round the inner circumference of the upper level, looking through each of the domes in turn.

No sign of Sophia, or the bomb. The other modules on this level were prototypes for different configurations of hotel suites. The first level checked, he descended and repeated the process on the second, largest deck. The habitation modules on this level seemed more technical in purpose, airlocks and tubular docks for future tourist submarines jutting out from them. He saw a couple more men repairing some piece of equipment in the first one he checked, nobody in the second—

Chase froze as he looked over the edge of the third section's dome.

Sophia.

Not just Sophia. Komosa was there too . . . and so was the nuke.

What had originally been Corvus's luxurious private suite was now being used as a glorified storeroom. The gold ingots recovered from the Tomb of Hercules were stacked in low piles along one curving wall, but the room's three occupants – as well as Sophia and Komosa, there was the man with the goatee beard whom Chase had seen with Yuen at the factory in Switzerland – were not looking at them. All their attention was on the bomb.

The bearded man knelt before it as if praying, carefully inserting an electronic device into the rectangular slot in the bomb's broad base. The device bore a small display screen and a keypad.

An arming system.

Chase's heart raced, bubbles frothing from his mouthpiece with each breath. He'd been right. Whatever Sophia was planning to use the bomb for, she was going to do it soon.

His options were now down to just one. Even if he used the underwater camera, by the time he had returned to the boat, reached land and sent Alderley enough evidence to convince him to talk to MI6, Sophia could have left. With the tilt-rotor, she could take the bomb anywhere within a thousand miles in three hours.

So he would have to stop her. Alone.

The curve of the dome distorted his view of the room below, but he could see the bearded man entering a code on the keypad, a long string of numbers appearing on the display. An arming code: a security precaution. Even terrorists and rogue states wouldn't want any low-ranking thug to be able to set off their expensive new toy.

The code entered, the man turned to Sophia and asked her something. He nodded at her reply and turned back to the keypad to enter another number.

Chase could see this more clearly. It was a time.

0845. Quarter to nine in the morning.

If Sophia planned to set it off in a city, that would be when the largest number of people were on the streets . . . and assuming the timer had been set for the current time zone, the bomb would go off in less than eleven hours.

The man turned a key in the arming device, and the screen went blank. He then stood and handed the key to Sophia. She regarded it for a moment, then said something that prompted a grin from

Komosa. With that, she closed her fist round the key and walked away, passing out of Chase's sight as she headed for the connecting module. The two men followed her.

He had to enter the base and sabotage the bomb.

He used the camera to take a picture of the room below anyway – if he couldn't get to it, at least he would have proof to send to Alderley. Then he swam downwards, heading for the concrete base.

He passed the third level and took a glowstick from his belt, bending it to mix the fluorescent chemicals within. Something loomed out of the blackness below in the murky orange light.

The base.

Chase quickly located the airlock hatch, right where Trulli had said it was. He brushed away a thin layer of silt and turned the protruding wheel to unseal it. The chamber below, barely large enough for a single person with a scuba tank, had flooded automatically when he started opening the hatch. He dropped into it.

Once the hatch was closed, he checked the airlock controls. A heavy lever was in the up position. He shoved it down, and air bubbles immediately surged up around him. The water drained away as air was pumped in. The hissing noise echoing around the small chamber was almost ear-splitting.

Chase endured the din with a grimace, waiting until the water was down to his ankles before facing the inner hatch. Another locking wheel awaited him. As soon as the hiss of compressed air stopped, he turned it until the seals were released and the hatch opened.

Beyond lay a dimly lit concrete corridor, dripping with water – not from leaks, but from condensation. The passage was cold, this part of the habitat being unheated. He quickly stripped off his scuba gear and laid it out ready for when he left, keeping only the knife and the camera. He wished he had a gun, but that was something Trulli hadn't been able to provide.

Metal hatches led to side rooms, but Chase ignored them, heading along the corridor to a circular chamber. A ladder led up to a hatch in the ceiling: access to the central core. He shook off as much of the water from his body and wetsuit as he could, then climbed the ladder and cautiously raised the hatch.

The cross-shaped compartment above reminded him of the interior of the control room, sleek and curvaceous despite its functionality, the futuristic space station vibe back in full effect. Hatches at the end of each arm opened into the connecting spokes leading to the bottom deck's habitation modules. Two of the bulkheads, Chase knew, housed power lines and life support systems. A third contained an elevator.

He went to the fourth – the emergency ladder – and carefully opened the hatch, listening intently for any sounds of activity above. All he could hear was the rumble of machinery.

There were at least eight people inside the habitat – Sophia, Komosa, the nuclear technician, the four men he'd seen, and presumably the tilt-rotor's pilot. Possibly more. And all he had to face them with were a knife and his fists.

'Doddle,' he told himself, starting his ascent.

The central chamber of the next deck was a carbon copy of the one below. He cautiously stepped through the hatch and padded to the door leading to the spoke adjoining Corvus's quarters. Drawing his knife, he opened the door a crack and looked through.

The tubular passage was empty. So far, so good.

Chase hurried down the corridor. A small porthole at the end looked out into the sea, with more doors to the left and right. He went right, the knife poised ready to strike . . .

Nobody was there. The gold ingots gleamed under the bright light clusters set into the ceiling.

So did the steel casing of the nuke. Apart from the addition of the arming device, the bomb was just as he remembered it from Switzerland.

He looked down into the base, between the three steel rails supporting the cap. A faint silver-grey sheen of uranium showed at the bottom. That was the slug, which would be fired up into the larger mass of uranium in the cap – but its path was currently blocked by two thick steel bolts. A safety measure, to prevent the slug from moving during transit and getting too close to the other uranium – which, while not triggering a nuclear explosion, would still release a lethal burst of radiation. Presumably the bolts would retract before detonation.

The whole thing was designed to be foolproof in function. What would be the best way to sabotage it?

The answer came to him in an instant, as brutally simple as the bomb itself. 'Just smash the fucker!'

Placing the tip of the knife against the timer's screen, he prepared to prise it off and rip out whatever wires he found beneath—

The door through which he had entered flew open.

Chase jumped up. Two men rushed in. One with black-framed glasses carried a crowbar; the other was unarmed.

Chase ran at them, the knife raised.

ANDY MCDERMOTT

'Get him, Gordon!' yelled the unarmed man. The man with the crowbar drew back his arm to swing it – leaving himself open to a strike at his lower body.

Chase delivered one, smashing the ball of his heel against the man's kneecap. Cartilage crunched. The man shrieked, the crowbar's swing suddenly abandoned.

Chase ignored him, already turning on the second attacker without skipping a beat. This man had received better combat training than his companion, balanced more lightly on his feet to dodge any kicks, arms raised to deflect a knife strike.

Chase stabbed the knife straight at his face, a crude and direct attack. The man almost mockingly swept up one forearm to knock the blow aside – only for Chase's other hand to snap forward like a cobra and clamp round his wrist, pulling it towards him.

Before the man had a chance to realise what had happened, the blade plunged down into his forearm, passing between the bones to burst through the bottom of his sleeve with a spurt of blood. Chase twisted the knife as he yanked it back out, ripping apart the muscles and tearing through tendons and arteries. More blood gouted from the wounds.

Even before the second man started screaming, Chase swung round and slammed his elbow into the first man's face, breaking his glasses in two and flattening his nose into mush. His head snapped back and banged against the compartment's outer wall. He slumped nervelessly to the floor, leaving a bloody trail down the bulkhead.

The other man was now desperately squeezing his arm to stem the bleeding, howling in pain. Chase didn't care, completing his turn by driving the knife deep into his throat. The howling

433

stopped abruptly. With no emotion beyond contempt, Chase twisted the knife again to sever the carotid artery. The man was involved in a plot to set off a nuke; he deserved whatever he got.

He pulled out the bloodied knife, and the man collapsed, twitching and gurgling.

The whole fight had lasted mere seconds. Maybe he still had time to destroy the arming device before the rest of the habitat's occupants arrived—

Clap. Clap. Clap.

'Oh, Eddie,' said Sophia in mock sorrow from the compartment's other entrance, 'he was only two days from retirement!'

Chase whirled to see her giving him a slow handclap. Komosa stood beside her, his Browning aimed at him. The nuclear technician was behind them both.

The knife was still in Chase's hand. He could throw it—

'Don't,' Komosa warned, quashing the thought before it could be completed. The gun's laser sight flicked on and danced across Chase's face, dazzling him. Reluctantly, he dropped the knife to the deck.

'Check the bomb,' Sophia ordered the technician before stepping further into the room. 'I have to admit, Eddie, I'm genuinely surprised and impressed to see you again. Did Nina survive as well?'

'She's fine,' Chase said coldly.

'What a shame. Still, lesson learned – next time, I won't assume that you're dead until I've actually seen your body.'

'There won't be a next time, Sophia. This is over.'

'So are you,' said Komosa. The laser spot slid down on to Chase's chest, then back to his face. 'I've been looking forward to this, Chase. Where do you want it?'

'Is little toe an option?'

Komosa snorted and fixed the laser between Chase's eyes—

'Not yet,' said Sophia.

Komosa gave her a look of disbelief. 'Sophia!'

'Just can't bear to live without me?' Chase asked sarcastically.

Sophia shook her head. 'Hardly. There's nothing I'd like more, but the fact remains that when I saw you last, you had no transport, no passport, no money and no idea where I was going. Yet twenty-four hours later, here you are.' She regarded him icily. 'You had help. Government help. Who else knows you're here, Eddie?'

'Oh, just MI6, the CIA, NSA, KLF and the RSPCA. They should all be dropping in about five minutes from now.'

'I don't think so,' said Sophia, folding her arms. 'If they knew *that*' – she nodded at the bomb – 'was here, we would have been blown out of the water by the Americans already. But you've told *somebody*. Who was it, Eddie?'

Chase merely shrugged. Komosa lowered his gun, bringing the laser down on to Chase's crotch. 'I'll make him talk.'

'We don't have time,' said Sophia. She looked over at the technician. 'Heinrich! Is it all right?'

'As far as I can tell, Lady Sophia,' he replied.

'Just out of interest,' said Chase, stalling for time, 'how did you know I was in here?'

Sophia smiled. 'This habitat has a very sophisticated life support system that warns the control room of any unexpected build-up of carbon dioxide. The first time you exhaled, we knew we had an extra person aboard.'

'I'll hold my breath next time.'

'As you said, there won't be a next time. But I still need to know who you've told about the bomb.' Chase said nothing. Sophia sighed and reached behind her back, taking something from the waistband of her trousers. 'You always were irritatingly stubborn, Eddie. Well, since you've forced me to advance my schedule, we'll have to continue this discussion later.' She brought her hand out from behind her back, holding an oddly designed gun.

'Hey, wait a—' Chase began, before a dart thumped painfully into his stomach. 'Oh, bollocks . . .'

Darkness consumed him.

'Something's happening!' Nina said, sitting bolt upright as she saw movement through the binoculars. People had appeared on the landing platform, standing out clearly in the glare of the spotlights. 'Oh, crap, it's Sophia! She's getting into the plane!'

She watched intently as more figures emerged from the habitat, two of them carrying something small but heavy between them. 'Shit! I think that's the bomb!'

The boat rocked as Trulli clambered forward. 'Are you sure?'

'Eddie told me what it looks like. That must be it.'

Trulli looked nervously at the water around them. 'Christ, I hope he got out okay . . .'

The blood froze in Nina's heart. 'He didn't,' she gasped. Through the binoculars, Komosa's giant form stood out clearly from the others – and she was intimately familiar with the man he was effortlessly carrying over one shoulder. 'Oh, my God, they've got him!'

She watched, helpless, as Komosa brought Chase to the tilt-rotor and unceremoniously dumped him inside its cabin before entering himself. Sophia, the bomb and the two men carrying it were already aboard. Less than a minute later, the hatch was closed, the landing platform was cleared and the oversized propellers were turning.

There was absolutely nothing Nina could do except watch as the tilt-rotor lifted off and rose into the night sky. Its engines pitched forward, and it sped off to the north, rapidly becoming nothing more than one more star amongst thousands.

'Oh, Jesus . . .' Nina whispered. 'I've lost him.'

27

Trulli raced his Discovery along the coast road from Marsh Harbour. 'Are you *sure* you'll be able to find where they've taken Eddie?' Nina asked.

'Pretty sure,' Trulli replied. 'All of Corvus's cargo ships have GPS trackers. Hopefully his planes do too.'

'And if they don't?'

The Australian didn't have an answer for that. Instead, he turned towards a cluster of industrial buildings along the waterline. A barrier and gatehouse blocked the road ahead. 'Okay,' he said, 'just try to look relaxed. Maybe a bit drunk, too.'

'How can I *possibly* look relaxed?'

Trulli stopped at the barrier. A uniformed security guard stepped out of the gatehouse.

'Evening, Barney,' Trulli said with exaggerated casualness. 'How's things?'

'Fine, Mr Trulli,' said the guard. He didn't seem suspicious, just curious. 'What brings you here at this time of night?'

'Well, I was gonna go for a midnight dip with my friend here,' he indicated Nina, 'and then I realised I left the bloody key for my outboard in the office!'

The guard looked through the window at Nina. Heeding Trulli's comment, she gave the man a languid wave. 'Hi.'

He nodded in acknowledgement, then turned back to Trulli. 'You're not going to be long, are you?'

'No, mate! Just got to find the thing. Should only take a few minutes.'

Barney considered this. 'She should really sign in, but . . . Okay, as long as you're quick.'

'You're a top fella,' Trulli told him. The guard smiled, then returned to the gatehouse. The barrier rose, and Trulli drove through.

They pulled up beside a large building at the end of a dock. Trulli jumped from the Discovery and hurried to a side door. Nina followed him inside.

Despite the urgency of the situation, she couldn't help but stop in surprise as Trulli switched on the lights. The building was a covered dock, a huge roller shutter at the seaward end cutting into the water. Isolated from the waves outside, the pool within the building was as smooth as glass.

That wasn't what had surprised her, though. It was a submarine, suspended above the water on cables, though its design resembled no sub Nina had ever seen before. If anything, she thought, it looked as if it ought to be piloted by Han Solo or Captain Kirk.

Trulli ignored it, considering it as everyday a workplace object as a chair. 'Up here,' he told Nina, clattering up a flight of steps to an elevated room overlooking the dock. She followed him into an untidy office, where a large draughting table covered with annotated blueprints dominated the space. 'Sorry about the mess,' he said somewhat sheepishly, sweeping empty cardboard coffee cups away from a computer on a smaller desk as he woke it up.

'What *is* that thing?' Nina asked of the submarine outside the office's windows.

'Hmm? Oh, that's my current project. The *Wobblebug*.'

Nina almost laughed. 'The *what*?'

'Well, that's not the *official* name. René wants to call it the *Nautilus*, but that's kind of a clichéd name for a sub. Although if he's dead, I guess it doesn't matter any more . . . Anyway, it's a supercavitator.'

'A what now?'

'It goes really fast,' Trulli oversimplified, before returning his attention to the computer. 'Okay, let me just log in . . . Great, I can get into the GPS network.' A few mouse clicks, and a list of Corvus's ships and aircraft appeared on the screen. 'You remember the tail number of that plane?'

She did; he entered it into a search field and hit return. 'Okay, it's got a tracker.'

The list was replaced by a map. Nina recognised the outlines of the Bahamas and the southern half of the eastern seaboard of the United States, from Florida up to Virginia. A line led north from Great Abaco to a point about a hundred and fifty miles off the South Carolina coast, a yellow triangle marked with the tilt-rotor's registration number at its northern tip.

'There,' said Trulli. 'Heading zero-eight degrees, speed two hundred and seventy knots, altitude ten thousand feet.'

'Where are they going?' Nina asked. 'Zoom out, show more of the map.'

Trulli complied. The screen now showed the whole of eastern America.

Nina felt a chill as she realised where the tilt-rotor's course would take it. 'Oh, my God,' she whispered, rummaging through the scattered papers on Trulli's desk to find a ruler. She held it against the screen, extending the course all the way to its final destination.

The chill intensified. She'd been right. 'Oh my God!' she repeated, more loudly.

'Jesus,' Trulli said as he saw it too.

The ruler sliced through New York.

Her home.

'She's going to New York,' Nina said, stunned. 'She's taking a goddamn *nuke* to *New York!*'

Trulli entered rapid commands on the keyboard, and a window popped up with more information about the tilt-rotor. 'No, she can't be. The Bell 609 doesn't have enough range, even with extra fuel tanks. She must be going somewhere else.'

'Where, though?' Nina looked back at the map. 'The only other place she comes close to on that course is Atlantic City, and why would she nuke New Jersey? Nobody would even notice!' Mind racing, she stared at the yellow triangle representing the current position of Sophia – and Chase. 'Can you show the positions of Corvus's ships on there as well?'

'Which ones?'

'All of them.'

Puzzled, Trulli did as she asked. After a few seconds, a couple of dozen new markers appeared. There were several in the Bahamas, where Corvus's shipping line was based, more either in or close to major East Coast ports . . .

And one on its own, off the Virginia coast. Directly along the tilt-rotor's course.

Nina stabbed her finger at it. 'That! What's that?'

Trulli zoomed in. 'It's the *Ocean Emperor!*'

Nina's mind flashed back to the party where she had first met Sophia. 'Corvus's boat?'

'Yeah. It's heading for New York, doing about twenty-three knots, so if it keeps up that speed it'll get there tomorrow morning, about nine-ish.'

'It's got a helipad,' Nina remembered. 'Is it in range of Sophia's plane?'

Trulli checked. 'Yes.'

'That's what she's doing. If she tried to fly over the city the air force would intercept her, and there are nuclear detectors on the roads – but she can land on the *Ocean Emperor* and sail the nuke right into New York Harbour without anyone knowing a thing until it's too late!'

'Jesus,' gasped Trulli. 'So what do we do? We've got to tell somebody!'

'Yeah, but who? I can't go to the authorities – I'm wanted for murder!'

He gave her a shocked look. 'You're *what?*'

'I didn't do it! But we can't just phone up Homeland Security – Corvus had friends in the government, they won't send the Coast Guard to pull over his boat on an anonymous tip.'

'Corvus is dead,' Trulli reminded her.

'Yeah, but they don't know that. Plus, if they *do* stop them . . . Sophia'll kill Eddie. I know it.' She looked away from the computer, through the office window. 'I've got to get on that boat.'

'Even if we had a chopper, which we don't, it wouldn't have the range or the speed,' Trulli protested. 'There's no way we can catch them.'

'What about that?' She pointed at the suspended submarine.

'Huh?'

'That. You said it was fast – how fast?'

'In theory, anything up to four hundred knots, but—' Trulli froze as he realised what she meant. 'No way, it's still experimental! I've never tested it at full power!'

'Well,' said Nina firmly, 'now's your chance.'

'This is a really bad idea,' said Trulli as he operated the electric winch controls. The *Wobblebug* slowly descended into the still water of the dock, the surface rippling gently around its curving hull.

'Noted,' Nina told him. 'If we sink, you can say that you told me so.'

'It's not sinking I'm worried about. It's blowing up.'

Nina looked more closely at the submarine. In some ways it reminded her of a wingless jet fighter. Two gaping intakes near the bow, currently blocked by metal louvres, led back to much narrower rocket-like nozzles at the stern. The bow itself, however, was oddly blunt where she would have expected it to be streamlined, as if somebody had sliced off the tip of the pointed nose. 'What do you mean, blowing up?'

'It's why I called it the *Wobblebug*. The original Wobblebugs were steam-powered cars from like a century ago.'

'It's *steam*-powered?' Nina said in disbelief.

'Yeah. It's not like it burns coal, though!' He pointed at the intakes. 'Seawater goes in the front and gets superheated by electric elements, and the steam blasts out of the back like a rocket motor. Most of the hull's full of polymer polypyrrole batteries – it's the only way to deliver enough juice short of using a nuclear reactor.'

'Wait, it can do four hundred knots just using steam? So why isn't everybody doing that? I thought submarines were pretty slow.'

'They are.' Trulli stopped the winch, the *Wobblebug* now floating in the water, and hopped on to its casing to detach the cables. He pointed at the blunt bow. 'But if you make the nose the right shape, when you hit a certain speed you get supercavitation – kind of a shockwave of air bubbles around the hull that cuts the drag from the water down to almost nothing. Like underwater warp drive. The Russians have had supercavitating torpedoes called Squalls for over a decade that can do two hundred and fifty knots, no problem.' The cables at the stern released, he made his way forward, balancing on the rocking hull with the ease of a tightrope walker. 'The reason nobody's used the technology for manned subs is that it's really hard to get the design right.'

'Until now.'

'Well,' Trulli said pointedly, 'that remains to be seen, doesn't it?' He unhooked the final cable and jumped back to the winch controls to raise the steel lines out of the way.

Nina regarded the vessel. 'But assuming it works—'

'Which is a big assumption.'

'—we should be able to catch up with the *Ocean Emperor* long before it reaches New York, right?'

'We should. Just a couple of problems, though – first off, you've actually got to get *aboard* the *Ocean Emperor* from the *Wobblebug*.'

Nina glanced over at the cage-like storage units beneath Trulli's office, which amongst other items contained coils of rope. 'We'll figure something out.'

'Uh-huh. The second problem is that it's a one-way trip. If the *Ocean Emperor*'s not where we expect, we're screwed. There's no going back.'

'Why not?'

'You need to get up to a certain speed before the supercavitation effect starts working. And the only way to do that's with a rocket. A *real* rocket, not a steam-powered one.'

Nina looked back at the *Wobblebug*'s stern. Recessed between the two nozzles of the steam jets was a third, broader opening. 'A *rocket*?'

'Yeah. It's a solid-fuel rocket, like the kind they use to launch missiles from subs. Once it's ignited it can't be stopped – and it only lasts for thirty seconds. When the sub slows down below supercav speed, that's it. It can't speed up again. It's got back-up pump-jets so it can manoeuvre, but they can only do twenty knots tops. Twenty-five, if you're not worried about them burning out.'

'The only things I'm worried about right now are saving Eddie and stopping my home from being nuked,' Nina said.

'Point taken.' Trulli switched off the winch and took the end of an electric cable from a reel, uncoiling it as he boarded the sub again. He opened the top hatch. 'Okay, I'll get everything prepped, and—'

'Mr Trulli!' They looked round to see the security guard, Barney, walking towards them. 'Is everything all right?'

'Er, yeah, mate,' Trulli said unconvincingly. 'No worries.

Just, ah . . .' He looked down into the open hatch. 'Think my keys might be in here.'

Barney gave Nina a suspicious glance, then walked past her to stand at the edge of the dock. 'Looks to me like you're planning to take this thing out.'

Trulli adopted a cheesy grin. 'Dunno why you'd think that.'

'You know that Mr Corvus has to give his personal permission for each launch.' Barney's hand moved towards his holstered gun. 'I think you should step back on to the dock and – unk!'

He staggered, then fell to the dock. The fire extinguisher with which Nina had just hit him over the head clanked down beside him as she put her hands on her hips and addressed Trulli. 'So, Matt. Are we good to go?'

'You've changed since I first met you,' he muttered, then dropped into the hatch, the cable trailing behind him.

Fifteen minutes later, the unconscious Barney had been tied up and locked inside one of the storage cages, and the large door at the end of the building raised. A cold wind blew in from the sea, the *Wobblebug* creaking against the fat rubber bumpers hanging over the side of the dock as waves lapped along it.

Trulli's head popped out of the hatch. 'Okay, we're ready. As we're going to be, anyway. I've hooked up a GPS receiver to the onboard computer, but it won't work until we surface, so if the *Ocean Emperor* changes course while we're underwater, we're screwed.'

'We'll have to take that chance.'

Trulli seemed dubious, but held out a hand to her regardless. 'Okay, then. Hop aboard. I warn you, it's a bit of a squeeze.'

She took his hand and stepped on to the *Wobblebug*'s hull. The sub wallowed under the extra weight. Once he was sure that she wasn't going to slip, Trulli dropped back inside the cabin. Nina carefully lowered herself inside feet-first.

'Jeez, you weren't kidding,' she said. The cabin was barely large enough for one person, never mind two. The small seat was crammed practically up against the controls. A steering yoke like that of a light aircraft jutted from the instrument panel, a fiendishly complex-looking bank of gauges and switches flanked by an LCD monitor screen with a keyboard duct-taped beneath it. Trulli was already in the seat, so she was forced to duck into the narrow gap to his side. 'So where do I go?'

'Right where you are, I'm afraid. You'll have to lie down and sort of wrap yourself round the seat with your backside against the aft bulkhead.'

'Oh, great.'

'Still want to do this?'

Nina squeezed awkwardly into the tight space. 'I don't *want* to do it. But I've *got* to.'

'I thought you'd say something like that.' Trulli flipped switches, checking the various gauges. 'Okay, the batteries are at full charge, and the booster's primed and ready to fire. Last chance to get out.' Nina frowned at him. 'Yep, I thought.'

He shut the hatch. Once it was secured, he tapped the keyboard and a video image of the dock ahead appeared on the screen. 'No room for a periscope,' he explained as he pushed a lever forward by a single notch. A soft vibration ran through the cabin, motors rumbling. On the screen, the walls of the dock slid past. Within thirty seconds, the *Wobblebug* was out in open water.

Trulli pushed the steering controls forward, increasing speed as he did so. Nina took a firmer hold of the seat as the submarine began its descent. The hull creaked ominously. 'How deep will we go?' she asked, suddenly nervous.

'Supercav works best when it's well clear of any surface turbulence, so probably around ten, twenty metres. Depends on the water conditions.'

'Have you taken it that deep before?'

Trulli hesitated before answering. 'Would you feel better if I said yes?'

'Oh boy.'

He flicked through several windows on the monitor in rapid succession. 'Okay, inertial guidance is set, I've got the waypoints programmed in. Hold on tight, it'll be bumpy.'

'How bumpy?'

'You know how bumpy a really big roller coaster gets?'

'Uh, yeah?'

He gave her a not entirely confident grin as he flicked up the protective metal cover over a particular button. 'Way bumpier than that. Okay, on three!'

Nina gripped the seat even more tightly.

'Two!'

She braced herself against the rear bulkhead.

'One!'

And cringed—

'Warp speed!' Trulli cried, pushing the button.

The response was immediate.

A thunderous roar filled the cabin. Sudden acceleration shoved Trulli back in his chair. Nina shrieked.

The *Wobblebug* shook violently as it surged forward. Nina had no idea how fast they were moving, but even through the roar of the rocket motor she could hear a rising hiss of water racing over the hull.

'This is the tricky part!' Trulli yelled.

'What do you mean?' Nina shouted back. She desperately wanted to put her hands over her ears, but if she let go of the seat she would be battered about like a pea in a whistle.

'I've got to time everything right! The rocket's only got thirty seconds of fuel, but if I open the seawater intakes too soon there won't be enough ram pressure and the engines will choke!'

'Too *soon*? What happens if you open them too *late*?'

'The heating elements melt and the sub will explode!'

'Perfect!' Nina wailed. The instruments were shaking too much for her to see any detail, but she could pick out a line of coloured lights flicking on one by one.

They advanced from blue into a zone of orange, approaching a single green light. Beyond it, the colour went straight to red – again with just a single light.

Presumably there wouldn't be time for a second red light to come on before the sub blew up.

'This is it!' Trulli gripped a lever.

Orange, orange . . .

Nina cringed again.

Green.

Trulli yanked the lever back as hard as he could.

Nina heard a clunk as the louvres covering the intakes flicked open and seawater from the leading edge of the shockwave burst in to hit the heating elements. There was a colossal hissing shriek, a furious banshee beside her—

The *Wobblebug* leapt again, another burst of acceleration crushing Nina deeper into the confined space. Even Trulli screamed.

The roar of the rocket stuttered, then with an almost frightening abruptness cut out. But the piercing hiss of the steam jets continued steadily. The push of acceleration gradually eased as the submarine reached a stable speed.

Nina opened her eyes, realisation that she hadn't been blown to pieces sinking in. 'How . . . how are we doing?' she asked, voice shaking.

'Hold on a sec,' said Trulli, sounding almost as surprised as she was that they were still alive. The sub was still shuddering, though not nearly as much as before. 'Holy crap, we made it. We made it!' He whooped with delight. 'We're doing almost three-fifty knots! Suck it, Russia! Australia takes the record!'

'And is everything working properly?'

Trulli's triumph quickly became more subdued. 'Battery drain's higher than I expected – must be from having two people aboard. The life support systems are drawing more power.'

'Will we be able to catch up with the *Ocean Emperor*?'

'I think so.' He double-checked the screen. 'I hope so.'

'So do I,' Nina said quietly.

28

The Atlantic Ocean

Even before Chase opened his eyes, he could tell from the rhythmic pitching motion that he was aboard a ship.

He could also tell there was someone else with him. 'Hi, Sophia,' he groaned.

'Again, I'm impressed,' Sophia said as he blearily forced his eyelids apart fighting to overcome the nauseating after-effects of the tranquilliser dart. She stood a few feet away, looking down at him. He tried to get up, but found that his arms had been handcuffed in front of him round a pipe running from floor to ceiling, in what appeared to be a cargo hold. 'How did you know I was here?'

'Your perfume. Chanel. It always was your favourite.'

'Hmph.' Sophia tapped one of her high boot heels on the deck. 'By the way, welcome aboard the *Ocean Emperor*. I seem to have inherited it from René. A shame I won't be able to enjoy it for very long, but needs must.'

Chase didn't like the sound of that. 'Where's the bomb?'

'Close by. Don't worry. It'll be even closer before long.'

He liked that even less. 'So what's it all about, Sophia? What're you going to nuke? And why?'

She arched a perfectly shaped eyebrow. 'Actually, I was rather intending to be the one *asking* the questions. Who helped you get out of Algeria? You might as well tell me – even you must realise by now that there isn't time to stop me.'

Chase brought his arm round the pipe to look at his watch. It was well after one in the morning – not much more than seven hours before the bomb was set to detonate. 'No, there's still time.'

Sophia sighed. 'Stubborn . . . to the last. Really, Eddie, Joe checked that pipe before he cuffed you to it. It's rock solid. The only way you're going to get loose is if you gnaw your own hand off. Who helped you?'

He ignored her and gripped the pipe, then braced himself and yanked at it. As Sophia had promised, it was solidly fixed in place, not even rattling. He tried again, with the same lack of result. Sophia made a 'tsk!' sound with her tongue. Defeated, Chase released the pipe and sank back to the deck. 'The dead guy you left in that room full of spears had a radio,' he admitted. 'I called MI6.'

Sophia looked confused. 'But it wouldn't have enough range to . . . Oh, I see. One of Mac's little tricks, I suppose. You couldn't have got support from the upper echelons, though, otherwise they would have taken action already.'

'They still might.'

'No, they won't.' She slowly circled him, a hint of victory in her smile. 'You keep forgetting, Eddie – I *know* you. Deception's not one of your skills.'

'Unlike you,' Chase shot back.

'It's a useful talent, certainly. None of my ex-husbands realised that I was using them for my own ends, and that includes you.'

'So what *are* your ends? I told you what you wanted to know, so now you can tell me – you owe me that much.'

She narrowed her eyes. 'I don't owe you anything.'

'Except your life.'

Although she tried to hide it, Chase could tell that his words had hit home. Sophia completed her circle as if about to exit the hold, then turned back to him. 'All right, if you really want to know, I'll tell you. It's only fair, since you're at least partly responsible in the first place.'

'How the hell am *I* responsible?'

She crouched, staring intently into his eyes, malice burning in her gaze. 'Because of *you*, Eddie, my family lost everything they had. All I have left is my title. Because of you.'

Chase tried to work out what she was talking about, but came up with nothing. 'Not quite with you there, Soph. You mind elaborating?'

'My father was completely opposed to my marrying you.'

'Well, yeah, I worked that out pretty early on. Like about five seconds after I met him.'

'No,' she hissed. 'You have no idea. He *despised* you, considered you on the level of vermin.'

Chase snorted. 'Now I don't feel so guilty for buying him those cheap cufflinks that Christmas.'

She jumped up. 'This isn't funny, Eddie!' For a moment he thought she was going to kick him, but she wasn't foolish enough to get within range of his hands or feet, even if he was cuffed to the pipe. 'I never told you, but while I was with you, Father practically disowned me, cut me off financially. And you didn't even notice, because you were so used to living on the cheap that it never even occurred to you just how much I'd been affected.'

'Is that what this is about?' Chase sneered. 'Poor little rich girl, Daddy cut up her credit cards?'

Again, she seemed about to lash out at him before intelligence overcame anger. 'You never did understand my family, what we did. Our business, our *wealth*, goes back generations, built up through diligence and reputation. We deserved it, it was our *right*. But then . . .' Her face twisted with disgust. 'The world changed. Suddenly, reputation and right counted for nothing. It all became about pure greed, just money, numbers flying back and forth between computers. Legacies were destroyed for nothing more than a quarterly profit statement.'

'Legacies like your dad's, you mean.'

'He was ill!' Sophia shouted. 'He wasn't thinking clearly, he made mistakes. Mistakes which if I'd been there to help him, he never would have made! But because I was with you, he was too proud to ask for my help – and when the *jackals* in the City and on Wall Street saw weakness, they charged in and destroyed him! They broke up his businesses, tore them apart to sell off piece by piece so that the banks and the stockbrokers and the lawyers could share it all out amongst themselves – and they left him with nothing! They left *me* with nothing!'

'And setting off a nuke somehow makes everything all right?' Chase asked. 'What the hell are you expecting to achieve?'

'I'll tell you *exactly* what I expect to achieve,' she said, her flood of emotion now replaced by a calculating coldness. 'The wealth of the people who destroyed my father is a sham, an illusion based on nothing more than the faith that their system works. I'm going to shatter that illusion, bring down the system. My target is New York, Eddie.'

'Jesus!'

She took in his shock with a degree of pleasure before continuing. 'Specifically, the financial district. At eight forty-five, just before trading starts, the *Ocean Emperor* will be in the East River at the end of Wall Street. When the bomb goes off, it will obliterate lower Manhattan – and completely destroy the hub of the worldwide financial markets. The financial crisis after 9/11 will be nothing but a *blip* compared to what will happen today. The American market will completely collapse, and take the rest of the world's stock markets down with it. All those people whose wealth and power is based on nothing more than faith, on pieces of paper and numbers in computers, will be left with absolutely *nothing*. Just as they left my father.'

'While you still have all the gold from the Tomb of Hercules,' Chase realised.

Sophia nodded. 'I have more men excavating the site right now. Nina was absolutely right – the value of *physical* wealth will multiply enormously following a financial crash. I'll get back what was rightfully mine – my family's wealth and status.'

'And screw everyone else, eh?' Chase growled. 'You're not only going to kill fuck knows how many tens of thousands of people when the bomb goes off, but what about all the millions of other people who'll lose everything too? Not just the fat cats, but ordinary people?'

'Why should I care?' Sophia sniffed. 'They're just the little people.'

'And what about me? Is that all I ever was to you?' She didn't answer him, not quite able to meet his gaze. 'What *happened* to you, Sophia?' Chase asked despairingly. 'Jesus Christ, you've murdered people in cold blood, and now you're going to set off a fucking *nuclear bomb*! How the fuck did you end up like this?'

Now she looked back at him. 'I have *you* to thank for that, Eddie,' she said. 'And I really *do* thank you, sincerely. If there's one lesson I learned from our time together, it's that.'

'What lesson? What the fuck are you talking about?'

Sophia stepped closer, just outside the range of his legs, and crouched down. 'My family always had power, Eddie, but it was the kind of power that came from wealth and influence. But when I met you, when you rescued me from the terrorist camp . . . you showed me another kind of power. The power of *life and death.*'

Chase couldn't answer, unable to do anything more than listen in horror as she went on. 'When you wiped out the members of the Golden Way, you taught me how to *truly* exercise power. The unwavering pursuit of an objective, without remorse. Anyone in the way of that objective must be destroyed.'

'You're fucking mental,' Chase finally managed to say. 'I went in to *rescue* you. I only killed people who were trying to kill *us*.'

'You can't deceive yourself any better than you can me,' Sophia snapped. 'You were ordered to *exterminate* them, Eddie. Not to drive off or capture, but to wipe them out. You were an assassin, a *killer.* You didn't feel anything when you shot them or stabbed them or slit their throats. I saw how you acted. I'll never forget it

456

– because it taught me that I needed to be like you. You were pursuing an objective, exercising power. Just as I am now.'

'I was on a military mission to rescue British citizens from terrorists,' countered Chase. 'What you're doing is mass murder for personal gain and . . . and fucking childish *revenge*!'

'You can say whatever you want!' said Sophia as she stood, voice rising to a shriek. 'You *made* me! All of this happened because of *you!*' She whirled and strode to the door, heels striking the deck like shots. 'Joe!' she shouted. 'Bring it in!'

'Don't do this, Sophia!' Chase said, pulling himself upright. Still trapped by the pipe, he could only move a couple of feet in any direction.

'You started all this the moment we met,' Sophia told him malevolently. 'It's only fitting that you should be here at the end as well.' Behind her, Komosa and the nuclear technician entered the hold, carrying the bomb between them. She pointed to one side of the room, well away from Chase. 'Over there.'

The two men carefully set the heavy device down. Komosa had something over his shoulder on a strap; at first Chase thought it was a weapon, until he saw that it was actually a bolt gun, six-inch steel shafts loaded into an open magazine protruding from its top. There were three holes spaced equidistantly round the bomb's metal base. Komosa placed the end of the gun into the first hole and pulled the trigger. A sharp crack of compressed gas, and a bolt was blasted through the deck with a piercing clang. Two more clangs, and the bomb was immovably secured. Komosa put down the bolt gun beside it.

Sophia went to the bomb, taking the arming key from a pocket. She inserted it, then with a dismissive glance back at Chase turned it. The screen lit up, still showing the time of detonation: 0845. A push of a button, and the display changed to a countdown.

Seven hours, two minutes, seventeen seconds.

Sixteen.

Fifteen . . .

She pulled out the key, but the display remained lit, the seconds flicking away. 'I think I'll pop up to the deck and throw this into the sea,' she taunted, holding up the key as she headed back to the door. The two men followed her. 'By the way, Eddie, the timer has an anti-tamper mechanism. If anyone attempts to stop it without the key, the bomb will explode. I just thought you should know.'

'Goodbye, Chase,' said Komosa, grinning his diamond smile. 'Enjoy the afterlife.'

The door closed behind them with a decisive thud.

Chase pulled and kicked at the pipe again, with no more success than before. Then he drew back his arms so that the chain of the handcuffs was around the metal and hauled on it with all his strength. Blood oozed from his wrists as the steel cut into his flesh, but the cuffs were too tightly fastened for him to slip his hands through.

But he kept trying. He had no choice.

'We're almost there,' Trulli said above the constant shrill of the engines. 'I think.'

Nina, stiff and sore from being stuck in her cramped position for over two hours, twisted to look up at him. 'What do you mean, you think?'

'The inertial navigation system isn't as accurate as GPS.

Especially when the ride's this bumpy – it throws it off. Worst case scenario, we could be nearly ten kilometres from where we think we are.'

Nina touched her pendant. 'Let's hope for the best case scenario, then. So what happens now?'

Trulli examined the instruments. 'Well, first, I've got to bring us out of supercavitation drive without squashing us like a cane toad under a road train!'

Nina's eyes opened wide. 'Wait, what, squashing? You didn't say anything about squashing!'

'I've never been this fast before!' Trulli explained. 'I can't just stop the engines, 'cause when the supercav shockwave collapses it'd be like running the sub into a brick wall. I've got to ease it down, get us to a safe speed before shutting off the steam.' He made adjustments to several controls, then took hold of the throttle. 'Okay. Let's give this a crack . . .'

Nina took hold of the seat and braced herself.

Trulli pulled the throttle back slightly. The noise of the engines didn't alter as far as Nina could tell, but the *Wobblebug*'s vibration changed, a snaking sideways motion slowly building up.

'Is that bad?' Nina asked.

'I hope not!' Trulli moved the throttle again. This time, the shriek from the engines lowered slightly in pitch. But the oscillation continued, the weaving sensation worsening. 'We're down to three hundred knots. It's working!'

'What about that shaking?' The sub's movement was making Nina seasick, but she couldn't help thinking that nausea was the least of her problems.

'I dunno why it's doing that – just have to hope it goes away on its own!' Another push of the lever. 'Two-eighty, two-seventy . . . Come on, you bugger! Two-fifty—'

The back end of the submarine suddenly slammed sideways as if kicked, only to hit something that flung it back the way it had come.

Another impact, and another—

Nina clung desperately to the seat as she was thrown about. Trulli fought with the controls, the submarine's stern swinging violently like the clapper inside a bell. '*Tailslap!*' he screamed.

'What?'

'The back end of the sub's bouncing off the inside of the shockwave! If I don't get us under control, it'll collapse!'

Trulli struggled to bring the *Wobblebug* back in line. The submarine lurched sickeningly, bashing against the edge of the swirling vortex surrounding it a few more times before its motion began to dampen down.

He reduced the throttle further. 'I think that's got—'

Skrench!

Something ripped loose from the bow and screeched back along the sub's length before being lost in the water behind them.

'What the hell was *that*?' Nina cried.

'We lost a fin!' The steering yoke bucked in Trulli's hands. 'I'm gonna have to risk backwash braking – whatever you do, *don't let go!*'

She had no idea what he meant, but his voice warned her that it was almost as dangerous as letting the shockwave collapse. She hugged herself against the seat as Trulli shoved a lever—

The louvres on the seawater intakes slammed closed.

For a moment, the shriek of the engines dropped almost to

nothing as the flow of water to the red-hot heating elements was cut off. The last of the superheated steam was blown out of the engine nozzles – then a surge of frothing bubbles from within the shockwave was sucked *into* the nozzles as the pressure inside them plummeted.

Without water to carry away the excess heat, the temperature of the steam elements had already shot up. The froth hit the searing metal, instantly exploding into superheated vapour—

Trulli pulled the lever again.

The intake louvres snapped open just as the expanding steam erupted through them, blasting twin jets through the supercavitation wave created by the submarine's blunt nose. The disrupted shockwave instantly collapsed, but the *Wobblebug* ploughed through it into the swirling mass of turbulence beyond, a buffer zone slowing the vessel rather than smashing it to an abrupt halt.

But it passed through the zone in barely a second . . .

Even with his seatbelt fastened, Trulli was slammed against the steering yoke as the sub hit dense seawater. If Nina hadn't been clinging to his seat with the strength of every sinew in her arms she would have been flung head-first against the forward bulkhead. Something on the cabin wall broke loose and smashed into the instrument panel. The lights flickered, broken metal beating at the hull . . .

The submarine slowed.

Trulli gasped in pain as he tried to lift his hand to the throttle control. 'Ah, shit!' he wheezed. 'Nina, help me, quick!'

Arms aching, Nina dragged herself upright. 'What's wrong?'

The Australian's face contorted. 'I think I've bust a rib! I can't reach the throttle – pull it back, shut off the elements!'

She hurriedly did as she was told. The hissing of steam from the engines died away, as did the last vibrations. The *Wobblebug* fell silent.

'Thanks,' Trulli gasped. 'Well, we stopped, and we're still in one piece, more or less. Guess that's something.' He examined the damaged instruments through pain-narrowed eyes. 'Don't think the sub's going to be going much further, though. Both the intakes are wrecked, and we're almost out of power.'

'How badly are you hurt?' Nina asked.

He grimaced. 'Won't be playing tennis for a while. I need to check where we are, get a GPS fix. See that lever up there?' He pointed at a particular lever on the cabin ceiling. Nina nodded. 'Pull it. It'll blow the ballast tanks, take us to the surface.'

She steadied herself, then pulled it. The submarine shuddered as water was forced out of the tanks by compressed air. Within a minute, a different kind of rocking motion took over – the swell of Atlantic waves against the hull.

Trulli tapped clumsily at the keyboard with one hand, the pain from his chest preventing him from moving his other arm. 'Okay, GPS signal is coming in . . . got it. Wow, we're not too far off.'

Nina looked at the screen as a map appeared. 'Where are we?'

'Off the coast of Maryland. About two hundred and ninety kilometres from New York.'

Nina instantly made the conversion to imperial measurements: a hundred and eighty miles. 'Where's the *Ocean Emperor*?'

'Give me a sec to see if I can get a satellite connection. It's not exactly like we've got wi-fi access out here . . .'

She waited anxiously first for the computer to link up to

Corvus's network, then for Trulli to log in. Compared to the system in his office, the satellite link was excruciatingly slow.

'Gotcha!' Trulli said at last. A yellow triangle indicating the *Ocean Emperor*'s position appeared on the screen. 'It's about four kays behind us, a bit farther offshore. Same course as it was on before, still doing twenty-three knots.'

'Can we catch it?'

'If the pump-jets haven't been completely screwed, then yeah. If we're quick.' He indicated one particular gauge. 'The batteries are almost drained. We've got maybe ten minutes of power left. But I'll need your help to pilot the sub. I can't do it with only one arm.'

Nina stared at the triangle on the map, so close to the icon marking their own position. *Eddie* . . .

She set her jaw in determination. 'What do you need me to do?'

29

Sophia stood on the *Ocean Emperor*'s bridge, regarding the view ahead. The lights in the room had been dimmed for nighttime operations, but even so there was little to see. The ship was almost thirty miles from shore, and there was nothing in sight but the ink-black sweep of the Atlantic and the starry dome above it.

She turned to the man beside her, Captain Lenard. The *Ocean Emperor*'s normal complement of forty had been reduced to a skeleton crew of just five for its final voyage, all of whom would be evacuated in the tilt-rotor parked on the helipad behind the bridge shortly before the ship reached Manhattan. 'And it hasn't reappeared?'

'No, ma'am,' said Lenard, a flint-eyed Frenchman. 'Whatever it was, it seems to have gone.'

Sophia looked suspiciously at the radar screens, then back out of the wide windows. Something had shown up on the *Ocean Emperor*'s radar almost directly ahead a few minutes earlier, then vanished again. It had been too large to be some piece of random flotsam, and considering the yacht's objective anything out of the ordinary had to be considered a possible threat.

But if it were a boat, it would still be visible on radar, and Lenard had already ruled out the possibility of its being the periscope of a submarine . . .

'Keep looking,' she finally ordered. 'If it reappears, call me at once. I'll be in my stateroom.'

'Yes, ma'am.' Lenard gave Komosa, lurking at the back of the bridge, a somewhat jealous look as Sophia gestured for the giant to follow her, then turned back to the radar.

The object the *Ocean Emperor* had detected was now much closer than its captain would believe. With Nina's help, Trulli had submerged the *Wobblebug* to a depth of just six feet, bringing it on a course to intercept the yacht. With two people working the controls, the confined space of the cabin was even more claustrophobic.

'Sorry,' Nina said again as she accidentally nudged Trulli with her elbow.

'No worries. At least you missed my ribs this time.' Trulli checked the monitor screen. At such a shallow depth, the computer was able to receive intermittent GPS signals, and the map showed that the *Wobblebug* and the *Ocean Emperor* were now less than two hundred yards apart. The submarine was almost directly in the huge cruiser's path, heading in the same direction but quickly being overtaken. 'Okay, she's nearly on us. I'll move us along her port side and then surface and try to match speeds.'

'How much time will we have?'

'Not much. Subs go slower on the surface, and I'll have to redline the pump-jets just to keep up. Even if they don't burn out, they'll still run out of juice real fast. And there's something else.'

'Figures,' groaned Nina. 'What is it?'

'With the bow wave that thing'll be kicking up at twenty-three knots, water's going to come in through the top hatch. A *lot* of water.'

'Wait, you mean it'll *sink*?'

'She's not going back home, whatever happens,' Trulli said, sounding disconsolate. 'Ah well. She gave us a good run, at least.'

Nina gave him a worried look. 'But what about you?'

'Don't worry about me. Long as you're clear, I'll be able to get out.'

'With a broken rib?'

'Life'd be boring without a bit of challenge, wouldn't it?' He squeezed her arm. 'You just get on to that ship, okay? Find Eddie, defuse the bomb and stop this crazy bitch!'

She turned as best she could in the tight space and kissed him on the forehead. 'Thanks, Matt.'

'No problem. If I get out of this, you just remember that job offer, okay?'

Nina smiled. 'You're at the top of my list.'

On the screen, the symbols representing the *Wobblebug* and the *Ocean Emperor* were almost overlapping, and she could now hear a new sound beneath the churning rush of the pump-jets; a low-frequency rumble coming through the water.

Powerful diesel engines. The yacht was upon them.

Trulli adjusted the steering yoke to bring the submarine closer to the surface. 'Okay, this is it! Start opening the hatch, but not all the way until I say.'

Nina turned the locking wheel as he guided the sub closer to the *Ocean Emperor*, switching the monitor to the camera on the hull. The image was almost completely dark and obscured by spray, but through the surging water bright spots were visible to the right.

Portholes. The *Ocean Emperor* was alongside them, the throb of its engines like the purr of a monstrous cat.

The *Wobblebug* bucked as it ran through the turbulent water thrown up by the ship's bow. Nina clung to the hatch, almost falling. Trulli battled one-handedly with the controls. More portholes slid past . . .

'Okay, open it!' he shouted.

Nina pushed up the hatch. Freezing water immediately sluiced in, drenching them. The *Wobblebug* bounced through the waves, more water and spume cascading in as it ploughed into each one.

She grabbed the coiled line they had hung beside the hatch and scrambled out to sit on the edge of the hull. At over twenty knots, the wind-chill instantly sliced through her sodden clothes like a knife of ice.

The *Ocean Emperor* loomed to starboard, a metal cliff face. The aft deck was closest to the water, but it was still over ten feet above the surface.

Gripping the open hatch with one hand, Nina fumbled with the line. A hook was attached to the end. If she was lucky, she would snag a stanchion or railing on the rear deck.

If she was lucky . . .

Another wave crashed over her, chilling her to the bone. Water poured into the cabin. The lights flickered.

'I'm losing it!' Trulli warned. 'The jets are overheating, and the water's shorting things out!'

'Get in closer!' Nina shouted back. She hefted the hook, ready to throw it.

The submarine edged towards the *Ocean Emperor*. The yacht's churning wake made the pitching worse, the *Wobblebug*'s bow leaving the water completely before smacking back down in the troughs between the waves. Even holding the hatch cover and using her legs to grip the edge of the opening, Nina could barely keep her position.

The yacht was overtaking them rapidly, the rear deck sliding towards her.

She drew back her hand. At the speed the ship was moving, she would only get one shot . . .

The interior of the cabin flashed with a blue electric spark, and the lights went out. 'Shit!' yelled Trulli. 'I've lost the—'

Nina threw the hook.

It arced through the air towards the rear deck, the line whipping in the wind behind it—

And bounced off a stanchion, dropping into the maelstrom between the two vessels.

Nina watched it fall in horrified disbelief, then frantically pulled the line back in. The hook clattered against the submarine's hull. Another wave crashed over the bow, the hatch now a circular waterfall rapidly filling the cabin. The *Wobblebug*'s engines were dying, and the *Ocean Emperor* swept past at an ever increasing pace as the smaller craft slowed.

She grabbed the hook again, and climbed fully out of the hatch, balancing precariously on the curved hull. Below, Trulli struggled to climb out of his seat as a ceaseless torrent of water pounded down on to him.

The yacht's stern passed Nina. She saw a surge of froth from its propellers swelling to consume them, the suction of the wake about to drag the submarine under the water—

Throw!

This time the hook cleared the hull, skittering over the rear deck before sliding back as the *Ocean Emperor* pulled away.

The *Wobblebug*'s bow pitched down into the froth—

The line caught.

Nina just barely had time to grip it before she was snatched off the submarine and dragged into the water behind the huge yacht.

Trulli was only halfway out of the hatch as the *Wobblebug* nose-dived, its stern completely clearing the water before the whole vessel plunged beneath the surface, dragged down by the weight of water flooding the cabin. Blue flashes cracked from below the waves as the massive batteries shorted out, then the sea went dark.

Nina had no time to think about the Australian's fate. Coughing and choking as freezing spray lashed her face, she pulled herself up the line, one hand at a time. The impact of each wave threatened to rip her loose and leave her to drown in the cold black ocean.

One hand. Then another.

Little by little, she brought herself closer to the yacht's stern. Every time her body smashed down into the froth she could *feel* the propellers whirling hungrily below.

The cold numbed her hands, pain the only sensation remaining. A few feet . . .

She gasped for air as spray exploded all around her, trying to shake the stinging water out of her eyes. The yacht's stern was a sheer wall of white-painted steel.

But there was something off to her side, above the centreline—

A ladder!

Access to the *Ocean Emperor*'s swimming platform when it was lowered and the ship was stationary. But Nina didn't care about its function – all she knew was that it was *there*, and she could reach it.

If she could hold on.

With a new burst of energy, she pulled herself along the taut line and finally reached the hull, her shoulder thudding against the metal. Muscles burning as she lifted her legs out of the water, Nina kicked against the stern, swinging herself sideways towards the ladder.

She was too low. Her legs dropped back into the water, the chopping waves like claws trying to drag her to her doom. With a yell, she pulled herself higher and tried again.

This time she cleared the frothing wake by inches. Feet slithering on the slick metal, Nina forced herself across the yacht's stern. The line bit into her hands. The ladder was just a few feet away, getting closer with each footfall on the wet surface, closer . . .

Taking all her weight on one straining arm, Nina grasped for the ladder. It was as wet and slippery as the hull, her numbed fingers unable to gain purchase. In a moment she would lose her grip on the line . . .

She kicked at the hull one last time, screaming in fear and fury—

Her fingers clamped round a rung.

For a moment she could barely believe it. Then, determination surging, she swung across to dangle beneath the ladder. Her feet hit the water, dragging in the ship's wake, but she pulled herself up and managed to hook her arm over another rung.

Shivering, she hung there for nearly a minute until sensation returned to her chilled fingers. Finally, she summoned the strength to climb the ladder, one painful rung at a time.

At the top, she flopped exhausted on to the teak decking, water streaming from her soaked clothing and hair. If anybody had been there to see her, there would have been absolutely nothing she could have done to fight them.

But the deck was empty. Slowly, Nina raised her head. Above, she could see the nacelles and tail of the tilt-rotor protruding over the edge of the yacht's helipad.

The sight energised her. If the aircraft was here, then so was Sophia.

And Chase.

Legs still shaking, Nina forced herself to stand. Some part of her mind noted with detached irony that she was standing almost exactly where she and Chase had fought at Corvus's party, an age ago. But this time she was here not to argue with him, but to rescue him.

She ran her hands firmly over her clothing before squeezing her bedraggled hair, trying to wring out as much of the cold water as possible. The rear deck might be empty, but the *Ocean Emperor* still had a crew aboard, and a wet trail through the ship's corridors would arouse the suspicions of even the slowest sailor.

As dry as she could get, she headed for the nearest door, trying to remember the layout of the ship. Three hundred and fifty feet long, someone had told her, with six decks. Enough cabins to accommodate over forty passengers during a cruise, in addition to all the crew quarters.

A lot of places to search.

She suddenly remembered Trulli and looked back over the stern. She had no idea whether he'd managed to get out of the submarine before it sank. For a moment, she thought she saw a small light flash amidst the endless darkness of the sea, but then it was gone.

'I hope you made it, Matt,' she whispered, clutching her pendant. Then she carefully opened the door and peered through.

It was a lounge, cream leather armchairs and a small bar. Empty. Nina crept into the room, its cosy warmth hammering home just how cold she had been in the water. She shivered, rubbing her arms, and paused to work out her next move.

First priority: find Chase. Once she'd freed him, they could take care of the next steps together, which were to locate and disarm the bomb, and then deal with Sophia and anyone else helping her.

So where would Chase be? He was a prisoner, so he was most likely to be somewhere that could be locked. That ruled out the staterooms, which were like hotel rooms in that the occupant could always open the door from inside. One of the holds, maybe?

She had to start somewhere, so it might as well be at the bottom and work up. A deck plan behind the bar showed emergency evacuation routes and the locations of the stairwells. She quickly went to a door at the forward end of the lounge. An empty corridor lay beyond.

Listening for movement ahead, Nina padded down the passage until she reached the stairs. She was about to descend when she heard something over the rumbling murmur of the diesels.

A moan?

It had come from the deck above. Nina cautiously crept halfway up the stairs and stopped to listen. It sounded like a man, possibly in pain. Chase?

She held still, anxiously waiting to see if the sound was repeated.

It was.

'Oh, for—' Nina hissed in angry exasperation when she realised what she'd heard. It *was* a moan, but not of pain. And now it was joined by another, a woman in the throes of ecstasy. *Sophia*. The man she'd heard was Komosa. 'Hope they both get the clap!'

Deciding that Sophia probably wouldn't be forcing Chase to watch, Nina descended the stairs. A glance at another evacuation plan confirmed that she was on the lowest deck, with the engine room astern and the holds forward.

On the assumption that the engine room would be manned, she scurried in the opposite direction to check each door in turn. The first was nothing more than a storage closet full of cleaning equipment, the second a darkened laundry. Undeterred, she continued along the corridor, making her way door by door up the length of the ship almost to the bow before taking a narrow connecting passage to head back down the starboard side. Holds full of stacked and secured cardboard boxes, a walk-in freezer—

One door was locked.

She froze, as if the rattle of the door might alert somebody. But the only sound was the thrum of the engines. She tried the handle again, still with no luck, then rapped quietly on the door. 'Eddie!' she said, as loudly as she dared. 'Eddie, are you in there?'

Silence. Then: 'Of course I'm in here, Sophia – you handcuffed me to a fucking pole!'

Nina let out a stifled gasp of delight. He was alive! 'No, it's me, it's Nina!'

Another silence. Then Chase spoke again, voice filled with utter incredulity. 'How the *fuck* did you get here?'

'I'll explain later.' Remembering that one of the closets she'd checked had contained tools, Nina rushed back to it and found a crowbar. She returned to the locked hold. 'Are you okay?'

'I'm bursting for a piss, but apart from that . . .'

'You're fine,' Nina muttered as she stuck the end of the crowbar into the door jamb and leaned against it, pushing hard. Wood creaked and splintered, then something inside broke and the door flew open.

Nina almost stumbled into the hold to see Chase standing near the opposite wall with his hands cuffed round a pipe. He couldn't hide his joy at seeing her. 'Bloody hell, it really *is* you!'

'Told you I'd come after you,' Nina said with a heartfelt smile. They embraced as best they could with the pipe between them.

Chase held up his wrists. 'Okay, pop these fucking cuffs off me and we can try to sort out the bomb.'

'You know where it is?' Nina asked. Chase pointed across the room. She looked round, and took a sudden step back when she saw the bomb less than ten feet away. 'Yeesh!'

'Don't go fucking around with it – Sophia said it's booby-trapped, and I actually think she might have been telling the truth for once.'

Nina lifted the crowbar, trying to work out the best way to get enough leverage to break the handcuff chain. 'Maybe we could just throw it overboard?'

'That would be very bad for the poor fish,' Sophia said from the doorway.

Nina whipped round, brandishing the crowbar – but saw that Sophia, her hair tousled and her face slightly flushed, had a gun pointed at her. Komosa, standing beside her wearing nothing but leather trousers, was armed too, as was an older man in a white uniform. 'Aw, crap.'

'I must admit, Nina, I'm even more surprised and impressed to see you here than I was to find Eddie poking around in my underwater base.' Sophia paused and looked thoughtful. 'Hmm. "My underwater base." That *does* sound positively Bondian, doesn't it?'

'How did you know I was here?' Nina asked, unamused.

'We picked up a distress beacon a couple of minutes ago, right behind us. The ship's computer told us that it was one of ours – one of René's, rather: that ridiculous submarine he wasted so much money on.'

'I dunno,' said Nina, 'it turned out to be a pretty good investment. It got me here.'

'For all the good it did you,' Sophia replied. She stepped fully into the hold, Komosa following, and gestured with her gun for Nina to put down the crowbar. Nina reluctantly obeyed, then raised her hands. 'As soon as we realised what it was, I knew it had to be you. No one else would be that *desperate*. Then one of the crew found wet footprints on the carpet in the aft lounge, so we just followed them.'

Nina sniffed. 'Well done, Sherlock.' She gave Komosa a brief look and saw sweat glistening on his bare chest and piercings, then turned her attention back to Sophia's untucked clothes. 'Too bad you had to interruptus your coitus.'

'Aw, I didn't need to know about that,' Chase complained.

Sophia smiled. 'It doesn't matter, Eddie – the end you always droned on about fighting until has finally arrived. Chain her up,' she said to Lenard, indicating Nina. He took a pair of handcuffs from a pocket and moved as if to secure her next to Chase, but Sophia spoke again. 'No, away from him. Over there.' She pointed to another vertical pipe across the hold.

'Can't we just *kill* them?' Komosa rumbled, clearly frustrated.

Sophia ran a hand down his chest. 'Now, now, Joe. I know you've been looking forward to doing it, but I want the satisfaction of knowing that the very first people who'll be killed by the bomb will be my ex-husband . . . and his *bitch* of a girlfriend.'

'You know,' said Chase, as Lenard locked Nina's hands around the pipe, 'most bitter ex-wives settle for cutting the crotch out of their ex's suits. Not nuking a fucking city!'

'Goodbye, Eddie,' Sophia said as she turned for the door. Lenard picked up the crowbar and followed her.

Komosa waited for them to leave, then stepped forward and punched Chase hard in the face, knocking him to the deck. 'My parting gift,' he said as he left.

'Are you okay?' Nina asked.

Chase spat out a gob of blood – and a tooth, the molar which had been loosened in Botswana finally knocked out. 'Well, he saved me a trip to the dentist. That's a gift worth at least two hundred dollars.'

'Oh, God,' Nina said quietly. She slumped to the floor, damp clothes clinging to her, and looked across the hold at the bomb. 'She's actually going to do it, isn't she? She's going to blow up New York.'

'This isn't over yet,' said Chase. 'Whatever Sophia says, this *isn't* the end. There's still time to do something. We've still got to fight.'

Nina rattled her handcuffs against the pipe. 'Any suggestions?'

'Well . . .' Chase looked up at his own pipe. He had tried everything he could think of during his captivity to break free – with not even the slightest hint of success. The pipe was too solidly fixed, the cuffs too well made. 'Actually, no. You?'

Nina shook her head disconsolately, then tried to move closer to Chase. He did the same, but with their arms secured, they couldn't even get their feet to touch. 'No,' Nina said, anger suddenly rising. 'No, dammit, *no!*' She flailed her feet, desperate to make any kind of contact with him, but he was just out of reach. '*Fuck!*' She gave up, pulling away and curling up against the pipe, hiding her tears.

'Nina . . .' Chase whispered sadly. All he wanted to do right now was hold her, comfort her, but even that had been denied him.

He turned away, to the bomb. The counter ticked down relentlessly.

Less than seven hours to detonation . . .

30

New York City

It was going to be a beautiful day.

The sun climbed above the eastern horizon, the cloudless red sky of dawn turning to blue as it ascended. Stark morning shadows cut across the sprawling boroughs of the great city, the eastern faces of the skyscrapers at its heart glowing in the golden light.

New York was already wide awake. By half past eight in the morning, the streets were a crush of cabs and cars, the dawn chorus of Manhattan not birdsong but horns. People flooded on to the island, filling every floor of each of the towers. The world's financial powerhouse was gearing up for another busy day.

Seven miles south of Manhattan, the massive span of the Verrazano Narrows Bridge, connecting the boroughs of Brooklyn and Staten Island, marked the dividing line between the Atlantic and New York Harbour. Dozens of ships passed beneath it daily, few of them ever attracting more than a casual glance.

The *Ocean Emperor* was one of them.

Sophia stood on the yacht's bridge once more, watching as the vessel made its way up the Narrows and rounded the jutting Bay Ridge district of Brooklyn. Ahead lay Governor's Island – and rising beyond that, the glittering spires of Manhattan, alight in the morning sun.

'They almost look like they're on fire, don't they?' said Komosa with a hint of awe.

Sophia smiled. 'They will be soon enough.'

Lenard turned to her from the controls. 'The autopilot has been set and locked, ma'am. The ship will follow the GPS waypoints to the East River, then turn for shore just before the bomb goes off. Even allowing for drift, it will be no more than fifty metres from land.'

'Good,' said Sophia. 'The closer the better.' She turned away from the window. 'I think it's time we left. Captain, get the crew to the plane. Joe . . .' She smiled. 'I've had a change of heart. Go down to the hold and kill Eddie.'

Komosa beamed back maliciously. 'It'll be my pleasure. What about the woman?'

'Leave her.'

He was surprised. 'Really?'

'I want you to make Eddie's death as quick and clean as possible,' she told him. 'I owe him that much, at least. But her . . . I want her to suffer.' She raised a hand to the deep scratch across her cheek. 'She can spend her last few minutes looking at the body of her dead love. I owe *her* that much.'

Komosa took out his silver Browning from under his leather waistcoat. 'Consider it done.'

'Quick and clean,' Sophia reminded him as he left the bridge, sunlight gleaming from his piercings. 'We take off as soon as the plane's ready. Don't be late.'

'I won't be,' he assured her with another diamond-tipped smile.

The timer reached 00:10:00, then continued its countdown.

'Well,' said Chase, 'now would be a good time for any last-minute brainstorms.'

'Afraid I'm out of ideas,' Nina replied glumly. They had tried every way they could think of to get free of their bonds, with no results except cut and bloodied wrists.

Chase rattled his chain against the pipe. 'I'm starting to wish I'd tried Sophia's suggestion.'

'What was that?'

'Bite off my own hand.'

Nina managed a tiny smile. 'Bit extreme.'

'It's an extreme situation.'

'We seem to have a lot of those, don't we?'

He nodded. 'Yeah, we've been through quite a lot together, haven't we? But . . .'

Something in his voice, an almost confessional tone, prompted Nina to sit up. 'Something you want to tell me?' she asked softly.

'Well, now's the time, isn't it?' He flicked a hand at the bomb. 'I just meant that, even though we had some problems . . . the last year and a half with you's been the best time in my entire life. I just wish I'd appreciated it more instead of acting like a selfish arse.'

'Aw, Eddie . . .' She gave him a sad, sympathetic smile. 'You weren't the only one being selfish. I'm as much to blame. But we did have some really good times, didn't we?'

'Yeah. We made a good team.'

'We were good matches.'

'Great matches.'

'Mm-hmm.'

They looked at each other for a moment. 'I, uh . . .' Chase began.

'What?' Nina asked.

'Nothing.'

'No, go on. As you said, now's the time.'

'Good point.' Chase paused, gathering his thoughts. 'There was a question I'd been thinking about asking you.'

Nina could guess what it was. 'Since we made up?'

'No, before that. I mean, not while we were in the middle of an argument or anything. But it'd been on my mind for a while.'

'So . . . go ahead. Ask me.'

He gestured at the bomb again. 'Well, there's not much point now, is there?'

'I suppose not.' Nina sighed. 'But . . .'

'What?'

'I think you know what my answer would have been.'

'I think I do.' He smiled, then let out a brief laugh.

'What's so funny?'

'Something just occurred to me. If we'd done it and decided to hyphenate our names, we'd be the Wilde-Chases. Sort of appropriate.'

'You only just realised that?' Nina said, laughing herself. 'I thought of that a year and a half ago!'

Chase raised an eyebrow. 'You were thinking about that right after we got together?'

'Well, it crossed my mind!' They both laughed.

And then the door opened.

Chase and Nina jumped to their feet as Komosa entered, gun in hand. 'Not quite what I expected to hear,' he said with mocking disapproval. 'But I can soon put that right.'

'You still here?' Chase asked. 'Sophia dumped you already, has she?'

'Actually, she asked me to put you out of her misery.' Komosa moved to stand between Chase and Nina, just out of reach of either of them. 'I'll be leaving with her in a minute. She has a good vantage point picked out on Staten Island.'

'Yeah, you can see all the best landfill sites from there,' Nina told him sarcastically.

'So, Sophia's finally let you come and kill us?' said Chase.

'No,' replied Komosa, pointing his gun at Chase, 'just you. She wants Dr Wilde to suffer much grief in her last few minutes alive.'

Nina's defiance was swept away by a wave of cold horror at the thought, but before she could react Komosa continued. 'But I have a better idea. I want you *both* to suffer – especially you, Chase. So I'm going to shoot you in the gut. You'll spend the last few minutes of your life in unbearable agony – and you,' he added, looking back at Nina, 'will have to stand there and watch.' He aimed his gun down at Chase's stomach.

'Don't I get any famous last words?' Chase growled.

Komosa smirked. 'Only "aargh!" ' He thumbed the chromed hammer back with a click—

Chase lunged at him, lashing out with his legs as the chain of his handcuffs rasped round the pipe. Komosa, caught by surprise, stepped back even though he was out of range.

He recovered his composure, took aim again, smiled – and lurched forward as Nina delivered a flying kick with both feet into his back.

She dropped hard on to the deck, cuffed arms outstretched above her head. Komosa staggered forward before regaining his balance—

Crack!

Chase leapt up and delivered a brutal headbutt that split the giant's lower jaw in two between his front teeth, a sharp edge of bone slicing through Komosa's gum and lip.

The Nigerian screamed, his mouth gushing with blood as Chase landed, head level with his chest.

Chase clamped his teeth round the silver ring piercing Komosa's left nipple and pulled back with all his might, dragging his opponent towards the pipe before the ring tore loose, ripping a chunk of bloody flesh out with it.

His own face streaming with blood from a deep gash on his forehead, Chase spat out the gory jewellery and swung round the pipe to grab Komosa's gun with his cuffed hands, pointing it away from him as he tried to twist it from the other man's fist.

But despite the pain, Komosa was recovering. Mouth hanging open, a revolting mix of blood and saliva drooling out over the now jagged line of his teeth, he lifted his arm . . .

And *kept* lifting.

Chase clung to the gun with both hands, but was powerless to stop himself from being hauled into the air, his chest thumping against the pipe as his feet left the floor. Tendons in the huge man's arm strained through his skin like steel cables, veins bulging as Komosa let out a gurgling snarl of pure rage.

His other arm drew back to strike . . .

Chase realised he would never be able to wrench the gun out of Komosa's hand – his grip was too strong, the steel clench of a vice.

Instead, he changed his hold, jamming his left thumb into the trigger guard over Komosa's forefinger. With his wrists together, the handcuff chain was slack – he flicked it up with his other thumb as he forced Komosa's finger harder on to the trigger—

Blam!

The bullet blasted the chain apart, pieces scattering across the hold.

Even though his hands were now free, Chase didn't release his grip on the gun – the moment he did, Komosa would shoot him. Still hanging from the man's raised arm, he slammed a knee up into his groin.

Komosa flinched back, the obstructing pipe preventing Chase from scoring anything more than a glancing impact. The blow from his other arm finally came. Chase tried to twist to avoid it, but the African's knuckles ploughed into his stomach with the force of a train.

He groaned, the sickening punch driving the wind out of him. His right hand lost its grip on the gun, setting him swinging wildly as Komosa abruptly moved back—

Chase's head slammed against the pipe with a dull *clong* of bone against metal. Stars of indescribable colours went supernova in his vision, new levels of pain searing through his skull.

His left thumb clenched again—

★

On the helipad, waiting impatiently beside the tilt-rotor, Sophia looked round sharply as she heard the faint sound of another shot from below. Then she jumped into the cabin. 'Take off! Quickly!'

The men already aboard looked at her in surprise. 'What about Mr Komosa?' asked the pilot.

'*Go!*' she screamed. 'Get us out of here, now!'

The only reason for her to hear a second shot was if something had gone wrong—

The bullet smacked into the far wall. His nauseating dizziness worsened by the ringing in his ears, Chase was unable to resist as Komosa bashed his left wrist against the pipe, trying to break his hold on the gun and knock him to the floor.

Another blow. Something crunched. His fingers were slipping . . .

Through a haze of pain, he saw Komosa's blood-streaked face. *Go for his eyes*, training and instinct told him.

Too far. Komosa's reach was greater than his own.

Which only left—

With a desperate burst of strength, Chase whipped up his right arm to stab at the gun with his thumb.

Not at the trigger, but the magazine release button behind it.

With a clink, the magazine dropped out. *Then* Chase went for the trigger, squeezing his left thumb for a third and final time to fire the remaining round in the chamber. The Browning's slide locked back.

Before the magazine reached the deck, Chase swung his foot and booted it across the hold. It hit the wall near Nina and clattered to the floor.

Komosa's eyes bulged with anger. He smashed Chase's wrist against the pipe again. This time, the pain was too much and Chase let go, stumbling and falling on to his back.

He was free of the pipe at last, but that was no consolation as the furious Komosa descended upon him.

The gun swung down at his head. Chase just barely brought his hands up in time to block the impact, but Komosa struck again, and again, the hard metal finally cracking against his skull. Chase's head thudded back against the deck.

He groaned. Through the blur of his vision he could make out the bomb about eight feet away, the clock still ticking down. From outside the ship he heard the roar of engines: the tilt-rotor taking off and rapidly peeling away.

Komosa got up, looking for the magazine. He spotted it and staggered towards Nina.

She saw Chase roll on to his side and crawl slowly, painfully, towards the bomb. Whatever he was doing, she had to give him more time.

She couldn't reach the fallen magazine with her hands. But she could with her *feet*—

Using the pipe for leverage, Nina swept around and kicked the magazine just as Komosa reached for it, sending it spinning across the hold to bang against the far wall. He hissed something incoherent, blood bubbling from his cut lips, then kicked her hard in the stomach before shambling after the clip of bullets.

Chase reached the bomb. He gripped the vertical rails, pulling himself forward.

Komosa scooped up the magazine and slammed it back into place, the slide springing forward to load another bullet into the chamber. He turned to take aim at Chase – and found Chase aiming at *him*.

'Pierce off!' Chase snarled as he fired the bolt gun.

With an explosive bang, the six-inch steel rod shot across the room. Designed to penetrate metal, the bolt met almost no resistance as it punched through Komosa's ribcage and heart before erupting from his back and slamming into the bulkhead. Pinned like a butterfly to a board, Komosa stared in shock at Chase before releasing a final bubbling wheeze. His head slumped forward, more blood running out of the neat hole in his chest to join the ooze dribbling from his broken mouth. The gun clunked to the deck at his feet.

'That was horrible,' Nina gasped.

'Fucker deserved it,' Chase said weakly, dropping the empty bolt gun and crawling towards her.

'No, I meant the pun.'

A noise escaped Chase's mouth that could almost have been a laugh. 'Are you okay?'

'Forget me, what about the bomb?' She squinted at it, trying to read the figures on the screen. 'Oh my God! There's only six minutes left!'

Chase changed direction, somehow finding the strength to push himself upright. Reeling, he went to Komosa's body and picked up the gun. 'You've got to get to the bridge, send out a Mayday – channel sixteen. Then turn the ship around, get it as far from land as you can.'

'What about you?'

'I'm gonna try and stop that thing from going off! Pull the chain round the pipe.'

She did as he said. 'I thought you said it was booby-trapped!'

Chase placed the gun's muzzle shakily against the chain, directing it as far away from Nina's hands as he could. 'I've got to do *something!*' He fired. The chain broke, Nina's wrists springing apart. 'Go on, get moving!'

With a worried look back at his blooded face, Nina hurried from the hold.

Chase staggered over to the bomb. 'Okay, what've we got?' The timer read 00:05:22. 'Five minutes to stop a nuke going off. I can do that. Yeah.'

Leaning on the cap for support, he looked down into the heart of the steel base. The thick bolts which held down the uranium slug had retracted. He reached into the hole, hoping that he might be able to pull the slug out from the rails, but the fit was too precise for him to get even a fingernail's grip round its edge.

If he couldn't get the slug out, then maybe he could block its path . . .

Fragments of information from his SAS briefings surfaced through the roiling dizziness. In a bomb of this type, the two pieces of uranium needed to be kept at least twenty-five centimetres apart to prevent them from reacting to each other and emitting radiation prematurely. That explained the gap separating the base and the cap.

So if he could jam the rails . . .

Winded, Nina entered the bridge.

As she'd expected, it was empty – everybody else aboard had left in the tilt-rotor. To her horror, the view through the wide windows was filled by the familiar outline of lower Manhattan: Battery Park a swathe of green to the left with the glass block of the Freedom Tower rising beyond the older brick buildings; to the right the ferry terminal and the South Street Seaport, the financial district's anonymous skyscrapers a sunlit wall behind the shoreline. The *Ocean Emperor* was making a slow turn, heading up the East River.

She ran to the wheel. The ship was obviously running on auto-pilot – if she could cancel it and turn back into the harbour . . .

The wheel spun in her hands, but the ship's turn didn't alter. The steering was operated electronically, not directly linked to the rudder, and the computer wasn't giving up its control.

'Shit!' She looked for a way to release the autopilot. Nothing jumped out at her, just ranks of indecipherable monitor screens.

The radio—

That was easy to find, at least, a push-button handset on a coiled wire. She turned one of the dials until '16' appeared in an LED display and took the handset. 'Mayday, Mayday, Mayday! This is the *Ocean Emperor* off lower Manhattan – there is a nuclear bomb aboard! I repeat, this is the vessel *Ocean Emperor* declaring a Mayday, there is a nuclear bomb aboard set to go off in four minutes!'

She waited for a response. Several seconds passed with nothing but the faint hiss of static. She was about to try again when a rather irate man's voice crackled from the speaker. '*Ocean Emperor*, this is the Coast Guard. I must inform you that making a hoax Mayday call is a federal crime carrying sanctions of up to six years' imprisonment and a fine of two hundred and fifty thousand dollars.'

'Fine, whatever!' Nina spluttered. 'Get your ass aboard and arrest me – just make it quick, 'cause I can't stop this boat!'

Another pause.

'Did you say . . . nuclear bomb?' the man asked.

'Yes! Nuclear bomb! B-O-M-B *bomb*! We've got Hiroshima in the hold and we don't know how to stop it! Call Homeland Security, call the President, call whoever the fuck you need to call, just do it in the next four minutes!'

Somebody else spoke in the background before the transmission cut off. Nina shifted her weight anxiously from foot to foot. 'Come on, come on, *do* something . . .'

Finally, a reply came. '*Ocean Emperor*, we are issuing a full alert,' said the man.

'Oh, thank God!'

'But if you *are* telling the truth . . . there's not really anything we can do in four minutes. It's up to you to stop it.'

Nina stared at the handset. 'Well, that helps! Thanks a lot!' She threw it down on to the console and ran back for the stairs. 'Eddie! We have a problem!'

Chase heard the distant shout. 'So what's new?' he said to himself.

He had collected what few items he'd been able to find in the hold – Komosa's pistol, the bolt gun – and attempted to wedge them inside the vertical rails to block the uranium slug's path. But they weren't enough. They could stop the slug from hitting the cap and achieving critical mass – but it would still get close enough to release a massive burst of radiation that would not only kill him and irradiate the entire yacht, leaving a huge piece of lethally radioactive junk adrift off one of the world's most densely populated cities, but possibly be powerful enough to affect people on land as well.

He needed more. But the hold was empty. Just him and the bomb.

And Komosa's corpse . . .

He checked the timer. Three minutes.

Less.

Chase stood, the pain in his head surging, and unsteadily made his way across the hold. The deck was rubber beneath his feet, like walking across a slack trampoline. He suspected he had a concussion, but couldn't afford the time to think about it. Instead, he reached up and took Komosa by the shoulders, trying to slide him off the bolt pinning him to the wall.

Dark blood oozed glutinously from the hole in Komosa's chest as he pulled, but the body only moved slightly. The bolt was stuck inside his ribcage.

Nina entered the hold. 'Eddie!' she gasped as she saw him manhandling the corpse. 'What're you doing?'

'Help me get him down,' Chase said.

'What for?' Nina began to ask, but then she saw the guns stuck through the rails separating the two sections of the bomb and realised what he had in mind. 'Wait, you're going to use *him* to jam the thing up? What is this, *Weekend At Bernie's*?'

'He's all we have! Come on, give me a hand. How long've we got?'

Nina checked the timer. 'Two minutes!'

She ran across the room to join him, suppressing her disgust as she took hold of one of Komosa's arms. Chase gripped the other. 'Okay,' he said, 'ready, and *pull!*'

They both braced their feet against the wall and leaned back, pulling as hard as they could. Komosa's head lolled, broken mouth agape. A horrible squishing, crunching noise came from somewhere deep inside the dead man's chest, but he remained pinned.

'The guy's still a pain in the arse when he's dead!' Chase exclaimed. 'Okay, *pull!*'

They hauled at his arms once more, straining to break him free. The wet noise came again, this time accompanied by a drier crackling. 'Come on!' Chase yelled at the body. 'Come loose, you fucking great—'

With a sharp crack of bone as the rib that had been impaled by the bolt finally snapped, Komosa jerked away from the wall and toppled over. Off balance with their feet against the wall, Nina and Chase fell with him. Nina shrieked as the huge man landed on top of her, his dead hand splayed over her face like a giant fleshy spider. She batted it aside, revolted.

Chase kicked himself out from under the corpse, then lifted it off Nina. 'Come on, we've only got—' He checked the timer. 'Shit! We've only got a fucking minute!'

They each grabbed one of Komosa's wrists, then pulled him across the hold. Too slowly. At six feet eight of solid muscle, he was no lightweight. Nina looked over her shoulder at the timer.

Fifty seconds . . .

'Are all – his bloody piercings – made of *lead*?' Chase grunted between each nightmarishly sluggish step. The bomb was six feet away, five, four . . .

Forty seconds . . .

'Okay!' Chase gasped as the corpse finally thunked against the bomb's solid base. 'Shove his arms in above the guns – we've got to block at least a foot of that gap!' He crouched and grabbed one of Komosa's hands, forcing it through the rails. Nina did the same with the other.

Thirty . . .

Chase reached round to grab Komosa's fingers and feed his hand out through the other side of the bomb.

It didn't move.

The Nigerian's forearms were too thick to fit between the rails.

'Oh, for fuck's sake!' Chase moaned. He shifted position and gripped the dead man's elbow, trying to shove his arm further through the gap. Nina let go of the hand she was holding to help him.

No luck. Only the first few inches of Komosa's wrist would go through before his bodybuilder's muscles wedged tight against the steel.

Twenty . . .

Nina switched her efforts back to the other arm, managing to get the hand and wrist into the gap – but nothing more. She jumped back and desperately kicked at his elbow, trying to hammer the arm in deeper, but with no success.

Ten . . .

'Fuckfuck*fuck*!' spat Chase as the timer dropped into single figures. Even with the two guns and both of Komosa's hands obstructing the rails, it wasn't enough to stop the uranium slug from reaching a critical distance. He needed something else, something at least ten centimetres thick.

But there *wasn't* anything.

Except—

Five . . .

'Get back!' Chase yelled at Nina, shoving her away from the bomb.

Three, two . . .

With a roar, Chase thrust his own left arm into the gap.

One . . .

Zero.

The explosive charge beneath the uranium slug in the bomb's base detonated. The can-sized cylinder of super-dense U-235 leapt upwards like a cannon shell, fire spewing out beneath it as it cleared the base and raced up the rails, hitting the bolt gun and the Browning and carrying them upwards with it.

They hit Komosa's dead hands, breaking bones with the force of the impact.

And slammed them up—

Into Chase's arm.

Still roaring, he had tensed every muscle to prepare for the pain he knew was about to come – but it was still beyond anything he'd imagined as his forearm was smashed against the underside of the cap. Even with Komosa's hands cushioning the impact, both the bones in his forearm broke as the slug flew up the rails towards the waiting supercritical uranium mass . . .

And stopped short.

Just over twenty-five centimetres from the cap.

It hung there for a moment, then dropped back into the base, a doughnut of acrid smoke billowing out around it. The mangled bolt gun fell after it and clattered on to the deck – even the machined steel of the pistol had been bent by the impact.

Komosa's hands were a crushed and bloody mess as they slapped down on top of the broken pistol. That just left Chase.

Eyes watering from the smoke, Nina scrambled over to him. 'Eddie! Oh, Jesus, Eddie! Are you okay?'

Face completely white, he very slowly and carefully moved his right hand between the rails to support his left wrist, then even more delicately slid both arms out. Nina clasped her hands over her mouth in horror when she saw his arm, a sharp spearhead of broken bone jutting through the mottled, purpled skin, trails of blood running from the wound.

He whispered something, but she couldn't make it out. 'Eddie, I'm here, I'm here,' she assured him, helping him support the injured arm. 'What is it?'

He whispered again, just loudly enough for her to hear. 'Now that's . . . sorted . . . think I'll . . . have a kip,' he said, before his eyes closed and his entire body went limp.

Nina kept hold of him, protecting his arm. 'You do that,' she whispered, kissing his cheek.

She stayed like that until an emergency search team in yellow radiation suits finally found them in the hold.

31

'Well,' said Chase as Nina helped him through the door, 'it's good to be home.'

'I thought you didn't like this apartment?' she asked mischievously.

'You know what? So long as you're there, we could live in a fucking cave for all I care.'

'Yeah, right. As long as it's a cave with cable, I bet. Oh, by the way . . .' She pointed at the coat hook behind the door.

Chase's bruised face split into a delighted smile. 'Oh, fucking awesome!' he cried on seeing the new black leather jacket hanging there. He kissed her. 'Thank you. Pity I won't be able to wear it for a while . . .' He held up his left arm, which was encased in a plaster cast and supported by a sling.

'It'll be there when you need it.'

'Fantastic. Don't suppose you got me a new Wildey as well?'

She smiled. 'You don't need to compensate for anything, Eddie.'

'Tchah!'

She laughed and guided him to the couch.

It was six days since they had been rescued from the *Ocean Emperor*, six days of hospital treatment and radiation exposure tests, all of which had been within safe limits . . . and six days of intensive questioning by Homeland Security and the FBI. The numerous agents finally convinced that they had stopped the bomb plot rather than been a part of it, Nina and Chase had at last been released.

From what they'd been told, the Swiss and Algerian governments had been contacted so that Yuen's factory and the remains of the Tomb of Hercules could be investigated. The Botswanan government had also been contacted, partly so that the uranium mine could be sealed off prior to a UN examination – but also, to Nina and Chase's intense relief, to see that the murder charges against them were dropped.

Also to Nina's relief, Matt Trulli had been rescued. The Australian had released the *Wobblebug*'s emergency beacon just before climbing out of the hatch, managing to don a lifejacket as the submarine sank. After spending a couple of hours adrift in the Atlantic before a Coast Guard helicopter located him, he had hypothermia to add to his cracked rib, but was expected to make a full recovery.

The only loose end was Sophia. After leaving the yacht, the tilt-rotor had landed on Staten Island close to the Verrazano Narrows Bridge so she could view the explosion from a safe distance – but once it became clear that the bomb wasn't going to go off, the aircraft took off again and headed for JFK airport. When its unusual behaviour and lack of a flight plan raised an alarm with air traffic control, it had hurriedly set down on an empty plot of land not far from JFK in the outer borough of Queens and been abandoned, its passengers fleeing. Two of them were later arrested in a stolen car, but of the others – including Sophia – there had been no sign.

She was now the subject of the biggest worldwide manhunt since Osama bin Laden. Engineering a plot to detonate a nuclear weapon in New York – and almost succeeding – had earned her the title of America's Most Wanted.

Chase started to put his feet up on the glass coffee table, then thought better of it, giving Nina a look. She grinned. 'No, go ahead. I'll let you off. Y'know, just this once. Seeing as you saved New York and everything.'

He glanced down at his immobilised left arm. 'Yeah, I should get a T-shirt made. "I saved New York and all I got was this lousy plaster cast" . . .'

Nina kissed him, then walked over to the kitchen area. 'I'm sure you'll get something more once all the secrecy clears. Do you want anything?'

'A pint'd be nice. Although I'll settle for coffee if you don't have one.'

'Coming right up,' Nina told him, taking a bag of coffee beans from the fridge.

'Speaking of secrecy, what's going on with the Tomb of Hercules? Have they told you if you'll be able to take credit for finding it?'

'I'd damn well better! Although I think it could take a while for everything to be sorted out.' She tipped the beans into the mill. 'The Algerian government wants to take full control, for a start. I bet their eyes went *ka-ching!* like something from a Bugs Bunny cartoon when they heard there was a treasure trove worth billions of dollars inside their borders. The IHA might have its work cut out trying to persuade them to open up the site.'

'Well, at least you won't have to deal with that.' Chase glanced back at her, uncertain. 'Or will you?'

She gave him a smile as she started the grinder. 'Not a chance. Right now? I'm on vacation. And so are you. And that's an official IHA decision.'

'I like the sound of that.' He stretched out, and was about to put his feet up when somebody knocked on the apartment door. 'Oh, buggeration. Never a moment's peace.'

'I'll get it,' Nina offered.

'Nah, it's all right,' Chase told her as he stood. 'I'll get rid of 'em. You keep grinding them beans.' He padded across the living room and opened the door—

Sophia stood in the hallway, a gun in her hand.

Before Chase had a chance to react, she fired.

A metal dart stabbed into his chest. Gasping in pain, he pulled it out . . . only for his shaking hand to halt mid-motion as the paralysing toxin spread through his body. Spasming, he fell on his back, plaster cast clonking against the wooden floor, the dart still clutched in his raised hand.

Sophia tossed down the dart gun and pulled a black automatic from her jacket as she slammed the door behind her. 'Hello, Eddie,' she said as she stepped over him. 'And Nina! I can't say it's a pleasure to see you again . . . but it will be in a minute.' She pointed the gun at Nina, summoning her out from behind the kitchen counter.

Heart racing, Nina eyed the knife block as she passed it. 'Don't even think about it,' Sophia warned her, stepping closer.

'What've you done to Eddie?' Nina demanded, looking across at Chase.

'Don't worry, he's alive – for the next few minutes, at least. I wanted him to watch.'

499

Nina stepped into the centre of the living room. 'Watch what?'

Sophia walked towards her. 'Watch you die, of course. God!' She stopped a few feet away and glanced scornfully around the apartment. 'You have no idea how much I despise you, you vulgar little American *bitch*. I can understand why you'd have some kind of hero-worship love for Eddie, but what he sees in *you*, I have absolutely no idea. Even someone as low class as him deserves better.'

'I don't love Eddie because he's a hero,' Nina countered. 'I love him for *being the man he is*. Not that you'd ever understand that.'

'Oh, shut up,' Sophia sneered, raising the gun towards Nina's face. 'Eddie, I hope you can see this. I'm going to kill your little tart. What do you think about that?' For just the briefest moment, her gaze flicked sideways to look at Chase—

Nina lunged forward.

She grabbed Sophia's arm with one hand as she twisted out of the line of fire, using the other to knock the gun from her grip. It hit the floor, a sharp edge gouging out a chunk of polished wood, and skidded under the coffee table.

Momentarily startled, Sophia stared after it before looking back at Nina, a mocking smile forming. 'Oh, you *have* been practising with Eddie, haven't you?' Her other hand snapped up and seized Nina's upper arm. 'But so did I,' she hissed, yanking Nina towards her and sweeping her right leg at the other woman's feet.

Nina tripped and fell to the floor, landing hard on her elbows next to the African statue. Old bruises flared with new pain. Across the room, Chase's eyes met hers, but he was powerless to help.

Sophia ran to the glass table, bending down to get the gun.

Nina jumped up, needing a weapon of her own, finding one—

Sophia's hand had just closed round the gun when the statue cracked down across her back like a baseball bat, so hard that the head of the sculpture broke off and bounced across the room. Before Sophia could respond with anything more than a cry of pain, Nina swung the carving again, this time hitting her shoulder. Sophia staggered and fell, the gun spinning from her hand.

Nina raised the statue, about to slam it down on Sophia's head—

Sophia kicked, catching Nina just above one knee and sending her stumbling backwards. Her calves barked against the edge of the coffee table and she fell on to the glass. It exploded beneath her, only her outstretched arms against the frame stopping her from landing on the broken shards.

Clutching her shoulder, Sophia got to her feet, hunting for the gun. It was on the far side of the room, near the balcony window. She rushed for it.

Nina painfully rolled over the side of the table's frame and crunched down on her knees amongst the broken glass, blood oozing through a dozen cuts in her back. She looked for Sophia—

She had the gun!

Nina threw herself behind the kitchen counter as Sophia fired, three shots blasting chunks of fractured marble out of its top. She crashed against the cabinets on the back wall, the door of one popping open to reveal an assortment of cleaning products.

She grabbed a plastic spray bottle, frantically unscrewing its cap . . .

The gun raised, Sophia advanced on the counter. She saw movement behind one end and turned to fire—

An arc of liquid flew from the end of the open bottle as Nina swung it, bleach splashing across Sophia's chest. The English-woman managed to bring up an arm to protect her face, but even diluted to act as a kitchen cleanser the chemical gave off a pungent stench strong enough to sear her nostrils, choking her. Sophia reeled, coughing and rubbing her eyes.

Nina jumped up, looking for another weapon. She saw Chase's Castro figurine on the counter and thought of hurling it at Sophia, then changed her mind and yanked the flex of the coffee maker out of the wall before flinging the machine over the counter. A dark spray of coffee grounds burst from the lid as it hit Sophia's gun arm, jolting the weapon from her grip and sending her staggering back against one of the armchairs.

Nina snatched a large carving knife from the wooden block and ran out from behind the counter. If she could reach the gun . . .

Eyes red and streaming, Sophia saw her coming and pulled the leather seat cushion from the armchair, raising it like a shield as Nina slashed the blade at her. The leather split open, sliced yellow stuffing bursting out like fat from a surgical incision.

The gun was on the floor between them. Sophia rammed the heavy cushion against Nina's face and upper body, knocking her back a step. Then she dropped, hand outstretched—

Nina kicked wildly at the gun. It skidded across the room to end up a few feet from Chase.

But he couldn't reach it, couldn't move anything except his eyes . . .

Sophia drove a fist into Nina's stomach, then threw the torn leather cushion hard into her face. Nina stabbed blindly with the knife as she staggered, but Sophia dodged it and clamped a hand round her wrist. She struck at Nina's fingers with her other hand, fiercely bending them back.

Nina screamed as joints crunched beyond their limits, nerve endings blazing. The knife dropped from her hand.

Still twisting Nina's fingers, Sophia brought her elbow up hard and smashed the point of the bone against Nina's temple, twice. Dazed, Nina fell on to the chair.

Sophia searched for the knife, but it had ended up amongst the broken glass from the table. Instead she turned for the gun.

Nina sat up, head spinning, seeing Sophia running from her.

And beyond her was Chase. Their eyes met, just for a split second. Then he looked away, not at Sophia . . .

But at his outstretched hand.

Nina instantly knew what he wanted her to do.

She flung herself across the room at Sophia just as she picked up the gun and spun to shoot—

Nina tackled her at shin height. Sophia wavered, then fell backwards, landing on Chase's hand – and the dart clutched in it.

Sophia's eyes went wide as she felt the metal spike stab into her back, knowing what it was, what was about to happen to her. 'No!' she cried, the shriek falling to a strangled gasp as the toxin took effect.

Nina released her legs and pulled the gun from her trembling hand. She threw the weapon aside, then looked down at Sophia's terrified face.

'Help me . . .' Sophia barely managed to whisper. 'Please . . . injection . . .'

'There's an antidote?'

'Yes . . . in dart gun . . .' Her eyes flickered in the direction of the abandoned weapon.

Nina checked it. Clipped under the barrel was a small metal tube. She opened the cap and tipped the contents into her hand; a syringe.

Sophia watched pleadingly, eyes begging her for help, but Nina just regarded her coldly for a long moment. 'There'd better be enough for two people,' she said, holding up the syringe. 'Because if there isn't, I'm going to sit here and watch you die . . . *bitch*.'

'Well,' said Chase, surveying the room from the couch, 'the apartment's fucked.'

'You know what?' Nina replied, curling up next to him. 'You were right. It's not really us. We can get somewhere nicer. And cheaper.'

'We've probably lost our deposit, though.'

She nodded at the bullet holes in the counter. 'Oh, ya think?'

The antidote had worked; it only took thirty seconds before Chase could move again. She had been sorely tempted not to give what was left to Sophia, but he persuaded her to deliver the life-saving drug – once he had retrieved the gun.

An alarmed neighbour had already called the police after hearing the gunfire, and it didn't take the NYPD long to arrive, finding Sophia tied up on the couch with Nina triumphantly holding the gun on her. There were some jurisdictional disagreements when the FBI and Homeland Security turned up soon afterwards over exactly who should take custody of the country's most wanted terrorist, but it was quickly decided they could be settled *after* Sophia was securely locked in a cell. She gave Nina and Chase a final hateful glare as she was handcuffed, then was hustled away, leaving them alone to contemplate their wrecked apartment.

'So,' Chase said, putting his right arm round Nina, 'any chance of that coffee?' She pointed out the broken coffee mill lying on the floor. 'Ah. Guess not. Why'd you throw that and not Fidel? You could've finally got rid of the ugly bugger.'

'He's not so bad. Thought I'd give him a second chance.'

Chase got her meaning. 'Well, probably a good thing. Coffee keeps me up all night anyway.'

'I can think of something else that'll keep you up all night,' Nina told him suggestively.

He feebly raised his broken arm. 'What, in this state?'

'Oh, you can just lie there, I'll do all the work. See? New position.'

They looked at each other, then both burst into uncontrollable laughter, the tension finally released. 'Oh, God,' Chase said at last, 'I can't believe we made it. After everything that's bloody happened, we actually survived. We're still here.'

'Still together.'

He looked into her eyes and smiled. 'Yeah. Still together. *Back* together.'

Nina seemed about to say something, then stopped. 'What?' Chase asked.

'I was just thinking . . .'

'What about?'

'The question of yours. When we were on the ship, you said there wasn't much point asking it.'

'Yeah . . .?'

'Well, we're not on the ship any more.'

'But we both know what your answer was going to be,' Chase said with a sly smile.

'I know! But . . .' Nina smiled back. 'I still want to hear you ask me.'

'Really?'

'Yeah.'

'You sure?'

'Positive.'

'All right, then.' Chase slowly and stiffly stood, then carefully lowered himself on to one knee in front of her. He winced as various bruises and battle injuries jabbed at him. 'Ow, buggeration and fuckery, that hurt.'

Nina raised an amused eyebrow. 'Those aren't *quite* the words I was hoping to hear from the man I love when he got down on one knee . . .'

'How about these, then? Nina Wilde . . .' He took hold of her hand, then looked into her eyes, his face and voice completely, totally sincere and heartfelt. 'Will you marry me?'

Nina smiled for a moment making a show of considering the question. But Chase had been right.

They both already knew the answer.